A SONG
UNHEARD

Books by Roseanna M. White

LADIES OF THE MANOR

The Lost Heiress
The Reluctant Duchess
A Lady Unrivaled

SHADOWS OVER ENGLAND

A Name Unknown
A Song Unheard

SHADOWS OVER ENGLAND ◆ 2

A SONG UNHEARD

Roseanna M. White

BETHANYHOUSE

a division of Baker Publishing Group
Minneapolis, Minnesota

© 2018 by Roseanna M. White

Published by Bethany House Publishers
11400 Hampshire Avenue South
Bloomington, Minnesota 55438
www.bethanyhouse.com

Bethany House Publishers is a division of
Baker Publishing Group, Grand Rapids, Michigan

Printed in the United States of America

Library of Congress Cataloging-in-Publication Data
Names: White, Roseanna M., author.
Title: A song unheard / Roseanna M. White.
Description: Minneapolis, Minnesota : Bethany House, a division of Baker Publishing
    Group, [2018] | Series: Shadows over England ; 2
Identifiers: LCCN 2017036157| ISBN 9780764219276 (trade paper) | ISBN
    9780764231469 (hard cover)
Subjects: LCSH: Man-woman relationships—Fiction. | Women spies—Fiction. |
    GSAFD: Christian fiction. | Love stories.
Classification: LCC PS3623.H578785 S66 2018 | DDC 813/.6—dc23
LC record available at https://lccn.loc.gov/2017036157

Cover design by Jennifer Parker
Cover photography by Mike Habermann Photography, LLC
Cover background: Hennepin History Museum, Minneapolis, MN

Roseanna M. White is represented by The Steve Laube Agency.

18   19   20   21   22   23   24   7   6   5   4   3   2   1

To my childhood piano teacher, Joanne Peto,
who taught me that a D♯ could weep, an E♭ could sing,
and a melody could be Jesus to a hurting heart
that would never listen to words.

ONE

London, England
September 28, 1914

The music seeped into her soul like fog over the Thames. Willa Forsythe leaned back against the grimy bricks and tilted her face up to the early-evening mist. It kissed her cheeks, cooled her, dampened her clothes. She let it. It was a reasonable price to pay for this.

Above her, the music spilled from the window, cracked open just enough to help it escape. Timpani and double bass, cello and bassoon. Clarinet and flute and horn.

And violin. She rested her head against the bricks and strained up onto her toes, as if that would draw her closer. She focused all her energy on that clear soprano voice.

The cellos missed their entrance. Again. And the rest of the group trickled to silence while the maestro shouted his displeasure.

Sometimes she imagined herself on one of those chairs with the other violinists. She imagined the heat that would sting her cheeks when it was one of her mistakes the maestro berated. She imagined exchanging a look with the other musicians that said . . .

She didn't know what it would say. Comradery with other musicians was as mysterious as the man she was about to meet. Which . . . She pulled out the cheap pocket watch she'd liberated from a drunken lecher last year. Ten minutes to make the seven-minute trek. Good. She would rather be early than arrive to find Mr. V already there.

With a friendly pat of thanks to the cold bricks for hosting her yet again, she slipped away from the symphony's practice chamber, out of the little alcove that the city had neglected, over the crumbling half-wall, and down the night-dark alley. If she were Rosemary, the shadows would make her shiver. If she were Elinor, the mist would make her reach to check the hair under her hat. If she were Retta, she'd pause there where alley met street to admire the slant of the sun as it made one final hurrah through the mist and fog, turning them to gold in one second and then vanishing in the next.

But Willa was none of her sisters.

For a moment, she almost caught a melody that danced its way through the sunburst. Almost. It was there one moment but then it slipped away, too fleet of foot for her ever to follow.

Her fingers itched for her bow. That elusive wisp of song wouldn't come when she had her violin in hand. But she could play that line the strings had been singing in the practice chamber. She wished she had heard the ending, but that bit between sections would do for one. After she met with Mr. V, she'd head back to her flat in Poplar and fetch her violin before going to the pub. They may not be a symphony-going crowd at Pauly's, but they always welcomed her to the little stub of a stage with hoots and applause. It was enough.

Even if it was never enough.

A toddler whined to her right as his mother hurried him along. A cab sputtered by. Someone coughed, and someone else shouted. In Flemish.

The crowds clogging the streets had shifted in the past two weeks. First it had been rosy-cheeked English lads in freshly pressed uniforms—like her little brother, Georgie—jostling and joking with one another and boasting about how they'd go and teach the Krauts a lesson for invading poor little Belgium. Then they had vanished, to be replaced with bedraggled refugees *from* poor little Belgium. Women and children who had escaped with only the clothes on their back. Men who stood about with their hands in their pockets, or reading the papers with perpetual scowls.

Willa turned the corner, trying to identify the newcomers by sight. Sometimes it was possible when they wore the country garb they'd fled their little communes in. Not so much when they were dressed like everyone else in the city. Until they opened their mouths and either Flemish or French spilled out.

Was it wrong of her to wish those English lads were here instead? Or Georgie, anyway. She missed his jests. His perpetual stretching of their family's rules.

The army would either straighten him out or crush him when he refused to be straightened. Either way, he wouldn't come home the same person he'd left as. Either way, it deserved some mourning.

She checked the street and crossed in front of a slow-moving wagon that was making motorists honk their horns and wave their fists. Not even a month officially at war, and already everything was changing. She could only hope it would be over as soon as the papers were predicting. A few months, they said, like the Boer War. That was all it would take.

Mr. V said otherwise. She turned into the little park where she was scheduled to meet him and breathed easy when she saw the bench unoccupied. No nondescript bowler hat. No careful grey suit. No placid blue eyes that seemed to see into the shadows of the past and future with equal, terrifying skill.

But he paid well. She could deal with a bit of fearsome omniscience if it carried ample pound notes along with it.

Her bench was damp, so she pulled a hankie from her handbag and swiped a spot dry before sitting. Then she stuffed the masking white square back in, overtop the wallet she'd slipped out of a gent's pocket an hour before, while he stood there spouting off at some poor street rat for not shining his shoes properly.

Served the lout right to be robbed. And she'd slipped the shoeshine boy one of the bills after the rich bloke blustered off, since he'd refused to pay the poor lad.

Street rats had to stick together.

"Well, good day, pretty Willa Forsythe."

The voice, laced with Flemish and increasingly familiar, brought her head around and her heart rate up. Not at the handsome face that greeted her with a smile full of even white teeth—at the fact that he was here, now, when Mr. V also would be soon. "Cor Akkerman." She forced a smile for her new Belgian neighbor. Her landlady had announced to them all not a fortnight ago that she'd be doing her bit for "brave little Belgium" and taking in a few refugees.

This one was trouble. She'd known it the moment he doffed his cap and grinned at her like he was doing now. The kind of grin that said he intended to make the most of his tenure in England, and that his "most" would involve charming some English lass into a compromising position.

Willa had never much cared for charm. And didn't trust any man who called her pretty. But *she* was in less danger of sliding into stupidity than, say, her actually pretty little sister Elinor. So better he keep his attention on her.

He motioned to the bench beside her. "May I?"

Cor Akkerman was trouble, no question. But she liked him nonetheless. She darted a glance over her shoulder. "Perhaps for a moment, but I'm afraid I'm meeting someone. My employer," she added. The last thing she needed was him thinking it was a beau she was meeting and deciding to take it as a challenge.

He sat, heedless of the moisture on the bench, and flashed that grin again. "I will not keep you long. But I could not pass up a chance to talk with the prettiest girl in London."

She snorted. She couldn't help it. But didn't bother responding to such obvious flattery with any other acknowledgment. "Were you out searching for a job again? You're rather far from home."

"*Ja*. I tried the utilities. The train stations." He made a face that, on most men, would have looked sour. Somehow on him it looked amused. "With so many men enlisted already, I thought there would be openings. But the desire to help my people extends only to the point where it does not hurt an Englishman, I think. They will give jobs to your countrymen before mine."

Reasonable, in a way. Though she understood the frustration it would give the refugees too. Willa flexed her fingers and tucked her handbag to her side—the side away from him. She'd turn the money over to Barclay—her eldest brother and leader of their patchwork clan—when she got home, and then she'd dispose of the wallet.

She felt as though she ought to have some advice for Cor. Suggestions on where else to look for a position. But she'd never much moved in the circles of the gainfully employed. "I'm sure you'll find something soon. Anyone willing to work, as they say, can." Though to her way of thinking, it was a complete waste to slave all day for some heartless employer, only to end up with barely two pence to rub together at the end of the day.

"Well. Perhaps my cousins and I will find our way to that pub you like tonight. Will you be there?"

Or miss one of the few square meals she ever got in a week? Willa nodded. "I will." Though if Cor would be too, she'd be sure to remind Elinor that it was her turn to head home early with the little ones again.

11

"Then I will say farewell now and see you later." He stood again and, not wanting to be rude, Willa did as well to see him off. He reached for her hand and raised it to his lips, angling his eyes up at her as he did so.

It was without question the most blatantly flirtatious move she'd ever personally received.

The question was, why did it feel so awkward? Other people engaged in such simple contact all the time, but on the rare occasions it happened to Willa with anyone but family, it always left her feeling stiff and uneasy. She reclaimed her hand, kept her smile cool, and waved him off.

Cor hadn't even turned out of the park before a more familiar voice came from behind her. "I'd steer clear of that one if I were you."

"Mr. V." She didn't turn, knowing he'd come to the front of the bench in another moment. No surprise seized her at his sudden appearance. No doubt he'd been there all along, waiting for Cor to leave. And he, at least, never reached for her hand.

Round the bench he did, though he wouldn't sit. He never sat.

Willa did, and made sure she looked far more relaxed than she felt. "And while I appreciate the concern, sir, you needn't worry. I wouldn't trust that one any farther than I could kick him. Though if you know something about him I should . . ."

Mr. V's gaze tracked Cor's figure as he disappeared from view. "Nothing particular. Though all I need to know."

Her brows knit. "Why do you say that? Just because he's a refugee?" She hadn't thought him the type to be prejudiced. But then, what did she really know of *him*? It seemed these days she passed quite a bit of time with absolute mysteries for companions.

"I was just in Belgium, recruiting refugees, Miss Forsythe. I assure you, it has nothing to do with his nationality." With Cor gone, he turned his icy gaze on her. "Though I am glad *you* do not seem opposed to them on principle. You'll be joining a few of them, if you take this little job."

Her fingers itched again, but not for her violin's bow this time. If he held true to the pattern Rosemary had shared with her, he'd have an envelope. In it would be instructions—and a bit of an advance on whatever he'd pay her for this *little job*. "Will I?"

"Mm." He drew it out and handed it to her.

Her pulse quickened far more over this plump, white rectangle than over even white teeth. Keeping her movements calm and deliberate, she reached for the envelope, stuck a finger under the flap, and ripped it open.

She didn't riffle through the bills, though she wanted to. One hundred pounds, she would bet. The same as he'd given Rosemary when she'd accepted her last job from him. She pulled out the paper instead, filled with precise type that told her nothing about him except that he liked order.

Her eyes skimmed the words. Snagged. "Are you quite serious?"

Mr. V clasped his hands behind his back. "Is there a problem? I rather thought you would enjoy this, given your . . . talents. It's why I've come to you with it rather than, say, your brother."

Her eyes were wide, she knew they were. But she couldn't regain her composure as she turned them on him. Not with *symphony orchestra* leaping off that page and scorching her. "You want me to . . . ? But the Belgians? Haven't they suffered enough? I don't steal from those who are worse off than I am, it's—"

"Do finish reading before you jump to conclusions, Miss Forsythe." Not a twitch of his lips. But she almost thought she detected a gleam in his eye. Perhaps. "This particular Belgian is not so badly off, I assure you. Or wouldn't be, if he could access his accounts. They're frozen, of course. The Germans have frozen all banking in Belgium. But it isn't money I want you to steal from him regardless."

Her breath caught as she read farther down the page. She

13

blinked, but it didn't change. That neat type still said *Lukas De Wilde*. It still said *Belgian Symphony Orchestra*. It also said *Aberystwyth*. "Wales?"

"There are wealthy sisters there who have recruited artists and musicians from among the refugees. To support them, and also to bring some culture to their neighborhood. You will be posing as a friend of theirs from school."

So the instructions said. Though she had to look at him again at that, her eyes still wide. "And how am I to do that? They'll obviously know I'm *not* an old school chum. Given that they'll have no memory of me."

There, a twitch of his lips. Perhaps. "The Davies sisters are . . . family friends, let us say. They know that you are about important business and have agreed to participate that far in this. They will not know your true purpose, of course. Only that you are there at my bequest."

She still wasn't entirely certain what his role in the world was—he had, it seemed, some connection to the government. Though what exactly that connection was she couldn't determine. All she knew was that if her family could continue working for him, they wouldn't have to haunt the streets anymore, looking for a likely mark. Or lie their way into balls to liberate jewelry. If they could keep working for him, Rosemary and her new morals wouldn't keep frowning at them all.

But they wouldn't have to completely change. He used them because of the skills they had honed over the years. Skills Willa had no intention of giving up, regardless of Rosie's insistence that they needn't steal anymore, that she and her new husband, Peter, would support the family.

Nonsense. Supporting twelve strangers was too much to ask of some bloke who hadn't yet been tested. What if such strain spoiled their marriage? No. Willa and Barclay had both agreed that, while it was fine to let Peter Holstein take the little ones on a holiday now and again, they would *not* be entirely beholden to him. They would support themselves, as they had always done.

In the *way* they had always done. Or nearly the same way. It was who she was. All she knew.

She glanced at the page again. "So what is it, exactly, that you want me to steal from Lukas De Wilde?" It took all her willpower to keep from crumpling the page, to keep her hands steady. To keep from seeing his face as it appeared on the poster she may have liberated from a rubbish bin and tacked to her wall. But he couldn't be so handsome in reality. It wasn't possible.

"I am not entirely certain—this is why I need someone with expert instincts to find it." Mr. V shifted a bit, no doubt to block her and his envelope from the view of a few passersby on a path two leaps away. "I can tell you only that it is a cypher key. It could be a ring, a piece of paper, anything really. Anything small enough to be carried always with him. But you will recognize it—it should have letters that align with a traditional alphabet and provide alternates."

She should be flattered, she supposed, at that reference to her instincts. But instead she frowned. "Cypher? You do know I'm no spy, Mr. V—just a thief."

"And I am not asking you to break any codes, Miss Forsythe— simply to obtain the device that will allow others to do so."

As if *that* were to ease her frown. "Why? Is he . . . is *he* a spy? For Germany?" The thought shouldn't make her stomach sink as it did. She didn't know the man, after all, aside from staring at his poster more than she ought.

Mr. V's lips twitched. "Does it matter?"

"Yes." She wasn't sure why—it shouldn't, not given the stack of pound notes. But it would be helpful to know who she was up against, wouldn't it? If he were a spy, a trained one who carried around encoding devices . . . Well, that wasn't just her average mark. He could be dangerous.

Mr. V chuckled. "No, my dear. He is not a spy. It is simply that his father had been doing work in the field of cryptography—coding and codebreaking. It is said he developed a cypher machine that could revolutionize the field. The Crown is very interested in procuring this machine, and finding this small device that Lukas De Wilde always carries with him is the first step." He lifted his silver brows. "Satisfied?"

She nodded. Aside from recognizing the thing, it shouldn't be too hard. Get into his room, snoop around. If all went well, it would take only a few days. At worst, a week or two. Although if he literally carried it *on* him, that would require getting close to him.

Willa Forsythe, rubbing elbows with a world-renowned violinist. With *Lukas De Wilde*.

She'd probably wake up tomorrow and find it all a dream.

He clasped his hands behind his back and eased a step away. "Time is of the essence. I've already made arrangements for your transport to Wales on Monday. Take tomorrow to get what you need to convince the world you are a gentleman's daughter off for a holiday with friends. Memorize the information I've provided. Have you any questions?"

Of course she had—the leading one being why he didn't just ask the man for this key, for the machine itself, if it was so important. And if he was *not* a spy for Germany. But she knew enough of her employer to guess that he wouldn't provide those answers. She had already pushed him for more of an explanation than she'd honestly expected him to give.

It wasn't her business anyway. She nodded and slipped the envelope into her handbag. "Consider it done, sir."

His nod said the meeting was over, so she stood, angling toward home while he turned in the opposite direction.

Her thoughts were a whirl as she hurried for the tube, as she rode the familiar train through the familiar tunnels, as she bustled toward her familiar little flat in dismal Poplar with its water-stained walls and rickety stairs. They could perhaps get something a little nicer, now that they had the payment from the last big job for Mr. V. But there was nothing better around here, and they never went more than a few blocks from Pauly's pub.

It was home.

And frankly, they could none of them square the thought of not being strapped. It was too new. Too unbelievable. And depending on how this job went, it could very well not last. So why get used to it?

She unlocked the door to the rooms she shared with Elinor and little Olivia, though she found the flat empty when she stepped inside. Rosemary had once lived in this bare little space with them too. Another something she couldn't square—that her oldest sister, her oldest friend, wouldn't be living here anymore. Wouldn't be a part of their world.

She was happy that Rosie was happy—she was. But sometimes it still cut. Was their life so bad that she could abandon it without a backward glance?

Willa looked around at the drab space, bare and ugly. They always had to be ready to move at the first sniff of the police, so their decorations were few. Their furniture all rented with the flat. A transient, temporary life.

No, she couldn't blame Rosemary for wanting something better. She just couldn't quite believe she'd found a way to get it.

Never mind all that though. Shaking it off, Willa deposited the envelope and pinched wallet in one of her hidey-holes, grabbed her violin, and rushed back into the dusk.

She could smell the food cooking at Pauly's from the end of the street, and it put more speed in her step. Another minute and she was pushing through those familiar doors, into the domain of the man who was the closest thing to a father she'd ever known.

Pauly was disappearing into the back as she walked in, but

he turned at the sound of the door and lifted a hand in warm greeting.

She didn't need a father anyway. Not so long as she had Pauly there, willing to play the part. Willing to love the ragtag bunch of street urchins he'd helped stitch together.

It was early yet, so the pub had only a few neighbors in it—and the family. None of them shared a drop of blood, but the bonds between them were all the stronger for being born of need rather than chance. They were at their usual table, the little ones all sandwiched between the older ones. She smiled to see Rosemary there, bending over Olivia to help her retie the ribbon on her braid.

Rosie would be leaving tomorrow, traveling to Cornwall with half the family, all of them who were twelve or under. It would do them all good to get out of London.

Still. London wasn't the same when all her family wasn't in it.

Then again, Willa wouldn't be in it either by Monday. Making sure her smile stayed bright, she bustled over to the people she loved best in the world. "Getting an early start tonight, are we?"

"And an early start tomorrow." Cressida, the oldest of the children going southwest in the morning, leapt up and greeted Willa with a mighty squeeze. "I'm so excited! I've never seen *anything* but London!"

Chuckling, Willa squeezed her back. "You'll have a grand time. Be sure to mind Rosie and—"

"We *know*, Will." Cressida added a roll of her eyes for good measure.

Little Nigel, the second youngest of their crew at seven, was bouncing on his seat. "I don't want supper. I want to go home to bed so it'll be *tomorrow*."

Willa chuckled and slid her violin case onto the floor under her chair. She looked over to the oldest of them—Barclay lifted a brow in silent question.

She nodded. "I have today's wages for you at home. And the meeting with Mr. V went well. I'll be going to Wales in a couple days."

Retta, blond hair smoothed back in some new style of chignon that made her look far more elegant than usual, leaned forward. "Wales? Whatever is in *Wales*?"

The words—those beautiful words—nearly stuck in Willa's throat as she sat. "A symphony orchestra. Made up of Belgian refugees, apparently, who are touring to raise money for the Belgian Relief Fund."

Lucy's mouth fell open, her dark, almond-shaped eyes going wide in her dusky face. "An orchestra! No wonder he came to you. You'll have a marvelous time, Willa!"

She would. Though truth be told, she'd never been away from the family for more than a few days. And never alone.

Across from her, Rosemary grinned. "I daresay I won't be able to convince you to come with us to Cornwall, then. I was going to try again."

That cut burned. It was good, what her sister was doing—taking the little ones for some fresh air and solid meals. She was, as they had always done, sharing freely what she'd found for herself.

So why did it feel like a betrayal? Like she was abandoning them all? Still, it was Rosie. Her oldest, truest friend. Willa leaned back in her chair. "You might have succeeded, if it weren't for this." She craned her neck around for evidence of Pauly's return. "Does he need help bringing the food out?" She'd eat first. Then she'd play.

"Nah, he said it would just be another minute or two." Barclay folded his hands over his flat stomach and surveyed the crowded table. "Our last night all together for a while. I'm glad you brought your violin, Will."

"Oh! The challenge." Grinning, Retta scooted forward on her chair. "I've just got it!"

Willa breathed a laugh—given that introduction, she had a feeling their little game was about to turn her way. "Now wait just a minute—I'm still not satisfied that you managed the one Rosie gave you. It isn't exactly stealing a train when you show up with a miniature in your pocket."

Retta's grin didn't dim. "She didn't say how *big*, did she? But trust me, I'll be more precise. You, Willa Forsythe, must steal . . ."

As usual, everyone around the table drummed their fingers against the smooth, worn wood, laughter punctuating their percussion.

Retta slapped a hand to the table, silencing the finger drums. "Music."

Willa blinked. "Music."

"Music—*original* music, never before heard by the public. I want to see a score—that's what it's called, right?—that has never been seen before by anyone but the composer."

Not quite as impossible as some of the things they challenged each other to lift. Not given where Willa was going. "Retta, that's hardly even a challenge. I'd barely even be able to call myself the best when I do that."

Retta's blue eyes didn't look at all uncertain. "I know for a fact most musicians aren't composers. And symphonies mostly play tried-and-true pieces, right? Betcha it'll be a far cry harder than you're thinking."

She may have a point. But surely *someone* among the Belgian orchestra composed something. Right? It would be a simple matter of finding out who. And seeing their work. Then *taking* their work. After making sure no one else had ever heard it.

Perhaps not quite so simple. But she pushed away from the table. "Piece of cake. I'll play it for you when I get home. But for now . . ."

Dinner could wait. She bent down, grabbed her violin case, and extracted the precious bits of wood and string. Amid the whooping and clapping of her family, she climbed onto the box of a stage Pauly had built for her. Lifted her bow. Closed her eyes. Called to mind that melody the violins had been singing from the practice chambers that afternoon, letting it fill her head until it spilled out into her veins and traveled to her fingers.

And she played.

TWO

Aberystwyth, Wales

The throb in his shoulder was a palpable thing. Lukas De Wilde didn't just *feel* the ache as he lowered his bow and gritted his teeth, fingers digging into the dense wood of his Stradivarius's neck. He tasted it—wine gone sour. He smelled it—metallic and hot. He saw it—grey edges to a world once colored.

As a boy, he had spent many an hour of practice staring with more longing out of his window than at his études. Even so, he had never been more glad for a practice to end than today.

Now he had only to make it back to his rented room without collapsing. And then to rid his mind's eye of that image of the garden outside his music room's window. The garden that was now a heap of rubble, smoking and smoldering still in his mind as it had been when he saw it a fortnight ago. His house—his father's house—destroyed.

But empty. If his lips had remembered how to pray, he would have offered a praise to heaven for that. Or perhaps a plea. Because he didn't know what it had meant that it had been empty, whether it was a good sign or a bad.

He hadn't found them on the road between Louvain and Brussels. Nor *in* Brussels. Not before the world collapsed upon him.

His colleagues were all standing, murmuring in English flavored with French or Flemish. A few of them who didn't speak English well would interrupt themselves with a huff and switch to their native tongue. Their friends would provide the needed English and answer in the words of their host land.

Another day—week, month, lifetime—it might have amused him, this polite insistence upon speaking English, even when there were no Englishmen in the room to hear it. Today, with the echoes of pain reverberating in his ears, he could not manage it. Careful to keep his right arm immobile, he stood.

Jules stood there in front of him, frowning. When had he even approached? He carried his cello with the ease of one whose arm was not screaming in hot, sour pain. But his eyes spewed hot, sour accusations. "You promised you would not push yourself too hard."

Lukas sidestepped his friend and turned to the wall. His case. The first step toward leaving and walking out into that still-unfamiliar street, to go to his not-his-own rooms. "It was only a practice. If that is 'too hard' then I had better tell our patronesses now that I am worthless to them and be sacked."

Jules muttered in that way of his. The one that had absolutely no discernable words in any given language, but a rather close resemblance to many in several that would have earned him a tongue-lashing from his mother. Or, for that matter, from Lukas's mother.

No. Best not to think about Mère until he was somewhere he could crumble in peace.

Jules elbowed his way past a cluster of nattering woodwind players to keep pace with him. He shot a glance back at the flautists though. There were a few young women in the bunch, and on another day, Lukas would have turned to see which had caught Jules's eye. But not today. And his friend soon redirected his attention anyway. "You're not even moving your arm. I can call the doctor again when we get back—"

"To what purpose?" The doctor would just give him that same impossible advice again. *Rest your arm. Do not play the violin for several weeks, until the wound has healed.*

He might as well have said, *Swim the Channel and then fly to Brussels under your own power.*

Lukas stopped in front of his case and bent down to open it. He couldn't contain the wince when he had to move his right arm—but he averted his face so Jules wouldn't see it.

Jules apparently didn't need to see it. "Then perhaps you should heed their *original* advice. A week or two of not playing will not lose you your place here. You know that as well as I do."

Perhaps it wouldn't actually inspire the Davies sisters to sack him—but they were getting paid per performance, with only a bare stipend between for living expenses. He had to perform on the weekends. And he had to, therefore, practice in between.

He could probably sneak back into Belgium with little more than the tuppence in his pocket, but getting back out again with Mère and Margot would require cash enough to line the pockets of whoever saw them, not to mention purchasing the actual passage—likely on some rusted fishing boat that could still escape the harbor at Antwerp without arousing German suspicion. And then he would have to set up his family in some quiet, out-of-the-way hamlet where they'd go unnoticed by English and Germans alike.

He set his violin into the molded case that fit it perfectly. Then moved the bow to its place. Blast, but it felt heavier than obligation. How could sixty grams be so hard to lift?

To Jules's observation about his position here he made no reply. Another something his friend didn't need. Jules's sigh was as fraught with meaning as his muttering. "How long will you be angry with me?"

Forever. Or until he knew where Mère and Margot were. "Why would you think I am angry with you?"

Jules crouched down too and flung his cello's case open with far less care than usual. "Would you just *shout* at me? Rant and rail as you usually do? I cannot handle this ice, *mon ami*. It is unlike you. It worries me."

Lukas closed his case, fastened it, and stood with it in his left hand. "There is nothing to rant about. You saved my life." And he couldn't forgive him for it until he knew it hadn't cost his mother and sister theirs.

Jules stood a moment later, his dark eyes flashing behind his spectacles. "You would have done the same had our situations been reversed. I looked for them—I did. But had I left you there, you would have died. Could you have found them, do you think, if you were dead?"

Rolling his eyes, Lukas turned away. Toward the orchestra hall door and the afternoon that stretched before him. He wouldn't have died in the streets. He had woken on the boat, hadn't he? He would have done the same had Jules left him at his Brussels home. Woken and found them and gotten them *all* to safety, not just himself.

But while he usually enjoyed a good, rousing row, he couldn't fight with his friend about this. Not this.

He angled for the door.

Muttering another almost-curse, Jules dogged his steps. "Hit me, if you like. Yell at me. Do *something* other than ignoring me."

"Do not be an idiot, Jules." His shoulder shot fire all the way down to his fingertips. It streaked down his back. If he listened, he could hear it galloping through his veins, pounding like the timpani. Each pulse was an echo of those German shouts that had battered him seconds before the bullet had found his shoulder.

Commotion at the door brought his gaze back into focus and his feet to a sudden stop. He looked up, but too late. Too late to wheel around and melt into the crowd of musicians. And he was too close to the door for the women coming in not to have spotted him immediately.

Spot him they did, the moment they came through the door. He had done a fine job of avoiding Gwendoline and Margaret Davies thus far, and he had intended to continue the practice. One of their representatives had made him this offer—safety, the chance to raise money for the Belgian Relief Fund, in exchange for coming here to Wales and touring with this orchestra.

He wasn't so sure it was another of their representatives who had made him the *other* offer. But he wasn't about to take any chances. If they had anything to do with the man who had introduced himself as V, then he wanted nothing to do with them.

With their gazes latched upon him, though, he had little choice but to smile and pretend his arm didn't hurt. Pretend he was still the same man he'd been a month ago, before the world turned inside out. The man who would have been quite happy to make their acquaintance.

The sisters exchanged greetings with those closest to the door, but he was quite clearly their aim. They maneuvered toward him quickly, always blocking his path to the door. Not that he was rude enough to go around. Though today, he rather wanted to.

Only when one of the sisters stood before him, a bashful smile curving her lips and a hand outstretched, did it occur to him that he quite literally couldn't be polite without pain. He had to concentrate fully on not moaning and grimacing as he lifted his right arm to receive her hand, to bend over it. "Miss Davies. A pleasure to finally make your acquaintance."

"Mr. De Wilde. What an honor. We saw you in Paris some time ago, when you were touring as a soloist." Miss Davies—he wasn't sure *which* Miss Davies—turned to her sister. "It was Paris, wasn't it, Daisy? Or was it Rome?"

"Rome, yes. We then went to Paris to buy a few pictures." The other Miss Davies—Daisy, though he hadn't thought that one of their names—stepped forward and offered her hand as her sister reclaimed hers.

Lukas repeated the torture of a greeting, his smile feeling as brittle as Mère's ancient china. "I am sorry we were not introduced then. It would have been a pleasure in Rome as surely as it is now."

They sounded like the right words to his ears. But they felt wrong on his tongue. Rome . . . Rome had been five months ago, the start of his tour. When the only guilt to claw his chest had been over leaving so soon after his father's death. When he had been able to assure himself that his mother and sister would do quite well without him, as they had always done. When Père's final words to him had seemed simple and impossible to fail at. When life had just been music and balls and beautiful women and sipping the finest wine.

When fame had been a blessing instead of a death sentence if he dared to go home.

The first Miss Davies linked her arm through her sister's. They both looked to be around his age, somewhere in the neighborhood of thirty years. Neither was what one would call a great beauty, though both were fair enough of face. Except that they looked as though they would prefer a quiet garden to a boisterous practice room. Why, then, had they come?

"Daisy and I were hoping to catch you today, Mr. De Wilde. You and Mr. Bellamy will join us for dinner tomorrow, will you not? We worried that perhaps we sent the invitation round to the wrong hotel, as we had not got a response from you. You are at the Belle Vue Royal, are you not? Or perhaps the Richmond?"

Yet another claw of the villainous guilt. Though to be sure, he was surprised Jules hadn't responded for both of them. "Forgive me." He forced his face into an expression of sheepish apology. "I have been recovering from a slight malady and neglecting my correspondence—I did not yet see this invitation or I can assure you I would have responded." With his regrets.

"With happy acceptance." Jules edged forward, *his* smile not looking the slightest bit forced. "It would be our honor, Miss Davies. We owe you much."

"Nonsense." Miss Davies shooed that away, but her smile had lost a bit of its reserve. "It is *our* honor to host such esteemed musicians. We pray that your presence will help enrich the culture of our dear principality."

Daisy nodded. "Our direction is in the invitation. We very much look forward to it."

"And you'll get to meet Miss Forsythe." The first Miss Davies sent her sister a pointed look. "She's only just arrived or we would have brought her round today."

"Yes, that's right. She was weary from the travel, but tomorrow she'll be right as rain." The second Miss Davies nodded. "She's a school chum. I'm sure you'll both enjoy meeting her."

Had he met them in Rome, the invitation and introductions would have been welcome. More acquaintances, more patrons, more of the wealthy elite to line his pockets and guarantee that he got to spend his life doing what he loved.

He gripped the handle of his violin case with his good hand and barely kept his smile in place through the timpani beating of his pulse down his arm. He let Jules deliver the expected answer about looking forward to meeting their friend.

Perhaps by morning his mind would be clear and he'd be able to think of an excuse to miss the dinner. Or perhaps his friend would bully him along as he'd bullied him to England and then to Wales, and he would sit down at an extravagant table that he would once have appreciated and make conversation that he would once have enjoyed and pretend he was happy to be there when all he wanted was to go home.

The ladies moved off to greet someone else. Jules nudged him toward the door, leaning close. His words were in low French. "Do not spurn them. Their resources got us out of Belgium. They could be useful in getting you back *in*. Have you considered that?"

Sunlight assaulted Lukas when he stepped out into the warm afternoon. He squinted against it, not realizing until that moment that the pain had moved up his neck, too, and lodged in his head. "I do not trust their resources."

Jules shook his head, incredulity darkening his eyes to twin shadows. "Why would you not?"

Because V knew more than he should have. Because the very memory of him made nameless terror course down his back. Perhaps the medication had heightened his reaction, but even so. Lukas wasn't about to accept help that obligated him to what that man no doubt intended. He would not trade one tyranny of his family for another—he would find them freedom. And if that meant scrimping and saving every pence he earned until he could do it alone, then he would.

They turned to the left, toward where their hotel lay a few blocks away, along the Marine Terrace with what was probably a splendid view of Cardigan Bay, if he could bring himself to note it.

Lukas's feet went no farther. A young lady stood in his path. Or not *in* it, exactly—he could have passed her by without incident. But she wasn't walking like most of the people on the streets of Aberystwyth. She wasn't chatting with a companion or in a bustle to get wherever it was she was going. She didn't have the look of one of the university's female students, with books in hand. She was just standing there, her dress white and simple and fashionable and hanging perfectly on a slender frame. Her hair, straight and apparently so silky that pins would not contain it, slipped here and there from beneath her hat.

But it was the look on her face that arrested him. She stood there surveying the building from which he'd just emerged as if seeing the girders and beams and foundation behind the façade.

Dissecting every stone and board. Making some account that he could not fathom.

His breath fisted in his chest. That was how Margot always looked at things. As if she saw what normal eyes could not.

"Lukas?"

"I just need a moment." He could blame it on the pain behind his eyes, down his neck, feasting on his shoulder, and that was what Jules would think it. He would let him. It gave him a moment to catch his breath and lean against the iron railing that separated the orchestra hall from the street. A moment to clear Margot from his eyes. To watch this stranger until he convinced himself she was nothing like his sister.

She was a decade older, for starters. Her hair was lighter. Her lips weren't moving in silent murmurs that, if one *could* hear them, would be but a collection of numbers. She didn't stand in that too-still way that Margot sometimes did, when the world within her head was so much louder than the world without.

But still, there was something there. Something more intense than the average person.

His perusal must have been less subtle than usual. The woman turned his way and swept that dissecting gaze over *him*. From head down to feet, back up, and arrowing in on his screaming shoulder for one quick, all-seeing moment. Then her eyes locked with his and she quirked a brow that said, *I dare you.*

Though *what* she was daring him to do he couldn't have said. Had they been in a drawing room instead of on a street, had he swept *her* with that gaze first, the look may have been an invitation.

It wasn't.

Jules chuckled beside him. "You are the one usually looking at women like that, not the other way around. Though I do not know why you are bothering—she is not your type. She is barely even pretty."

Wasn't she? Lukas blinked, but still he could not see her eyes so much as the way they were looking at him. He could not see her face so much as the challenge on it.

"Not to mention that she is hardly turning to a puddle as your conquests usually do." Jules nudged him in his good arm. "You must be off your game, *mon ami.*"

He had no interest in the game just now anyway. Beautiful women—or *not* beautiful women—could wait until he had Mère and Margot out of Belgium. Until he could lift his bow without wincing. Until the world wasn't quite so upside down, backward, and inside out.

Still. When she just blinked at him and turned away, as if he were nothing but an insect she had decided to ignore rather than swat, pride bullied its way through the pain. Women might not all turn to a puddle as Jules liked to tease, but they never just dismissed him so quickly.

Maybe she was married.

A thought that lasted all of a second, until the Misses Davies stepped back outside and one of them said, "Miss Forsythe! I thought you were resting."

The intensity snapped clear of the woman's eyes, replaced with an easy light and a quick smile. She was a different girl entirely as she shifted her stance and moved toward his patronesses, one all light and breezy and what one would expect of a wealthy school chum. Not like Margot at all.

She motioned toward the street and spoke in a voice full of stiff English syllables. "Walking seemed preferable after being on the train. I paused when I saw your car."

Jules nudged him again. "We had better either be introduced or leave. Hovering here is rude."

He nodded. Turned. And walked away with as large a stride as his arm, his friend, and their instrument cases could manage. Tomorrow would be soon enough to be introduced to Miss Forsythe.

31

Tomorrow they would see *which* Miss Forsythe she chose to be—the one who was what one expected, or the one who saw beneath the flesh to the bones of a thing.

Tomorrow he would decide which one he *wanted* to see.

Today he would take a bit of that medicine the doctor had given him and fall into blessed oblivion until it was time to pretend again that he was well.

THREE

Brussels, Belgium

Margot stood at the window as she had been doing for the last sixty-two minutes. The streets were far too empty for the middle of a business day. And those out upon them were all wrong. German uniforms instead of neat suits with crisp ties. German shouts instead of Flemish or French. German soldiers with their ridiculous march, like they were made of iron and could not bend their knees.

A few boys had made fun of that march—and had been arrested.

Margot's nostrils flared. That made thirty people she knew personally who had been arrested. Thirty. Eighteen had been released, but the other twelve . . . Eight were sent to Germany. Four were awaiting trial.

She gave them a seven percent chance of emerging from that trial with their lives. And that was probably optimistic.

"Margot, come away from the window," Maman said for the eighth time.

Margot did not so much as twitch. She hated Brussels, had always hated Brussels. And it was worse now, when they could not even live in their own house. Too dangerous, Maman had said. They were blessed that they had fallen in with old Madame Dumont along the road on that long, terrible walk here from Louvain. That she had offered them a place to stay when it became clear they could not go to their own house—not with the Germans swarming through it.

But it was unfamiliar. Margot hated the unfamiliar. She hated this house belonging to Madame Dumont, where her room was upstairs rather than down. She hated this city, with its too many buildings and too many lungs all trying to breathe the same air. She hated that she couldn't even say her full name anymore, lest German ears hear it.

She wanted to go home, back to Louvain. But there was nothing left of their town. Not that mattered. Her chest hurt when she thought about the number of books destroyed when they burned the library. Paintings too, and other art she couldn't even count.

But the books. *The books*.

Papa would have wept had he seen those precious collections going up in flames. If he had witnessed the clouds of smoke choking the air, choking them all. It would have broken his heart.

Perhaps it had been a kindness on God's part to take him when He had.

Her fingers curled around the faded velvet of the curtains. "He's coming."

"He is an hour early. I suppose it is good you *didn't* come away from the window." Maman's black skirts rustled as she stood. She would be putting away all evidence of how they'd spent their day—the few books of Papa's they'd dragged here with them would go back into hiding, along with the letter Maman had been writing to one of her old friends from Louvain—and her knitting would come out.

Margot should help. But her fingers wouldn't uncurl from the velvet. And her gaze wouldn't leave the figure striding down the street.

She knew, intellectually, that she was supposed to love her enemies. God said so, and He was the one authority figure she felt compelled to listen to—the one authority figure she knew without question deserved her respect. Who never talked down to her. Who outsmarted her. God told her to love Generalleutnant Wolfgang Gottlieb. To pray for him. To fast for him.

She would rather spit in his eye. Which was so typical a response of a fourteen-year-old girl that it shamed her. She wasn't typical in anything else. She wouldn't be here either.

Even if she *did* want to add a kick to his shins just for spite. Though doing so would no doubt land her in jail. Other girls her age had been arrested for supposedly desecrating German corpses. As if any of them really went so near a dead body to poke it in the eye.

Though Margot wouldn't blame them for *wanting* to do so.

"Margot! *Now* come away from the window. I have your scarf out."

She hated knitting nearly as much as she hated the officer striding toward this house as if it were his. Maman was determined she know how to do the things a young lady should know how to do, but the needles felt so awkward in her fingers.

Turning away from the bleak scene outside the window, she released the curtain and tried to ignore the hollow feeling in her stomach. Food, Maman said, would be getting scarce soon. They and Madame Dumont had agreed to ration what they had left. Otherwise they'd be forced to rely on the good graces of Gottlieb just to eat.

And they were *not* going to rely on the good graces of Gottlieb.

Their aging hostess had retired for an afternoon nap, leaving the two of them in her cozy upstairs parlor where they'd taken to spending most of their days. Margot sat in the chair beside Maman's, made her posture perfectly imitate her mother's. But she felt like a marionette, not a proper girl. No matter how perfectly she mimicked the curve of Maman's neck or the way she held her arms, she could not make her fingers do what they should. They wanted a pencil, not knitting needles. She picked up the length of red wool that she was supposed to be turning into a scarf for Lukas.

Lukas would wear whatever she made him—but he would be more than a little embarrassed to wear this thing in its current state.

"Your pattern isn't turning out right, *mon chouchou*."

Maman was a master at pointing out the obvious. "I know." Intellectually, she loved the patterns in knitting. So long as it was in someone *else's* knitting. "I lost count."

Maman's breath was eighty percent exasperation and twenty percent amusement. "You can go on for hours about logarithms and algorithms, but you cannot count two-three-two?"

"I got distracted." She'd been musing about whether they could work a secret code into knitting somehow. A letter assigned to every stitch. *A* for a knit, *B* for a purl, *C* for a yarn over, *D* for a make-one-left. She'd come up with a whole alphabet. . . but was no good at actually telling what she'd done just by looking at the finished product. Someone else could, perhaps. Someone who had years of experience with knitting.

If she were trying to get a secret message to her grandmother, she'd be set.

As it was, her scarf now had holes from those Cs and was uneven from the Ds, and she was going to have to rip out the last three rows and do them over. Correctly.

She hated knitting.

From the open window came the dreaded clomp of Gottlieb's polished black boots. With each footfall, Maman sat a little straighter, her arms went a little stiffer.

Margot clenched her teeth together. They wouldn't be in this mess if her mother looked like her friend Claudette's dowdy matron. Gottlieb would have taken one look at her and decided to find his lodgings elsewhere. He was one of the highest ranking men in Brussels and could have demanded any of the grand houses he wanted—it was pure bad luck that brought him to their door.

Bad luck and Maman's beauty. With that thick dark hair and those striking brown eyes and perfect features that Lukas had inherited—it was really no wonder that Gottlieb had followed them home and demanded lodgings. He was just a puppy nipping about Maman's heels for attention, that was all.

A puppy with the power of life and death in his hands. And a pistol at his hip. And thousands of men willing to do his bidding.

Suddenly she didn't like puppies either.

"You just pulled out five rows instead of three, Margot. Pay attention."

She *was* paying attention. The front door had opened, and already four steps had fallen on the stairs. He was coming up, toward them, rather than going straight to his room downstairs. And he was coming quickly—more quickly than usual. It usually took him ten full seconds to march his way up to the landing. Now he reached it in six. Another six and—

The door swung open with such force that it smacked into the bookshelf behind it. Maman jumped and splayed a hand over her chest.

Margot didn't flinch. She focused her gaze on the row of woolen loops needing to be caught by her needle again and refused to acknowledge Gottlieb with even a glance.

Maman stood, and it wasn't fear coming off her in waves. It was the particular kind of fury that Margot knew best—that which came from a blatant disruption to the peace her mother loved. "Generalleutnant! My mother and I have opened our home to you—you will pay me the respect of not destroying the furnishings my grandfather handcrafted, or you will find your lodgings elsewhere!"

Now Margot *had* to glance up. Would the puppy pout?

No. The puppy snarled. "Your *mother*, is it? Very strange, Fräu Dumont—if that is your name. I have just had the opportunity to glance through the city records and have found that your *mother* has no children. No son that you were supposedly married to." He swept his gaze down her black dress. "It does beg the question then, does it not, of whose death you mourn?"

Did he know how ugly he looked when he wore that expression? How red his face grew under his white-blond hair? The way his eyes bulged? Even if Maman weren't in mourning, even if there were room in her heart for anyone other than Papa, she would have run away from a face like that.

Not that Maman ever ran away. She planted a hand on her hip and snarled back. Though *her* snarl, like everything else about her, was somehow beautiful. "Do you honestly believe every record of every birth is to be found in one archive? My husband was born to his mother in Louvain—go and find the records there, if you require them. No, wait . . . you cannot. Because your men destroyed everything of value in our hometown."

Gottlieb's eye twitched. A vein pulsed at his temple. One more pascal of pressure and his head might just explode.

What a shame that would be.

"You speak as if there is blame to be cast upon the German army for our behavior in Louvain. But I assure you, the city was filled with *franc-tireurs*. We destroyed exactly what had to be destroyed for our own protection."

"That is the most ridiculous thing I've ever heard." The words tumbled out before Margot could think to bite her tongue.

Maman sent her The Look. The one that begged and pleaded with her to just *be quiet*. It was a look she knew well. Ripe with temper but tempered with love. Margot was fairly certain she'd been receiving that look since she was a year old and starting to string words together.

Gottlieb turned on her. For most of the ten days he had been living here, he'd simply ignored her presence entirely. Too late to go back to that, she supposed.

"And why is that, *fräulein*? Enlighten me."

She put on the sweet smile Maman had made her practice in front of a mirror and batted her eyes like Claudette used to do when trying to sweet-talk her father into buying her something. "I daresay I haven't time to truly *enlighten* you, sir. But I can correct you rather quickly about this."

Gottlieb folded his arms over his chest. He was about the height Papa had been, but far too narrow. Too thin. With none of the softness that had made Papa's side such a welcoming place to be. And his hair was too light and his eyes were too blue and—

"By all means."

"You have obviously not seen Louvain for yourself. You would have seen the number of houses ruined and know it was simply not possible that so many—ours included—housed hidden snipers. And the library! Do you really think *it* was being used in such a way?" She shook her head. "Many mistakes were made that day."

His too-chiseled chin tilted up. "The German army does not make mistakes."

A snort slipped out. Usually Maman would have chided her for it, but just now she was too busy loosing a snort of her own. Margot slipped another red loop onto her needle. Probably twisted the wrong way, but she didn't much care. "You will really claim that not one of the thousands of soldiers, many of whom had never seen combat before they marched into Belgium, could have made a mistake? Have you any idea the odds of that?"

"Margot." Maman's invective was not, she knew, over challenging Gottlieb this time. It was over talking of mathematics. However vaguely.

Gottlieb's nostrils flared. "The German army is a machine, *fräulein*. Each part performs exactly as it was trained to do."

"Then you admit it was the *aim* of the German army to destroy Louvain? Since they never make mistakes, it must have been purposeful." Though so far as she had seen, the German High Command denied any responsibility for it. Not that many papers had made their way to her.

She missed the papers. Missed them as much as she hated knitting. The two may, in fact, be directly proportional.

"Louvain was filled with enemy combatants."

"Louvain was filled with merchants and scholars, nothing more."

He lowered his arms. "Shots were reported."

"*Your* men's shots." And even if a few old men *had* tried to defend their homes, since when was that a crime? Belgium was obligated to protect its borders. Legally required to do so by the very terms of its neutrality, of its existence.

Gottlieb knocked his knuckles against the tabletop. "Weapons arsenals were found at churches."

It was so ridiculous it hurt. "Where people had taken their hunting pieces when they heard the army was coming so that they would not be found in their homes, so that they could not be accused of being a combatant!"

Was that a twitch at the corner of his eye? It was, though she didn't know him well enough to say whether it was from frustration or if, perhaps, he saw her point. "Your homes had loopholes for gunmen to shoot from."

It didn't just hurt, it *itched*. Her shoulder twitched. She switched her words to Flemish so that he wouldn't understand more than one word in six. "Maman, he's too *stupid*. I can't stand it."

"Margot." But a smile hid in the corners of her mother's mouth. She kept her words in French. "Generalleutnant, the holes in our walls—in the walls of nearly every building you'll find in Belgium—are not loopholes. They are merely holes for the scaffolding. For house painters. Surely you have such things in Germany? They do not even go in more than a few inches. This is something any soldier could have discovered had he bothered to pick up a stick."

Gottlieb tugged on his jacket. "We are at war, madame. We haven't time to plunge sticks into every random hole in a wall to see if it's hiding a sniper."

"No, far quicker to assume. And then claim an inability to have possibly misjudged." Margot gave up on the stupid knitting and tossed it back into the basket between their chairs. Then she stood. If she spent another moment in the room with this man, she might say something she regretted.

She would go to her room. She would find a book or a newspaper—one of the issues Madame Dumont had given her, or one of the few she had carried all the way from Louvain. She would read until the itch died away. Perhaps work some more on her theorem, if she dared with this monster under the same roof.

But Gottlieb made no attempt to remove himself from her path. Instead, he blocked the doorway more fully and narrowed his eyes at her. "You have a sharp tongue for such a young girl."

She was *fourteen*. Hardly an infant, if still a year or two away from lengthening her hem. And oh so tired of being judged for her braids and pinafores when she could out-think every single adult she'd ever met. Except, perhaps, Papa. She lifted her chin. "You'll find that in Belgium, even the children have brains. We're not, you see, just part of a *machine*."

Something glinted in his eyes. Were she to see such light in Papa's or Lukas's, she would have assumed it amusement. But in Gottlieb, it was probably a dark joy at the thought of tormenting her. He nodded toward the chair she'd just vacated. "For whom are you knitting the muffler, *fräulein*? It looks masculine."

Did it? Perhaps her pattern wasn't as terrible as she'd thought, then.

Maman stepped closer. "It is for—"

"I was asking the girl." For once, he didn't even glance at beautiful Maman. No, he kept his gaze on Margot. As if the stare of a self-important lieutenant general could unnerve her.

Don't ever mention Lukas. Maman's whispered words from two weeks ago still filled her ears. They'd been huddled together, just two among the thousands trudging their way from the burned-out shell of Louvain. The priest at the head of their column had been accosted by a German soldier, tied up, and forced away somewhere or another, just for being Catholic.

That was when it had really hit them—the ferocity of these people who had bludgeoned their way into Belgium. That was when they realized that their invaders would show no mercy based on such trivial things as age or gender. If they would dishonor men of God, then . . .

That was when Maman had insisted that Margot never breathe a word about her work with Papa. When she insisted that they must do all they could to appear to be like every other Belgian family, nothing special. When they had agreed to pretend to be Madame Dumont's daughter-in-law and granddaughter, to deny who Papa had been and what he had been working on. To deny that Lukas, whose face and name and parentage was known everywhere in Europe, was anything to them.

They had prayed with every footstep that he would stay safely in Paris. But he hadn't, of course. He had rushed home to try to save them. And now there was some pompous German soldier parading about Brussels, claiming to have shot and killed the famous violinist.

But he was still alive. He *had* to be alive. She would know it if he weren't, wouldn't she? She would have felt that tug of emptiness again, like she had when Papa had breathed his last.

He was alive, and he was outside of Belgium, and he would come back for them. He would find them somehow, even though they were staying in this house they'd never seen before their arrival, with a woman they hadn't even known until that horrible two-week trudge through the countryside. He would find them. They had only to survive until he could manage it.

Margot produced another sweet smile. "The scarf is for my grandfather—on Maman's side. His always end up with burn marks from his cigars. I thought if I make him something, it will be ugly enough that no one will mind if he ruins it."

Gottlieb studied her, probably watching for a flinch or a tic or some other sign that she lied.

But a lie was just a matter of mathematics—the correct proportion of truth and falsehood, delivered at the correct rate, with breaths and blinks interspersed at correct intervals. Lies were easy.

Until one had to confess them to one's priest. But surely it wasn't a sin to protect one's brother from the Germans. She was ninety-eight percent certain that God approved.

Gottlieb nodded and eased to the side. Not enough that she could pass comfortably, but enough that she could pass.

She made it only to his side before he halted her with a hand on her shoulder. "You would do well to mind your tongue, young *fräulein*. It could land you in hot water indeed with a less measured man than I."

She shrugged away from his touch. "Your warning is noted." And he was probably right. But it was rather like asking a cat not to meow.

The hallway felt like freedom as she stepped past him and followed its lines to her room. She had spent the first week in this house getting to know it. How many rungs of banister her fingers could brush between the stairs and her room, which boards creaked, how many steps it would take to reach her chamber if she measured her steps just so. She had learned how far she could go and still be able to hear the conversation in the parlor clearly.

But there was nothing to hear today. Gottlieb said, "Fräu

Dumont—" That was all he got out. Maman must have raised a hand to stop him. And then sent him a glower that said she wouldn't speak to him. Maman could keep a whole town silent with one of those looks.

Except they weren't quite strong enough to overcome Margot's need to speak when that need arose. Because sometimes things needed to be *said*. No matter who told her she shouldn't say them.

Her room was dim and warm and stuffy. She hadn't wanted to open a window—not when it meant hearing the shouts of German officers wafting up on the breeze. But comfort won out now, so she pushed up the frame and breathed in the breeze that pushed its way in.

The itch had moved to her fingers. She needed a pencil. Paper. Newsprint. She needed something to read. Something to solve.

After closing and locking her door, she pulled the box from under her bed. So little. So little left of their life with Papa. The only things she had been able to save. The rest had burned. This was all she had left, these few books and newspapers and treatises from last summer, before he died.

At least it contained her favorite cypher. She pulled out the newspaper, which had been folded and unfolded so carefully but still was getting ragged at the edges. Almost afraid to touch it, she nevertheless unfolded the sheets. She *had* to. She had to see proof of him, that he had been. That *she* had been something more than she could be now.

He had never told her when he'd planted a cypher for her. She had to read every newspaper, every day. Every page. And if she missed something, he wouldn't tell her until the next day, with a raised brow and a chortle that shook his middle. He'd ask her if she had enjoyed such-and-such an article. He would say that his friend so-and-so had done the typesetting, and she would know. She would know she hadn't paid enough attention.

This one she had nearly missed. Usually she knew to look

for a message in an article because Papa would leave a key for her somewhere on the front page, within one of the headlines. Or more than one, to keep her on her toes. He hadn't this time. He had been trying to trip her up. Testing her. Because, he had said, knowing how to break a cypher when one knew the key was child's play. Being able to break a cypher without the key . . . that was what they dealt with in the real world.

She was still not certain who *they* were. Governments, she suspected. Those whose purpose was in figuring out what *other* governments were saying. Telegrams, for instance, were easy to intercept—but how to translate coded messages within them if one didn't know the key?

Margot's gaze ran over the article for the seventy-third time since this newspaper had appeared at her place at the table. It looked like a normal article—nothing to tip her off that secrets lay within. None of the words within it lacked sense or meaning. There were no characters a bit bolder than the rest.

She had nearly turned the page that first day. But then . . . something had stopped her. A pattern had caught her eye.

Intuition—that was where it started. But intuition, as Papa had said, was only the first step. The second, always, was mathematics. It wasn't enough to know *that*, not when it came to cryptography. One had to know *how*.

She had spent two full days working it out, to the exclusion of all else. Maman had begun to fret and fuss at her and to chide Papa for his game. Lukas had tried to tell her she was chasing a shadow, that nothing was even there.

But Papa had said nothing. So she had kept working.

Now she could see it so clearly. When she looked at the print covering the page, the encoded letters leapt off and flipped in her mind's eye to their counterparts, their hidden meanings. She could read the *real* message trapped within the false one.

When you can read this, you are ready to help me.

Her lips couldn't decide whether to smile or to quiver. How many times had he put this message in a paper and it had slipped by her? Too many, she suspected. She had too long missed it. If she had noticed it at ten, at twelve, then she would have had years to work by Papa's side. If she had just grown up a bit faster, or not been distracted by regular schoolwork or the stories Claudette told her to make her laugh . . .

She would have had more than six months, then, working alongside him. And everything would be different now.

FOUR

illa had spent almost the entirety of her twenty-three years in London. She knew every street and alleyway and tube tunnel and could navigate with all the skill of a cabby. Not knowing her way around wasn't an option, not when one was in a line of work that required quick getaways.

So her first order of her first full day in Aberystwyth was to explore. To get lost. To wander around until all the strangely spelled street names were stuck in her mind. Until she was fairly certain she could find her way around the city—which, really, was so small it hardly deserved the name, regardless of the cathedral that meant it was one, technically. She could navigate easily to the house the Davies family had let for the autumn. Where the orchestra met. Where they would perform a few times before the tour began in November.

Hopefully, Willa would be done with her job long before then, before she had to learn another city and more odd names.

Uneasiness still stalked her when she finally stepped back inside her borrowed home. Usually learning her way about would assuage that feeling, but not today. Not given the certainty that someone had been following her.

Eight different times she had turned quickly to try to glimpse whoever it was, and seven times she'd seen absolutely nothing. Once, she'd caught the flash of a brown jacket as someone ducked into an alley. The back of her neck still tingled from that being-watched feeling.

It couldn't be a bobby, or any kind of inspector. If it were, she'd have seen him—they liked to hide in the open, not in alleyways. It certainly wasn't Mr. V—she wouldn't have spotted him at all.

Who, then? Who else knew she was here? Or if it was an Aberystwyth local following her, *why?* She certainly didn't look wealthy enough to warrant such attention, despite the lovely gown Rosemary had made for her.

It was the job. It *must* be the job. She had rather thought it little more than a lark: come, hear the orchestra, steal the cypher—and some original music—and then be gone. But if someone was following her, it meant this was more than a well-paid holiday. It could mean rival thieves, or enemies.

Danger, either way. She'd have to be on her guard. If she made a mess of this simple job, Mr. V might never bring their family more work, and then they'd *have* to rely on the charity of Rosemary and her new husband, or go back to subsisting on what they could fence.

Neither was an option she much fancied.

"Oh, there you are, Willa. I was beginning to think you'd got lost."

She pasted on a smile and closed the front door behind her. Margaret Davies—who went by Daisy—stood just inside the drawing room door with a pleasant smile of her own and waved Willa in to join her.

She still couldn't fathom why these two sisters had agreed to host her as they'd done. Mr. V had called them family friends . . . but that didn't fit either. What cause would he have to be friends with two ladies surely young enough to be his daughters?

Always questions. Never answers. And Willa detested unanswered questions.

But she couldn't dislike Daisy or Gwen. They may have buckets of money, but they were so blasted *sweet* that it was hard to resent them for it. She obeyed the wave of Daisy's hand and slid into the drawing room.

Given that it was a let house, the somewhat ostentatious appointments didn't reflect the sisters. Both women had fair brown hair, and neither was particularly remarkable. Their dresses, though of good quality, weren't as prettily made as this one Rosemary had stitched for Willa. Daisy settled into a chair with a little cough, and Gwen was rubbing at her fingers.

Willa took a seat. "Thank you again for having me, Miss—"

"Oh, none of that. Not between old friends." Gwen grinned and darted a glance toward the door. "You must be Willa and we Daisy and Gwen or we'll never pull this off," she added in a whisper.

Daisy's smile went strained against her pale cheeks. She wasn't, she had said last evening, particularly unwell at the moment. She just always tended that way. Which was part of what led the sisters to a quiet life apart from the society they could have afforded to frolic in. "It *is* unsettling though. I can't remember the last time we had a secret from Miss Blaker."

Willa shifted on her chair, which wasn't nearly as comfortable as it had looked like it would be. "I am sorry for the secrecy. If you wish to devise a different story—"

"Oh no. It's quite all right." Daisy's countenance relaxed again. "We are neither of us fond of falsehoods, but sometimes the Lord asks us to do the unexpected for a greater cause. We are helping Britain. We know that."

Were they? If they were certain of that, then they knew more than Willa did. As to the claim that the Lord had some sort of hand in this . . . that just went beyond comprehension. Never in her life had Willa really heard anything about God that made any sense. But now all of a sudden Rosemary was spouting a bunch of nonsense about Him, and apparently she'd be getting the same sort of rot from these two.

"Well, I am grateful for your hospitality. And looking forward to seeing the workings of the orchestra."

Gwen's eyes lit, and she sat forward, dropping her hands into her lap. "They are a remarkable group—simply remarkable. Our trustee, TJ, and his colleagues outdid themselves in collecting the best artists from Belgium. I could scarcely believe it when they returned with Mr. De Wilde."

Willa's throat wanted to go tight, but she swallowed to convince it to behave normally. Yes, he had been every bit as handsome as his posters indicated when she saw him on the street yesterday. And a great deal more besides—more moody, more intense, more . . . dangerous. The same kind of dangerous that Cor was, with the added deadly elements of style and money. "I look forward to meeting him."

The sooner she did, the sooner she could set about her job. And the sooner she could get home to London and streets with names she knew how to pronounce.

"Gwen used to play the violin, you know." Daisy reached up to check her hair, which appeared to be styled for the evening already. Though the style was muted and a bit frizzy. "She was quite good."

Willa turned her gaze on the older of the sisters. "Used to?"

Gwen stretched out her hands. "I can't any longer—it hurts too much. My fingertips, you see, have gone so very sensitive with this nerve ailment I have."

"She's resorted to the organ. I'm afraid this house doesn't have one, but when at home she practices daily. Perhaps at some point you'll get to hear her."

"I hope so." The words came easily, but Willa was stuck on the previous statement. She couldn't quite imagine giving up the violin. She hadn't even been able to travel without bringing hers along, as that would mean possibly weeks without it. Unthinkable.

"But the violin will always be my first love. I hope to convince Mr. De Wilde to do some solo performances in Wales while he is here, as well. If I cannot do it myself, I can at least take joy from another's far greater talent." Gwen's smile took on a note of mischief—though so quiet a note Willa wouldn't have even noticed it in anyone else's smile.

She couldn't help but grin in return. "Perhaps we could even convince him to let you attend a few practices." So that Willa could tag along. Somehow or another, she had to get close to the man. Befriend him, if necessary. She could find her way to his rooms without any personal connection, but if he carried this cypher key on his person . . . Well, then she had to be near the person.

"Who's to say?" Still smiling, Gwen stood. "We had best get dressed for dinner. Our guests should arrive soon."

The sisters chatted as they led the way out of the room—something about a new painting that Daisy was working on giving her trouble. Willa didn't pay much attention. She wasn't sure how best to gain the confidence of De Wilde. Her original plan had been to play the wide-eyed society girl who was awestruck by his brilliance . . . but she could hardly do that now. Not after that silent little exchange in the street yesterday.

She hadn't been able to help herself. There had been something in his gaze, something far too intense to go unanswered. Something that had left her only two choices—to step back and look away, admitting weakness. Or to return the challenge.

Stupid, stupid decision, Willa. Had she shown weakness, she could have played it up. Used it against him. But no. Survival instincts had flared up, drowning out her plans.

She shook it off and mounted the stairs behind her hostesses. Her borrowed room was the size of her entire flat in London.

The chamber was roomy and ornate and had a canopy bed the likes of which she'd only ever seen in storybooks. A table sat beside it, and in the corner were a beautiful washbasin and bowl. Against the far wall stood a wardrobe so large she could have fit her own clothes in it and Elinor's and Olivia's besides.

Willa bypassed all that and moved to the window, careful to come up to it from the side so that her silhouette wouldn't be visible through the gauzy curtain if anyone happened to be looking. Easing the fabric aside just a bit, she peered out to the street below.

No brown-clad man stood out there watching. Not within sight.

She let the curtain fall back into place and turned to the wardrobe. There was really no time to be thinking about whoever had been following her anyway—she had to focus on the encounter to come. On Lukas De Wilde and how to find whatever this key thing was.

Only two evening gowns hung within the armoire. Both had been designed by Rosemary, so they were pretty and in vogue and looked like much more than they had cost. She chose one at random—a pale yellow and blue—and changed into it as quickly as she could manage. At home, Ellie would assist her. To get such aid here, she'd have to accept the help of a maid. And that just rubbed her all kinds of wrong ways.

Willa sat on the plush little bench in front of the dressing table and shook her head. She'd sooner struggle for an hour on her own than let the Davieses "lend" her their shared maid. Though granted, it *was* a struggle to get her hair to stay up.

It hadn't used to be, when it was longer. She pulled out the pins already jabbed into her low chignon and let the locks fall to her shoulders. Last year for Christmas, she and the other girls had decided to pool their resources and buy some heavy wool for a coat for Barclay—he always gave what they had to one of the younger ones before he saw to his own well-being, and it had been particularly cold that winter. But family policy said nothing stolen could be given as a gift.

So Willa had cut her hair and sold it. She still wasn't sure how the others had managed the coins they had donated, but they'd no doubt all been creative. And they'd done it—they'd bought some good, thick wool and cloth for lining it too. Rosemary had cut the coat, pinned it, and they had all helped stitch. Then they'd gotten to see Barclay's eyes light up.

And go wide with shock, too, when he saw Willa's shorn locks. Her lips quirked up now to remember it. There was nothing so fun in the world as rendering Barclay speechless.

He wouldn't be now though, were he here—he'd be snapping at her to get a move on. She had a job to do.

She was jabbing in the last pin when she heard footsteps in the hall, along with Daisy's soft laughter. And then a bell from downstairs.

Time was up. And her stomach had the knots to prove it.

She would take a moment more though. Just one. After waiting to make sure the sisters didn't knock on her door to fetch her, she moved over to the wardrobe again and pulled out the valise stashed in the bottom beside her violin case. Barclay had altered the thing for her, building in a false top in which to hide the papers from Mr. V—one slender enough that no one would look at the thing and think, *There isn't as much space within as there should be—something must be hidden.*

It took her fingers a moment to remember the trick to unlatching the compartment. Then another minute to flip through the file and find the photographs Mr. V had provided of known cypher keys.

A ring, one of them. She'd already studied it closely, even using a magnifying glass to try to see how in the world someone could have hidden any secret messages within the gold. There were symbols though—it had the look of a signet or seal or some such nonsense.

The second photo was of a children's book. More specifically, the end leaf of a book, which had letters in a seemingly random arrangement, as if to look merely playful. That seemed to be the common thread here—an alphabet in some form or another.

That, then, was what she'd look for on De Wilde, or in his room.

She slid the pages back into their place, the valise back into its place, and dragged in one last breath of ease before squaring her shoulders and striding to the door.

Once in the hallway, she could hear strains of everyday music— laughter and voices, and the *chink* of something tapping against a glass. The clear tenor of a man's voice. A baritone of another. A high, feminine laugh that couldn't possibly belong to either Gwen or Daisy and so must be Miss Blaker's. Willa had met the sisters' former governess and current companion only briefly the night before and hadn't known quite what to make of her.

With any luck, she wouldn't be here long enough to form a solid opinion.

Padding along in her new pumps, Willa hurried down the stairs and followed the voices toward the parlor. But then she paused in the shadows outside the door and looked in. Daisy and Gwen, of course, were playing hostess and pouring something or another from a crystal pitcher. It wouldn't be the traditional spirits—not here. They had already mentioned last night that theirs was a temperance household. But lemonade, perhaps? With berries? It was pink rather than yellow.

And unimportant. Her gaze skimmed over Gwen, Daisy, and Miss Blaker, who sat primly in a chair. Settled on the two dark-haired men who stood in the center of the room.

De Wilde stood beside the same man who'd left the concert hall with him yesterday. If Mr. V's notes could be trusted, he was Jules Bellamy, a cellist and De Wilde's closest friend. He was a bit taller than her mark, slighter, with what she could only term a scholarly look about him—hooked nose, intelligent eyes,

54

hollow cheeks, spectacles. Pleasant enough in appearance, but unremarkable.

Which made a marked contrast to Lukas De Wilde. He was about the same height as Barclay—just above average. A trim but solid figure that hinted at muscle whenever he moved. Rich dark hair, eyes so deep that from here they looked black—and piercing. And his face . . . his face was just as it had been yesterday. Utter male perfection.

Willa granted herself a moment to draw in a breath. To tell her stomach to behave itself and her nerves to be calm. He was a man like any other. It didn't matter that he was handsome. And rich. And quite possibly the best violinist alive today. He was a mark.

A mark who swung his gaze over to the doorway when she slid into it and yet again gave her that look that had ruined everything yesterday. Intensity masking challenge.

Her spine eased into the perfect alignment she and the other girls had practiced amid much laughter before they decided to brave the society functions in search of a few sparklies to liberate. Her chin came up a notch. Or two. But she forced her face to remember itself. Pasted on what she hoped looked like an easy smile and stepped into the room.

"And here is our guest." Gwen handed one of the glasses she held to Bellamy and the other to De Wilde. "Allow me to introduce Miss Willa Forsythe. Willa dear, this is Mr. Jules Bellamy and Mr. Lukas De Wilde."

She enlarged her smile and nodded at each of the men with a polite "How do you do?"

Bellamy returned the greeting, along with a murmured response. De Wilde was reaching for the glass—but his movement was uneven. And pain flashed, dark and stormy, in his eyes. His smile remained neutral and easy, but . . .

He was injured—his right arm. Probably his shoulder, given

the way he was moving. How in the world could he play if it hurt him so? Had he pulled a muscle, perhaps? Pinched a nerve?

If so, he must have done quite a job of it, because that pain didn't clear from his eyes as he returned his arm to his side and switched the glass to his left hand. He ought to have reached for it with that one to begin with—and no doubt was thinking the same thing even now.

Their hostesses didn't seem to notice. They continued their chatter, inviting everyone to sit if they so desired, assuring all that the meal would be ready shortly. Daisy pressed a glass of pink stuff into Willa's hand.

She moved toward a sofa but had no intention of sitting unless she must. She thought better, observed better, on her feet. Moving in the general direction of the sofa would hopefully suffice. Likely would, given that Miss Blaker had asked some question or another of Mr. Bellamy, and he remained where he was standing to answer her, gesturing with his glass.

"I am *so* glad you could join us, Mr. De Wilde." Gwen stepped into the space beside him, looked from him to Willa.

Willa took a step toward them, effectively joining their group with that small movement. And making a mental note of how seamlessly her hostess had achieved the inclusion.

"I used to play the violin myself—though of course I never achieved your level of skill and talent." Gwen looked perfectly at ease, despite the fact that she wasn't exactly what one would term fashionable. She wore a high-necked gown that bordered on dowdy, though she moved about with confidence. But then, this was her world.

De Wilde only glanced at Willa once, for the briefest of moments, before turning his smile on Gwen. But it was enough to scald her. "I have heard that you played, *mademoiselle*. And have heard, too, that you are modest—that you were quite good. Would that I could hear you."

Gwen sighed, her smile sad. "Would that I could let you convince me—however embarrassing it would be. I don't think I will ever cease missing it." She rubbed at her fingers, much as she had been doing earlier.

Another flash of his eyes. Not exactly the same intense pain as before, but something similar. Then he leveled that gaze on Willa. "And you, Miss Forsythe? Do you play an instrument? Piano perhaps—I know it is the preference of many society ladies."

She'd plinked a few keys on the old upright Pauly had. But whatever fluke of nature had enabled her to pick up a violin and a bow and just *play*, it had not translated to the piano. Hence why she had often thought, in those early days, that her violin was magical. That the music rested in it, not in her.

She ought to claim no musical experience whatsoever. Because really, how much did she have? The only instruction she'd ever received was what she could steal from someone else's lesson, hovering under open windows and straining upward to listen. For a year or so, she'd found an actual violin instructor who gave lessons in a ground-floor room of his house. Willa had listened outside the window whenever she could manage it.

Then he'd up and moved, the blighter.

De Wilde lifted a brow, so subtly she almost missed it.

Her shoulders went back. "I also play the violin. A bit. I've never had formal instruction though, so my skill is certainly nothing deserving of bragging."

There was nothing wrong with her words—neither in the ones she'd chosen nor in their inflection. Their correctness was proven by Gwen's expression—a bit of pleasant surprise at the revelation itself, but a smiling kind.

Why, then, did that challenge burn in De Wilde's gaze? "Do you? Then you must play for us later, after dinner."

"Oh, I hardly think so." And why would he want her to? So he could laugh at her? But no, that didn't seem right. There was nothing *cruel* in his eyes. Just . . . just . . . she didn't even know the word for it. But she didn't intend to indulge him. "I don't even have my instrument with me in Wales."

A lie, of course, but she was most certainly not going to pull out that scarred old thing. Love it as she might, it wasn't befitting her assumed role.

"No matter. You can play mine." He motioned to a case she hadn't even noticed sitting there, under a side table. "I brought it to show Miss Davies, knowing she appreciates the instruments crafted by Stradivari. I thought perhaps she would like to see mine."

Gwen's eyes went as bright as a summer sun. "Oh! How good of you, sir. Yes, I most assuredly would."

He had a Stradivarius? *Idiot.* Of course he had a Strad—all the best of the professional string players seemed to have one. Willa forced a swallow past a throat gone dry and looked to that case again.

He had a Stradivarius. *Here.* And he'd offered to let her play it. All for the low cost of her pride—and really, what did pride matter in this? When else would she ever have the chance to actually touch an instrument so fine? To *play* it? Her head bobbed slowly. "Very well, Mr. De Wilde. After dinner—so long as you promise not to laugh."

His smile was quick. Mischievous. And nearly curled her toes. "*Bon.* I shall look forward to it."

Willa took a sip of her drink—definitely lemonade with some sort of berry in it—and silently thanked the servant who appeared in the doorway and announced dinner. With any luck, she would end up seated as far from this man as possible during the meal and . . .

No. She needed to be close to him, to see what he might carry on his person that could have an alphabet on it. He wore no rings, so that option was ruled out. But perhaps . . . something else. A cufflink was probably too small, wasn't it? But he could have a pocket watch. A pocket watch could easily have an inscription on it.

Daisy was moving toward the door, her smile clear and bright and young. "You gentlemen can escort Miss Blaker and Miss Forsythe—my sister and I shall lead the way."

Escort them? Willa took a step back, even as De Wilde crooked his elbow her way. She may have made a show of insisting that Gwen have that honor, but the sisters were already moving toward the door.

And pain was pulsing again in De Wilde's eyes. He ought to have offered his left arm instead—but she was standing on his right side. It would have, she supposed, been odd.

Blast. She couldn't well refuse without looking rude. But oh, she wanted to refuse. Her smile no doubt looked as strained as his gaze when she reached out to rest her gloved fingers against his arm.

The fabric of his jacket was smooth and fine. The arm beneath it was firm—as she expected of someone who spent most of his days with his bow raised. The subtle scent of sandalwood drifted to her nose.

And something more than the usual uneasiness skittered its way up her spine at the contact.

"Shall we, then?"

Rather than look up at him again, she kept her gaze on the others as he started them toward the door. His accent was different from Cor's and the other refugees' she'd met in London. French rather than Flemish. But faint, bespeaking a long education in English, she would guess.

"Are you from Wales as well, Miss Forsythe?" His accent may be slight, but her name still sounded strange coming from his lips. Or maybe it was just that so few people called her *Miss Forsythe.*

She shook her head but kept her gaze on Daisy's back. "No.

London. I've lived there all my life, other than when I went to Highfield School in Hendon—just on the outskirts of Town. That's where I met Daisy and Gwen." They were older than she—which meant, if anyone wondered, she'd have to claim to be nearer their ages than her own. She could perhaps get away with twenty-eight and still have gone to school with them. But certainly not her twenty-three.

But De Wilde didn't question her age. He hummed and led her through the door. "I have always liked London. I performed there just a few months ago."

"I know. I was there." On a catwalk above the symphony hall, where she'd listened for a full hour to him play—as much time as the coin she'd slipped a stage boy had bought her. She'd had to climb down at the intermission and steal back out into the cold winter air.

But it had been worth every dizzying moment of being perched up so high. Not that she meant to tell *him* that.

From the corner of her eye she saw his head turn toward her. And she felt his smile. "Were you? You should have arranged for an introduction. I would have enjoyed meeting you."

An incredulous snort slipped out. "I hardly think so, Mr. De Wilde."

His step slowed, which somehow pulled her gaze up to his. She found his brows knotted into a question. "And why would you say such a thing?"

This was a mercy of the false story Mr. V had created for her—he must have known she would prefer it to pretending to be actually *rich*. "There were two dukes in the audience that night." Those whispers had reached even the catwalks. "If anyone were to get an introduction, it would be them and their wives. Not a girl of middling means who only aspired to Highfield because of a scholarship."

He chuckled. She heard the charm in it, felt it weave itself around her. Felt an echoing anger rumble through her. No one had a right to be so handsome *and* talented *and* charming. It set her teeth on edge.

He leaned closer. "I did indeed meet the Dukes of Stafford and Nottingham that night—along with their lovely wives. But I *always* have time to meet intriguing young ladies as well."

A laugh slipped from her lips—the kind that was too short to speak of genuine amusement. She couldn't help it—it was so obviously *wrong*. "Except, sir, that I am *not* intriguing."

"Are you not?" They'd reached the door to the dining room, awash with bright electric lights. "I believe *I* get to be the judge of that, *n'est-ce pas?*"

"Think what you will." Especially since she would no doubt fade from his mind altogether once they were out of each other's company. That was the way of men like him—a way that transcended class and station. Handsome, charming men were all the same. Flirting with a woman long enough to get what he wanted from her, then flitting off to the next. Leaving the poor girl in a state of panic that could last for a year. *Years.* And never once bothering to come back and see if she had survived his leaving.

Sometimes she could still see her mother, searching hopefully through every male face. Never seeing the one she wanted. Murmuring, ever murmuring, about how handsome he was. How he'd loved her. How he'd called her pretty and told her she was the best girl in the world. *His* girl.

Willa could appreciate handsome faces as much as the next woman—when they were safely flattened onto a poster to tack upon her wall. But in flesh and blood they were suited to be marks, nothing more.

She let go of his arm and didn't bother looking at him as she made her way to the same chair she'd sat upon last night. She would study him, yes. She would learn where he took his rooms, when he was gone from them. She would take whatever it was Mr. V wanted. She would play his violin later.

And, yes, she would enjoy besting him—because he quite obviously deserved it, thinking as he did that he had only to smile at a woman to have his way with her.

Well, he had never met Willa Forsythe. He had no idea what he was in for.

FIVE

e had no idea what to expect—and when handing his most precious possession to a veritable stranger, that caused Lukas more than a bit of concern. He lifted his violin from its case with his left hand, tilting it, as he always did, into the light. To see how the illumination in this room, this house, played on the gloss, drew out the impossibly tight wood grain.

It had taken him years to earn enough to buy this. *Years.* It had been his goal since he was a boy deciding that he rather liked this violin thing after all. To own a Strad. To know every time he touched bow to string that he held a masterpiece in his hands.

To know that if there were a fault in the music, it was *his* fault, *his* shortcoming, not his instrument's.

"Oh, it's beautiful." Gwen Davies perched near him on the edge of the sofa, leaning forward to study the violin. "Look at the scrolling, Daisy."

Daisy scooted closer to her sister so she could lean over to see. Their hair was within a shade of each other's, that color of brown caught halfway to blond but not.

Lukas obligingly held out the violin to them. "You may take it, Miss Davies. I trust you." She knew the value of a Stradivarius.

Gwen took it as carefully as one would a kitten, stroking a gloved hand along its curves. "Gorgeous. I never fail to be awed by Stradivari's workmanship."

Her sister made some reply, but Lukas paid it no attention. He glanced instead toward Miss Forsythe.

She was an enigma. Scarcely looking his way during dinner, playing the part of smiling guest wherever the conversation went. But there was more to her, of that he had no doubt. The way she'd been studying that building yesterday . . .

The way she studied the violin now, from her stance behind the sisters' sofa. She didn't reach for it. Her posture said she was perfectly at ease—nearly bored even.

But her eyes were hungry.

His father and his sister could spend days studying a mathematical enigma—Lukas had never shared that particular love of theirs. But a puzzle of a woman he could study for an eternity.

He drew his bow from its bed and held it out to her. "Here you are, Miss Forsythe. Whenever you are ready."

A smile danced over her lips, vanishing again even as she reached for the bow. Yet even then, her gaze was set on seeing more than what he held out. She stared at his left shoulder, the one he'd used, and then at his right, which was yet again on fire. He'd had no choice but to use that arm during dinner—though his knife had never weighed so heavy.

But he'd been so careful about guarding his expression. Even Jules hadn't whispered a question about how he felt as they made their way back into the parlor—he'd only said, "Are you certain you want to let her play your Strad?"

Certain? No. But he was curious. Not so much about how she played, but about how she might look when she did so. What light might be in her eyes. Whether she would focus upon the instrument with that single-minded intensity, or whether she'd approach it as she had her meal—without any care, it seemed, as to whether she ate a carrot or meat. Whether she played a grace note or a whole.

Her gaze swept from his thundering shoulder to his face, as if to say, *I know your secrets. And I'll use them against you when-ever I please.*

Intriguing indeed.

She ran her fingers over the bow, studying it, weighing it. Leaned over the sofa back to see whatever Gwen was pointing out on his violin now. Tugged off her gloves. She wouldn't be able to play with them on, he knew. And it wasn't an action she per-formed with any visible intent to make a show of it. No meeting his gaze as she did so, suggestion in her own. No careful, sensual tug of satin from fingers. She did it absently, as his mother might. It shouldn't have been so interesting to watch.

Her fingers were long and slender, her palms lean. Good hands for the violin, to be sure. And her gaze went even hungrier.

Perhaps she would have tea with him if he invited her to step out. Or accompany him to the opera, or to a play, if this miniscule Welsh city had such things to offer. A moving-picture house was probably out of the question this far to the west.

Gwen turned on her cushion, smiling, and held up the violin. "Here you are, Willa. Play something lively for us."

Miss Forsythe took it, holding it for a moment to study it. Took another long moment to position it on her shoulder, under her chin. Backed up a step.

Her eyes went closed. The bow came up.

Lukas held his breath. The instrument was one of the best—but it could not make a master from a novice, and she had made him promise not to laugh. It didn't bode well.

But she only played a scale, slow and steady. To get a feel for the instrument, he knew, to test the tension and tune of the strings. Both of which were faultless, but likely different from what she was used to. And sometimes people didn't care about the quality if it was too different.

But that smile played at the corners of her mouth again. She nodded, turned away from them—not deliberately, from the looks of it. More as if she'd forgotten they were there. And then she played.

He recognized the piece—*I Lombardi alla Prima Crociata*. He'd played it himself three years ago, when the Conservatoire presented a season of Verdi on the tenth anniversary of the composer's death. It was, as Miss Davies had requested, lively. And challenging to play beautifully.

But her fingers never stumbled over the quick notes. Her bow never hesitated in its back-and-forth glide over the strings. And the song came to life in her hands. Even without the rest of the strings to provide the beat and background, it skipped through the high, lighthearted sections and then sobbed its way through the minor phrases.

When he'd practiced it at home, he'd always missed the accompanying strings, the percussion, the woodwinds. He'd always felt this was a piece that needed the harmony, despite the violin having the melody.

He didn't think so now.

Jules sidled up beside him and spoke in low French. "I assumed she would be an amateur. But she could give you a run for first chair, Lukas, were she to audition for it."

She could. And where usually the thought would have ignited a flame of jealousy, his chest had no room for that just now. Not given the appreciation surging through him. He could only hum his answer.

Jules chuckled. "I didn't think I'd ever see the day when a woman struck you dumb."

"Gloat later. Just now I'm listening to a master." He nudged his friend aside and moved to get a better view of her face as she played.

Her posture could be improved. And she was still playing to the wall more than to her audience. But the skill . . . her skill was unsurpassed.

Perhaps his staring had unnerved her—she brought the piece to an end far too soon, using a cadence from the middle part to do so. The others all burst into applause. Lukas lurched another step forward, all but whimpering.

Oh yes, Jules would be gloating later. But that didn't matter. Lukas spread his hands. "Why did you stop? Please keep playing. I would love to hear you finish the piece."

Miss Forsythe leapt back a step when she saw how near he was. What was the matter with this girl? He was still a large stride away, by no means too close.

She seemed to realize as much and eased half a step closer again, clearing her throat. "I cannot, sir, though I thank you for saying so. But I don't know the rest of it. That's all I heard."

Jules edged closer too. And his brows were wearing the same frown Lukas felt tugging on his. "All you *heard*?"

Her eyes had gone back to the violin, her gaze stroking over it like a caress. "Yes, I heard the London Symphony practicing it last week. But I couldn't stay long enough to hear the end."

His friend held up a hand. "Wait. You *heard* someone practicing it—the complete ensemble, no less—and can then play the violin part so perfectly yourself?"

Her cheeks flushed such a becoming shade of pink that Lukas decided then and there he would have to elicit blushes as often as he could. "Well, I don't know that it's *perfectly*."

"I do." Lukas tucked his hands behind his back to keep from reaching out when a lock of hair slipped from her style to frame her face. If she was the kind to be so startled at him standing an end-table's length away, she would probably bite him if he made a move like that. Not that he went about touching the hair of women he barely knew. Except when he was trying to know them considerably better. In which case they usually purred at him and turned their faces into his hand and . . .

Not likely with her.

He slid a step to the side. "So you play by ear?" He could pick out a melody, of course. Work out something he'd heard. But he certainly couldn't re-create a piece that complex, so perfectly, having only *heard* it a time or two. "But you surely read music too. I can get you the rest of the fantasia. I have it with me, in my rooms."

She slid a step to the side as well—the one away from him. And nodded. "I do, though not nearly as well. I had to teach myself and—"

"Teach yourself?" Jules's laugh was half snort. "You surely studied under a master. Joachim?"

Her brows knit. "Who?"

"*Who?*" Lukas nearly laughed. Until he realized she was quite serious. Or pretending to be. But how could a violinist of her talent not know of the greatest violin master of their day? He looked to Gwen Davies. "Perhaps you can tell us, since your guest will play coy. Under whom did she study? Or perhaps you took lessons together at school?"

Miss Davies wouldn't meet his gaze. And her fingers twisted the fabric of her dress. "I . . . I didn't actually know she played. She was a few years behind me at the academy, you see. And apparently quite a bit ahead of me on the violin."

Miss Forsythe shoved that slip of hair behind her ear with far less care than he would have used on it. "Now look, I won't have you making fun of me. I may be an amateur, but—"

"Amateur!" Jules laughed outright this time, going so far as to turn to include Miss Blaker in his mirth. "Listen to her. As if she does not know quite well that she could put Lukas out of a job."

Lukas shot his friend a glare. "There is room in the world for more than one violinist, Jules." But he had to look back at her.

Had to. "Why are you not in an orchestra somewhere? Perhaps it is beneath your station?" But she'd said she'd gone to school on scholarship. So then, this should have been a logical step. Any ensemble would be grateful to have her, even if her sight-reading skills were far beneath her by-ear skills.

"Now you're teasing me." And she looked none too happy about it. "I wouldn't know the first thing about . . . about auditions or whatever would be needed for that."

"Your instructor could surely have led you through the process." She looked ready to snarl.

Lukas held up a hand before she could. "My apologies. I seem to be probing a sensitive subject." Which he intended to probe more fully. But subtlety was obviously called for. "Perhaps you will play us something else? What of . . ." He searched his mind for another of the most complicated pieces, eyes on the plasterwork of the ceiling. "Bach's *Chaconne* from *Partita No. 2 in D Minor?*"

She simply blinked. "I'm afraid I don't know that one. Not by title, anyway. What does it sound like?"

Gwen Davies was pushing to her feet. "Oh, I have it! I never could play it well, but I have the music. It was always my favorite. I brought that box of music with me, didn't I, Daisy? Isn't that the one we stored in the spare room?"

"Oh, I believe you did." Daisy Davies pushed to her feet too. "But you put it in the attic with the trunks, I think."

"No, I'm quite sure it was the spare room."

"You check there, I'll look in the attic. Just a moment, Willa. We won't be long."

The two sisters sped from the room, Miss Blaker moving after them. "They'll never find it there. I'm all but certain all the sheet music is in the upstairs parlor. Excuse me for a moment."

Miss Forsythe's eyes went wide as the three women abandoned her, and she reached out with the hand still holding the bow. "Oh, but . . . wait . . ."

Lukas exchanged a bit of a grin with Jules. And made a point of *not* stepping closer again, though he wanted to. "My parents hired a music tutor from the time I was four. I imagine you began just as early, *oui*? And you must practice hours each day."

A war raged through her eyes for a moment—a war he knew well. Women's eyes often had such battles in them. The question of whether to be truthful or to lie. Her shoulders sagged. "I didn't pick up a violin until I was twelve."

"Twelve!" A late start indeed for having such skill. "Remarkable. You must have taken to it quite naturally."

She gave one quick nod and cast her glance between him and Jules. "I did. I . . . I picked up that battered old violin that day, and it felt as if . . . as if I'd finally found a part of myself I hadn't known was missing."

"Your family must have been very proud of your natural talent, to have encouraged you to reach such skill. And your instructor must have been delighted to have such an intuitive pupil." Jules offered an easy smile, but Lukas, at least, knew quite well he was fishing for more information. Jules was as passionate about the teaching process as the music itself. One of these days, in another year or two, he meant to open up a school of his own. Once he'd achieved fame enough to have his pick of pupils.

Lukas had never shared that particular desire. Perhaps someday he would settle down to such morose things. But just now the thought of children who would as soon duck out of a lesson as have one set his teeth on edge.

The move of her eyes was exasperated. "I have never had an instructor, so do stop trying to wheedle a name out of me."

"Never?" Jules frowned. "*Incroyable*. You play with far too much skill to be untaught."

And she went stiff as ice. "Some people don't need to be *taught* in order to learn."

"Very true." Was that not what Père had always said about Margot? That it wasn't like *teaching* her at all—it was like reminding her of something she already knew but for which she hadn't quite had the words.

He had always thought music similar. That his favorite compositions were capturing something he'd always known existed and putting it to paper. Giving voice, giving words to those soaring notes of joy, the pulsing beats of temper or pain.

But it had taken teaching for him to learn how to bring those notes to life on an instrument. For everyone he knew, it was the same. Oh, he had met musicians who played by ear, to be sure. But not like this. "So you began at age twelve. Teaching yourself. And now you can re-create the most challenging pieces after hearing them . . . how many times?"

She shifted, glanced at the incredulous Jules again, back to him. Shrugged. "It depends on the piece. Once, sometimes. Twice or thrice always suffices."

Once. Or twice.

Jules fell to a seat on a chair. "*Incroyable*," he muttered again.

Lukas just held that gaze she'd shifted back to him. It *was* incredible. Unbelievable. "You are a . . . a prodigy." He'd never met one, not really. Children with talent, certainly. But *this* talented? Never. Miraculous, his family would say. God-gifted.

He'd not given much thought in recent years to gifts from God. And these last few weeks, he wouldn't have bet God was still even imparting gifts, given the state of the world. But what else could one call this? *Her?*

Jules was shaking his head. "You could be a professional. You realize that, do you not? You could have an illustrious career. Win awards. Set tongues to wagging about your skill."

She gripped Lukas's bow, his violin, and looked to be sliding right back into irritation. "I don't want fame. Or awards or . . . I just want to play. That's all. To have the music."

The music. It had been about that, once, for him. The pure love of it. The desire to spend his days courting it, being courted by it.

He'd nearly forgotten what it felt like—but now it was searing heat in his shoulder, traveling to his gut. He wanted that again. To remember it, but not only that—to live it. To be reminded day in and day out why he spent his life with a bow in hand and strings under his fingers.

She could remind him. And he could teach her. Between them . . .

He drew in a quick breath and put on his best grin. "Will you marry me?"

Jules narrowed his eyes.

Willa Forsythe blinked. "Are you out of your mind?"

Probably. But he kept the grin in place. "Think of it—how well suited we would be. You with your natural fire for the music, me with all I've learned. We could teach each other, remind each other of why we love it. Travel together. Tour. Play. Until children come along, then we'll limit the traveling, of course. But just think of them too—how remarkable they will be."

Surely he *was* mad, because he could almost see it as he spoke the ridiculous words. Strads in both their hands, sitting together in a small ensemble, trading off the lead. Then a dark-haired tot between them. Grinning up at him and calling him *Papa.*

Perhaps the injury had addled his brain as much as his shoulder.

He angled a step closer. "We can spend part of the year in London. Part in Brussels, part in Louvain."

No. The jest struck a note of pain. There was nothing left of Louvain to speak of. And Brussels . . . Brussels was lost to him just now.

His shoulder pulsed again. Not just Brussels was lost. Mère, Margot . . . where were they? What if . . . *Non.* He wouldn't entertain such thoughts.

Willa shook her head and turned away. "I'd heard you were a ladies' man. I *hadn't* heard you went about proposing to girls you just met."

"He does not." Jules glared at him. And switched his words to Flemish. "And why would you begin doing so now? This kind of jest isn't like you."

He shrugged. "If marriage is too much to ask just now, then perhaps a different offer." He stepped closer again, around the end table between them. "Let me teach you."

"Teach me?" She spun to face him. "Make up your mind, De Wilde. Am I a prodigy or a child needing a teacher?"

"Who says prodigies need no teacher?" He spread his hands, ignoring the continued pulse of his shoulder. "You have the talent. The skill. But I can teach you the theory. The posture. The details. I can turn you into the best violinist of the century—and even if you have no desire for fame, you must realize you would appreciate the music all the more with proper instruction."

Jules must have taken to his feet again, for he appeared in his periphery, scowling. "Why would you do that?" Flemish again. "You'll make her better than you—you know that, don't you?"

"Why would you do that?" English, of course, from Willa—and flavored with an accent she hadn't displayed before, though he couldn't quite place it.

Because he saw his father, standing in their old schoolroom, looking down on what Margot was scribbling—what Lukas had assumed to be nonsense. And he saw that realization dawn in the eyes of the man he'd always most looked up to. The realization that what he had worked years to understand, to achieve, came so naturally to this tiny girl. That she would surpass him. And that the best thing he could ever do for himself, for the world, was to help her do so.

Lukas had always thought it possible for a man of Père's pride to do it solely because Margot was his daughter.

But now he understood. It wasn't because of the bonds that already existed. It was because of the bonds that *could* exist, if they were forged through a mutual love. It was because Père had found that day someone who would understand him.

It was because he recognized that she would better the world.

As this woman before him could do. She could bring such beauty into the dark places. And he could help her.

He swallowed all that back and let his eyes slide shut. Let his arm scream. Let the years of *Lukas De Wilde, world-famous violinist* fade away until he was just a boy again, possessed by what was, for him, that most basic love. "For the sake of the music." He opened his eyes again, captured her gaze, and held it fast. "What say you?"

Footsteps sounded in the hallway along with feminine laughter. The Davieses and Miss Blaker would return in seconds. And who knew whose side they'd take in this—probably not his.

She dragged in a long breath. "Lessons, yes."

Victory. He would teach her whatever she didn't know. Get to know her in the process. Decipher what made her so very intriguing.

And then decide if he was jesting or not about more.

The ladies entered again, chattering and waving sheet music about, Miss Blaker carrying a music stand.

Lukas retreated back to Jules's side.

His friend was scowling at him. "What the devil are you about?"

He sat in the chair beside Jules but kept his gaze on Willa as she looked over the music. "Exactly what I said."

"*Non*. Impossible. Because you said *marriage*, and that is a word you have avoided like the plague. I have seen you with my own eyes parry every thrust your mother has made in recent years about settling down with a nice girl."

Who knew he could torment his friend so fully simply by proposing to a young woman? It was worth maintaining the jest just to watch the temper in Jules's eyes. "Well, I'd never met *this* girl."

Jules mumbled. Then shook his head. "You are drunk on the pain medicine."

"I didn't take any."

"Idiot. Then you are drunk on the pain."

"Maybe." But not just that of his shoulder. As Willa positioned the sheet music on the stand and studied it with furrowed brows, Lukas sighed. The truth of the admission burrowed deep. "Maybe I *should* be. I have lost my father. My home is destroyed. I have no idea where my mother and sister are—or if they yet live." He looked over and met Jules's familiar eyes. "It *should* hurt. To realize that I have built nothing to last. That now, with one German march, I've lost everything that matters. And for what? To chase fleeting pleasures?"

He looked back to her again, held his breath as she positioned her fingers on his violin's strings and launched into the opening measures of one of his favorite songs. "No more, Jules. No more."

SIX

She wouldn't go. Willa paced to her window, then back again to the door. She ought to leave now, to get there on time. But she wouldn't go. It was stupid and foolhardy and utterly ridiculous to think that Lukas De Wilde, arguably the most prominent violinist of their day, was really interested in teaching *her* about the violin. He must have an angle. Everyone always had an angle. And from the file Mr. V had given her, his angle seemed to be charming everything female.

Not that she could determine why he'd decided to charm *her*, female or not. She wasn't anywhere near as pretty as the women he'd been photographed with before. But if his game wasn't so simple, then what *was* it?

Well, she wouldn't find out. Because she wouldn't go. That was that.

In the street below her open window, children's laughter floated up to her. If she didn't look out to see the unfamiliar faces, she could pretend it was Nigel and Olivia and Jory out there, playing and teasing and acting like every child. She missed them. Five days away, and she missed them. She wanted to go home—except they wouldn't be at home; they'd be in Cornwall. She'd have to go *there* if she wanted to put her arms around the little ones.

Blast Rosemary for changing everything on them. Even if it *was* for the better—which remained to be seen, really.

Willa strode to the too-soft feather bed and sat on its edge. She had to go. Not home, and not to Cornwall. She had to go to the Belle Vue Royal Hotel, whose direction De Wilde had scribbled down for her last night, and she had to meet him in the reception room he said he had permission to use for practicing. And she had to *learn*.

She wanted to learn.

She dreaded learning—what if he wanted to change everything about how she played? He would no doubt teach her *rules*. And she detested rules. What were they but contrivances created by the powerful to keep the masses in line? Even in music. He would try to tell her to stand a certain way, fill her mind with nonsense about . . . about *mathematics* or something, and it would ruin it all.

But she had to go. She had to go, because it was where he was living, and she'd be close to him, and she could do her job while there. She could find out what room was his and determine how and when to slip into it to search for this blighted key.

Find it. Go back to London. Hand it over to Mr. V and . . . and go home to her empty flat that would have only Elinor and no little ones, and that was assuming that Elinor hadn't decided to stay with Lucy and Retta while the children were all away.

Her fingers dug into the mattress. The world had gone mad. Not just with the war, with *everything*. Utterly, infuriatingly mad.

She got up again and strode to the wardrobe. Not set on grabbing a hat for the trek she had to make, but to pull out that battered violin case. She set it on the bed and extracted the equally battered violin.

Poor thing. It looked like a rag next to the memory of the Stradivarius she'd held last night. Dull and scarred and . . . lighter even, as if the wood were too thin. Perhaps it was. Still, it was one of her oldest friends, and her fingers caressed the familiar curves and corners, ran along the strings.

A tap sounded on her door along with a soft, "Willa?"

Gwen, she thought. Though she and Daisy sounded rather alike. "Come in." She ought to put this old thing away first, but . . .

Gwen, yes, and she slipped in with a smile. "I had a feeling you were having second thoughts."

She had no business having feelings about Willa after knowing her for so short a time. And certainly no business being *right*. Willa sighed. "I'll go." She must, for the sake of the job. That didn't mean she had to like it, or that she had to listen to a blasted thing he said. She only had to *pretend* to.

Gwen clicked the door shut and eased her way over to the bed. She was wearing another high-necked gown without the least bit of fashion to it. Her eyes were on the violin. "Is this yours? It has the look of an old friend. Well loved."

Willa breathed a laugh and flicked a fingernail over the deep scratch that had been there when she found the thing. "Well abused before I found it and loved it. It was tossed out. Junk." She'd known the feeling.

Gwen smiled and sat down too. "My first violin wasn't much better. It had been my father's as a lad, and he'd not been gentle with it. But I loved it. I almost hated to replace it with a better one—almost."

Willa smiled in return and put her old friend back in its case. "I didn't want to bring it out last night. That's why I said I hadn't my instrument with me. I can only imagine what Lukas De Wilde would have said if he saw it."

Gwen chuckled. "And more, he let you play *his*. Not that I'm condoning a lie, of course, but that must have been a heady feeling. And your playing—you're amazing, Willa. I had no idea. And I had to confess to a bit of jealousy in my prayers last night."

Never in her life had anyone ever been jealous of *her*. Willa eased the lid of the case shut and latched it. "Do I . . . Do I need a teacher? Lessons?" She wasn't sure what answer she wanted.

She had a feeling Gwen would give her the truth, no matter whether she wanted it or not. The woman tilted her head, gaze focused on some spot well past Willa. Her eyes were a simple brown. A common color, but filled with warmth and . . . peace. A rarity these days. "I saw nothing wrong with your form or execution. But I am not the expert that Mr. De Wilde is. What I do know is that he has never once offered to tutor anyone. He has never offered a lesson. He must have seen something very special in you to do so."

Nonsense. She might not know what his angle was, but she was certain it wasn't as simple as what he'd said. She tapped a finger to the case.

Gwen stood. "I don't know why Mr. V sent you here, Willa. But unless this interferes with your true purpose, I say you'd be a fool to let such an opportunity pass you by. No one else in the world can claim to have had instruction from Lukas De Wilde. But *you* will be able to do so."

And more, this *was* her purpose in coming. Or a means to it. With a nod, Willa stood. "I know. I'm going. I just . . . What do you know of him? Beyond when he's appeared in the gossip rags?" Which was far too often, apparently. Not that she read the things normally, but clippings made up a good portion of that file Mr. V had given her. Far too often, with far too many beautiful society girls. And beautiful actresses. And beautiful opera singers. And . . .

Gwen's face pinched. "His reputation *is* rather scandalous, isn't it? But Daisy and I both agreed he was of no danger to us. For all his wild ways, he comes from a very decent Christian family. He may not live by such guidance himself just now, but he knows it and respects it."

Willa shifted from one foot to another—and heard Barclay in her head, from back in the day when they'd decided to target society marks and that they'd do so best by learning to blend in with them. *"Stand still,"* he'd said time and again. *"Your fidgeting will give you away in a heartbeat. Be at ease."*

She stood still. But she couldn't be at ease, not with that talk. "I'm not . . ." She had no reason to confess, did she? Except that she had to. "I'm not what one would term religious. I realize you and Daisy are, but . . ."

From what Mr. V's information had told her, they were Methodist or something equally odd and strict.

But Gwen smiled. "Our faith is the rock we stand on, Willa— but we don't demand anyone else stand here with us. Though if ever you wanted to, there is plenty of room."

Willa relaxed. What had she expected—for this quiet young woman to launch into a sermon of fire and brimstone? "I'm honestly not even certain there *is* a God. And if there is . . . well, I've never seen any evidence."

Gwen didn't look offended. Her smile remained in place as she stood and angled toward the door. "God is real, my friend. And I daresay you *have* seen Him—you just didn't know it." She moved to the door, then paused with her hand on the latch. "I hope you don't mind if I pray for you."

Rosemary claimed to be doing so as well. Which was just bizarre. What made these people think that, if there were a God, He wanted to be troubled with her? But she offered a tight-lipped smile. "I don't mind." She just didn't think it would matter a lick in the grand scheme of things.

"Good." Gwen sent a pointed gaze to the wardrobe. "Now you had best get your hat and gloves and get moving, young lady. You'll be late for your lesson." She slipped out the door.

Willa's gaze kept darting as she moved toward the violin case. Part of her wanted to bring it—but she'd already planted her lie last night, claiming not to have it with her. And she didn't need

De Wilde scoffing. *And* she could only assume she'd get to play *his* again, since he didn't think she had hers.

"No offense, old friend. But you've earned a bit of a rest, don't you think?"

Her violin remained accusingly silent as she slipped from her room and hurried down the stairs. But she'd make it up to it later. Perhaps she'd come home with a new piece to play. For that matter, Gwen said she could borrow any of her music she liked. She'd brought it with her solely because she'd known there would be musicians about, she said, and one never knew when her collection could be needed.

Bully luck for Willa. Not that she meant to be here long, but even if only for a few days, she would enjoy going through it all. Figuring out if she'd heard any of the pieces before, which would make reading the music easier. Picking her way through the unfamiliar ones until the melodies took on life in her heart.

The sun was scant when she opened the door, playing hide-and-seek as it was with a cluster of white-grey clouds. It could well rain this afternoon, given that the clouds on the horizon were mostly grey and more solid sheet than balls of fluff. She grabbed a brolly from the rack before shutting the door behind her and starting out.

She hadn't needed the direction to the hotel. She'd spotted it yesterday on her scouting expedition—only a fifteen-minute walk from the rented Davies home. With purpose in her stride to cover up the hesitation still squeezing her insides, she set off.

A whole street had sped by before she felt it again. That tingling at the nape of her neck, that tightening of her gut. Someone was following her.

If yesterday's pattern held true, she'd not see them if she turned. Why waste the time, then? She'd have to be cleverer than that to catch them at it, to get a glimpse of whoever wore that brown jacket. For now, she did her best to project an air of oblivious focus and kept to her path.

Once, she turned a corner quickly enough to get that glimpse, that flash of rusty brown. But only once. Then the hotel loomed, and that tightening in her stomach could no longer be attributed to someone following her. It was who waited for her that brought it on.

Just a mark. Just the job. She recited the words as she emerged onto Marine Terrace with its views of the slate-grey bay. In the height of summer, there would no doubt be crowds of seagoers rambling about the bathhouse at the end of the promenade, but with autumn's winds blowing today, only a few bundled people dared to step onto the beach. Willa took account of them—two women with three children between them, one old man tossing bread to the gulls—and then bustled her way into the hotel and inquired at the front desk as to where Mr. De Wilde was holding his practice.

But such mundane observations couldn't dislodge the unease. Marks weren't supposed to study her as closely as he'd done. And praise her playing. And offer to teach her.

And they certainly weren't supposed to *propose*. He'd been joking, she knew, but still. Who in the world would propose to a woman, even as a joke, within an hour of meeting her?

The desk clerk directed her toward what he called the Ocean Function Room, though she wouldn't have needed instruction on reaching it. A few steps down the corridor and the music seeping from beneath its door was a siren song all its own.

He was playing something slow and mournful. Pausing outside the door, she stood there rather than interrupt. Just listened.

He hadn't played this one at the concert she'd bribed her way into last winter. Nor had anyone else at the others she'd sneaked into, or whose practices she'd overheard. She couldn't even recall hearing it on one of the old rubber records she'd found to play on her equally ancient gramophone—a device she'd rescued from a rubbish bin and which Barclay had managed to repair for her after a few months of tinkering.

And she'd remember if she'd heard it before. It was the kind of soul-searing melody she loved best, the kind she only ever played in the solitude of her flat. Certainly not the kind to share in the pub—no one could clap their hands or stomp their feet to the beat of it.

No one would want to. It was the type of melody that spoke of sorrow and pain and a longing for something always out of reach.

It sounded almost, *almost* familiar. As if she knew the voice but not the words. As if she'd heard another line of it before, but not this particular refrain.

The door was muffling it a bit. The low notes, and some of the richness of them all. But he was expecting her, wasn't he? It wouldn't be rude to simply slip in.

With all the stealth she had mastered for survival, she turned the knob, slid silently into the room, and closed the door again behind her.

His back was to her, his jacket draped over an armchair, his white shirtsleeves rolled up past his elbows. His forearms, she quickly noted, were muscled and sinewy, strong. But he was still favoring that right arm, not sweeping the bow out as far as she would have expected him to do. Wincing, nearly bobbling the whole melody, when he tried. And this was a slow song—how would he play a quick one if he was in such obvious distress?

No concern of hers, really. For now she listened, her throat tight when he lingered on that D sharp. Her nostrils flaring when the melody danced upward for one glorious, major-key moment before it gave a final weeping cry of beautiful despair.

Silence underscored the last note. He held perfectly still until the echo of it had died completely away. And not until he moved did she move too, softly, just a step. "Beautiful. I've never heard that one before."

He didn't jump or start or otherwise seem surprised at her presence. Merely turned, slowly, with a smile that tried to melt her insides.

Tried. Didn't succeed. Much.

"You would not have. A friend of mine composed it last year, for a quartet."

She nearly grinned. An original composition—and if she couldn't have heard it, perhaps that meant it had never been played in public. She could win Retta's silly little challenge without any effort at all.

He lowered his right arm, too slowly. "We have only performed it once, a few months ago. In Brussels. Where I believe you said last night you have never been?"

Well, blast. But no matter. Perhaps he had another of his friend's pieces, one that had never been performed. And if not, it hardly mattered. The real job came first. The lesson second. Retta's challenge a far third.

"I've never been out of Great Britain," she confirmed in response to his half question. Her gaze sought the music stand and the sheets of paper upon it. "Is that where you're from though? Brussels?"

"In part." His voice sounded odd. Strained. Pained. "We have a house there—my family. It is technically mine now that my father has died, though it still feels like my mother's home. But most of my growing-up years . . ." He cleared his throat and held out his beautiful violin and its matching bow.

She took them, but she kept her gaze on his face. Just as beautiful, in its way, as the Stradivarius. But just as pained as his words, and not in the same way as it had been last night after he'd used his sore arm too much. Perhaps a kinder woman would let the subject drop.

She'd never claimed to be particularly kind. "Your growing-up years? Where did you spend them?"

He didn't meet her gaze. "Louvain."

A word that made her breath stick in her throat. *Louvain* had been in all the papers—Louvain, the proof of Germany's barbarism. Of their cruelty. Louvain, all the evidence Europe needed to hold the Kaiser's army in utter contempt. "No. Have you family there? Your mother?"

His jaw ticked once, twice; he must have been clenching his teeth. She thought he wouldn't answer. Thought it all the more when he spun away from her and busied himself by pushing the music into a stack and flipping it so its face was to the stand.

Then his voice cut its way into the room like a mournful D sharp. "My mother and little sister were both there when the Germans marched on the town."

"No." She could think of nothing else to say. No assurances to give. No bandage for what must be a slicing sorrow. "Are they all right?"

"*Je ne sais pas.* I do not know. I . . ." He squeezed his eyes shut, shook his head, cleared his throat again. "You came for a lesson, not my story."

"I've enough time for both." Not that she'd anticipated feeling this sympathy for her mark—and not that she'd let it bother her, ultimately. She couldn't.

But she knew what it felt like to wonder whether one's mother was living or dead. She knew that question. How it could eat a body from the inside out.

He waved it away. Her offer to listen, or the thoughts themselves? He said only, "They were not there when I went back. Not in the house, which was burned. A neighbor said they had left. I will find them."

How, when he was here in Wales instead of there in Belgium?

He pointed at the violin. "Play for me, *s'il vous plait.* What I was just playing."

She measured him a moment more. Decided that this was the kindest thing she could do for him, and that at the moment she felt like being kind. She would let it drop. "All right, but I didn't hear the beginning. So if you would turn that music back around . . ."

"*Mais non.*" His smile went from forced to a grin in a blink—and as impish as any of Georgie's ever were. "From memory."

"I was a bit late—I only heard a few minutes." But if he meant to confound her with the removal of the music, he was going to be disappointed. "I can only start from what I heard."

"*Naturellement.*"

She shot him a halfhearted glare. "And I don't speak French."

His brows lifted. "Was it not taught at your school? Miss Davies—both of them—assured me they know it."

Blast. She shrugged. "I was never very good at it and haven't used it since. So what I once knew, I've forgotten."

"Then I beg your pardon." He produced another too-handsome smile and nodded toward the violin. "As this is not a French lesson, I will strive to speak only English."

"I don't *mind* when you speak French—I just want you to realize that I won't understand much, so if you launch into instructions in it . . ."

He kept those brows raised. "Are you stalling, *mon ange?*"

Was she? *Why* was she? And what in the world did *mon ange* mean? Shaking her head, she positioned the violin under her chin, marveling yet again at how smooth was the chin rest. Raised the bow. Called to mind the first strain of the song that she had heard clearly enough to re-create. And began.

What had the other three instruments in the quartet been playing while the violin sang this melody? Mere accompaniment, or did they have melodies of their own, a counterpoint to this one? She hadn't so much as glimpsed the title on the sheet music to see if it was a concerto or a sonata.

But she could hear it as she played. The low thrum of bass,

underscoring. The trill of a woodwind, highlighting. Accenting. Playing a sweet note here, to offset the mournful one. Near dissonance there, as she held a long note.

A story of loss and longing wove its way through her as she played. Almost—*almost*—the tale of her beginnings. Or of the beginnings of her life as an orphan, anyway. Almost. But not quite, not with that hope woven through it here and there.

No, it was more . . . more like how she'd felt a few weeks ago when Rosemary had said she was finished. Finished with the life they'd worked so hard to be masters of. She could be glad that her sister had found something that made her happy. Glad that she wanted to share it with them.

But it couldn't erase the missing of her. The feeling that things were changing, and that no matter how much *better* they might look now to someone from the outside, it was still loss. A world at war, determined to change every bit of her life.

There was still hope—she still had Rosemary, and she *was* glad for her. There was that major-key climb upward. But then the realization that it had taken someone *else* to give her sister that happiness. That Willa, and the family they had forged from necessity and sheer grit, wasn't enough.

She was never enough.

The last note faded away. And her eyes felt damp enough that she had to blink a few times and draw in a long breath before she could bring herself to look around for her new teacher.

He stood leaning against the wall opposite her, watching her as he'd done last night, as if he expected her to sprout wings and fly about the room. For a moment, he didn't so much as twitch. Then one corner of his mouth pulled up into a crooked smile. "My apologies."

Well, *that* wasn't any of the responses she had expected. "I beg your pardon?"

"When I awoke this morning, I found myself doubting that

you had truly picked up that fantasia simply by listening, so I devised this test." He motioned to the backward-facing music. "I knew you could not have studied it beforehand."

Was that amusement or irritation plucking at her? She couldn't quite make up her mind . . . but then decided she would be generous, since she was currently holding, for the second time, a Stradivarius that probably cost as much as her entire neighborhood in Poplar. She smiled. "Satisfied?"

"More than." He pushed off from the wall and turned to a box taking up residence on a chair. "Our lesson, then. This is a fairly simple étude that you will be able to play without trouble." Brandishing the fluttering sheets, he put them on top of the others on the stand. "Begin whenever you're ready."

She took a minute to look over the music first. It had taken years to be able to read music, to learn the language of what had at first struck her as strange little blobs of ink on strange little lines. She probably never would have cracked how to do it if Pauly hadn't found her a book on the subject. Even so, learning how on her own had been a challenge she'd nearly given up on.

But after a few years of struggle, something inside her had seemed to click. And once it had . . . it was beautiful, really. That those small black circles could tell a story that could then be translated into the most beautiful part of life. *Music*.

She was still not all that proficient at sight-reading. But this étude *did* look simple. Straightforward. Satisfied that she could play it with only minor fumbles, she raised the bow again.

And got no more than ten measures in before hands landed on her back. She jumped away, a squeak of protest in her throat as she spun on him, ready to use his bow as a weapon if she must.

Lukas De Wilde held up his hands, laughter in his eyes. "I was only trying to correct your posture, Miss Forsythe. I beg your pardon if I startled you. I should perhaps have warned you."

"*Perhaps?*"

He chuckled. "Forgive me. I am new to this teaching. But I promise you, this is purely professional—what my tutor did for me as a boy. I will save my flirtations for after the lesson, you have my word."

She hesitated another moment, then turned around again to face the music stand.

"There now." He eased closer. *Too* close, whether he meant it to be flirtatious or not. Put his hand on her back, which most assuredly did *not* make tingles dance their way up her spine. Pressed, forcing that not-tingling spine to straighten another notch. "Are you always so . . . what is the word? Skittish?"

Her shoulders edged back. "Yes."

"Good—the shoulders, not the skittishness. That is how you should play, whether sitting or standing."

Highly uncomfortable. And her spine would likely forget to keep itself so erect as soon as her mind was taken over by the music. But she wasn't going to waste her breath arguing with him.

"Now. Again."

He didn't move his hand, as if he *knew* her spine would curve the moment he did. And how in the world was she to play, to get lost in the music, with him *touching* her the whole time?

"Or we can stand here all day, *oui*? Simply enjoying each other's company."

"Has anyone ever told you you're insufferable?"

"*Oui*. But they usually say it with a laugh and a flutter of their eyelashes."

She could well imagine. Though she had no intention of fluttering her eyelashes at anyone. Certainly not someone who expected it. "Well, I say it in seriousness."

"Noted. Now begin."

Because it seemed preferable to debating his charm, she raised the bow and focused her gaze on the opening bar again. This time, once she'd gotten past the first two lines, his hand eased away. He still stood too close—she could feel him there, just behind her, looking over her shoulder—but the playing was easier without the touch.

And the music, though only an étude, was lovely. She felt the smile of it as she played, enjoying the way it pranced up and down, the way her fingers felt as they shifted on the strings.

Then his *hand* again, pressing against her spine. Her fingers stumbled.

"*Continuez*. Keep going."

She did and managed to do so without the stumble after his next retreat-and-return. Though by the end of the étude, she had little choice but to release a sigh of exasperation. "It's no use—I've been playing too long to suddenly learn new posture."

"Nonsense. We can always learn something new." He was grinning. She didn't turn around to see it, but she could hear it in his voice. "Again, from the beginning."

They went through it thrice more, and then again, seated. At least when she was in the hard wooden chair, he only tapped a finger to her back as a reminder. Still. If she concentrated on the music, her back wouldn't stay straight—and if she concentrated on her back, she knew well her playing was only mediocre.

Her frustration was compounding with each touch. Frustration with herself rather than with him.

So then, she would focus on something else altogether. After completing the étude, she looked up at him. "What time is it?"

He reached into his pocket and pulled out a gold watch, flipped open the front of its case.

It was engraved, but not with words that she could see. Just a filigree design. So far as she could tell, no cypher key could be hiding in those twists and turns. And the back was unmarked.

There could be something within the case, though, or even behind the works.

"Three o'clock. Have you had enough for our first day?"

Did he have to phrase it like that, as though she were giving up? She leaned down to set the violin in its case. "I had better get back—I promised to accompany Daisy to a hospital she is considering supporting."

He closed the watch again.

She narrowed her eyes at it. "May I see your watch for a moment? It looks a bit like my grandfather's. Is it a Patek Philippe?" Those were so valuable they couldn't be fenced—too easily traced. But she'd lifted one for a client once who had paid her directly and made a pretty penny.

De Wilde unhooked the watch from his fob and held it out to her. "*Non.* Cartier. My father gave it to me when I gained a position with the Brussels Conservatoire."

Cartiers were far easier to move. She nodded and opened it, noting the engraving on the inside of the cover. It just looked like a simple inscription—how was she to know whether it was something more? "What does it say?"

"'To mark the achievement of your dreams.'" He chuckled. "My father was the best of men, and a genius, but not with words. So my mother had him add this."

He reached down, his fingers brushing hers, and opened the case still more, revealing the inside back, behind the gears.

More writing. This time he didn't wait for her to request a translation of the French. "'If they are a fraction as bright as our love for you, you will soar to the highest heights.'"

If it was the key, he wouldn't show a stranger so easily, would he? And all the ones in the examples Mr. V had given her hadn't made sense in and of themselves. These appeared to be actual words. Not that she knew French, but it *looked* like real words.

She handed the watch back. And had a feeling she'd need to find her way to his room before this was over.

SEVEN

L ukas slid the watch back into his pocket, more than a little surprised that she'd shown interest in something of his—and had not jerked away when their hands brushed. But then, she must be accustomed to men taking her hand.

She'd looked ready to skewer him with his own bow for touching her back though. He tried to tamp down a grin. "There now. Lesson complete. Time for the flirtation."

She narrowed her eyes at him and jumped to her feet. "Don't waste your breath. I'm immune to it."

"No flirtation, then. Just honesty." He took a step toward her, knowing well she'd just back away. Which she did, sidestepping the music stand. "I want to get to know you better. Will you have dinner with me? There is a lovely restaurant a few streets from here. Or tea—you English love your tea, *n'est-ce pas*? I have seen tearooms, with young couples coming and going without chaperones. This is appropriate here, I assume?"

They danced another step, him advancing and her retreating. Her gaze remained a glare. "I'm not going anywhere with you."

"Why not? My intentions are honorable." He may not know

exactly what they *were*, but they were unlike any intentions he'd ever had for a woman before. He wanted to get to know her. Sort her out. Determine why he reacted to her as he did.

She snorted. "You seem to forget that your exploits are plastered across all the gossip rags, Mr. De Wilde. I well know your reputation, and how honorable it's *not*."

"Hmm." He'd taken another step, but now he stopped. It took him a long moment to identify the waves of feeling swamping him. *Regret.* "Mère was right."

She stopped too, fingers digging into the unfortunate back of a stuffed chair. "What?"

"My mother. She always said I would regret my hedonistic ways when I met a young lady about whom I was serious." But he'd never really believed her. Or perhaps never believed he'd meet anyone who could inspire him to seriousness.

Willa Forsythe all but snarled at him. "As if you're serious about *me*. We just met! And we both know I'm not the type of lady you usually spend your time with, so—"

"But that is the point, *non*?" She was unlike anyone he knew— hence why he must become better acquainted. He'd never expected to meet someone with the intensity of his sister, the withering stare of his mother, and the dedication of his father. Someone with a talent that challenged him and a face he could watch intently for hours on end, just to see what flitted across it—and what didn't.

Now, for instance, her countenance had gone blank. She squared her shoulders as she ought to do when she played and lifted her chin. "I'm leaving now. And when I come back, you're going to cease with this ridiculousness. Do you understand?"

Her eyes were the loveliest shade of blue. Or perhaps green. Or some combination thereof. "Sorry. My English no good. *Je ne comprends pas.*"

There, a twitch of her lips. And a breath that sounded far

more like laughter than she probably wanted it to. "How do you say 'idiot' in French?"

He grinned. "*Mon amour*. Try it out."

She rolled her eyes instead—apparently even *she* knew that it meant "my love." But the twitch had definitely settled into a small, beautiful smile. "Goodbye, Mr. De Wilde."

"Lukas. Only my closest friends call me Mr. De Wilde, so if you do not want to give me ideas, you had better call me Lukas."

Another laugh-breath. A shake of her head as she strode past him. "I'll see you tomorrow. In the meantime, rest that shoulder, or you're going to be an absolute wreck for the concert on Saturday."

"Some of us have to practice our music to get it perfect—and memorized."

She tossed a look over her shoulder that *was* flirtatious, whether she would admit it or not. Perhaps she would label it only as teasing. She opened the door. "My sympathies. Really."

He wanted to follow her. See if he could earn a full-fledged laugh, a real smile. But he'd probably pressed his luck enough for one day, so he settled for moving to the window. She'd have to pass by it if she was going back to the Davies house.

It took her a moment to navigate out of the hotel though, of course. Which he spent looking about the street, still largely unfamiliar to him. But it looked like any other seaside street. Nannies and mothers bustled about with babies in prams, children's palms in theirs. Men strode along with business on their faces. Here and there someone paused, looking at a building number or out to the bay.

Or leaned against the railing that separated street from sand. He'd have thought nothing of it—Marine Terrace was full of people stopping to take in the view—except that one particular man happened to come to attention just as Lukas's gaze slid across him. And then the man started across the street.

Again, it would have been nothing more than a passing thing

to note, if Willa hadn't hurried by the window just then. And the man's gaze was locked on her. He jogged the remaining distance across the road, dodging a horse and carriage, his eyes following her progress down the sidewalk.

Alarm rose. She'd never been here before, she'd said last night—she knew no one in Aberystwyth—so it could not be an acquaintance waiting for her. So then who? And why?

He'd have yelled a warning to her, but a mother with a squalling toddler paused just in front of his window. It left him only one choice.

He spun for the door at a run.

———◇———

Willa heard the footsteps racing toward her a second after she felt that invisible finger-brush over the nape of her neck. Someone was following her—and this time they weren't being subtle about it.

She had a split second to decide how to handle it. Which was all she needed. A quick glance around to gauge the crowds or lack of them, where on the street she was, what was nearby.

She was only steps from where the promenade was intersected by Terrace Road, so it was a simple matter to turn onto it, her eyes open for any handy alley—of which there were far too few in this city. She had to settle for the nearly empty Stryd y Gorfforaeth. A few strides, then a quick turn into the cubby that led to the hotel's back entrance. She pivoted, her hand ready to strike.

A smiling, far-too-familiar face paused just out of reach. "Pretty Willa Forsythe. You do not look happy to see me."

Familiarity didn't make her lower her fist. Fear did. Because this man should *not* be in Wales, watching her. Watching her like *this*, coming from a meeting with Lukas De Wilde.

Something she hadn't properly felt in years snapped its teeth into her stomach. *Panic.* "Cor Akkerman? What in blazes are you doing here?"

His gaze swept her from crown to shoe, noting no doubt the quality of her dress, of her jewelry, of her pumps. Quality that certainly didn't belong on someone who lived where they did in London.

He was going to ruin everything. *Everything.*

And he smiled about it. "Looking for work, of course."

"A hundred and fifty miles from your flat in Poplar? That's quite a long way to commute, don't you think?"

He'd followed her here. He must have.

Cor chuckled and slung his hands into his pockets, dislodging his buff jacket—which, come to think of it, was higher quality than what *he* usually wore in London too. He looked almost like a gentleman, except for the hair that was a bit too unruly.

"Well worth it," he said in that Flemish accent that suddenly grated rather than sounding charming, "to spend time with *you.*"

Why did he follow her here? He didn't like her that much—she was just a new face, one of the countless he'd been flirting with, she was sure. Nothing special to him, that he should have followed her.

Her stomach cramped. *How* had he followed her? All these arrangements had been made by Mr. V with the utmost secrecy.

She was in so much trouble.

"Willa!" New footsteps pounded, and another voice spoke her name with an accent she didn't much want to hear right now.

A few choice words vied for a place on her tongue. She leveled a finger at Cor Akkerman's chest. "You cause me trouble and I will pluck out every hair on your head and make you eat them."

Cor merely narrowed his eyes and half turned. "Have a new beau already? You move quickly, Willa Forsythe."

He was about to see how quickly she could move her fist into his eye. Or her knee into his groin.

She stepped past him to lift a hand, palm up, to the man who came to a halt at the corner of Terrace and the unpronounceable street she'd opted for. "I am well, Lukas." Perhaps the use of his first name would calm him.

Or perhaps it would make possessiveness flare to life in his eyes when he saw how Cor lounged against the hotel's rear wall.

Men were all such oafs.

"I saw someone chasing you. And as you do not know anyone here—"

"Oh, but she does." Cor straightened and stepped to her side, actually slung an arm around her shoulders.

She jerked, that instinct rising to step away. But his fingers bit into her shoulder, holding her fast. Her teeth clenched.

Lukas's eyes narrowed.

Cor chuckled and pulled her tight against his side. "We are old friends from London. So naturally, I dropped by when I arrived in Aberystwyth. Is that not right, Willa?"

She suddenly wished Lukas were stupid—stupid enough to believe him, anyway. But he obviously wasn't. He measured Cor as if taking full stock of him in two seconds flat.

What did he see that she hadn't when they were safely in London?

"Odd. How can you possibly be *old* friends when you surely did not arrive here in Great Britain any earlier than I did? A few weeks ago?"

Cor stiffened. Not enough that her eyes probably would have noticed it, but she felt it in the muscles of his arm. "You assume much."

"It is an easy assumption. Your accent is clearly from the Antwerp province—and I know when the Germans invaded that region. You could try to convince me you were here already, I suppose, and are not a fellow refugee. But I would not believe you." He looked like some lord, standing there at the alley's end with his chin raised and disdain dripping from his eyes.

Perhaps that was how all the French Belgians viewed the Flemish—how was she to know? Or perhaps it was just because he had wealth and fame and thought it made him better than the rest.

Or perhaps he was jealous. Odd thought, that. But it matched the burning in his eyes.

Cor chuckled. "I see you are an open-minded and fair man, Monsieur . . . ?"

Rather than provide his name, Lukas held out a hand toward her. "May I see you home, Miss Forsythe?"

It called for a quick calculation—which of them would it be riskier to offend? Lukas, who was the entire focus of her reason here? Or Cor, who knew too much of who she really was?

The hand left her shoulder. "Go ahead, pretty Willa. I will call on you later." *I know where you're staying*, he might as well have shouted. He offered her a handsome smile. "We can reminisce together. Tell your hostesses all about London." *I'll blow your cover if you don't do what I say*, his eyes screamed.

Blast him. Teeth still clenched, she stepped away from his side and put her fingers in Lukas's palm. It felt warm and a far cry more welcoming than Cor's hand had on her shoulder. But then, De Wilde had come out here solely to try to help her. Not to threaten. Or blackmail. Or whatever it was Cor intended.

Part of her wished he really were just lovesick, following her like a too-clever puppy. But she knew better.

Lukas drew her hand through the crook of his elbow and just held her there by his side for a moment, while Cor whistled his way past them and back to Terrace, hands still in his pockets.

Willa drew in a long breath and tried to convince her jaw to relax. "Who is he?"

She had no qualms about lying—but didn't rightly know what lie to tell. So had little choice but to settle for the truth. "Cor Akkerman. A new neighbor of mine in London."

He'd been watching Cor cross the street and walk toward the row of shops but turned his gaze now on Willa. It was dark and rich and far too intent. A shiver coursed up her spine despite the sunshine currently brightening the day. "He is courting you?"

A scoffing laugh passed her lips before she could stop it. "I scarcely know him."

"This matters very little when a woman has caught a man's eye, *ma cherie.*"

Why was she standing so close to him? His gaze was disconcerting enough from a few feet away. This close, it was downright unnerving. She put a few more inches between them. "Yes, well. I never trust a man who calls me pretty."

Now those dark eyes snapped and sparkled, and the corners of his mouth tugged up a degree. "And why is that?"

"Because I'm not. So anyone who would say so is a flatterer, and I've no use for that sort."

"Ah." He led her back toward Terrace. "Thank you for the advice. Though I cannot say as *pretty* would have ever been a word I would choose to describe you. You are far too interesting to be pretty."

It was just the sun heating her, not the odd bit of praise. She looked across the street to see Cor disappearing into an ice cream shop. And pulled her hand from Lukas's arm. "You probably left your violin unattended in the function room. You should go and see to it. I'll be fine."

The mirth left his eyes. "I will walk you home. We will simply go and put the Strad away first."

Though it was on the tip of her tongue to disagree, Willa nodded. *Away* would mean in his room. Which meant she could see where it was without any need for the underhanded. She'd be a fool to pass that chance by.

And she was already enough of a fool, having dismissed Cor as basically harmless—to all but gullible women—when he was quite clearly *not*. So she followed De Wilde back into the hotel, into the parlor where his violin still rested happily in its case. She stood there and let him talk about nothing as he gathered all his things—instrument case, box of music, and stand—and then took the box from him, above all his protests. She hadn't missed his grimace as he lifted it in his right arm.

Then she followed him to the stairs and up them to what must be the topmost floor. Fourth door on the right. Not exactly ideal for sneaking her way into—it wasn't on the end or around a corner. Shouldn't a musician of his caliber have been given a better room? There would be too many people coming and going here.

She didn't go in, of course. He'd think it strange—or an invitation she was *not* making—if she did. But she glanced past him and saw that the room was a suite. This door opened into an outer chamber with a sofa and table and chairs, a fireplace unlit. Another door stood shut to the right.

Which was the one where he stored his secrets?

He set down his gear and turned again into the hall, locking the door behind him and sliding the key into his pocket.

That she could lift easily, when it was time to search his room. Or she could no doubt borrow the hotel's master key with minimal trouble.

They were back on the promenade, Cor nowhere in sight, when she interrupted his musings about Paris this time of year with, "What happened to your shoulder?"

She wanted to know—but more, she wanted to make him stiffen and pull away, to decide to let her walk herself home.

Instead, he swallowed and covered the hand she'd rested again on his arm with his other one. Anchoring her there. Creating a bond where there ought to be none. "I was shot."

Shot? She tried to pull her hand away—it was tucked into the crook of his injured arm, after all—but he stopped her

100

with that second hand. "How? When?" She didn't have to ask where—he'd already confessed he'd been in Belgium since the invasion, looking for his mother and sister. When else could it have happened?

He glanced down at her, but then focused his gaze straight ahead. "Two weeks ago, in Brussels. I had gone there when I did not find my mother and sister in Louvain. But the Germans were waiting for me. Watching for me."

Her throat went tight. "*You* specifically, or refugees from the countryside in general?"

"*Me*. My father, you see . . . Before his death, he was doing important work. Work the Germans wanted. I daresay they did not realize they had burned it all in Louvain, but they know I am his son. One of the soldiers recognized me as I was making my way to our house. Tried to detain me, so . . . I ran. And was shot."

It aligned with what Mr. V had told her of this family—the father, the work. But why in the world would he admit it all to her? "Did they think you were involved in this work?" *Or that you had bits of it on your person?*

Lukas shook his head. "I cannot say. It would be foolish to think so—I am a musician, not a mathematician as he was. They presumably thought I knew where he had stored it all. Which I do—in the house they burned to the ground. It is all gone now, but the Germans . . . they would not have listened had I told them that. They seemed to think every Belgian a spy or a *franc-tireur* or . . ." He shook his head again.

She might as well fish for whatever she could. "What was he working on? Your father, I mean."

He flicked a gaze down at her, one that shone with intelligence that he quickly covered with a charming grin. "I could not tell you if I wanted to, *mon amour*. I am a musician, not a mathematician. And it was all mathematics."

So then, he had *some* sense when it came to baring his soul to strangers. Good for him, if bad for her. She returned the grin. "Did you just call me an idiot? I ought to storm away."

His laugh brought the gaze of every female pedestrian their way.

Blast, but it would be hard to blend into the shadows if she spent any more time in his company.

EIGHT

Margot smiled into her friend's giggle and tried to determine what, exactly, was so funny about Claudette's older sister saying what she had to a German officer. It had been stupid, in Margot's opinion, to flirt with him. Risky.

But she wouldn't say so. Certainly not today, the first time she'd seen her friend in a month. Their mothers had bumped into each other yesterday, and Maman had whispered where they were staying and the name they were using. She wouldn't have trusted most people with such information—but Claudette's father had worked with Papa.

Claudette's father had been arrested.

They understood the need for discretion.

And now here they were, in Madame Dumont's upstairs parlor, their mothers speaking in whispers on the sofa, knitting needles clacking, while Claudette giggled and Margot pretended to understand why, when really she was looking out the window.

The afternoon was waning. *He* would be back soon. And she hadn't even had the chance to work on her theorem today, what with their visitors.

Not that she wasn't glad to see Claudette again.

Her friend sighed much like their mothers were wont to do. "Have you heard a word I said?"

Margot blinked and focused her gaze on Claudette rather than the windows. She looked as she always had—deep brown curls pulled back in a sky-blue ribbon, flounces on her dress, a smile hovering about her lips.

Except for her eyes. Her eyes weren't the same carefree brown they'd been before. They were shadowed now. Hard. They knew what it was to lose a father, even if *she* had hope of getting hers back someday.

It wasn't something Margot had wanted to share with her friend. "Of course I have. Do you want me to recite it all back to you?"

"*Non!* You always make me sound so ridiculous when you do that." She giggled again, but this time Margot heard the strain in it. The false note. And then it died away altogether, and she scooted closer to where Margot sat on the window seat. Focused her gaze out the window. "How many bricks are in that house across the street? The red one?"

A game they had been playing for years. Usually it made her grin. Today . . . it made her want to. Almost. "Five thousand two hundred twenty-six."

"Really?" Claudette pursed her lips. "I thought for *sure* it was five thousand two hundred twenty-*eight*. Are you sure you factored in the chimneys correctly?"

Margot rolled her eyes. And let silence speak for a beat, two, before she said, "Are you frightened for him?" She kept her voice at the barest whisper, so their mothers didn't hear.

Claudette focused still on that redbrick house, but her fingers worried the lace edge on her skirt. "They're sending him to Germany. They'll try to make him work for them."

"He won't." She found her friend's fingers, covered them with her own. There weren't many people in the world she would touch willingly, but Claudette she had known since she was a baby. She was more sister than friend.

Her attempt at comfort brought tears up to pool in Claudette's eyes. "But what will they do to him if he doesn't? I don't want my papa to die, Margot."

This was why she hated conversation. What could she possibly say to such a thing to make it better? There was nothing, no comfort to offer. Claude Archambault would either help the Germans and betray his country, or he wouldn't and they would kill him for it. A traitor or a ghost—neither was what anyone would want for a father.

Margot squeezed her hand again and gave up on words.

Their mothers rose from the sofa, goodbye in their postures. They embraced, kissed each other's cheeks, and were making promises already to visit again next week.

"You can come to us next time, Sophie," Madame Archambault said, gripping Maman's hands.

Maman shook her head. "I am sorry, Marie—I do not dare. It is too near our house, and they will be looking for us there. This is risk enough."

Claudette's mother sighed. "You are right, of course. But . . . do you really think you will be able to keep your name secret for long? Someone will recognize you on the street and call out a greeting. And the wrong German ears will hear it."

Now Claudette turned her hand under Margot's so she was squeezing *her* fingers.

Maman lifted her chin, though the show of strength didn't quell the trembling in her lips. "We will do what we can, while we can. Until Lukas comes for us."

Madame Archambault nodded, but her mouth was a tight, straight line, and doubt filled her dark eyes. She didn't say that Lukas was gone, dead, shot by the Germans and never to return for them. Not with words did she say it. But with her eyes she did.

"He is not dead." Margot whispered it because she must. Must push it out into the room to counteract the doubt.

"He is not dead." Claudette's echo was just a whisper too. But she too spoke it. And then she stood and smoothed out her skirt. "I will see you next week, Margot *Dumont*."

"*Oui*. Until then, know I pray for your papa. And for you." She said a prayer now, in the way that made her feel closest to her God, who so perfectly ordered the universe. *Two, four, nine, sixteen, twenty-five, thirty-six, forty-nine* . . .

Madame Dumont came in as their guests were leaving, giving them her wrinkled smiles and well-wishes, promises to pray. Once they were gone, the old lady settled in her favorite chair by the unlit fireplace, her gaze focusing on Margot. Her smile looked genuine. "It is a blessing to me to have you two here. Bringing laughter and friends into this house again."

Maman patted the Madame's shoulder. "It is a far greater blessing to us, Mère Dumont. Without you . . ."

Margot added a small smile to the conversation but could manage no more. Her gaze went back out the window, where their friends were exiting the house and making their way quickly down the street.

It was good of the lady to protect them like this, yes. And no great difficulty to call her Grand-mère and show her affection and respect when Gottlieb was around. But Margot wanted her *own* life.

A group of soldiers strode by on the street below their window. Proof that no one had their own life just now. Not the ones they used to know.

Another pair of soldiers came into view after the first group had disappeared. One was Gottlieb—and he carried a box.

"He is coming." Margot frowned out the window, her eyes on that box. She didn't know what could be in it, but it made her stomach cramp. It was something new—and these days something new always meant something bad.

The second soldier kept walking when Gottlieb peeled off.

Behind her, Maman and Madame Dumont turned their conversation to when the weather might cool and how much food was left in the shops. Margot listened to the door open and then shut. To Gottlieb's footsteps. Would they turn into his room?

No. They were on the stairs, sounding light and quick. *Happy*. A happy Gottlieb was surely bad news for the rest of them.

A few moments later he was striding into the parlor, *sounding* happy too as he wished them all a good afternoon. There came then the sound of something sliding onto the table.

Margot finally looked his way, saw that box. He was opening it, a smile on his lips.

"I have brought you a surprise. Something to entertain us all as the days grow shorter and autumn turns to winter."

The cramps squeezed tighter. How could he speak so glibly about being here so long? Months? Whole seasons?

He drew out two wooden bowls fitted with lids and then a square of wood about a foot wide. It looked almost like a chessboard, except that the squares painted upon the top were only outlines, none of them colored. And where some of the lines intersected, there were little dots painted as well.

Maman kept on knitting. "A game?"

"*Ja*. It is called Go. From the Han Chinese empire, but it has become quite popular in Germany." He took the lids off the bowls, revealing black stones in one, white in the other. "It is a strategy game."

Margot turned fully to face the room.

Maman's needles clacked together. "I have never enjoyed such pastimes. Perhaps Mère will play with you."

Madame Dumont chuckled. No doubt because they all knew Gottlieb didn't want more of *her* company. "These old eyes could not even see the board. Perhaps young Margot could learn it."

Dual strings pulled taut within her. The one insisting she

refuse out of principle, because why would she want to be so near him for so long? The other drawn like a moth to the flame of that game board. What were its rules? Its aims?

"No." Maman's voice was nearly too quick, too alarmed. "Margot has enough to fill her time. Come, *mon chouchou*. This scarf will not knit itself."

Gottlieb tossed the second lid to the table—a bit more forcefully than necessary. "*Someone* will play with me. I insist."

Silence met his demand. Margot dug her fingers into the plush cushion of the window seat. Of course Maman would forbid her from playing. Of course. But . . .

"*Fräulein.*" Gottlieb leveled a finger at her and then pointed at one of the chairs at the table. "You will learn. Call it part of your education, since you have not gone back to school."

School was hardly an option here—and she had already learned everything the lower schools could teach her anyway. She had been enrolled in classes at Papa's university in Louvain. *Before.*

She looked to her mother.

Lips pressed tight, Maman was obviously weighing the options. After a moment, she nodded. But she needn't speak for Margot to hear the warning she'd be issuing.

She could play—but she couldn't play *well*.

Slowly enough to demonstrate a reluctance she only half felt, Margot stood and moved to the table. Took a seat.

Gottlieb tossed the box to the floor and sat too, with a smile. "There now. You will enjoy this."

She positioned her chair and regarded the board. Nineteen squares in each direction. "Is it like chess?"

"The rules are simpler but the play more complex." He slid the bowl of black stones over to her. "Black plays first, so the beginner has that honor. The object is to surround the most territory with your stones, by placing them on the points of intersection on the grid. You cannot move them once placed. But your opponent can seize your stone by surrounding it with his own."

Simple, yes. But there would be virtually endless possibilities. Her mind raced, and that knot in her stomach eased. "When does the game end?"

"When one of the players decides to make no more moves. It can last for hours or days or weeks." He smiled, baring white teeth that would likely not hesitate to snap at her. "It will take you some time to get the feel for it, but I think you will like it. You are a clever girl."

Clever she was allowed to be, to an extent. But she could feel her mother's gaze drilling into her back. *More than clever* she must be careful to avoid.

Just another challenge to enjoy. She would play two games, that was all—one in her head, with the moves she would make if she were playing with Papa or Lukas. Another on the board with *him*.

She reached into the bowl and plucked out one of the smooth black stones. It hardly even mattered that she would have to lose, at least at first, and be sure never to win by much. She would get to *think*.

It was more than she had expected today.

Willa slid into the study that was rarely used, the yellow paper crumpled in her hand and her gaze casting over her shoulder. None of the ladies would purposely eavesdrop, she was sure. But any one of them could happen by, and while she may have obtained permission to use the telephone, that didn't mean she wanted them to overhear.

But then, they were the least of her concerns. *Anyone* could overhear a phone conversation. The operators, to be sure. And anyone else on the party line. Which made her wonder why the telegram in her hand had instructed her to use one.

Well, there was nothing for it but to place the call and guard her tongue while doing so.

Still. As she picked up the receiver on the candlestick telephone, something was bothering her. Not the call. Not the telegram. Something to do with the reason for it.

She'd left again the moment De Wilde delivered her home. Rounded the corner to the nearest telegraph office. Her message to Barclay had been simple: *Cor followed me.*

His message back, delivered just twenty minutes ago, had been no longer. *Ring Hammersmith-1528 at 7.*

She gave the operator the number in a calm voice, but it was a lie. Too many questions warred within her. Were telephones really a wise way of communicating? Why would Barclay have instructed her to use one? And where in the world was Hammersmith-1528? It wasn't their end of London.

Why, *how*, had Cor Akkerman followed her here? And what the devil could she do about it?

It wasn't a moment before a cheery "Hello!" sounded across the miles, tinny and half-covered with static. Willa gripped the telephone and sank into the chair behind the desk. "Retta? Is that you?"

"Oh, do relax, Barclay, I'll only keep her a moment!" This was barely audible, obviously not aimed into the receiver. Then, "I just wanted to say hello. I've never used one of these things."

"Neither have I." Willa traced a finger along the edge of the desk. "Where are you?"

Retta's bark of laughter came over the line with no trouble. "Where do you think? We're at Rosie's new place."

Of course—who else did they know with any claim to a place in Hammersmith? But it was beyond comprehension that her sister suddenly had *two* new houses, in both London and Cornwall. "Why? Did they come back already?"

"Of course not. But they offered us the use of the London house

110

while they're all in the west country, and it just made sense. There were only the four of us here so long as you're gone, so we don't need three flats."

So they'd let the flats go? Willa's fingernails dug into the wood of the desk. It wasn't unusual for them to move about, but they usually did only in case of emergency. Not just convenience. And never before had Willa not been part of the decision-making process.

"Hey! I hadn't finished!" Retta's voice was even more distant now.

Then Barclay's filled the line. "I know what you're thinking, but stop. You know very well this was reasonable—or you will, once you get over your pique at not being involved in the decision. We would have been stupid not to accept this offer. Free housing, Will."

Sometimes it was annoying to be known so well. "It's awfully far from Pauly's."

"But the rent we're saving more than makes up for the price of a tube ticket. Now—tell me about this puppy that followed you home."

Willa rested her forehead on her hand and sighed into the mouthpiece. Every time she closed her eyes, she still saw him, and tried to see something she'd missed before. Some glint in his eye or tell in the quirk of his mouth. "I don't know how he did." Which was terrifying, but she daren't say that over the phone lines.

Barclay's sigh gusted over hers. "Ellie ran back to your old flat when we got your wire. The other mutt's still there. Landlady thought Cor was just seeking what he could in other parts of London."

The truth, or was Cor's cousin just covering for him? He could be involved. They shouldn't assume he wasn't. "What do I do? Should we contact Mr. V?"

"Are you out of your mind?" Barclay had a way of saying that—

it had been grating on her and Rosie since they met him. Always so superior, and so confident that he was right. Made worse by the fact that he usually *was*. "We'll never work for him again if we let him know you're taking in stray dogs."

"I'm not *taking him in*." But he was right, blast him. She squeezed the bridge of her nose. Mr. V knew too much about them already. And they knew far too little of him, except that he paid well and had, occasionally at least, some tie to the government.

Which was every bit as terrifying as Cor following her here. More. They'd tried all their lives to *avoid* the authorities—how had they come to be working for them, however indirectly? And what would he do if they failed him?

Lack of future work would be the least of their concerns. He could arrest them. Destroy them. Rip the family apart.

No. "So what do I do?"

"Did you pet the pup? Or just see him across the street?"

The code words were likely to get a bit ridiculous if they kept this up. "He came over nipping at my heels. But my new friend joined us and shooed him away within moments. Still. He'll no doubt have sniffed out where I'm staying."

"Regular bloodhound, apparently. I'd thought him just a mongrel."

"So then?"

A static-filled hum crackled into her ear. "Maybe he just likes you. Maybe it's nothing to worry about."

A ridiculous statement that hardly deserved a reply. "Dogs don't just *like* me, Barclay. Not enough to follow me home."

"I daresay that's not exactly true—but in this case, we're not talking about following you a street or two, so I'll grant the greater point. I—what?" A moment of muffled noises. "Retta has a rather cogent suggestion. For all the friends V has, he must have some rivals as well. And those rivals may have some well-trained pets of their own."

Her stomach would never unknot again. What was she involved in? And why had it seemed so much better than just lifting wallets from overfed, upper-class marks? "Do you think he's dangerous?"

"We oughtn't to assume he's not. But keep your head. Learn what you can about him, but otherwise focus on your purpose there. And for heaven's sake, don't let him smell your fear."

"I'm not afraid of some stray dog." Much. Just uneasy, that was all.

"Right." The distance did nothing to cover his amusement at her expense. "Well, listen. Ring me here whenever you need me—I'll try to be home every evening at this time, me or the girls. And when I meet with V tomorrow, I'll probe a bit. Much as I can."

"Meet with V?"

"Apparently he's work needs done in London yet too. He was at Pauly's last night. Doesn't pay as well as your job, but . . ."

But they'd be fools to turn down whatever he offered. Who knew how long it would last? But in the meantime, they could perhaps save a bit for a rainy day.

And they had scads of rainy days.

"All right." She straightened and drew in a long breath. "I'll just do what I do, then."

"How's that going?"

"Well enough. I met Lukas De Wilde yesterday." Her eyes slid closed. "He gave me a violin lesson this afternoon."

Were it Retta or Lucy or Elinor or Rosemary, a squeal would have come over the line. But it was Barclay. He offered only a scoffing laugh. "You don't *need* lessons. You're the best."

Her lips turned up. Sometimes she loved his scoffing. "Apparently my posture's rubbish."

"Always looks fine to me."

"Well, what do you know?"

He laughed, minus the scoff this time. "Granted. Hey, Retta asks if you've found any original music yet."

"Almost. Tell her De Wilde has a composer friend—I'll have got one in no time."

"All right, well. Listen. If you need any of us, just give the word. We'll be there. Help you get control of this pup."

Of course they would. Because they were family. "I know. Tell Luce and Ellie I said hello and all my love and all that."

"Mm. Be careful, Will."

"Carefuller than careful." But theirs wasn't a safe, careful life—he knew that. Their family motto was all about danger: *With the greatest risk comes the greatest reward.* Even so. The greatest risks meant the greatest preparation, the greatest planning, the greatest caution. That was the only way to master them.

They said their farewells, and Willa set the receiver back into its hook. Then just sat there for a long moment, staring at the deep, warm brown of the desk.

Her brows knit. *Brown.* The man following her yesterday and earlier today had been wearing a brown jacket.

But Cor's had been buff. Closer to white than brown.

Her stomach knots knotted. Either he'd changed his jacket during her lesson for some bizarre reason or . . .

Or Cor Akkerman wasn't the only man following her about Aberystwyth.

Music filled the cavernous room in a way she hadn't realized was possible. Willa had thought she'd known how big the world was—or how big *her* world was, anyway. But as she sat in the darkened symphony hall on Saturday, in an actual seat, beside other music lovers, having gained entrance with a ticket rightfully paid for . . .

The world grew. It expanded well beyond questions of Cor or Mr. V or men in brown jackets, pushed all those dreary concerns from her mind. It unfurled wings that sounded like melodies soaring to the heavens and plunging to the deepest depths.

She wore the second of her evening gowns, lovingly stitched by Rosemary into a prettier style than the ones her hostesses wore, and she'd jammed pins into her hair until it didn't dare slip out. She knew she looked like the others around her—not the elite of London, but someone who could afford to sit in one of these chairs legitimately. And for the first time in her life, she almost wished she rightfully belonged here. So that she could experience this again and again, with her family beside her.

The catwalks hadn't done it justice. And that beloved alley outside the practice chamber—that barely held a candle to this, where the high ceiling caught the sound and made it more.

She felt, as she listened to the ninety musicians following the motions of the maestro into a frenzy of musical bliss, as though she were seeing true beauty for the first time. She felt bigger and smaller all at once. More alive. Closer to death. Fear and peace, love and sorrow. She *felt* like she never had before. And it left her with energy coursing through her veins, stinging her fingertips.

Could she really play as those people on the stage did?

Her gaze traveled through the darkness and to the platform awash in golden light. Traveled along the other sections until it caught on the *only* section—the violins. There were many of them, all looking equally talented as their bows drew along the strings, as their fingers pressed and flew.

Lukas, of course, sat on the end of the row closest to the audience. The position of honor—first chair. His posture perfect, his arms moving with the same ease and mastery as his colleagues.

Only because the Davieses had gotten them seats so close could she see the expression on his face. The pain hiding in it. It had progressed as the night went on. Now, as their second encore came to a rousing end and the audience gave a standing ovation, he smiled as the rest of them did. But the pain lurked there in his eyes.

He looked her way, though she doubted he could see her through the stage's lights. Then he stood along with the others, bowing.

The maestro bowed deeply, hushed the audience with a hand, and bowed again. "This evening is dedicated to Miss Gwendoline Davies and Miss Margaret Davies, with the sincere gratitude and appreciation of this orchestra. It is because of you, ladies, that we have a hope of helping our beloved Belgium. Thank you. And again, thank you."

Applause roared through the hall. Willa joined hers to everyone else's, chuckling a bit at how the bashful sisters flushed. She could have sworn she could feel the heat of their blushes coming off them.

Or maybe it was something else. She glanced toward the stage again and saw that Lukas De Wilde was most assuredly looking at *her*. Not the sisters. Her.

Never mind that. Chatter sprang up from a hundred places as the house lights brightened, and Willa didn't need to remind herself of her cover story to smile. How could she not smile? At this moment, she didn't think she'd ever stop smiling.

If only Rosemary had been here to share it with her. And Barclay. And Retta and Lucy and Elinor.

As it was, she had only Miss Blaker to turn to as the sisters were pounced upon by some eager couple in overdone evening wear. "That was lovely," she breathed. The understatement of the century, but she had to be careful not to gush too much.

Miss Blaker nodded with enthusiasm though. "Indeed. Such a talented group! I have never heard *Symphony in D* played so well. The maestro is quite a visionary, don't you think? I was enthralled by his interpretation of the first section by the time he reached the cadence."

Cadence? Wasn't that just a beat—how could one *reach* the

cadence? Willa cleared her throat. "Indeed. *Visionary* is exactly the word I was thinking."

"And the piece they played by one of their own—he is no Bach, of course, but the motivic transformation was rather splendid."

The . . . what? "Yes, I imagine he has quite a future as a composer." Willa edged a few inches away from Miss Blaker, toward the Davieses. Perhaps the sisters were using normal words.

But one of them was saying something about "the tutti." And the bloke in the row behind them was chiming in with something about "a well-placed échappée." And bit by bit, Willa's smile required force.

It wasn't fair. Not even a little. This was her language, her greatest love—music, dazzling in its brilliance.

So how could these people manage to take what she knew by instinct, from that place deep inside her, and make it confusing?

Her gaze went to the stage again, where the musicians were filing off to put their instruments away. Decked out, each and every one, in the most elegant of clothes. Posture perfect. Instruments of the highest quality.

They would know, every one of them, what a tutti was. And an échappée. They would know, the moment she opened her mouth in their presence, what Willa was *not*.

She was not one of them. Whatever Lukas De Wilde might tell her, she'd do well to keep that truth always in mind.

Willa Forsythe belonged in the alley outside their practice chamber. On the catwalks overhead, backstage. She could fake her way into the audience, apparently.

But never upon the stage. If ever she tried it, they'd all see her for exactly what she was: nobody.

NINE

The knock on his door brought Lukas's eyes open, but he hadn't the energy to rise. His shoulder was on fire, sending aches coursing all down his arm. And his back. And up to his head. And, if he focused on it, all the way down to his toes.

The wound was festering. He'd given in and called for a doctor again this morning, and the man had poked and prodded around inside his shoulder, pulling out a few fibers that had apparently not been removed along with the bullet on the boat.

He'd soon be "right as rain," the man had claimed.

Lukas didn't know what was so right about rain, but he wasn't inclined to believe the mustachioed man with the round belly, given the torment he had inspired with his blasted pincers.

And why would that blasted knocking not *stop*?

"Lukas! I know you're in there." French words. Jules.

Lukas hooked his not-screaming arm over his eyes. How could it be so bright in here when he hadn't any lamps lit and the sun was on the other side of the building? "Go away."

"You don't really want me to do that." A moment of silence, and then the jingle of a key brought Lukas's arm down again. Had the man finagled the master from the front desk?

Partly, he saw as the door opened and Jules strode in. The

118

clerk had walked him up and unlocked the door for him. And didn't have the good grace to look abashed about it. What kind of attendant was he, letting people into other people's rooms? He ought to get the man sacked.

Jules strode into the living area, a stack of something or another in hand. "Don't be angry with him—the doctor gave him instructions to check on you if you did not come down for luncheon. I convinced him I would do the job for him."

Lukas grunted and covered his eyes again. "Go away. Let me die in peace."

The stack of something or another slapped the low table before the couch on which Lukas rested. "You're always so amusing when you're sullen."

"I'm not sullen. I'm in agony. I'm about to gnaw this arm off and be done with it."

"Mm-hmm." Jules lifted Lukas's good arm and looked from one eye to the other. Though what he was checking for was anyone's guess. "Did you take the medicine he left for you?"

And fog up his mind before his lesson with Willa? "*Non.* I don't need it."

"You'll just gnaw off your arm instead."

"It would be more effective."

Jules rolled his eyes and straightened. "I sent a note round to the Davieses, letting Miss Forsythe know you're in no condition to give her a lesson today."

"You *what?*" He strained toward sitting—then collapsed with a groan back onto the cushions behind him. How could one little bullet wound in one little shoulder make his whole body useless? "Send another one round then, saying you were mistaken."

"Perhaps I would, if I were." Jules helped himself to a seat in the chair adjacent to Lukas's sofa. "Don't be an idiot, Lukas. You need to rest. You were all but in tears by the end of the concert Saturday night—"

"I was not."

"—and then you were stupid enough to try to practice yesterday when you ought to have been resting."

Well, he'd *had* to practice. He'd messed up the section at Bar 180 in Bach's *Symphony in D* on Saturday night, and that wouldn't do. And since Gwen Davies had informed him that there would be no lessons on Sundays and that they were already engaged for dinner, how else was he to fill his time?

He'd barely gotten to exchange two words with Willa on Saturday after the performance. He'd scarcely spoken to her at all since walking her home on Friday. How was he to know if that Cor fellow was still bothering her, if he never got to see her? If her hostesses and then his idiot friend got in the way?

"Lukas. You won't want some strange girl you're trying to impress to be here for this." Jules leaned forward and picked up the stack. Envelopes, now that Lukas blinked his eyes clear and actually bothered to look. Quite a few of them. "The hotel in Paris finally forwarded your post. There's a letter from your mother. Postmarked before the invasion."

"What?" Now he *did* sit up, agony be hanged. And stretched his left arm out for the letters. "And you let me go on about my arm?"

"Because two minutes will make all the difference?" Shaking his head, Jules held tight to the stack rather than hand it over. "I can stay. Or I can go. But I need your word that you'll meet me in the dining room at seven, either way. You'll eat, and you'll be reasonable, and you'll not fall into a brood or worse, and you'll certainly not go off on another tear."

He hadn't been the only one to go off on a tear when the news had reached Paris of the Germans' invasion. They both had. The only difference was that Jules had actually found his family, safely escaped to France already, while Mère and Margot seemed to have vanished with the wind.

No, there were two differences—the Germans hadn't been

lying in wait in Brussels for Jules, hiding in his townhouse with weapons drawn.

Lukas nodded, hand still outstretched. "You have my word. Dining room at seven. And I would like to be alone."

Jules set the stack onto his palm but didn't release his gaze. "This won't answer your questions. Don't expect it to do so. She wrote it before any of this happened."

"I know." His questions could only be answered by *being* there, by finding them. Or by somehow getting in touch with them now. But telegraphs had been shut down in Belgium. Post wasn't going through. Newspapers weren't even being printed—which must be a special kind of torment for Margot.

The German army had his country in a stranglehold.

If only Jules had left him there, he'd know by now. He'd know whether they were alive or dead or . . . He'd have found them and brought them *all* to safety.

Jules rose. "I've new ammunition now, so for that I thank you. You do realize, I hope, that if I hadn't brought you here, hadn't accepted the offer from the Davieses on your behalf, you never would have met your Miss Forsythe."

His friend had a point. Though, intriguing as the young lady was, he never would have traded his family's security for a pretty—or not so pretty—face, no matter how masterful she was with music. Even *before* the world fell apart. Though if he were looking for the proverbial silver lining in his current situation . . .

Jules shook his head. "You're utterly incomprehensible, do you know that? All the most beautiful girls in Europe throw themselves at you—girls with money and family names and influence—and you set your sights on some nobody from London at whom no one else would ever look twice."

If no one else looked twice, it was because they were fools, all. And he was happy to let them be.

But it wasn't exactly accurate either. That Flemish farmer

parading about in a jacket that didn't fit him had obviously looked. There was something about that Cor Akkerman that put Lukas's teeth on edge—and it wasn't just the way he'd treated Willa. Though granted, that was a large part of it. It was . . . It was . . . *something*. Perhaps when pain wasn't fogging his mind, he would be able to pinpoint it.

Jules muttered a mild near-curse and shook his head. "Whoever would have thought that Lukas De Wilde, playboy extraordinaire, would fall in love at first sight with someone like her?"

"It wasn't love at first sight. It was intrigue at first sight." He flipped through the stack of envelopes, not caring a whit about any of the others. Just seeking that familiar handwriting. "Love at first *listen*."

Jules snorted. Which had rather been his point in saying it—a tease that, in turn, proved him not *quite* out of his mind with pain, didn't it?

There. His mother's script, elegant and easy. His hand shook as he plucked it out and let the other letters fall where they may. "All right, perhaps not *love*. But she is something special. Would you have me ignore that? What if she is the one meant for me?"

His friend folded his arms over his chest. "My mother always says that the one you're *meant* to marry is simply the one you *do* marry—it's not a matter of romance, it's a matter of deciding to love and make it work."

"And how do you decide who to marry in the first place, hmm?" He studied the words on the envelope, though they were nothing noteworthy. His name, the hotel in Paris he'd been staying at, the direction. He flipped it over and tore open the flap.

"Well, you certainly *don't* decide when you're out of your mind with pain from an injury and upset about your family on top of it. You are in no state to make any life-altering decisions just now, Lukas."

It wasn't as if he'd put a family jewel on her finger. It had only been one little proposal—why did it bother Jules so?

Lukas pulled out the folded paper, covered on both sides with small, neat words in French. "Would you leave now? Please?"

Jules loosed a sound that was half sigh and half growl. And spun for the door. "I give it a month before you lose interest. So just don't *marry* her in that month, and you'll both come out of this well enough."

Making no response, Lukas waited until the door clicked shut behind the naysayer and then lifted the sheet of paper to his nose and closed his eyes.

Mère's letters always smelled like her, from the bit of perfume she touched there, to the upper-right corner. Just now it seemed a scent from a different world. A world still sane and understandable and steady. So very different from this chaos into which the Kaiser's army had plunged them all.

He opened his eyes again, but the words were too blurry to read. The questions were too blinding.

What if these were the last words of his mother's he ever read? What if something had happened to them on the road between Louvain and Brussels? What if it were years before he knew anything of their whereabouts or well-being? Or if he *never* knew?

An invisible hand curled around his throat and squeezed. Another pressed on his chest until he thought he'd scream from the pain of it. Something inside him pulsed, stretched . . . but what? Toward what?

He'd failed. Failed the only people in the world who really mattered. Failed at the last promise he'd made his father. He hadn't kept them safe. He hadn't been there the one time they really needed him. And now what could he even do? Here from Wales, where he could not search, could not do anything but play the violin and moan in pain? What hope did his mother and sister have, if they were still alive to hope at all?

Nothing. Certainly not *him*. He could do nothing.

The hand gave up squeezing and seemed to claw his insides instead. Red, blinding agony . . . and then something softer whispered over him. Something that cooled the fire a degree and made him open his eyes. It felt a bit like Mère's touch always had on his forehead as a boy. The way she'd sweep his hair from his brow and press a kiss there.

He unfolded the letter.

I do not know when this will reach you, my boy, or if it will. But surely by the time it does, things will have changed in our world. We just got the news of that letter sent to the king from the Kaiser, claiming that he has heard France intends to march through Belgium and that we had better accept an alliance with Germany now. Lies, as every Belgian knows. Lies that will rip at our lives. The king would never negate the very conditions of our independence—alliance with any country. The army has been called out to defend our borders and our neutrality.

But we all know the army is more for parades than fighting. I cannot help but think they will not last long against the German war machine. By the time you receive this, no doubt the outcome is known.

You will worry, I know, and so I pray this reaches you quickly and stays your hand. Remain in Paris, I beg of you. Out of harm's way. If Germany invades . . . It is too much to hope for that they will not seek us out, hoping to find your father's work. Especially—we did not tell you this. You were on tour, and we did not want to worry you. But a month before he died, the German government had contacted him. They were trying to convince him to move there, to bring them his work. Of course he refused. But they know who he is. They know what he was doing. They will want it, even with him gone.

You know what this means. They will seek us, and they will seek you.

I am already preparing to leave, but it will take time. Margot is reviewing all of his work so that if any is lost . . . We will destroy it before the Germans can get their hands on it. And then we'll go. I do not yet know where or how, and it is best I don't. Best I rely not on my own reasoning, which they will be able to deduce, but on the Lord.

He will deliver us, Lukas. I know He will.

"Did you? Did you deliver them, God?" His hands were shaking, the paper fluttering in them, making the words blur again. Lukas set it down on the table for a moment and pressed at his eyes. Sniffed.

He didn't expect an answer. God had never answered him—though to be fair, Lukas had probably never really listened. Never really *expected* any kind of response. Had rarely prayed beyond the words uttered by rote during Mass. Something he'd done less and less over the years as he traveled.

It had never mattered. Until now, when it did. Because it must. Because there was no one else in the world who could help them. "Lord . . . I don't know you. But they do. They do, and they love you. Protect them, please. I beg of you."

He didn't hear the voice of the Lord. But he heard Margot—sarcastic, too-smart Margot, looking up at him with that gaze of hers that would have unnerved him if he didn't love her, love it, so much. She'd been, what, ten at the time? When she had cornered him on one of his visits home to Louvain.

"Do you even believe in anything? You don't act as though you do."

He'd laughed, waved it off. Or tried to. "Of course I believe in something."

"In yourself, perhaps. You know how it hurts Maman, don't

you? Your behavior? Seeing all those articles in the gossip columns about you? You break her heart."

It hadn't been what he'd wanted to talk about, certainly not with his sister, fourteen years his junior, who ought not to even know anything about the kind of behavior their mother so despised. "You shouldn't read those parts of the paper" had been the only retort he could think of making.

She'd rolled her eyes at him in that way Mère had tried, and failed, to break her of.

Lukas had studied her for a moment. She'd always looked like any other girl her age. Average height, straggly hair, neither too thin nor too heavy. But she could drill holes through him with her stare. He'd thought, perhaps, to challenge her that day. Or perhaps to defend himself. He still wasn't sure of his reasoning.

"If you're so smart, why haven't you reasoned your way to the realization that there is no God who cares about the minutia of our lives?"

She'd snorted. "I'm so smart I've reasoned my way *to* Him. Because there are things I don't understand. Things I never will. But He does."

"So a Creator-God, then."

"Lukas." She had a way of saying his name. She didn't drag it out as Mère did when she was frustrated with him. She just changed the pitch—high on the first syllable, low on the second, hitting that K with an accent. "Let me put this in terms you can understand. Can a man compose a symphony without paying attention to each individual note? Can he put together an orchestra without caring about each musician in it? It's ridiculous to posit a Creator who stands back, unconcerned. If we grant a God, we have to grant a *complete* God."

It wasn't that *he* believed in a God who was Creator only . . . but he'd almost wanted her to. To have that thing he could point

126

to as a fault in her. A failing in their parents' eyes that they would worry over, rather than always focusing on *his* soul.

But that had been stupid and selfish. He was glad she had her faith in God. More now than ever was he glad.

And for the first time, he wished he understood it a little better. That it was more to him than his sister's faith, or his mother's, or his father's.

He wished he had that Someone to lean on, as they always had. He picked up the letter again.

I know you tire of hearing that I pray for you. But perhaps now, with trouble upon us, it will mean a little more. I pray that you turn to the Lord, Lukas, before it is too late. I pray that you follow His guidance to safety, as we will do. I pray that someday I see you again, and that I see you with His light in your eyes.

If this coming storm is as dark as I fear, then the future of the De Wilde family is uncertain at best. Your father was a good man, a godly man, a man who obeyed the call on His life. But he talked too much of all his work, and he gained the attention of men he ought not to have. And now we will all pay the price of it.

I know he told you to protect us. But you cannot, my precious son. We are in God's hands, and God's alone. War is knocking on our door, and it is bigger than any of us. But the Lord is bigger than war. He will take care of us, if it is His will. And if it is not, then it will be to His glory. Rest in Him.

Rest? Where was *rest* to be found in any of this? Lukas set the letter down carefully upon the table, knowing he'd want to reread it later. Then he covered his face with his hand and leaned back against the couch.

He'd always had some intention of settling down to a life of which his parents would approve. In that nebulous *someday* of the future. *Someday* when he was older and ready to be boring. *Someday* when the star of his fame had dimmed. *Someday* when he cared more about pleasing them than about pleasing himself.

It had never once occurred to him that there wouldn't *be* a someday—which proved what a fool he was. That his father would die so suddenly. That his mother and sister would be lost to him. That everything he once sought would grow pale and inconsequential under the shadow of war.

This, then, was what Margot had meant. God had known. God had always known. Man might not, but the Lord did. And perhaps, if one were on good terms with the Almighty, that would bring comfort rather than resentment.

God had known—and had done *nothing* to stop the horrors.

Again, Margot's voice in his head. Or his heart. "What would you have Him do, Lukas? He warns us of how not to act, but we disobey—like that time I climbed the tree when Papa had told me not to. But how is mankind railing at God any different than when I screamed at Papa for not catching me when I fell, even though I'd done it deliberately when he wasn't nearby?"

He scrubbed his hand over his face. He could still remember her screams of pain when she'd fallen. And the look on Père's face. He had held her and he had wept and he had said he was sorry for not being there, never pointing out that it would have been avoided had she obeyed.

Did man's actions grieve the Lord so in heaven? Did He ache for them, even as they tore themselves apart?

Would it all be different if more people heeded His advice, as Margot implied?

Of course it would be. He didn't have to know God personally to recognize that basic truth—that if everyone lived by those principles of right and wrong, the world would be a much better place.

Though that meant . . . Lukas's heart twisted. Or perhaps his stomach. Or his diaphragm. Something that robbed him of breath and made him double over.

What lives had *he* ruined in his blind quest for his own pleasure?

"Oh, God. I cannot put it all to rights. I don't know how. I don't know where they are or remember their names or . . ." He hadn't cared who those women were or why they were there, slipping room keys into his palm. It had only mattered *that* they were there and willing and beautiful.

Something foul and thick and tangible slithered about inside him. Something that had long been there—but he'd been blind to it. Until now. Now he thirsted for something pure and bright. Hungered for a feeling of cleanliness.

His parents had taught him the answers to all his questions, surely. But he'd buried the knowledge under too many years of disdain. Now he couldn't call them back up from whatever depths he'd banished them to. God forgave, he knew that. Jesus had come to earth for that purpose.

But how did one go about turning filth over to a God of purity? How did one get to know His voice? How could one ever escape the fear that one's sins had ruined more lives than one could ever put to rights?

He pushed to his feet, groping for the jacket he'd slung over the back of a chair. He needed a priest. There was surely a Catholic church somewhere in the city. He'd seen spires while out walking. He had no idea what church they belonged to, but he'd head in that direction. It would have a man of the cloth in it or near it. Someone who could answer his questions.

Shoes—he needed shoes. He found his lying helter-skelter beside the armchair and slid them on, then slid out the door. He'd forgotten to grab his hat, but he hardly cared about that. A slow trek down the stairs and then he was surging through the lobby, gaze on the front door of the hotel.

He nearly bowled over Daisy Davies, who was just turning from the reception desk. She gave a little squeal and slapped a hand to her chest, her eyes wide. Her hair looked a bit frazzled, perhaps from the weather. Or perhaps because it always did.

Lukas steadied her with a hand to her elbow, muttering apologies all the while. In French, but she didn't seem to mind his lapse. A smile soon replaced her surprise, only to melt away again into what could only be termed alarm.

"Mr. De Wilde, you look terrible! What are you doing out of your room? Why, I only dropped in to leave you a note assuring you we were praying for you—we were all a bit worried when Mr. Bellamy said you were too much under the weather for Willa to come today."

Praying? Lukas blinked, stepped back a few inches. That was right. Someone had said something about how religious the Davieses were. "It is injury, not illness. I will be well. But I have a question for you, if you would, Miss Davies."

Her smile returned, though it lit her eyes more than it curved her mouth. "Of course. What is it?"

Though he opened his mouth, it took him a moment to find the words to say. Never in his life had he sought out a man of God of his own free will—he'd rather avoided them, always certain they could see his sins and would judge him for them. "I have just had word from my mother, from before the invasion. I would seek a priest. Perhaps you know of one? I have seen some of my colleagues leaving for Mass, but I never went with them, and . . ." He could have knocked on one of their doors, he supposed. But at this point that would require going back *up* the stairs.

Miss Davies's eyes filled with calm. "Of course. You will be looking for Father Baggaley, at Our Lady of the Angels. He is a good and godly man, and I know he has been a great comfort to the other refugees. He and our own reverend are good friends, and I have met him several times. I can take you to him."

His head bowed. "I would be grateful."

"You look ready to fall over." She touched a hand to his arm, a quick press-and-retreat. "Please, sit and wait just a moment. The car is parked a few streets over, but I'll go and fetch the driver and we shall deliver you to the church—it is very near my own, as it were, and I was about to go that direction. You don't look as though you could handle a walk."

It was on the tip of his tongue to argue, but she may have a point. That light touch had sent him swaying. "I thank you. I shall just . . . just wait outside in the fresh air."

"Very well." She tucked her hand into the crook of his elbow, and he got the distinct feeling she did so to steady him, not so that he could lead her toward the door.

The rain-scented breeze was a welcome slap in the face when they stepped outside. It wasn't raining here, not yet, but the clouds were dark over Cardigan Bay, and low. Certainly damp enough to account for her frizzing hair.

Miss Davies released him. "I'll return posthaste. Do rest, Mr. De Wilde." She waved a hand at one of the benches dotting the promenade on the other side of the street.

He nodded. Even crossed the street toward the bench.

But then a flash of beige caught his eye.

He waited until Miss Davies was out of sight—he was fairly certain she wouldn't hesitate to turn back and scold him—before he wove his way through the pedestrians, toward that figure lounging against the seaside railing.

Cor Akkerman. And he didn't bother darting away at Lukas's approach. Nor did he bother straightening. He just gave a snarling smile. "Have another lady friend already, do you, De Wilde? I am sure Willa will be interested in learning of it."

And she would probably believe the worst of him, given his history. She would be right to do so, in general. But in this particular case, Miss Davies would no doubt tell her about their run-in well before Cor Akkerman could insinuate anything.

Lukas touched a hand to the railing to steady himself. "How long since you left Belgium?" The only other refugees he'd seen were the ones he worked with every day—and they'd all come over on the same boat he had. They'd all been in Brussels when the Germans invaded, and they'd seen little. They knew less.

Akkerman quirked a surly brow, probably at his daring to speak Flemish. Or at the slight French accent that colored it. "What's it to you?"

"I thought perhaps you may have news I haven't heard yet."

"And why would I tell it to you if I did?"

Lukas's eyes slid shut. "Please. We have common enemies, *n'est-ce pas*? The Germans. They chased you out of your home as surely as they chased me out of mine."

Akkerman snorted. "From what I hear, you *musicians* weren't chased—you were lured here by a couple of rich sisters with promises of safety and money."

"Money to send home." He opened his eyes again. "You know as well as I that the food in Belgium will run out in a matter of weeks. If people don't send money and food—if the Germans don't allow it—our people will starve by Christmas."

The cockroach before him just shrugged. "You have a point?"

His fingers curled over the top edge of the brick under his hand. He wanted to walk away, send the insect scurrying. But of whom else could he ask these questions? The other Belgians he saw daily knew no more than he did about the plight of others, and they couldn't leave to search out answers any more than he could.

This man, though. He was clearly a bit of a wanderer if he had followed Willa here from London. "Do you know where there are more refugees? Have you heard where they've gone? I seek my family."

Something shifted in the man's eyes, though Lukas's mind was too cloudy to put a name to it. Straightening, Akkerman shoved his hands in his pockets. "Quite a few are in London. I've heard there are camps and towns being set up in other parts of England—and of course, a resistance army forming, alongside the French. I don't know any details." He took a step, brows arched. "I could find out. If you cared enough to help me do so."

Lukas didn't much care for the sort of man whose loyalty could be bought, but that sort could prove useful—so long as he never shared any information with him that he wouldn't mind someone else purchasing from him in turn. He drew in a long breath. "How much will this 'help' cost me?"

A corner of Akkerman's mouth pulled up in a nasty little smile. "Fifteen pounds."

"Robbery."

"Then find someone else." Another careless shrug. He turned away.

Blast him. It would eat up a goodly portion of the stipend the Davies had paid him for living expenses. It would keep him that much longer from going back to Belgium.

But they could be out of Belgium already. God could have led them to England—to Wales, even. Why not? "Ten pounds. I will leave half of it for you at the front desk—and give you the rest when you come back with information."

Akkerman turned again. "Twelve. With eight now."

"Twelve, yes. But only half up front. I'll not budge on that."

The man pursed his lips and then nodded, pulling out a too-bright smile. "You have a deal, *monsieur*." He put such a ridiculous accent on the French that the mangling could be nothing but intentional.

Lukas couldn't bring himself to smile. His head was too light. And his arm too burning. "The money will be there in the morning."

"Excellent. That'll give me tonight to let my girl know I'll be away for a week or so."

The implication charged the air between them. Lukas didn't deign to respond. The look in Willa's eyes the other day when this fellow had put an arm around her shoulders hadn't exactly been warm and inviting. She was *not* Cor Akkerman's girl, whatever he might claim.

Though she hadn't exactly melted at Lukas's touch either.

But he'd think about that later. Turning without any acknowledgment of the claim, Lukas spotted Miss Davies's car rounding the corner. He had other things to focus on just now.

TEN

She'd have an hour, at the outside. That was all. Willa glanced once more into the dim, narrow hotel hallway and eased the door shut behind her. From what she'd been able to glean with the ten-second glance at the guest register she'd managed yesterday, this floor was filled with Belgian musicians. Which meant that it should be empty now. And would remain so until their second concert was over two hours hence.

Missing it was in part a sharp, hollow ache in her middle, making that elusive, unheard melody weep through her heart, only to vanish again before she could take hold of it. And in part, it was a relief. No reminders, tonight, of all she wasn't.

Just a focus on what she *was*.

A lamp had been left on in the outer room of the suite, which may have caused a burst of panic had she not already verified that Lukas had indeed gone with his colleagues to the symphony hall. It would hurt him—his shoulder had still looked stiff and painful to her eyes during their three lessons this week—but he would never admit it to the world at large.

Willa cast her gaze around the room as she slid her lock-picks back into her bag, along with the skeleton key that had, happily, worked without her needing to use the more skilled tools. Noting

135

the distance from window to door, she drew herself a mental line on the floor, beyond which she'd be visible to anyone on the street below. The curtains were drawn, but lamps meant shadows.

The room was well appointed but impersonal. Few belongings were taking up residence here in this outer room. A pair of everyday shoes. A hat. The crate of music that she saw at their lessons. She bypassed all these normal things and padded to the writing desk in the far corner, well out of view of the window and street below.

A stack of correspondence sat on the surface, envelopes slit but still enclosing the missives. All to him, but with a direction to the Hotel Elysées Union in Paris. She flipped through them, looking for any hints of the covert.

There were none, not to her eyes. The only English one was a request to visit New York City on his tour. A few were clearly invitations to events, all out of date. One, toward the bottom, was what appeared to be a love letter, though she couldn't read many of the French words to be absolutely sure. But she spotted a few of the phrases he kept spouting at her. *Amour. Ma cherie. Mon ange.*

There were two more in the same script, but he hadn't even opened those envelopes. Whoever this *Em* was who had signed that first letter, he was apparently happy enough to ignore her.

One little part of Willa felt a bit of smugness at that. But only one *very* little part, and only for a moment. Because she knew well that she wouldn't keep his affections either. And didn't want them anyway. The very fact that he had these love letters sitting here . . . He was the type of man she most despised. She might recognize his charm, but she'd sooner hand herself over to Scotland Yard than fall prey to it.

Her fingers stilled on another letter. This one was outside its envelope and sat in a corner of the desk all its own. Flipping it to see the signature, she didn't need to know much French to realize it was from his mother.

He'd mentioned this one on Tuesday. When his face was still so haggard with pain, when he could barely lift his arm, when shadows circled his eyes from what must have been a sleepless night.

It would make sense, wouldn't it, for a key to be hidden somewhere in this? A message from his family. Sent just before war broke out. If his mother had suspected what was coming, mightn't she have included hidden instructions on how to reach them and hence get his father's work?

But Lukas hadn't seemed to know how to reach them. And if he could fake that level of despair, then he ought to be acting on the stage, not just playing violin.

She reached into the bag looped over her shoulder and pulled out the box she'd slid inside it this evening, when she'd told her hostesses that she had a headache and wouldn't be joining them at the concert tonight. She'd never actually operated a camera before, but the shop girl had told her it was easy—meant to be, so that busy mothers could take snapshots of their children. Then all she had to do, the girl had said, was send away the film and she'd end up with beautiful photographs.

Risky. Someone could steal the camera and whatever evidence she committed to the film. Or steal the photographs themselves.

But it was the best means she had been able to think of for getting her employer a glimpse of this correspondence. She couldn't just take the letter, not if she wanted De Wilde to remain off his guard. And she didn't trust herself to copy it, not with it being in French. She could misspell something vital and not even realize it. This way, he could see for himself if there were anything important on the paper.

Assuming she managed a focused photograph. She went through the steps as the sales clerk had instructed, praying all the while for a decent result.

No, not *praying*. Wishing. Hoping. It was entirely different.

Teeth clenched, she put the camera back in her bag and the letter back where it had been. Even *he* was talking of prayers now, which was just infuriating. Of all the people in her life to start spouting religious nonsense, who would have expected it to come from the man renowned for his ungodly lifestyle?

It didn't matter. He wouldn't be in her life for long anyway.

And besides, she could almost understand why he'd have a sudden crisis of conscience, given his family's situation. She just highly doubted it would stick.

Shaking it off, she went systematically through the rest of the desk, snapping photographs of anything that looked promising. It took her another fifteen minutes to check every possible hiding place in this outer room, careful to leave everything exactly as she'd found it. Then she turned, with a deep breath, toward the door that stood shut. Into the bedchamber.

She'd taken only one step toward it when a noise made her halt, made her brows scrunch up. A door closing. If she wasn't mistaken, the heavy door at the top of the stairs, not the lighter swing of a room's door. Someone else had just arrived.

"Blast." It wasn't him, surely. But it shouldn't be *any* of them on this floor, and if someone *was* coming back, it very well could be the one struggling to recover from a gunshot wound. He could walk right through those doors in another minute and . . .

It was probably some flautist who had forgotten something. Right? It wouldn't be him. Not with his determination to deny his injury. Still, she plastered herself to the wall beside the door so she could listen.

Footsteps. Soft, but not light. A man's step, trying to go unheard.

The padding of the invisible feet stopped outside the door, blast it all. Willa pressed her lips together.

It wasn't Lukas. Couldn't be. He wouldn't walk with such a mincing step to his own door.

A scratch, a tap of metal on metal.

Another sound she knew well—but not a key in the lock. A *pick* in the lock.

Apparently she wasn't the only thief in Aberystwyth trying to steal from Lukas De Wilde. But she was sure as blazes going to be the only one who succeeded.

With a quick, silent movement she reached into her bag and pulled out that magical skeleton key. Then, breath held lest she make a sound, she slid it into the lock. Not all the way—she didn't want to bump into the picks and thereby shout that someone was in here foiling the would-be thief. But most of the way.

Another moment, and then a soft curse from the other side of the door. Willa smirked even as the masculine mumbles out there turned to more insistent scraping and scratching.

She kept her hand on the key, more for her own peace of mind than because she feared the intruder would somehow dislodge it. Jamming a lock was a guaranteed way to interfere with a lock-pick.

The real question now, though, was who was on the other side of the door.

She drew her lip between her teeth, eyes on the peephole. She could look, of course. But if she did, she'd block the bit of light coming through the hole, and if Whoever He Was happened to look up just then, he'd know someone was in here.

No, she would be patient. Wait until he was walking away and then steal a glimpse.

Easily decided. More difficult to carry out through the interminable minutes he kept trying with the pick. What, did he not realize it was jammed? Did he think himself merely inept?

Amateur. Any thief worth his salt knew the difference between a difficult lock and a jammed one. How long would this bloke keep trying?

Minutes, apparently, upon minutes. She glanced at her cheap

watch at one point, and the story its hands told her made frustration simmer in her stomach. He was wasting all her time. *All* of it.

She ought to leave the key to do its job and continue her own business.

But even with the utmost care, she could make a noise. He could hear her. And if he realized someone else was in here . . . Well, he may be an inept thief, but who was to say his skill level in violence?

She'd just stay right here until he left. It was the safest bet. And she could always come back during the next concert to search the bedroom.

She'd have to, at this point. She hadn't time enough to make a good go of it. Drat it.

And drat it all the more, but what was she to do about this idiot outside now? She couldn't very well let someone else beat her to the punch. Mr. V would be livid if that happened. Should she somehow warn Lukas that there was a thief about?

No, then she'd be interfering with her own job.

Follow this bloke when he left?

Risky. And while the greatest rewards came with the greatest risks, she saw no real prize waiting in that scenario to make it worthwhile.

She pressed her lips together. Maybe the smartest choice would be to tell Mr. V. See what he said to do. Though it rather pained her to consider such a move. Would he keep giving them work if they couldn't handle the simplest of jobs without running to him for help?

Finally, a curse came from the other side of the door. She didn't recognize the word, just the sentiment. Was it even English? Perhaps Welsh? Then a gusty exhale and what she convinced herself was the sound of a shoe pivoting on carpet.

She waited another second, two, and then eased up against the door. Waited yet another second, and then put her eye to the peephole.

The man was walking away. She caught only a glimpse of his

back, distorted by the curve of the glass. But it was enough to make her brows tug together.

Average build, average height. Middling brown hair covered by a derby. And a jacket in a deep, rusty brown.

She drew in a long breath and listened for the heavy fall of that stairway door. Cor may have disappeared again this week, but her other shadow was apparently still in Aberystwyth. And was, without a doubt, linked somehow to this job concerning Lukas De Wilde. More, he'd been following her before she'd begun coming here for lessons, so he'd known from the start what *she* was about.

Gripping her bag, she counted out two minutes and then let herself out, relocking the door behind her. And wished, for the first time in years, that she had a weapon in her bag more effectual than a camera.

She scurried to the stairs and slid silently into the dim space, hurrying down to the ground floor. Then pulling to a quick halt.

A familiar figure approached the front desk, in a buff jacket instead of a brown.

She may never stop frowning at this rate. Moving smoothly to avoid catching anyone's eye, she rounded the steps and ducked in behind them, where the ornate railing would hide her from view.

Cor Akkerman leaned onto the counter with that charming smile of his. "Good evening. Did Mr. De Wilde leave an envelope for me? Cor Akkerman."

The man behind the desk flashed an impersonal smile along with his "Just a moment, sir" and then bent down to search beneath the desk.

Willa eased a bit more into the shadows of the stairs. Why would Lukas have left anything for Cor? She would have sworn they didn't know each other—there had been no recognition in either's eyes last week when they met. What was Cor's angle? He had to be out to gain something.

141

And gain something he did, when the clerk stood back up with an envelope in hand. "Here you are, sir."

Cor took the envelope with another smile and handed a different one to the clerk. "Thank you. And this is for him."

Interesting. And frustrating. What business did these two have? She held her ground for a moment, watching as the clerk greeted another man in hotel uniform and then gave his place behind the desk to him. The first bustled off, disappearing quickly through the same back door Willa had entered through.

She then glanced to where Cor had drifted to a halt across the lobby, nearer the doors than the desk. He'd opened the envelope and was flipping through it. She couldn't hear anything he may have said, but he spun back around with jaw clenched. Then startled at seeing a different man behind the reception desk.

Still, he strode back toward it, making Willa glad she hadn't emerged. He slapped the envelope onto the counter and utterly failed at wiping the anger from his face. "Pardon me. I just left an envelope with your colleague for Mr. De Wilde. I need it back, if you please."

The new clerk blinked. "I beg your pardon?"

All semblance of charm had vanished from Cor's face—though to her way of thinking, he'd have better luck with this particular fly if he kept the appearance of honey. He tapped a finger to the counter. "Your colleague. Where did he go?"

The new clerk bristled. "His shift was over, sir. I am certain I can help you with anything he could have."

Now Cor put his smile back on, though it was likely too little too late. "Of course. My apologies. I just left a letter here for Mr. De Wilde that I need back, if you please."

Willa pressed her lips against a grin as the clerk did that *blink* again. "I'm sorry. I cannot hand over anything belonging to our guests."

"It does not belong to your guest. It belongs to *me*, and I—I left the wrong one."

She rolled her eyes. Surely a man who could follow her all the way to Wales could do better than *that* for an excuse.

The clerk, of course, didn't budge through the next two minutes of wheedling. Though he *did* offer to have Cor escorted out of the hotel. At which point the Belgian sneered and stalked off.

Very interesting. She may have been tempted to try to lift the envelope herself to see what was in it, but the clerk slid it into his inner jacket pocket the moment Cor walked away. And with the desk between them, it would be hard to slip out again. She could probably lure him from behind it . . . but she suspected there was an easier way to discover the answers to this particular question.

On silent feet, she slid from her hiding spot and hurried out the back door, darting down the dark street until she could peek around the corner of Terrace, toward Marine.

Yes, as she suspected—Cor stood at that corner, leaning into the row of buildings. Lying in wait. Which meant she could too, back here. He would confront Lukas when he returned, and all she had to do was stay here for another fifteen minutes or so, and she'd hear all about it.

Under normal circumstances, the wait would have been as easy as getting caught in the rain. But tonight her eyes kept searching the darkness, looking for that rusty-brown coat. Her fingers tightened around the straps of her bag.

Lukas had better tread carefully. It seemed that he had far more enemies on the streets of Wales than a musician ought.

ELEVEN

It may have been easier to change his life if Lukas's friends didn't continually stare at him as if he'd shifted into an ogre every time he made a sound decision. With a huff, he lifted his violin case. And scowled at Jules. "Why do you look at me like that?"

"You must be feverish. From the wound. I thought you said it was feeling better." His friend actually reached out as if to put a hand on Lukas's forehead.

He batted him away, only slightly wincing. Which, given the strain from the concert, was a true accomplishment. "Just because I want to go back to my room, I am ill?"

"It isn't like you." And something unhappy, perhaps even irritated, flashed through the depths of Jules's eyes. "You haven't been yourself since . . ."

"Since I discovered that my family has vanished?" His own irritation sparked, fanned up into a flame. Not quite the same kind of flame Jules was accustomed to, but not quite the silent, brooding one that had held him in its grip since waking up on British soil either. "Do you really expect such things not to change me?"

Jules darted a glance at the other musicians milling about— most of them going out for a late supper somewhere or another,

144

some to the homes of the rich patrons who had filled the concert hall.

Yes, he usually would have been among them. Out eating and drinking and flirting and indulging in whatever pleasure he fancied. Funny how he didn't long for that even a bit right now. Didn't have any desire to feel like his old self.

His friend stepped near and pitched his voice low. "I expect you to search for them. To find them. To pursue that like a hound on the trail of a fox, because that is your way. But not to turn into a monk in the meantime."

With a shake of his head, Lukas began the process of weaving through the milling musicians. Jules would follow. Or not. Just now, he hardly cared which. If his friend wouldn't support him in this change he meant to make to his life, then . . .

Then what? They would simply cease being friends?

It left a hollow feeling in his chest, that thought. Jules had been a constant in his life for decades. The one always happy to tag along, to check him when he ventured too close to out of control, to be measured when he was not.

But then, really, why had he spent all those years at Lukas's side? Why had he never insisted on his own path when Lukas dictated their every move?

He paused a few feet from the door and looked back.

Jules was only a step away, thunder in his brow and cello case in hand. He pushed past Lukas into the cool night. "One of these days I'm not going to follow when you walk away in the middle of a conversation."

"I'm sorry."

The words—simple, small—brought Jules's feet to a halt. "I beg your pardon?"

Was it that odd for him to apologize? Lukas tried to think of another time when he'd said those little words in a similarly serious tone—about his own behavior—and came up blank. Blast, but it was a wonder he had any friends at all. He shook his head and indicated they keep moving. "I said I'm sorry. For assuming you will just follow. For always assuming it, in every part of life. The truth is, Jules . . . The truth is, I don't know what I'd do without you. You have always been there to guard my back. To keep me in check. To . . . to save my life. I owe you a debt I can never repay."

Rather than move, Jules just stared at him. A long fifteen seconds later, he shook his head. The serious lines of his mouth pulled up just a bit. "Perhaps I *do* like this new Lukas. Despite scarcely recognizing him."

His own smile felt tight and strained. "The question is why you ever liked the old one."

"If you're looking for flattery, keep looking." Jules motioned him forward, down the path that was growing increasingly familiar. "You've people enough singing your praises without needing my voice added to the mix."

"I'm not after flattery." And Jules had never offered any, to be sure. So perhaps Lukas wasn't *that* bad a friend, to have always appreciated the honesty he got from him. "I'm after the truth. Do you not think me capable of changing? Of putting aside my wild ways and settling down?"

Silence walked with them for a few steps, though it was the thoughtful, musing kind, not the stormy, brooding kind. And then Jules tilted his head, keeping his gaze straight ahead. "Capable, yes. Of course. I always assumed you would, eventually. But this isn't a change to which you were won over or slowly grew accustomed. It's too sudden—wrought by circumstance, not some internal epiphany. It's the war that's done this to you, Lukas. And so, what happens when it's over and life returns to normal in a few months?"

Lukas shook his head. "Life will never return to normal. Or . . ." Of course it would—to some semblance of it, anyway. "It will be a different normal, after the war. We will never be able to forget. I

will simply be a different normal too. The kind that can appreciate the gifts God has given."

"Now you sound like our mothers."

And their fathers. Men, both of them, who had found a way to
be strong and successful and happy living quiet, family-oriented
lives. Lukas could do the same.

Funny—of the two of them, most people probably thought Jules
the more likely to settle down first. Yet here he was, incredulous
and unwilling. It made a grin tug at one corner of Lukas's mouth.
"I'm not asking you to change with me, you know. You can go on
living the epicurean life."

Jules halted and then pivoted. Moonlight and streetlamps illu-
mined his face—caught in an expression of realization. "You know,
you're right. Just because you're eschewing all the best invitations
doesn't mean *I* must." He smiled and took a step to the side, putting an extra foot of space between them. "You go ahead and rest.
Pray, or whatever it is you mean to do these days. I'm famished."

He hadn't expected him to just turn and leave quite so quickly.
Did it point to something in Jules, that he would do so? Or some
other, yet unrealized shadow in Lukas, that he would expect his
friend to keep following?

Perhaps he *would* go back to his room and pray. Try to straighten
all this out—who he was, who he could be, and who his friends
were. It would likely take a lot of practice before he really understood what the answers to those prayers were, but his parents
and Margot had always insisted that the more one spoke to God,
the better one could recognize His voice in return.

For now, he forced a smile. "Enjoy, *mon ami.* I will see you
tomorrow."

A few seconds later, he was alone on the street. And feeling
another brood coming on. He didn't like to be alone—and rarely
was, until all this began in Brussels, when pain had been too
constant a companion for him to want another.

147

Another flaw he needed to examine? Should he be content with just his own company and the Lord's? Or was it simply a personality trait, one that was neither good nor bad?

Perhaps the latter. And so perhaps the logical thing to do was to marry. Ensure a companion for all his days and nights. Children to fill the hours with laughter and argument—two things he had always loved.

His lips quirked up again. It wasn't a distasteful idea, really. And if he wanted some entertainment, he could propose to Miss Willa Forsythe again on those grounds and see her reaction. He had a feeling it would be every bit as volatile as the one she'd made to his suggestion that they marry for the sake of the music. And if he wanted to see her in an outright panic, he could probably achieve it with words of romance and affection. That seemed to alarm her more than anything else.

The strains of a record drifted out an open window toward him, the gramophone's silhouette visible behind the thin curtains when he glanced up. *Music.* That, if nothing else, he did indeed have in common with the skittish woman.

But he wanted to convince her to spend some time with him *without* his violin in her hands too. To talk to him. Get to know him. Let him get to know her. That was the only way to discover what this intrigue she ignited within him really was. Whether it would pass or whether he could happily spend a few decades trying to decode it. *I would value your advice on how to convince her to give me a chance, Lord.*

He listened as he walked. But he heard only that fading note from the gramophone. An auto rumbling by a street over. A horse neighing from up ahead.

Where was God's voice in these everyday noises? Perhaps learning to pick it out would be akin to finding that one voice in an orchestra—a particular cellist or horn player. It was by no means easy when the whole point of the symphony was to hear a creation somehow greater than the sum of its voices. But it could be done when one had a practiced ear.

He had never been as skilled at it as, say, Willa seemed to be. Did *she* hear God's voice amid the noise of life? He would ask her. If she was such a good friend of the Davieses, then chances were good she shared their faith. Perhaps she could help him rejuvenate his own.

He strode along the final few feet of Crynfryn Row until it terminated at Marine Terrace, his eyes by rote searching through the streetlamps' glow for the familiar stretch of white building a few doors down. His arm was much improved, but the healing process was more exhausting than he'd ever supposed. He was ready to collapse on his bed and spend a few hours in oblivion.

Which apparently would have to wait. He was just outside the circle of the hotel's lights when a somewhat familiar shadow emerged from the far corner. Dread curled through him, twined with relieved expectation.

Please let him have worthwhile news, Lord. His prayer felt as rusty and stiff as his arm, but he was at least trying. Much as he *tried* to position a welcoming smile on his lips, though he really didn't like the man. He moved to the corner, since the other made no attempt to come to him. "Akkerman."

The lights did nothing to banish the shadows on Cor Akkerman's face. "Do you mean to cheat me?" He spoke in Flemish, harsh and low.

Lukas fought the urge to reply in French, just to irritate him. His brows drew together. "I beg your pardon? Why would I do that?"

As he waved a hand at the hotel, Akkerman's face darkened still more. "I got your envelope—empty, let it be noted, of the money. Our agreement was that you would leave it at the front desk."

"No, our agreement was that I would leave the *first* bit at the front desk. Why would I leave the rest there for you to claim regardless of whether you did the job or not? You show me answers, I pay you." Simple enough. Though the hunch of his companion's shoulders had him looking around for escape routes. He wasn't usually a pushover, but with one arm injured and the other holding a violin worth more than a house, he wasn't exactly in a position to put up a fight.

The man gritted his teeth for a moment, then visibly relaxed and drifted at a seemingly leisurely pace up Terrace Street. "I left you a letter with all I found, but I can tell you now as well. There are refugees spread all throughout Great Britain, and rumor is that there will be thousands more before the month is out. They are most heavily concentrated on the east coast—logical, since it's closest to the Continent. But other ports like Bristol are full of them as well."

Them. Did this man feel no unity with his fellow countrymen who had been ousted as surely as he had been?

Lukas nodded and kept pace. "Are they integrating into the local communities or setting up their own?"

"Both. In the cities, they stay where they can. But a few camps are already springing up in the countryside, with purpose-built buildings." Akkerman folded his arms across his chest and halted at the next small junction. This must be the way back to his rooms. Or he wanted Lukas to think so, anyway. "You gave me vague instructions—I can give only vague answers. If you want more specifics . . ."

It would cost him more. Lukas had the urge to grit *his* teeth as well.

How much did he really want to tell this man about his family? Would he be a fool to trust him with even a sliver of the truth?

But he didn't know who else to send out in search of answers. And if he kept it vague enough, it would look like no more than what any other man in search of his mother might do. "Right."

He set down his instrument case and reached into his pocket, pulled out his wallet. He extracted a twenty-pound note with a sigh. "The rest of this payment, with some for the next. I need to know if any of these communes have newspapermen. And if they will be starting up their rags here to distribute to the refugees."

Akkerman reached for the note, all smiles now. "It'll take a bit of time to find that out. I'll have to talk to some cousins I have scattered about."

"Then talk to them. But I want all the information you can find about it—if, and who would be running them if so. And how to go about subscribing and placing advertisements." He hoped—he *prayed*—that one of Père's friends would be among the refugees. One who would help. Who would let Lukas put a message in his paper for Margot and Mère. It was his best hope of finding them.

Please, God. Please.

Yet even as he prayed it, something inside went heavy, sank. The chances were so slim—that he'd be able to get a message to them at all, that they'd receive it, that it would *work*, that they could get one back to him. That he would have the means to go and save them.

It felt, just now, impossible. But impossible was all he had to hope in.

Akkerman stuffed the money into his pocket, nodded, and took a step past him. "I'll report as soon as I know anything useful."

Lukas nodded as well and picked up his violin again, turned to watch him go. Praying the money he'd had with him in Paris would fund Akkerman long enough to find him the information he needed. Praying his family was out there somewhere, searching for ways to find *him* too. Praying—

A tingle brushed the back of his neck, made his throat go tight. Someone was watching him . . . though he wasn't usually one to note such things. It never really struck him as this did, but now his head jerked to the side, his gaze searching the shadows of the quiet street to his right.

Some street rat? A thief waiting to pounce, who had seen that exchange of money? He should hurry back to the safety of the promenade, the hotel doors, and the light. He should . . .

"Willa." He wasn't sure what, exactly, made him certain it was her in the shadows. Some shift, perhaps, that caught the light? But no, all was darkness in the alley. His eyes gave him no message that *anyone* lurked there. Perhaps he'd caught a whiff of her citrus scent. Or perhaps, if he were being romantic and believing his own stories, his soul had simply recognized the nearness of hers.

His lips curved as she stepped from the shadows. Perhaps he ought to give his soul more credit.

She didn't smile. "How did you know I was there?"

Her voice was cold calculation. And her eyes were those measuring, all-seeing windows again. Gone was the polish, the ease, the sweet smiles of the society girl.

Who *was* this woman? Perhaps in a lifetime he would find the answer.

It would be a start, anyway. And would prove entertaining for years. Still grinning, he shrugged and moved toward her. "True love knows when the object of its desires is near."

At that, she rolled her eyes, as he'd known she would. "What utter rot. I certainly hope you don't actually *believe* such nonsense."

Maybe he did. Or was beginning to. And perhaps, in a decade or two, she'd believe it too. For now, he looked past her, down that dark street. "What are you doing out at this time of night, *mon amour*? Miss Davies said you were unwell." She didn't *look* unwell. She looked perfectly at ease. A little bit angry.

And absolutely perfect.

"I stepped out for some air and saw *he* was back." She used her chin to indicate where Cor had been. It wasn't a ladylike gesture. Had, actually, a bit of the masculine to it. Where had she picked it up? And, the better question, why did it suit her so well? "Thought I'd follow him."

She turned her blue-green gaze on him. It was grey in this light, but no less piercing. "Do you really trust him to find information for you?"

He probably should have told her sooner that he'd hired her would-be suitor for the task. But he hadn't wanted to fill what few minutes they had together without the violin with talk of *him*.

And he wasn't yet accustomed to the thought of including someone else in his decisions. He would have to change that, if he meant to pursue her seriously. And just now, he felt as serious as a bullet wound, that tingle of her nearness still fresh.

In answer, he shrugged. "I think I can trust him exactly as far as the money goes, and not an inch farther. But as long as my silver holds out, I think he can be useful. Plus," he eased closer, just to watch her spine straighten, her feet shift half a step away, "it keeps him away from you, *n'est-ce pas?*"

She was all angles and planes and straight lines. And if he hadn't just turned over a new leaf, he would deem it a much-desired challenge to make her melt into a few delicious curves draped around him.

Her chin came up. "I can take care of myself."

"*Je sais.*" His affirmation emerged on a chuckle. Because he wouldn't have expected it from a girl in her position. But it had been clear from the moment he first saw her. "Of this I have no doubt. But if a friend can help you, then all the better, *oui?*"

He must have leaned closer to her, though he didn't realize it until her hand landed with a thud against his chest and pushed him back. "You are not my friend, Mr. De Wilde. It takes more than a ten-day acquaintance to earn that title."

"True. At least when the ten-day acquaintance is filled only

with music lessons and your determination to keep your distance."
He made sure to keep that space she liked between them—but
he caught her hand as it tried to drop away, and eased his violin
case back to the ground. "You do eat, do you not?" He may have
questioned how regularly she did so, given her slenderness, were
it not a strange question for a well-to-do girl.

She huffed and tried to pull her fingers free of his.

He held them all the tighter. "Have a meal with me. Tomorrow,
after Mass. I will arrange a picnic. That will be charming, *n'est-ce
pas*? Relaxing." And inexpensive—not that he didn't want to shower
her with all the good things his fame had earned him, but all those
things were cut off from him just now, and he had to be wise.

"I am not interested in *relaxing* with you." Yet as soon as she
said it, she drew in a sharp breath and averted her gaze.

Was it because of the way he'd run his thumb over her knuckles? Or was that giving himself too much credit?

"Shall I beg? I can. I perfected the art as a boy."

The wisp of laughter that escaped her lips sounded like bugles
and cymbals and trilling flutes—*victory*. "I bet you did."

He bent his elbow, raising her hand and drawing it to a halt
against his chest again. "Please, *mon ange*. Grant me an hour or
two. Do not decide to dislike me before you even give me a chance."

Her eyes skimmed his face and then focused beyond him,
across the street. Much as he watched her expression, he saw
no shift in it. No softening, but no hardening. No resignation,
but no determination.

Still, at length she nodded. "All right. A picnic, tomorrow. Call
after church." Once again she tugged on her fingers.

He didn't relinquish them. "You will not regret it. The Davieses'
church and mine are all but next door to each other. We can meet
there and then fetch the food from the hotel kitchen."

Now her face went utterly blank. "Directly from church? I can
just meet you at the hotel."

"Nonsense. We will both be walking back, we may as well walk together."

But that blankness on her face was interesting. He had a sneaking suspicion it was what panic looked like on her.

Yet another tug of her fingers. "Will you please let me go?"

"Of course I will. After I have determined why you are so afraid of touching me."

There, a flash in her eyes. Apparently Miss Willa Forsythe didn't like her bravery being questioned—and looked to be the type to rise to the challenge. "Just because I don't like being touched doesn't mean I'm *afraid*."

A point he would normally grant. But it hardly suited him to do so now. "No? I think if I were to kiss you, you would flee in terror."

She had to see through him—she was too smart not to. But apparently whatever ghosts in her past made her sink her teeth into a challenge were stronger than her common sense. He saw it flash through her night-greyed eyes.

Then the fingers he held to his chest went from resistant to insistent, knotting in his shirt. She jerked him closer and stretched up on her toes to press her lips to his.

In that moment of racing thoughts, he knew a moment of his own fear—that the self he had so recently set away would come roaring back, dragging him into that thought-world that cared only for his own pleasure. That he would take too much, press too far, without consideration for what this woman in his arms really needed from him.

But something new happened as he slid his bad arm around her and drew her close, as his lips moved over hers, softening the kiss that had been forceful and hard. Desire still burned, yes, deep in his stomach. But stronger, filling him from top to bottom, was a warmth that was far different. A . . . longing. A yearning. Not to take, but to give. To give something more than an hour of pleasure. To give her a day or week or month or perhaps even a lifetime that would make her realize there was more to the world than what her eyes could ever see. That there was hope and there was laughter and there was love that could swell and sway like a fantasia. That could make them soar like a sonata.

Her back didn't jerk away from the hand he spread against it. Her cheek actually leaned into his left hand, which he'd moved to cup it. For a moment, her mouth was pliant and receptive and followed where he led.

Then something flipped, and she all but jumped away from him, her eyes just a little bit wild. A little bit accusing—as if *he'd* been the one to start it.

It probably wouldn't benefit him to smile. But he wanted to. He'd have to remember the trick of challenging her, assuming it would work for him again. Though he had his doubts.

The wildness faded behind the clear, hard look he'd come to expect from her eyes. She lifted her chin and took a step to the side, past him, then toward Terrace Street. "Good night, Mr. De Wilde."

Somehow, seeing her in the light made him aware of the darkness all around them. He let the flirtation slide from his face and reached out, though he didn't touch her. "Let me see you home. It is dark and unsafe for a young lady."

The curve of her lips mocked his concern. "You needn't worry for me. I told you I can take care of myself, and I mean it."

"I would be less than a gentleman if I did not worry for you in such a situation."

Yet she lifted her brows and took another step away. "Good. I've no patience with gentlemen. I think many men would benefit by being less of one." As if hearing how that could well sound, her eyes went wide. "Not that I mean in *all* respects, mind you. That wasn't some kind of invitation to be a rake. I just mean in matters of acknowledging a female's independence."

He could hardly resist grinning again. And could hardly insist on seeing her home now, when it would likely undo what progress he had made tonight. So he settled for a compromise as he picked up his instrument case again. "I will hail you a cab, at least. Will you argue with that too?"

She sighed and walked with him back toward the promenade, where a cab waited, as usual, in front of the hotel. "I can hail my own."

The grin simply wouldn't be tamped down. Margot would love her and her every insistence that she was the equal of any man. Mère, on the other hand, wouldn't know quite what to think. There was, she would say, a beauty to the order that had been in place for centuries. There was a reason for it.

She admired strength though. Softness, she'd always claimed, should have a spine of steel hidden inside it.

Willa had the steel—it just wasn't much hidden.

Who would have guessed he'd find that so appealing? He took her hand and walked with her toward the cab, largely to be sure she didn't just pivot and stride away from all thoughts of safety. And she only tried once to tug her fingers free.

He chuckled and got a better grip on his violin case's handle. "When we are married, will you still insist on walking home alone?"

"You're an idiot, Lukas De Wilde."

"You and your sweet talk. Is it any wonder I am smitten?" He lifted her hand to his lips even as the cabbie came to attention and opened the door for her. "I will see you in the morning, *mon amour*."

She freed her hand and turned to the taxi. He thought she intended to get in and go without another word, but she paused with one foot inside the car and looked back at him. "Lukas . . . be careful. With Cor and . . ."

Her words trailed off into the night, urging his brows to lift. "And?"

Her gaze flicked to his violin case. "You left that sitting on the sidewalk for a full two minutes. Which is utter idiocy."

She had a point. "It was all but leaning against my legs. And I am certain if someone tried to steal it, you would intervene. Surely a girl who can take care of herself so well can help protect a violin too, *oui?*"

Margot would have narrowed her eyes at him and declared him mocking. Willa simply gave him a cool little smile. "Your violin, yes. Though if some thug had thought to bash you about the head first, I'd have let him while I grabbed the Strad."

It probably shouldn't make him laugh. "So long as you would play it for me while I convalesced."

Her gaze flicked to the violin with far more affection than he'd yet to see her direct at a person. "I'll see you tomorrow, Lukas."

His name was music on her tongue, with its clipped London accent. He savored its cadence long after the cab's engine roared to life and drove her away from him.

Yet he couldn't shake the thought that it wasn't his careless ignoring of the Strad that she had really wanted to warn him about. She had some other concern for him but hadn't wanted to admit it.

A chill danced up his spine as he turned into the hotel lobby. He had concerns too—but he'd do his best to keep her well out of those.

TWELVE

I kissed Lukas De Wilde last night.

Willa tapped her pen against the paper, absent any clue of how to follow up that statement. And not entirely certain she meant to send it to her sister anyway. Rosemary had thoughts enough filling her head right now—all the little ones with her in Cornwall, the new home, the new husband. She no doubt had her fill of kisses and bubbling emotions and all those things Willa had sworn never to fall prey to.

And she wasn't prey. *She* had kissed *him*. It was different.

A fun tale to tell her family, nothing more. She'd let Barclay growl about it, and she'd claim it was nothing more than being able to say she had done so. Lukas De Wilde, world-famous violinist and equally famous playboy, at her mercy. Her *own* claim to fame. On her terms.

She balled up the letter and tossed it into the wastebasket beside her small desk. She could fill her words with all the bravado in the world, but Rosemary would see through it. She would know that it had left her shaken. And she wasn't about to admit that weakness to anyone, even those she loved best. Especially those she loved best.

She'd write a new letter to Rosemary and the little ones later. After the picnic. After *church*.

Grimacing at that thought, she reached for her hat and moved to the mirror to pin it into place. She'd declined the invitation to join the Misses Davies at services thus far, but De Wilde had boxed her in. She couldn't very well admit to him that she'd never darkened the door of a church in her life. It wouldn't fit with the cover story she was to live while here.

Well, she could suffer it for one morning. How bad could it really be?

She had her answer half an hour later, when she was sitting shoulder to shoulder with Gwen on one side and Daisy on the other. Listening to the reverend drone on and on about what a loving father God was.

It took every ounce of control she possessed to keep her fingers from biting into her legs. A *father*, was He? Yes, perhaps so. Absent. Invisible. Someone who set a life in motion and then disappeared, leaving his family to fend for themselves and spend their every second longing for him. To be with him again, in her mother's case. To know who he blasted *was*, in hers.

Yes, God was *just* like a father. Never there, except when it was to rob her of what little she had. To stack the deck against her from the moment she was conceived until she learned how to wrestle control out of His hands.

If either of them ever stood before her—her earthly father or this so-called heavenly one—she'd tell him exactly what she thought of his *love*. And perhaps deliver a kick in the shins for good measure.

But she never would. Because neither was ever there. Neither, for all intents and purposes, was real. Not to her. Not anymore.

Those thoughts were a hot, boiling mess inside her by the time everyone stood to sing some song she'd never heard and could only pretend she knew because she had a book in her hand with the notes blessedly written out for her. They threatened to seethe over as she followed the smiling Daisy and Gwen out into the aisle. To leak right through the corners of her fake smile and spew onto a few unsuspecting Methodists.

It clouded her vision so much, she scarcely even noticed when Lukas eased up to her side in the church foyer—she might not have seen him at all had he not made his presence known with a light touch on her elbow.

Instinct made her want to jerk away. But he anticipated that and took her arm gently, tugging her toward the door. "Come, *mon ange*. Outside."

She may have argued, if she dared to open her mouth just now. But who knew what might come out? And much as she would enjoy letting all these thoughts cudgel the religious fuddy-duddies about the ears, she owed some respect to Gwen and Daisy.

They may be rich—and religious—but they had opened their home to her and treated her like a friend, no matter that she'd never proven herself such. So she'd have to prove it now. She wouldn't make a scene in their church.

Lukas tugged her out into the cool breeze of early October and the clouded-over sunlight. It wasn't raining, which was about all she could say for the day.

As for the man who led her down Queen's Road . . . he had no business knowing that she was upset. None. No one but her family could ever tell when she was angry, and he was most assuredly not family. She didn't even like him. And if she'd lain awake last night remembering the feel of his arm around her and his lips on hers, it was just because she was frustrated with herself for doing something so stupid. Her own terms or not.

He'd manipulated her, and she'd been fool enough to let him. To rise to a challenge she'd known very well was meant to benefit *him*, not her.

"We shall walk it off, *oui*? Head back to my hotel for the picnic basket and the car I hired for the day."

Her jaw still wouldn't unclench, though she sent a look over her shoulder. Gwen and Daisy must still be inside the church. She couldn't just walk out without telling them.

"I told them I was stealing you away now. They will not worry." He slid his fingers down her arm, lifted her hand, and wove it around his elbow to rest on his forearm.

When had he told them that? The steam escaping from her ears must have deafened her to those whispers. Which wouldn't do. Anger was all well and good until it dampened one's senses. Then it could make one stupid.

And Willa Forsythe would *not* be stupid.

She faced forward again. And caught, again, a flash of brown out of the corner of her eye. Here, even here outside the walls of the church, someone was watching. Following. Whose steps was he tracking today though? Willa's or Lukas's?

She swallowed back the question and matched her stride to her companion's. If God were real, were such a protective *father*, one would think He'd at least keep His own churches safe from spies or thieves or worse. In which case, He should have kept *her* from walking through the doors, she supposed.

Lukas made no attempt at conversation, not at first. Just held her hand against his arm and led her at a moderate pace along Queen's Road—which was most assuredly not the fastest route back to the Belle Vue. They ought to have turned down Bath, which intersected Terrace Road. But she wouldn't complain. She wasn't ready to be there yet. This tangle of thoughts had to seethe a little first—and she wanted the chance to see if that flash of brown followed them all the way.

Queen's Road eventually terminated at Marine Terrace, at which point Lukas turned her back toward the correct direction. The wind whipped at them, and at the water of the bay, and at the hats of the pedestrians littering the promenade.

Lukas pulled her a little closer to his side. "So is it God with whom you are angry or your father?"

Her nostrils flared, though it was the only tell that slipped out before she caught herself. She kept her gaze where it had been, straight ahead toward the curve of the bay and the distant pier, even though she'd rather have looked away. "What makes you ask such a question?"

"I heard the others say what the sermon had been about. What makes you dodge the question?"

Blast him. Dratted man. She glanced up at him. If he were grinning at her . . . But he wasn't. His eyes were dark and serious and endless, and his lips held a straight line. He looked concerned. And something more—something that went beyond mere concern. She had no word for it.

But it made her stomach seize and her throat go tight. Just like last night when that brown-coated stranger had been at the very door. *Danger!* screamed her every nerve.

She wasn't one to run from it. But she didn't toy with it either. "I'm not dodging your question. I just don't know why you'd assume I'm angry with God *or* my father." The absent snake. The invisible tyrant.

A little hum of disbelief came from his throat. "I grant you have a very good . . . what do they call it? A poker face, I think that is the term. Perhaps the best I have seen. But I have a sister who once tried to find the mathematical formula behind a convincing lie—rate of blinks, angle of gaze, in proportion to speed of breathing. Everyone in my family had to get very skilled, very quickly, at reading impassable faces."

His sister sounded like a girl she could like. "Is she near your age? Your sister?"

He angled her a look that said he knew well she was trying to change the subject. "Fourteen years my junior."

"So much?"

He lifted a shoulder. "There were others that did not make it past infancy. A couple that never drew a breath. We were all very relieved when Margot thrived. Thrilled. I admit that I thought at first she would not seem much like a typical sister to me, our ages being so different. But . . ." Now he grinned. And she didn't mind it at all. "She was every bit as pesky as she would have been had she been born a decade sooner."

Willa's lips tugged up too. For a second.

"Have you any siblings?"

Back down they came. Rosemary had talked with no trouble of the family when she was working the job in Cornwall over the summer. But look how *that* turned out. She'd ended up too close to her mark to finish the job.

A mistake Willa wouldn't have duplicated, even if the story Mr. V had provided for her hadn't already answered this question.

She shook her head. "I'm an only child." And she needn't any formula for lying to deliver the statement. It was, if one discounted the family she had chosen and gathered to herself, the truth. So far as she knew. Though chances were good her no-good father had sired a few other children on naïve young girls struck dumb by his charms.

The snake.

"And there is that anger again. Why?"

Her gaze snapped to his. "How . . . ?" But she didn't even know how to finish the question without verifying his assumption. And if there was one thing Lukas De Wilde needed no more of, it was confidence.

Yet he didn't look arrogant just now. He still looked more-than-concerned. "I keep telling you we were made for each other. It should come as no surprise that we should understand each other well, then, *non*?"

She gritted her teeth. "If you must know . . ." Just enough to appease him, to quiet him. That was all she would say. It wouldn't agree with the story Mr. V had given her, but so long as she kept her own consistent, it would do. "My father walked out before

I ever even knew him. It was just my mother and me and his hulking memory." Until Mum had followed him.

Her fingers curled into his arm for half a second, then she forced them to relax.

"That must have been difficult. I cannot imagine those early years without my father."

And she could not imagine early years *with* a father. Or with a mother who wasn't looking for him every time they stepped out of their flat. It had struck her as sad for a while there, when she was old enough to realize that it wasn't quite normal to always be searching for what never showed up.

Then he had. Sort of.

Willa couldn't even remember seeing him across the crowded street. She just remembered the way Mum had sucked in her breath. The way the fingers around hers had gone painfully tight. They'd stood there, in the middle of the road, holding up traffic, for too long a moment. Until someone jostled them out of the way.

Until Mum had seen where he'd gone.

Then she'd bustled Willa back up to their flat, told her to be a good girl and that she'd be back directly. With Papa.

Willa had put on her best dress, though it was far from pretty. She'd combed her hair and washed her face and sat on their faded sofa in their faded front room. And waited. And waited. And waited. Day had turned to night; exhaustion had overtaken her.

She'd been six. Just six. Being left for a few hours was no new thing for her, but when she'd startled awake the next morning, she'd seen the note on the floor.

Mum had taught her to read. He would expect it, she'd said. He was a man of intelligence, of education. She must make her papa proud.

She could still remember the feel of that paper—expensive, thick, rich. Better paper than Mum ever could have purchased. She could still feel the way her heart pounded as she opened it up. It would tell her to meet them for breakfast, perhaps. Or to pack her things, because he would be taking them with him in a few hours.

She could still see the words swimming before her in Mum's hand.

I'll come back for you when I can. You're a clever girl, you'll get along. Mumma loves you, Willa.

"Willa? Are you well, *ma cherie?*"

"Just ducky." She shook off the memories, the emptiness. The anger. Her mother had made her decision. And Willa had decided then and there that she wouldn't be like Mum, always waiting for someone else to show up and make her life better. She hadn't waited for her mother's return. She took what she could, and she left too.

If Mum had ever come back, Willa hadn't been around to find her. She'd forged her own path. Made herself into her own person.

But she knew in her gut that her mother had never come looking for her. And her father had never wanted her. And if either were still alive—which she sincerely doubted—then they deserved whatever ills befell them.

Only when the light shifted did she realize they had reached the hotel, and that Lukas had led her inside the lobby. She had missed the other half of the walk as surely as she had the first.

Acceptable only if she were walking with Barclay or Rosemary or the rest of her family. Not when she was arm in arm with her mark. The man in brown could have jumped into their path, and she wouldn't have seen it.

Stupid.

Lukas's smile was small. That particular degree of warm that said he understood and would make no demands on her.

But he shouldn't have understood. He *couldn't* have understood, with only the few words she'd given him. And the fact that he'd grown up with loving parents who had sent him to school and hired him a violin teacher and given him pocket watches with sappy inscriptions when he finally grasped hold of his dream.

She stood and waited while he disappeared to fetch the picnic basket, wrestling her wayward thoughts into control. No more preoccupation. She had a job to do, and it didn't include ranting at God. Or her parents. Or kissing Lukas De Wilde.

It would be back to London after she found this key. Back to bribing stage boys to let her sneak in for a few stolen minutes of music. Back to her trusty alley outside the London Symphony's practice chamber. Back to that stubby little stage in Pauly's pub, where everyone knew her and cheered her on and had no idea if she was playing an Irish folk tune or a masterwork by Vivaldi or Paganini.

Her gaze swept the lobby with its elegant appointments and rich colors. She didn't need this life. Didn't want it. All the fine things came with high expectations, with demands on one's freedom and very soul.

But the music. She would miss the music when she went home. Miss sitting in the audience and hearing the notes soar overhead, even if the conversation baffled her afterward. Miss being invited to sit in on rehearsals. Miss sifting through that box of sheet music that Lukas had at their lessons and choosing whichever she wanted to try to learn.

A melody echoed through her head now, some elusive combination of the sorrow and the joy. Inspired, no doubt, by what those others had written before her. Probably some odd combination of their compositions. She could almost, almost, hear it clearly today. That aching sadness of what she'd never had—minor notes, long and smooth. That raging anger at those who had decided her fate for her—quick staccato, heavily accented.

A hand touched her elbow, and the notes broke through with startling clarity for one moment. Then went silent.

"Are you ready?"

She could manage no smile, but she nodded and let Lukas lead her back outside and into the overcast, wind-whipped day.

An auto sat at the curb, and this he moved toward, a lopsided grin on his face. "One of these days, when I am in a given city long enough to justify it, I will have one of these. What make, do you think?"

"Rolls-Royce." Perhaps she picked the most out-of-her-grasp one she could think of. Perhaps because she knew it was out of *his* grasp as well.

But the blasted man wouldn't be offended. He chuckled. "I daresay not. Although that concert in London, when the dukes were there—the Duke of Stafford was telling me about his Rolls-Royce."

She gave a heavy blink. "You were talking to a duke about *cars*?"

"Why not?"

"Because . . . because it's so *normal*. And he's a *duke*."

Lukas chuckled and opened the passenger door of this car for her. She couldn't have said what make it was, but certainly no Rolls-Royce. "He is just a man, *mon amour*. With a wife who is determined to have a Renault."

A couple who could afford *two* high-priced automobiles? She shook her head and slid into the closed cab. "And there are children starving in the streets."

Lukas paused with his hand on the door, ready to close it behind her. His eyes were sharp. Not the kind of sharp that sliced—the kind that considered. "They are generous benefactors to many—the Staffords."

She lifted a brow. "I daresay they give only what doesn't make them feel a pinch. And how is that *generous*? It is only worth noting if it *hurts*." Like Pauly, who gave what he didn't really have to keep orphans from starving. *That* was benefaction worth touting. But no one ever would, because he didn't make his donations with a newspaperman on hand to sing his praises.

"Hmm." Lukas's lips pressed together, but he didn't look at all put out by her pronouncement as he rounded the car and got in on the driver's side, sliding the picnic basket to a rest between them. "I suppose I'll prepare myself for a life of feeling pinched, then, *oui*? You will apparently give all our surplus to the poor." He made a show of tilting his head. "It is a good use for it. And I daresay there will be many poor in Belgium after this war—perhaps you will approve us helping them?"

Of all the . . . "You are infernally exasperating. There is no 'we' or 'us' to help them. But *you* are certainly welcome to give all you can." It was a fine idea, really. If the papers told it true, the Germans had obliterated many a town and village when they marched through the tiny nation. It made her stomach sink to think of all the children now homeless. All the mothers who would now be struggling to feed and clothe them.

"Well, look at this." He reached out the open window and touched a hand to a mirror. "To see behind us, I suppose? I have never driven one with mirrors."

There was one on her side as well. Willa leaned toward it to get a better angle. How interesting. Perhaps with this she could get more than a fleeting glimpse of the rusty-brown jacket. "But you *have* driven before, correct?"

"Do you not trust me, *ma cherie*?"

"Trust is earned, along with friendship." The street behind them had another car puttering down it and two carriages drawn by horses. Most of what was to be seen, however, were people milling about in their Sunday best, tugging children along with them.

She missed the little ones. Having one of them scramble up onto her lap and loop an arm around her neck. The way they looked at their big brothers and sisters with complete trust. *Earned*, to be sure. They'd taken them in when they had no one. Fed them as best they could. Clothed them. Taught them how to survive.

Now they'd be taught new things—properly educated, thanks to Rosemary and Peter. Taught things like history and philosophy along with the basics of reading and writing and numbers.

She was glad. Glad they'd have chances she never had. And yet . . . it was only because of someone else's generosity that they could give them that. Rosemary's new husband. And, in part, Mr. V, who had paid the family quite a handsome sum to guarantee their loyalty to him.

"And off we go." Lukas pulled onto the street. "Though we are not going far. Just to the castle—we could have walked, were it not for the hamper."

The drive would take only five minutes, yes, but it took them up onto a hillock that would offer a very different view than the close-set walls and buildings of the little city. Willa set her eyes on the crumbling turret as soon as she could, and beyond to the green hills of the countryside. So that she could pull the images out again during the bleak London winter, along with the strange sights she had seen on the train into Wales—sheep grazing on hillsides, hills rising all about them, heather and yellow-flowered scrub plants vying for dominance.

"It does not look too busy today." Lukas pointed ahead, to where the old castle tumbled in upon itself.

She drew in a long breath. London had its share of ancient sites, to be sure—but not like this, left to the wind and weather. Her city hadn't patience enough to let a building crumble naturally. "Beautiful."

"The cook at the hotel said it is a perfect spot for picnicking."

Her shoulders relaxed against the back of the seat. "Perhaps this day won't be so terrible after all."

Lukas chuckled. "Good to know you were so looking forward to our afternoon together."

She certainly hadn't been. But she had a job to do, and she aimed to finish it as quickly as she could. Another week, perhaps. She would get back into his suite and search his bedroom. They had no concert this week though. She would have to risk it during daylight hours, while everyone was at one of their practices.

Her gaze latched onto the mirror. That same automobile from the street outside the hotel was still behind them, though the carriages had vanished in some other direction. What color was the jacket of the driver? It was too shadowed in the car's interior to make it out. "I'm not much for the getting-to-know-you nonsense. I hardly know how to do it."

"It is easy. You tell me a bit about you, I tell you a bit about me."

Easy. Right. "You start."

"All right." He kept his gaze ahead of them as he puttered up the hill toward the castle grounds. "What would you like to know about me?"

Where you keep your secrets. She waved a hand. "I don't know. Your family?"

"Ah." A smile overtook his lips. "A good subject, to be sure. You will like my family, *mon amour*. I only wish you could have met my father."

She rolled her eyes at the idea of ever meeting those who remained. "What was he like, beyond being a brilliant mathematician?"

"A brilliant mathematician." He chuckled and angled an amused gaze at her. "It was what everything came back to with him. Mère says that she tried for weeks to get his attention when they first met, but she did not succeed until she decided to embroider a theorem into her sampler. *That* he saw, though he had walked by her blindly for weeks."

Willa's lips twitched up too. "Why was she so determined to

171

catch his eye?" He must have been wealthy. That was the usual reason, wasn't it?

But that answer didn't match the softness in his eyes. "To hear her tell it, she knew the moment she was first introduced to him that she wanted to spend her life with him. She was a great beauty in her day—she still is, quite honestly—and she had her pick of beaux. But she said they all bored her. When she met Père, she knew he would not."

"She wouldn't be bored by *mathematics*?" Willa shook her head. His mother must have been rather inclined to it herself, if that were true.

"There is something so very alluring about genius." He sent her a teasing gaze, a crooked smile. "I suddenly understand that."

She narrowed her eyes. "So I am the genius and you the pretty one in this equation? And you think if we can re-create your parents' circumstances, we can re-create their happiness?" She snorted her opinion of that.

It did nothing to dampen his smile. "So you admit you find me handsome?"

As if he could draw her into a trap so easily. Willa sent him a glare. "You know well you are, but don't try to make something of it that it's not. I'm immune to handsome faces."

"Ah, but it does not matter, *n'est-ce pas*? I have already found the equation that will secure your attention." He pulled into an empty lot near the castle ruins. "You want to keep playing my Strad, you must keep spending time with me."

"Hmm." That car behind them continued straight ahead, but it slowed more than the road required. Watching them, she'd bet. Just as she'd bet the man inside had middling brown hair and a rusty-brown jacket. "That may result in affection for your violin. It does not necessitate affection for *you*."

"You pierce me through, *ma cherie*. But I am relentless. I will win you over by my sheer determination."

She couldn't see the car anymore as Lukas killed the engine and reached for the door. But tension possessed her shoulders again. "You'll waste your time, and then I'll be gone. I'm only here for a short visit, Lukas. Then it's back to my own world while you stay in yours."

"But we share a world. Music."

How wrong he was. But then, their worlds were overlapping for another reason too. One she would never admit to him. Then there was Cor, who came here following her and was now working for him.

And the man in brown.

She drew in a long breath as Lukas came round to open her door for her and shot her a warm smile. He was a man with a bull's-eye on his back, and did he even realize it? Did he realize that the same danger that had met him in Brussels was stalking him here too? Well, perhaps not the *same*, but it was surely linked.

His father, brilliant as he may have been, had made the De Wilde family targets.

She didn't return his smile, warm or otherwise. "Are you afraid for them? Your mother and sister?"

Pain overshadowed that too-handsome face. Like, but not like, what had been in his eyes due to his shoulder. "Terrified. But I will trust, as my mother begged me to do. I will trust there is a God strong enough to see them to safety. And I will find them."

"I'll help you, if I can." The words were out before she could stop them. They hung there in the air, accusing her of stupidity—this was not her job, was not why she was here.

But she could do her job *and* help him find his family, couldn't she? Not because she was going soft. Just because she, better than anyone, knew the pain of not knowing where one's mother was. And could imagine that echoing note that came when it was not by one's mother's design. And when a sister was missing too.

173

If any of the family were to vanish, she would turn the world upside down looking for them. They all would.

His fingers gripped hers long enough to help her out, but then they drifted away. He was respecting her boundaries right now, though he seemed happy enough to push them at other times.

"Thank you, Willa. I do not know how you could help, but . . . thank you."

She was more capable than she intended to let on. But for now, it was enough to offer a small smile. To look around at the nearly empty site that would probably fill as the afternoon wore on and more picnickers left their church pews and sought recreation. To note that moving, man-shaped patch of brown on the far side of the castle.

Oh yes, she could help him more than he knew. And it was going to start by turning the tables on her follower.

THIRTEEN

Margot placed a black stone on the game board and wished she dared to put it where she *really* wanted to. When the war was over, she would have to find someone trustworthy to play Go with her, so that she could at least once be good at it. Lukas could learn. He may claim not to be interested in such things, but she hadn't been able to beat him at chess until she was eight—and even now, he occasionally won a game.

He was more than he let on most of the time. Just like Maman.

Across from her, Gottlieb hummed, thoughtful. He wasn't quite so hideous when stationed at a game board rather than trying to charm her mother. He would be even less hideous if he were wearing normal clothes rather than that awful uniform.

But no. He probably slept and bathed in the thing. She'd never seen him without it.

He flipped a white stone between his fingers as he debated his options. She had chosen the position he wanted, she was sure. It was one of the reasons she had put her piece there. Even a dunce could have seen it was his next move.

"Your skill is improving, *fräulein*." He offered a small smile and leaned back in his chair as he surveyed the board. "It is a pleasant pastime for a lazy Sunday afternoon, is it not?"

Every afternoon was lazy now. Lazy and tense. Because they didn't dare fill them as they once had and never knew when the next tragedy would strike. They'd gone to Madame Dumont's church this morning for Mass—Maman with a black veil over her face lest anyone recognize her—and even the familiar Latin words had seemed all wrong. The priest had been too young, his voice too deep. His homily too . . . too . . . measured. As if he knew the enemy could well be listening and taking account of every syllable.

Wise of him. But still. She wanted to hear old Father Pudois again. Speaking from the heart.

In reply to Gottlieb, she said, "It is not completely boring."

He chuckled—which sounded all wrong coming from him. "Careful, *fräulein*, or you may make me think your hatred of me has dimmed a degree or two."

It pierced. More, probably, than he meant it to. She kept her gaze on the board. "I do not hate you. God forbids us to hate."

He snorted and set his white stone down in an utterly predictable spot. "You believe all that drivel, do you?"

Her fingers curled around her next stone, her gaze darting to the sofa and chairs. Maman had gone to lie down with a bad headache. Madame Dumont was here still . . . but she had dozed off in her rocking chair.

No one to scold her, then, for letting a few honest words slip past her lips. "You think God is drivel?"

"I think the idea of God and morality is a construct of civilization meant to keep the masses in line. I think those of superior intellect are capable of moving beyond such constructs."

Now *she* snorted. "Why not just proclaim 'God is dead' and be done with it, if you are so fond of Nietzsche?"

His stillness screamed for a long second. Then his "You are familiar with Nietzsche?" blistered her.

One of these days, she would be old enough that people would not look at her like she was an aberration for being well educated. One of these days, she might even be respected for her mind.

She longed for that day. How many more years? Two? Four?

Assuming she survived that long. Which, if she kept saying foolish things with Germans around, she might not.

She sent him her best scowl. "I have heard his works discussed. My father, God rest his soul, enjoyed entertaining his friends and debating with them. I would listen through the vents."

"Ah, yes. Your sainted father. He was a . . . ?"

"History professor in Louvain." It was the story they had agreed upon, the one they had decided was least likely to trip them up. Madame Dumont did have a nephew who had taught history at the university; he had run off to join the military outside of Belgium rather than evacuate to Brussels, and he had taken his family with him to settle them with distant relatives in France. If anyone bothered to check their story, there was enough fact there not to raise alarms.

And it at least meant claiming her father was in academia. A bit of truth that made the lie easier to say.

"Ah, yes. And he discussed Nietzsche with his friends?"

"He did."

"And his conclusion?"

"That a man who died of syphilis ought not to be the trusted voice on the value of ignoring morality."

His laugh boomed out, filling the room and rousing her false grandmother. Though Madame settled back down again in half a second.

Gottlieb's chuckle kept rumbling. "A clever man, your father."

She nodded and slid her game piece onto the board. It was, perhaps, a bit too smart a move. But by her calculation, she could make one or two too-smart moves a game and he would chalk it up to the luck of the ignorant.

"He does have a point, that there are natural consequences for our actions. And that the constructs of morality are designed to spare us from some of them. Cages are always meant to keep their prisoners safe."

"Or to keep the world safe from *them*." She rested her fingers in the bowl of stones and let their even, smooth surfaces soothe her. "Nietzsche may have claimed that only the most evolved men had moved beyond good and evil, right and wrong, but what man would not claim to be among the superior? And if everyone were to let his deepest, darkest desires reign, then . . ." She lifted her chin, met his gaze. "Then we would have a world full of selfish monsters stomping on anyone in their path. Destroying what society has worked centuries to build. Killing for no reason."

Joining the German army, in other words.

He heard her silent accusation. She could see it in the narrowing of his eyes. "Careful, *fräulein*."

"Of course. My apologies. If you do not think it immoral to punish or kill a young lady for speaking her mind, then I could easily get into trouble, could I not?"

He shook his head, a muscle in his jaw ticking. "You do not anger *me* with such words, Margot. But there are less measured men than I about, *ja*? I would not have you in trouble with *them*."

Right. *Them*. He would not punish her because it would ruin his chances of winning Maman's attention. She grunted. "It is your move."

"I am thinking." He settled a fingertip on top of his next stone and twirled it in a circle on the tabletop. "Something I am beginning to believe you do too much, my young friend. You should get out more often. Visit friends. Go to school. It is not healthy for a child to be trapped always in her own mind."

"My friends have been scattered. My schools have been closed."

"So make new friends. Enroll in a new school."

She opened her mouth to retort, but a loud growl from her

stomach beat her to it. And made heat stain her cheeks. Their rationed stores were growing pathetically small already. What would they do when winter came?

Gottlieb smiled—no doubt at the thought of having them at his mercy, reliant on what he could provide. "If you need a break to get something to eat, feel free."

"Need more time to think of your next move?" She forced a hint of teasing into her tone. Well, she hoped she did. "Or do you mean to rearrange the board when I leave? No, thank you. I'll stay right here."

He pretended affront. Well, she hoped it was pretend. "Have it your way, then."

She folded her arms over her stomach in the hopes that it would hush up. Let the silence tick by for a long moment. Long enough that it wouldn't seem strange to return to their previous topic. "I find your views on God and morality rather odd for a man whose very name means 'God's love.'"

"It is just a name. Yours means 'from the mountain.' It hardly implies you can live nowhere else."

Actually, her surname meant simply "the wild." And she could well resort to such behavior if nothing changed in the next few months. "Names can have power. If it were not so, we would not take such care with them. And you would not strive to earn new and better ones, *Generalleutnant*."

"A rank is different. I earn that. My name . . ." He waved a hand. "Something that perhaps an ancestor took seriously. But it has no meaning anymore."

"How sad that you think so." She glanced again at the Madame, who was snoring softly now. At the window with its fading light. At the world beyond it, where soldiers marched without bending their knees, citizens avoided the streets, and neighbors whispered with disdain about those who had abandoned their homeland and taken refuge in other, freer countries.

If their own neighbors were here rather than Madame Dumont's, would their disdain be directed at Lukas? Or would they not believe he still lived and instead whisper that he had died trying to save them?

No. He was alive, out there somewhere, and he would come for them. Somehow. Eventually.

She pulled out a handful of stones to see how many she could stack before they tumbled. "It is a very convenient philosophy for a soldier, to be sure. To be able to do whatever you please, thinking yourself above such things as law and morality."

"You are a cruel judge, *spatz*. Just because I do not feel the confines of what *others* tell me is moral does not mean I have no compass inside myself pointing me north. And it certainly does not mean I think myself above the law. I agree to abide by it when I accept citizenship, do I not?" He rested his elbow on the table and his head in his hand. His gaze remained glued to the board. "That was a very good move. I will need a moment."

Margot, deciding to ignore the *sparrow* endearment, balanced a fourth stone on top of the third, though the round tops were making it quite a challenge. "What, then, of when a whole nation breaks a law? An agreement between nations? Is it not right for *them* to be held accountable?"

"You speak of Germany invading Belgium?" He tapped a finger to his chin but didn't look at her. "We had no choice. Had we not done so first, France would have. It was *Kriegsraison*."

Her German was good, and she understood the two words that were put together, but that they'd created a new term for it gave her pause. "Excuse me?"

"*Kriegsraison*. The right of a government to disobey a law if it is to accomplish a wartime objective or avoid extreme danger."

She just stared at him.

Gottlieb glanced up long enough for their gazes to tangle, and he must have read utter disdain in hers. He sighed. "You obviously do not see it that way, being the unfortunate victim in this particular war. But Belgium . . . A nation has only the rights it is strong enough to protect. Yours, *fräulein*, cannot stand on its own. And so it can offer its people no rights."

It itched so much it burned. "It is God who gives us our rights."

"*Nein*. It is the state. And when your state is weak . . ." He shrugged. "But I do not see why the thought of Belgium being weak should upset you. Your people have no national pride beyond what is fashionable to tout on feast days."

Her hand curled around the stack of stones. She wished they were sharper, so they could bite into her palm and distract her from that terrible burning itch inside her chest. "Excuse me?"

There was nothing hard, nothing taunting in his gaze. Just . . . fact. Or what he mistook for it. "We Germans fought for our unification. For our identity. Most countries did. But not Belgium—is that not so? You fattened and grew rich because of a peace others created for you. All the money you make off the delicacies you grow, all the bragging about your superior workforce, but the Belgians will not spend so much as a franc on their own defense."

Her nostrils flared.

Gottlieb weighed his stone in his hand. A corner of his mouth pulled up. "Your country only exists at all because Europe agreed that it should, as a neutral land, so that no one country could claim its prime strategic location. If ever you had wanted to be more than that, you would have to be willing to fight."

"And yet if we try, *you* cite it as undue aggression and kill any civilian who looks at you wrong." Her lips curled up. "Is that your *Kriegsraison*? Exception to the law?"

His lips twitched into a smile. "*Nein*. That *is* our law. The ordinance of 1899 gives the military the right to kill any civilian who is assisting the enemy or their allies."

Her blood ran cold. "Define assisting."

He shrugged. "There is no definition. It is entrusted to the soldiers to determine that in the moment."

A chill wracked her. The killing was far from over, then. And they would do it with impunity. Killing any citizen who did not kowtow to them, able to say any resistance was aid to the enemy.

Gottlieb chuckled. "Relax, little one. We are civilized men, not monsters."

"I must ask you to prove that, Generalleutnant."

Another laugh. "And so I shall. I will share my bread with your family. I will see no one harms the lovely ladies of the house of Dumont. I am a friend."

Ha. She clamped her teeth down on her tongue to keep from making a response. But a jumble of numbers, random and unorderly, clouded her mind.

Silence rewarded her restraint. It stretched, uncurled, and would go on, it seemed, forever. Gottlieb had pursed his lips as he continued to study the board.

A full minute later, raucous laughter from the street penetrated the windows. Margot frowned. The voices were shouting in German. And from the sound of it, they were jeering at someone, not just in general.

Since Gottlieb would apparently take another century to decide on his move, she got up and went over to the window, looking down to see who the soldiers were tormenting now. Her breath caught when she saw the familiar brown curls. "No! Generalleutnant, stop your men!"

"What is it?" He was at her shoulder, peering over her head to the street. He sighed when he spotted the four soldiers prodding at Claudette.

What was she doing here? And alone?

For a moment she thought Gottlieb would do nothing. But then he unhooked the latch and opened the window. "Klein! Schmidt!"

The men—the two he named and their companions—snapped to attention.

Margot didn't wait to hear what he'd say to them. She dashed out of the room, down the stairs, and threw open the door to the street just as Claudette ran toward it. Margot pulled her friend inside. "What are you doing here?"

Claudette's cheeks were flushed a rosy pink, and indignation sparked her eyes into flames. "Just coming for a Sunday visit. I *thought*."

A Sunday visit? They both knew the days for those simple pastimes were long gone. She would have a reason beyond that.

Of course, Claudette was no fool. She wouldn't just shout her reason here, where German ears could overhear.

Margot shut the door. "Without your mother?"

"She's ill today. And my sister is caring for her, so . . ." She glanced past Margot to the top of the stairs and made a little curtsy. "Good afternoon, sir."

Margot spun. Gottlieb was, of course, standing just outside the parlor door. And he was *smiling*. "Ah, you found one of your scattered friends! *Gut*. You need it. You two go ahead and visit, *ja*? We will finish our game later." He started down the stairs. Perhaps he meant to go and join his men outside. Find another schoolgirl to harass.

They stepped aside as he neared the entryway and then scurried past him, up the steps, as he aimed toward his room. Margot curled her fingers around her friend's arm and tugged her toward her own room.

Only once the door had clicked shut behind them did she dare to whisper, "What is it? Why are you really here?"

Claudette gave her a dimpled grin and reached inside the jacket she wore, though the day wasn't all that chilly. It had apparently, however, allowed her to conceal . . . treasure. Treasure, pure and simple.

Manners forgotten, Margot snatched the newspapers from her friend's hands. "Where—how?"

Claudette laughed and sank down onto Margot's small borrowed bed. "Lucille brought them home." She leaned forward, making her voice the barest of murmurs. "Her beau is helping smuggle them into Brussels. There will be more, Margot."

More. *Life*. She sank down right where she was, onto the floor, and spread the first of the two out before her.

They were both in English. It made her brows pucker. She could read English and speak it, but it required thought. And Papa had rarely ever hidden anything for her in an English paper, so she'd little practice at seeking codes in them. Though it was the same principle, regardless of the language.

And irrelevant. Papa was not here to hide messages.

Lukas, though. Wherever he was, he would know this was the safest means of contact. He'd still have the key she had devised. He may have thought it a game, but he would have kept it. Because that was Lukas—more sentimental and serious than he liked to let on.

But the chances of anything being in *these* papers?

Her heart sank. She didn't know how many newspapers there were in the world, but even a rough estimate produced ridiculous odds for the right ones finding their way to her.

Claudette knelt beside her. "Why are you sad? I thought you would love this."

"I do. I *do*." To prove it, she leaned over and rested her forehead, for just a moment, against Claudette's shoulder. "It is just . . . how will we ever find him?" She didn't dare to say his name.

She didn't have to. Her friend knew, and she sighed. "I don't know. But you will. And he'll get you out of here, away from all this."

"You can come with us—you and your mother and sister."

"Maman will not leave. She says it is our duty to stay in our home and make the best of what may come." Claudette smoothed back one of Margot's stray hairs. "It is different for you though. You *must* leave. As soon as he comes for you."

It was good to know that Claudette, at least, would not judge her if she did. But whether that could ever happen remained to be seen. She turned back to the paper, frowning at the headline. *The Rape of Belgium!*

A rather crude choice of words. She read through the article— slowly, as she worked the rust off her English.

Perhaps it was more than a little rusty, because the words didn't seem right. Her brows knotted and then knotted again. "Did you read this?"

"Maman translated it for us. It is nonsense, of course— exaggeration. Meant to sell newspapers. Maman said it was called . . . sensationalism? Something like that. But it is still news! And it is in our favor, isn't it, for the world to think we've been treated so poorly?"

They *had* been treated poorly—but this article made it sound as though no woman or girl was safe from the savage passions of the German soldiers. As if any citizen who dared to step into the street was attacked.

She was no friend to the soldiers and would be the first to enumerate their cruelties—but it was nowhere near *that* bad.

She shook her head. "When does exaggeration ever work out well, Claudette? When it is pointed out, people will then think it was a complete lie, that there is *no* truth to it."

And if Lukas saw articles like this . . .

Act with reason, she bade him across the miles, praying God would deliver the message to him. *Not on emotion. We are well.*

For now, at least.

FOURTEEN

It had taken Willa an hour to circle around to the back of her follower. To be sure enough of his position to know where to circle to—and to be tricky enough to make him think she was already inside the hotel for her lesson, which she had in fact requested be later than usual today.

But she'd done it. She felt that surge in her veins as she came round the final corner and saw that familiar rusty-brown jacket sitting on a bench.

The man in it was nothing to note. Hair a middling brown. Weight a middling twelve stones, she would guess. Skin a middling pale.

He didn't look up from his newspaper as she approached, but he was aware of her. His fingers tightened around the paper just a bit.

She sat beside him and crossed her ankles, looking out over the town that, in her opinion, shouldn't really be called a city. But then, she'd grown up in London, which the Welsh would probably deem *too much* of a city. The question was, where was Mr. Brown here from? "If you wanted to remain unseen, you oughtn't to have followed us yesterday."

186

His chuckle was all sunshine and rainbows, and the disarming scent of pine drifted to her when he shifted. "Why would you assume that my goal? Perhaps I wanted just this, Miss Forsythe."

A chill skittered down her spine, digging in its claws as it went. It was one thing to realize someone had been following her—different, somehow, that he knew her name. Even if it *were* easier to discover just now, when she was the guest of known sisters and on the arm of a celebrity, than it would be in the anonymity of home.

And his accent. It was almost, nearly a normal London cadence. Perhaps, if her ears weren't so practiced at noting nuances in sound, she wouldn't have noticed it.

He wasn't from England.

She didn't let it change anything about her posture. "If you wanted this, then congratulations on your success. Now what?"

"Now . . ." Mr. Brown flipped a page amid much rustling. "We make a deal."

"Oh, do we?" She could give a deceptively bright chuckle as well. "I cannot think what deal I would want to make with you."

"Then your imagination does not match your skill in . . . other areas." He smoothed a crease in the fold. "I was following you in London, you know. Seeking the best thieves to assist me, and everyone I asked said the same thing—if I want the best, then I want Barclay's crew."

He'd been following her at home? And she'd failed to note it? Something that burned of failure sizzled through her veins. She sent her mind back to those last weeks at home, to the pub, searching her memory for any unfamiliar face that had set her instincts buzzing.

"For weeks I haunted that bleak little back-alley pub where your crew meets. Watching you all, determining which of you would best fit my needs. But there was no question. And so I ought to have known the Admiralty would set you on the same

187

task for which I wanted you—your talents are too uniquely suited to this case."

The burning sank teeth in. None of them had noticed him. They'd been too distracted with Rosemary turning their world upside down. Or *she* had been, anyway. Her own fault, and now she'd pay the price.

"I knew the moment you booked a ticket to Wales that we were about the same business. And so, my offer. The key, Miss Forsythe—give it to me rather than your employer when you find it, and I will pay you double what he offered."

Double? Pound signs danced before her eyes for a moment before falling to the ground and dashing themselves to pieces. "Who are you? Or perhaps the better question is, who are you working for?"

"Does it matter?"

Did it? How many times had they claimed, with cynical smiles and flip words, that their loyalty was to the coin and not the monarch upon it? But that was before they went to war. Before Georgie had signed up. Before Rosemary had married a man who was an actual friend to the king. That was before Germany had begun their march of destruction across Europe.

She wasn't completely sure she understood loyalty to a mere place. But she understood being opposed to something—and she was perfectly comfortable saying she was opposed to Germany.

That was the accent. German. This man beside her was . . . what? The spy she'd claimed not to know how to be?

She folded her hands, clad in pretty little white gloves, in her lap and watched a bird fret over something stuck at the edge of the pavement. "How do you even know how much I have been paid?"

The man laughed again—a short, soft bark of it this time. "I am familiar enough with how much your government grants for such tasks. It would have been about two hundred pounds, correct?"

The bird pecked at the ground. Willa might as well too, just to test things. "It was a thousand, actually."

"Ha! Ridiculous. What kind of fool do you take me for?"

She shrugged. It wasn't strictly true—but V had paid that much for the last job. "It was to guarantee the family's loyalty and establish a relationship. If you'd like me to give it to *you* instead, then . . ."

A grumble rumbled between them, and this time that careful accent disappeared into German words. Then, "Fine. Two thousand pounds."

Easy. *Too* easy. Her stomach soured. Not at the supposed deal, but at the thought that this man wanted that key so much. Would toss all that money her way to get it. It must be far more important than she'd supposed.

But why? Professor De Wilde was already dead—what could this key he'd made really accomplish without him? How could it possibly lead these people to whatever machine he'd created? She hadn't the foggiest notion and didn't really know how to discover it. Cryptography, or whatever it was called, was well beyond her.

She hummed in supposed consideration. "I don't know. My employer is a dangerous man I don't mean to cross."

He snorted. "Shadows generally are. But he never needs to know. Whatever you find, simply supply me with a photograph or rubbing or some kind of copy before you return to London to turn over the original." He flipped another page of newsprint. "Simple."

Hardly. "Why not just get it yourself? Why were you looking for a thief to begin with?"

"It is not my skill set."

A little breath of laughter slipped out. He was right about that—not understanding that the lock had been jammed. He was definitely not a thief.

Which meant . . . Clawing chills wracked her. She was sitting a foot from a spy. A German spy. Someone who ought to, by all rights, be in prison right now. According to Rosemary, the government was quietly rounding up anyone suspected of espionage and locking them away.

Though to be fair, *she* ought to be in jail too. If she were judging on that criteria.

And really, why had the government let foreign agents run about freely to begin with? Why wait for war to arrest those they already knew were guilty of it?

Stupid, if you asked her. Which no one ever did.

Regardless, this man had thus far escaped the notice of the government, or evaded them. Which meant that, while a lousy thief, he was apparently pretty good at being a spy. Still, she ought to have spotted him in Pauly's as she had on the streets here. She ought to have known he didn't belong there.

Should she leave her options open? She couldn't imagine putting herself in league with the Germans just now, when they were shooting at her little brother. When this key could arguably lead to something that would harm him there on the front. But what if she could somehow use this man? He could, perhaps, help her identify what the key even was.

A dangerous game, to use him and yet keep the thing from him. A dangerous game if she refused, though, too. What might he do if she *didn't* agree to help?

She glanced over at him just long enough to catch the gaze he flicked her way. His eyes were hazel. Shuttered behind little round spectacles that would provide a shielding glare from the sun on days when it bothered to shine. But just now, she saw his eyes clearly.

And they were hard. Cold. Calculating.

Remove her. That was what he would do if she didn't help him. He would get her out of his way—he certainly would *not* let her report to Mr. V with the key.

Best to play it safe for now. Let him think whatever he wanted

. . . while *she* thought of what to do about him. "You had best stop following us around—Lukas is smarter than he lets on. He'll notice eventually, now that his arm is healing and not distracting him."

"I will not *need* to follow you, if you agree to meet me with the key."

Somehow she doubted he would trust her that fully. But let him think her so naïve. "How? How would I meet you, I mean. If you're no longer following us."

"Send a note to Mr. Black at the Gogerddan Arms Hotel."

Mr. Black? No, she'd stick with Brown, in her thoughts at least.

He folded his paper with more care than it called for. Stood. "We'll meet here again, the day after you send the note, at precisely eleven o'clock in the morning. Agreed?"

Well, she wasn't going to *disagree.* "And you'll have the two thousand pounds."

"Of course." His smile though—meant to look like a polite farewell to a stranger—was as warm as a knife blade. "And more to come, if you wish. Whatever your government asks of you, give it to me first. And you, my dear, will be paid twice for it. A rather tidy arrangement, do you not agree?"

Profitable—but far from tidy. Double agents were no doubt the most hunted people in a war, and she didn't much fancy having a death sentence hanging over her. She gave him a tight-lipped smile and said nothing.

He walked away, his paper folded under his arm. Just another man about his day.

She held her seat for a long moment more, letting it all sift through her mind. Her line of work was never exactly *safe.* But Mr. V had led them into a whole new ocean of turbulent waters. Where the lines between thief and spy grew ever more blurred.

It was a line she didn't relish crossing. Thieves dealt simply in *things,* which could be replaced easily enough by the marks who lost them. And in the case of their family, they made it a policy only to steal from those who could well afford the loss. Spies sold information that got people killed. And one couldn't just replace a life, no matter how deep one's pockets.

But two thousand pounds. And double on any future jobs. It was a fortune.

Once two minutes and a half had ticked by, Willa stood too and meandered her way back to Lukas's hotel. Just another girl about her day. Not one anyone would think was debating loyalties and danger and risk.

With the greatest risk comes the greatest reward.

It was a truism their family had proven time and again. But which was the bigger risk here—working *with* the German or against him?

And could that really be her gauge on what to do? It shouldn't be, should it? She should have some gut feeling that told her *this is right* and *that is wrong*.

But right and wrong . . . they got fluid after a while in this life. When you were so hungry your stomach was turning inside out and stealing was the only way to eat, then you quickly decided it couldn't possibly be wrong to steal some food. And when you then had other mouths in your care to feed, bony little bodies to clothe, rent to pay . . .

Her feet came to a halt at the street corner, though she wasn't quite sure why. It took her a moment to realize that something felt odd. And a longer one to realize *what*.

It was too quiet—not the street. Her head. Usually when she thought long and hard about something, there was . . . not noise. Something more melodic than noise. Something akin to the soft, mood-setting music an orchestra played during an opera when the actors were moving about, engaged in action without words. A backdrop as adept as the painted one at setting the stage.

She could never translate that music in her head to her fingers, but it was always there. Sometimes rising to a level that was surely nearly audible to anyone standing nearby, sometimes so quiet she herself had to strain to hear it. But *there*.

It wasn't now. When she was debating whether it could possibly be right to double-cross Mr. V.

But if it weren't, if she admitted it, if she drew that line in the sand, didn't that then mean she was admitting there was a side she was on? Something greater than herself or her family that was worth fighting for?

That was dangerous. That could lead her to make decisions that put something *above* her family. Like Rosemary had done, though she'd deny it.

Her glove-clad fingers curled into her palm. No. Nothing was more important than the family they'd pieced together. Nothing. Not England, not Germany, not war or intrigue or money. Nothing would *ever* make her choose to follow her own path away from those children.

Someone bumped into her—a mother with two chattering tots. The woman gave her a harried look and a muttered apology, though they both knew it was Willa's fault for just standing there like a dunce on the street corner.

She offered an apology of her own and forced her feet forward. Down the familiar walk to the hotel, through the familiar door. A nod to the familiar clerk at the desk, then the quick turn down the hall to the function room with the sea view that they'd claimed as their own.

No music greeted her. Combined with the silence within her own head, it was striking. And made her nearly, for one half of a second, fight back the urge to let tears well. She could handle loss and risk and cold and hunger, but *this* she couldn't do—she couldn't lose the music. Whatever decision she made, it must be one that brought the melodies back.

The door stood open, and when she turned into it, she spotted

Lukas right away, at the table that held his crate of sheet music. His fingers stilled in their flipping when she entered, and he shot her that grin that had no right to make her stomach quiver as it did.

It was a shame, in a way, that she couldn't take his talk of a future together seriously—his would be a fine face to wake up to every day. If he weren't so blasted charming and untrustworthy . . . But he was. Which meant she'd have to be content with the version of him she had tacked to her wall. The one before her now was far too dangerous to keep so near her. And no doubt about as faithful as her own father had been.

"Hello." She tossed her handbag onto a chair, tugged off her gloves to toss on top of it, and unpinned her hat. "How's the shoulder today?"

"Driving yesterday took a toll—though it was worth it." He rotated his arm, wincing only a little. "Did you sleep well, *ma cherie?*"

"As always. What are you teaching me today?" The Stradivarius called to her especially loudly given her otherwise empty ears. Her gaze focused on where it rested, elegant and beckoning, in its case.

"*Non*, no playing today. We must spend some time on theory."

Her heart lurched. "I fail to see why."

"Because last time when I mentioned the G augmented chord, you had no idea what I meant." He folded his arms over his chest and raised a brow. "You could be the best violinist of our day, Willa. But not if you cannot speak the language."

As if she needed to speak the language to play on the only stage she ever would—the one Pauly had built for her. "I don't care about being the best of our day. I just want to play."

The silence pounded in her head.

And his eyes shown dark and serious. "There is a saying, I believe, about hiding our lights under a basket. Perhaps Jesus

194

was talking of our faith, but I believe it applies to the gifts He has given us as well, *n'est-ce pas*? This miracle He has given you, *ma cherie*—you must not hide it. You must share it with who you can and spread that light. The joy that only music can bring. I like to think it is a sacred duty. A . . . calling."

She shifted from one foot to the other, stifling the urge to spin away from such talk and leave. "God, if He is real, is not calling me to anything."

"No?" His smile looked sad. "I think you are wrong. But as I doubt I will convince you through mere conversation . . ." He sighed and straightened. "We will compromise. I will let you play now—a reminder of this thing we both love—but then we will teach you the vocabulary you need to know, and I will send you home with sheets on it you can study. For now, we can work on how you hold your bow."

It took everything in her not to bristle at the implication that there was something wrong with the way she did it now. Or perhaps *everything* still wasn't enough, because he laughed, bright again, and sidled near with eyes twinkling.

"Your form is by no means bad, *mon amour*. But we could all use a bit of refinement, *n'est-ce pas*?" He waggled his brows at her. "And it will give me an excuse to touch your arm and make you jump."

He'd certainly taken every excuse yesterday as they'd strolled around the castle ruins after they ate. A hand on her arm, on her back, fingers catching hers. She'd almost gotten used it. Almost. Though she'd never admit on pain of death that it was more pleasant than not.

Still, she did jump when he came right up to her and touched a finger to her chin. And no doubt the scalding gaze she set on him told him clearly what she thought of that action.

He'd already grown as adept as Barclay, however, at ignoring her glares. His eyes were narrowed. "What is the matter, Willa?

You look upset today, and it cannot be merely over my suggestion that we study theory."

She may have argued, if she weren't infinitely aware of the crumpling of her own features just now. Because it wasn't right that he should be able to tell that with a glance. And it was certainly all wrong that she wanted to lean into his hand rather than away from it. And it was absolutely terrifying that the internal music had again with that one little touch from his fingers.

She sank onto the chair positioned in front of the music stand. Safely away from him. "Do you ever hear it? The music in your head? Or is it just me?"

Crouching down in front of her, Lukas somehow made a frown look handsome and compelling. "Do you mean a song that has got stuck in there, or something else?"

"Else. I think. I don't know—it may be bits of existing songs pieced together, perhaps."

"Ah." The frown transformed into a smile every bit as handsome and compelling. "My friend Eugène speaks of such things—the composer. Perhaps, *ma belle*, you have a song in there you need to put to paper."

She shook her head. "I can never get it from head to fingers. And I thought I warned you against calling me pretty."

"*Belle* is not *pretty*. It is *beautiful*. The Alps compared to . . ." His lips twitched. "To these Welsh hillocks they so optimistically dub mountains."

She could imagine Gwen and Daisy huffing at the affront to their beloved landscape. But that was beside the point. "I am not beautiful."

"That is, as they say, in the eye of the beholder. And I could behold you all day with great joy." He took her hand in his and lifted it, pressed his lips to her knuckles.

No flirtatious glance up at her as he did so. Just a seriousness, almost a reverence—though that was absurd.

"We should get to work."

"*Oui*," he said. He released her fingers, but rather than stand, he touched her chin once more. "Will you let me kiss you again before you leave today?" Now the grin again, though it was still not exactly flirtatious. Odd, given his words. "Perhaps it will cheer you."

A roll of her eyes was absolutely necessary. "Isn't it laborious to drag that head around all day, being so full of yourself?"

"Unbearably sometimes." He stood, holding her gaze all the while. "You did not say no."

"I also didn't say yes."

"But you did not say no. This is progress."

He was so ridiculous. It shouldn't make her want to smile. "Focus, Lukas. We both know I'm only here for the sake of the violin."

"Mm." He moved off the two steps it took him to reach the case and then crouched down to open it. "You do realize that when you marry me, it will be half yours? Incentive."

"Ha. Incentive to poison you and keep it all to myself?" Now *she* was ridiculous, playing along. Sort of.

"Oh, we can come up with a more creative means of getting rid of me than that, if it is your goal." He straightened with the Stradivarius and bow in hand, eyes twinkling. "Though it will not be, once we marry. I will make you happy."

Hand out, she gave him the same look she did Georgie when he pushed too hard against the rules. "Music. Not marriage."

"We can have both. Though it may require buying you your *own* Strad, now that you mention it. So we can play duets."

It shone, sparkling in the air like stolen diamonds for as long as it took to blink. Then she shook it away and reached for his instrument. "What happened to your promise that you would not flirt during lessons?"

"The lesson has not yet begun." He handed her the violin,

though, with a grin. "*Now* the lesson has begun, and I will cease with such—"

A knock on the open door cut him off. "Pardon me, Mr. De Wilde. There is a Mr. Guillaume here to see you, quite insistent that you will want to meet with him straightaway."

She glanced over her shoulder long enough to verify that it was the clerk at the door.

Lukas sent his gaze heavenward. "My composer friend—always so impatient. Do you mind, Miss Forsythe?"

It sounded strange to her ears now, that formality, after nearly two weeks of endearments and the liberty he'd taken of using her first name. Willa offered a tight smile every bit as formal. "Go right ahead, sir." Perhaps he'd return with an original composition—how lucky would that be?

"You go ahead and choose what you will play today." He motioned to the crate of music and followed the clerk from the room.

She first took a few minutes to tune the Strad, reveling even in those boring notes. Her ears were beginning to grow accustomed to its smooth tones, her fingers to its tension and weight. Her own violin, when she pulled it out in her room at the Davies house, felt light in comparison. Like a child's toy.

But as sweet as one too. As full of memories.

His music selection was ambrosia, each piece she flipped through tempting. She felt a bit like Barclay had looked in that bookstore the week before she left London. With finally a few pounds in his pocket that he could spend on anything he wanted— something *new*, which was unprecedented for them. He'd spent hours just moving among the shelves, his head tilted to the side so he could read title after title.

He'd regretted *that* later, to be sure, whining about the crick it had given him. Whining with such exaggeration that the rest of them had no choice but to laugh.

She pulled out a few pieces and took them to the stand, going through the first bars of each to see which caught her attention today.

The first was pretty. Slow, though. Not quite what she was looking for. The second was fast and scattered, bringing to mind leaves dancing on the autumn wind—something she would love to play, but she'd probably make a wreck of it without having studied it first—and especially every time Lukas touched her elbow.

The third—the third didn't deserve to be called music. She made a disgusted noise within ten measures.

Lukas's laughter grew louder with each step he took into the room, ending at her shoulder. "What—you do not like atonal compositions?"

"Do *you*?" She may lose all respect for him if he did. It sounded like nothing but a collection of random notes rammed up against each other like strangers on the tube.

"I despise it. But I thought I should at least attempt some before dismissing it completely, so I purchased a few selections." He motioned to the sheet music. And then swept it off the stand and back into its box. "My conclusion was much like yours. That next piece may do though."

She played through the first few lines and nodded. May have let loose a satisfied sigh, too, at how blessedly harmonious it sounded in contrast to that jumble of nonsense that had preceded it.

Setting her eyes back on the beginning, she got into her normal stance—except with a straighter back than usual—and waited. Lukas slid into position behind her and adjusted her bow arm so minutely that she growled. "That is not even a change!"

"It is. A subtle one."

"So subtle as to be a waste of time."

"It will make a difference, *ma cherie*, in the long run. Begin."

She began. Though she wasn't sure how she was supposed to remember to keep her arm a new way when it didn't even feel *new*. So she simply played, and managed not to jump when he

199

touched her elbow again halfway through the piece, and managed not to growl when a hand to her shoulder indicated some problem with *that* near the end.

"Again."

She craned her neck around to look at him instead, where he stood half behind her. "What was I doing wrong with my shoulder?"

"Nothing, but I was not certain of it at first. You are too thin, *ma belle*. I could not tell if it was your normal shoulder blade or if you were contorting it." He slanted a glance at her back.

Too thin? She was exactly as fat as she could afford to be. "You've never noticed before how my shoulder looks?"

"You have never worn this dress to our lessons before—it drapes differently. I would add that the shade of red is becoming, but that might be too close to flirtation." He looked as though he wanted to smile but held it back. "Now, again."

Her rebellious streak came to the surface, though she'd done a fine job of ignoring it in their lessons overall, she thought. "Did your composer friend have anything new to show you?"

"Feeling chatty today? All right." He eased back a step, wearing his amusement like a stylish hat. "No, only a question. He is always wanting the violin to play more notes at once than is reasonable."

"Have you anything he's written here? That hasn't been performed?"

Those well-shaped brows of his arched. "Why that has not been performed?"

She could just tell him about the challenge, leaving out the bit about thieving. And calling Retta a friend rather than a sister—technically true, she supposed. But it didn't seem quite sporting, so she shrugged. "It would just be fun to play something so few people had."

"If you want to do that, *mon amour*, then perhaps you should write something yourself."

"I told you—it won't come out of my head."

"Convince it." He eased closer again. "Music is like a person, *oui*? You must make friends. Court it. Listen to it speak, let it find its voice."

For someone who claimed not to have it living in his head, he certainly seemed to know a lot about it.

Willa sighed and turned back to the sheet in front of her. "I listen. But it hides when I do."

"Hmm. Hidden treasure is always the most precious—once you lure it out, I think it will be brilliant."

Words. Just words. But her soul soaked them up. Even if she couldn't quite believe him. "Assuming I ever *can* lure it out."

"What is hidden can always be found, *mon amour.*"

Found, yes. She raised the bow and focused her gaze on the opening bars. And she *was* a thief. Once she found a thing, she knew how to take it. It was just a matter of finding it. And maybe . . . maybe she was in the right place to do that.

FIFTEEN

Lukas pulled his coat tight and buttoned it up against the cold wind blowing in off Cardigan Bay. Autumn had descended upon them in full force this morning, making it suddenly apparent that October was well underway.

Last October he'd been in Louvain, spending a relaxing two weeks with his family through his mother's birthday. Père had still been alive, laughing one moment and contemplative the next, teasing Mère, devising new "games" for Margot. They hadn't known then that he would be gone within months. But if they had, they wouldn't have spent those weeks any differently.

Now Père was gone. Their house was rubble. Mère and Margot had vanished. What a difference a year made. This time next year, would the war still be dragging on, or would it be over as everyone hoped? Perhaps they would be picking up the pieces and fashioning a new mosaic of a life from them. No father, no house that he'd grown up in, but a family reunited. With, perhaps, a new addition. If he could convince Willa to let him past those walls she had always around herself.

Jules would say he had just begun to believe his own jest. But it was more than that. Perhaps it had *always* been more than that.

He turned down the street, away from the bay and its hotels

and holiday houses. He didn't really fancy going to the rougher part of the small city to meet Cor Akkerman. But he didn't really fancy the man coming always to the hotel either.

He craved news in a way he'd never understood Margot doing. Up until now, newspapers he could take or leave. He would glance at the headlines, learn enough to be able to talk sensibly, and then happily return to his music or friends or invitations.

These days, though, he read the headlines much more intently. He winced at the descriptions given of the Germans running roughshod over his countrymen and prayed with all that was in him that it was exaggeration. Prayed that women and children hadn't really been treated as cruelly as the journalists reported.

Prayed somehow, in some newspaper somewhere, he'd find that word to make him take note.

"Lukas!"

He took note, but this certainly wasn't a message from Margot. He turned, brow furrowed. Jules had barely exchanged two words with him in the past week. Those they *had* exchanged had been distracted, rushed.

His friend now hurried down the sidewalk, wearing a frown of his own. "What's the blasted hurry? I've been trying to catch up with you for five minutes."

"I am feeling the cold." And it made his shoulder ache anew, though he wasn't about to whine about it. He'd had his fill of listening to his own complaints. He offered a grin. "You should have shouted sooner."

Jules sent his gaze heavenward, to where the wind chased the clouds across the sky like a swift-footed fox. "Where are you going?"

He actually paused for a moment to consider how much to say. Which just proved how at odds they had been with each other this week. He had never hesitated to share anything, everything with Jules.

And he wouldn't begin now. "I have become acquainted with another refugee who is gathering some information for me—where there are camps, newspapers, the like. I am meeting with him."

He must have expected Jules to nod and motion him forward again, falling in beside. He must have expected it, because that was what he always would have done before. But today, the man just stood there. Nodding, but absently.

"Looking for news of your family, I trust? I hope you find them." Jules shifted, touched Lukas's arm. "Listen, I have a favor to ask of you. I need you and Miss Forsythe to have supper with Enora and me."

He would dismiss the search for Lukas's family so quickly? So entirely? That wasn't like Jules. And why? "Enora." The cause of this new, distracted state apparently. Lukas knew the name was familiar. But for the life of him, he couldn't place it. Perhaps because he was too busy staring at his friend and trying to pinpoint what had shifted between them.

One of the clouds from overhead settled on Jules's face and darkened. "Enora Peeters. We have played in the same orchestra four of the last five years, Lukas. Do not tell me you do not know who she is."

It clicked into his memory then, thankfully. Enora Peeters, renowned Flemish flautist—a woman he knew very little about despite moving in the same musical circles. But the image of her round pink cheeks and bouncing curls gave him confidence enough of the face that belonged to the name that he could roll his eyes and try a tease. "Of course I know who she is. It's just that I never imagined you seeing a *woodwind* player."

And he didn't want to talk about a potential romance right now; he wanted to talk to his friend about the search for Margot and Mère. Get his advice. Seek his opinions. But that would only make him look more selfish. And he wouldn't be. If Jules wanted to talk about Enora Peeters, then they would.

The rigid line of his friend's shoulders relaxed. A bit. "And I'll not be seeing her for long if I can't convince her that I haven't been unduly influenced by *your* ways over the years."

A slice of guilt . . . though it was followed by simmering frustration. "Did you not just recently rejoice in the fact that you could still pursue those ways, even without me, when I said I was finished with them? You now want to convince a woman that you never did?"

"What did I ever do but follow behind you, keeping you out of trouble? *I* was not the one with the endless string of women. I enjoyed the food and wine. Nothing more." Chafing his hands together—gloves apparently forgotten—Jules eased back a step. "I simply need you to come tonight. Talk of how boring I have always been, perhaps. And demonstrate yourself fully in love with Miss Forsythe—I have been telling Enora how you've turned over a new leaf for her."

"Not just for her." But that was beside the point. Lukas sighed. "You know I am happy to help you convince Enora Peeters to give you a chance. But *tonight*? You think I can actually convince Willa to have supper with us tonight? I can barely cajole her to lessons thrice a week."

Jules eased back another step. "You're Lukas De Wilde. You'll manage."

"Yes, I am. And that's the problem now for both of us, isn't it?"

But Jules chuckled and waved that away. "Convincing women of whatever you wanted them to believe has long been one of your gifts. Employ it now on my behalf, Lukas. That is all I ask."

Convincing the flute player that he'd turned over a new leaf would require only the truth. Convincing her Jules had always been the staid one would require only slight exaggeration. Convincing Willa, though, to come with them . . . "I will try. That is all I can promise on such short notice. But she may have plans already with the Misses Davies. If tonight does not suit her, is there another time?"

"Friday, I suppose. But aim for tonight."

He barely had time to mumble out an agreement before Jules had pivoted and strode away.

Should it hurt that things were changing, when he was the one who had set those changes in motion? Should it sit as heavy as grief that his friend was a step further away than he'd been in a decade?

He turned too, more slowly than Jules had done, and continued on his path. He wanted his friend to be happy. To find a special someone with whom he could make a life. Jules would make a fine family man—be a devoted husband, a doting father. He would travel a bit more and then settle down without a backward glance to a life of lessons and schools.

Or at least Lukas *thought* he would. Though at the moment, he didn't much trust what he knew of his oldest friend.

The houses he passed grew dingier. Smaller. The shops sported no luxuries in their windows, just necessities and food.

Mère and Margot. They had to be his top priority.

He spotted Cor Akkerman through the wide front window of the bakery at which they'd agreed to meet. He sat at a small table, a steaming cup of something before him and a pastry in hand.

Lukas pulled open the door and rode the gust of wind inside, happy enough to shut it out again. He ordered himself a cup of coffee and took it, black and steaming, to the other chair at the circular table.

Akkerman barely glanced up to greet him. He rather took another enormous bite from the pastry. Or maybe it wasn't a pastry—savory scents drifted toward him rather than sweet ones. "Have you tried their sausage rolls? Not bad."

Lukas took a sip of his coffee. Winced. "Would that I could say the same for this." He should have gotten tea, he supposed—the British were masters at that. But he was getting tired of it. He needed a good cup of French coffee. "Have you any news?"

"*Ja.*" He didn't offer it though. Instead, Akkerman took a long draught of his own coffee and another bite of the sausage roll.

He wouldn't get irritated. It wouldn't help. Lukas instead sighed and looked out the window. "I have heard that the Americans have put together a relief organization. That they have sent a ship full of food for our people."

Akkerman snorted. "And the Brits will not let it leave their ports again—did you hear that part too?"

He had, in fact. "They will not hold it for long, surely." It could make the difference between life and death for hundreds of thousands of Belgians. Surely Great Britain, which upheld the "plucky Belgians" as a standard to inspire their own boys to enlist, wouldn't be complicit in their starvation.

Akkerman lifted his brows. "You have more faith in them than I do." He jammed the last bite of sausage into his mouth, not seeming to notice—or to care—that bits of the pastry crust clung to his lips.

Though his tongue objected, Lukas took another sip of the awful coffee, just to have something to do. "Have you family still in Belgium?"

"Getting chummy now, are we?" Akkerman wiped off his mouth—with his sleeve—and leaned forward. "Look, me and mine are no concern of yours. You wanted information on refugee movements and newspapers—that is what I bring you." He reached into his pocket and pulled out a rumpled, folded sheet of paper. "Here."

It landed in the middle of the table, and Lukas reached for it with all the calm he could muster. In barely legible handwriting, Akkerman had made two lists. The first, town names—presumably where camps or Belgian villages were being set up, or where large numbers were integrating into the English towns themselves.

The second bore names such as *L'Indépendance Belge* and set his heart pounding. "So there are some—newspapers." Though the list was short, with only three names. Two had "London" scrawled beside them. One, Brussels. He tapped that one's name. "This is still running at home? Under the noses of the Germans?"

Akkerman's shrug bordered on insolent. "Someone had a copy of it, dated a week ago. My impression is that they do not manage many editions. And who knows how many of those few make their way here?"

"What about the reverse—how many of the editions from those in London make it back into Belgium?"

Now Akkerman's lips curled up into a mean little grin. "There is high demand. For that and even for foreign papers. I have a cousin who helps smuggle them in—for quite a sum too. He says English penny papers are selling in Brussels for fifteen francs apiece. I am thinking I may get in on this trade."

"Hmm." He certainly wouldn't stop the man from that—it would, shame of shames, take him to the east coast of England and across the Channel. Well out of Lukas's way. And Willa's. He squinted at the rest of the information scrawled under the papers' cities. "These are the names of the owners?"

"*Ja.*"

"Fleming . . . Van—what does this say? Rompu?"

"Van Rompa. And Allard."

Allard. That one sounded familiar. Was he one of the many newspapermen with whom Père had made friends? He could well be. His was the name beneath *L'Indépendance Belge*, which was obviously a French paper. That meant Allard was either from Brussels or Wallonia—the French-speaking south section of Belgium—like the De Wildes.

"Thank you for this." Lukas pulled out the rest of Akkerman's wage and set it on the table. "If you hear anything else interesting, do let me know. Or if you relocate, I would appreciate word on how to reach you, in case I need your services again."

The man pocketed the cash and stood. "I will be here for a

while yet." His grin was wolfish. "Unfinished business of my own still, you know."

Willa, he meant. Lukas bit back a response and stayed perfectly still until Akkerman strode through the door. She could no doubt take care of him herself, if he came sniffing around her again. But Lukas would warn her that he was back in town.

And beg her, for Jules's sake, to dine with them tonight. Perhaps she'd be inclined to mercy if it was for someone else.

He checked his pocket watch and stood. Still plenty of time to call on her at the Davieses' before he had to get to rehearsal. With a bit of luck, she would be home and not out calling on someone else at this time of day.

The wind greeted him when he stepped out of the bakery, and it inspired him to hurry along his path. These first cold days were always the worst, making him fantasize about a tour that would keep him in the Riviera during this time of year. Or perhaps Africa. South America. Somewhere hot and languid.

Though Willa wasn't in any of those places, so all in all, he was rather happy to be in Wales.

Or would be, if his family were here with him.

His step slowed as he rounded the corner. Would they be safe here? If he stayed with the orchestra—the only way he knew to make money enough to support them—everyone would know where he was. And, by extension, where *they* were. Which would mean that those looking for his father's work would know.

V would know. And would no doubt come knocking on his door again, that careful smile in place over those careful words. *"I can help you,"* he had said that first day when Lukas had stepped off the boat, barely conscious until that snapped him into awareness. *"I can keep your family safe. Work with us, tell us how to find your father's work, and we'll protect you all."*

Give England his father's secrets willingly, in other words, and they wouldn't take them by force.

Lukas's hands fisted in his pockets. It wasn't an option. Not that he didn't prefer England have them over Germany, but . . . but it wasn't as simple a matter as handing V a file of papers or a mechanical device.

It would mean handing him his sister.

Only when his teeth ached did he realize he was clenching them, that his jaw was so tight the muscle in it was ticking. Did V understand what he was really asking? No, he wouldn't. Couldn't. No one outside of the family and a very few of their closest friends realized that Père's mysterious cypher machine was no machine at all. It was a young girl too smart for her own good.

It was his duty as her brother to protect her. From Germany, from England, from *anyone* who would treat her like a weapon. A tool.

She was so much more than that. Deserved so much better. She deserved a *childhood*, one full of idle days and escaping from lessons and laughing with friends and . . .

Though Margot hated all those things. Her mind was never idle. Lessons, when they could actually teach her something new, were her favorite sport. And the only friend she had ever had to laugh with was Claudette.

Claudette's father had been Père's closest friend and colleague. *He* knew how crucial it was to protect Margot. Perhaps she and Mère were with the Archambaults, perhaps *that* was how he could find them.

Though he wasn't sure who he trusted enough to uncover that information for him. Certainly not Akkerman or any of his "cousins." But he didn't know how else to get news of or to his home.

Blast the Germans.

The city grew statelier with every step, the houses better kept and larger until he turned onto the street where Willa made her temporary home. Lukas paused a moment before going up the steps to ring. It wouldn't do to see her with all these thoughts ricocheting through his head—she would know and call him on them. And while he would someday love to share them all with her, he couldn't afford to do so now.

He was falling in love with her—that was the simple and unvarnished truth—but that didn't mean he could trust her. Not fully. Not yet.

He wasn't a fool.

A deep, cleansing breath. A silent prayer that the Lord would take the worry from him and replace it with wisdom, and with knowledge on how to find and rescue his family. Then, when his face felt calm and clear, he rang.

A servant opened the door to him a moment later and, apparently recognizing him, ushered him in with a smile.

Lukas fished a card from the case in his pocket and set it on the man's silver salver. "Lukas De Wilde for Miss Forsythe, if she is in."

The servant gave a short bow. "Of course, sir. Have a seat in the parlor and I shall fetch her."

"Thank you."

The man turned for the stairs, leaving Lukas to step toward the room he'd visited before when he was here.

But his feet halted a few steps from the doorway. His ears strained.

Willa's voice. Faint, and he couldn't make out the words, but he recognized the timbre. She wasn't upstairs, she was down. Somewhere.

He should undoubtedly just take a seat and let the servant search her out. It was the polite and logical thing to do.

His feet apparently didn't receive that message, as they started down the hallway of their own volition. They followed his ears around a corner and down a side hallway to what must be some sort of study, given the sliver of desk that came into view through the open doorway.

211

She stood at the far side of it, facing the window, speaking into the telephone that she carried. He leaned into the doorway, figuring that those instincts of hers would note his presence in just a second or two, then he could motion to her that he would be waiting in the parlor and leave her to her conversation.

Except that she didn't turn. She gripped the stick of the phone like she fancied strangling it. "I know the difference between a German shepherd and an English mastiff, Barclay."

Barclay? She'd never mentioned a Barclay, much less indicated she knew one well enough to ring him up at considerable expense.

Though come to think of it, she'd never really mentioned *anyone*. Not by name.

And *dogs*? Why was she speaking of dogs? He'd never seen her with one.

So little he really knew of her. It made a chord of loneliness echo long inside him. Those people he did know were all too far away— physically or emotionally. And this woman who had somehow managed to capture his being with hers . . . she was a stranger.

Willa gripped the phone tighter and all but growled. "If I were of a mind to do something stupid, do you think I would tell you first? And do give me a bit of credit, will you? I am many things, but I am not—" She turned just a bit, showing him part of her face, her thinned lips that suddenly pulled into a smile. "Well, if I've said it so many times, perhaps you ought to remember it and stop assuming you're the only one in the family with an ounce of intelligence. I—"

She spun toward Lukas, obviously having just seen him in her periphery. Her smile grew. "—should go. Lukas apparently decided to pay me a call."

He didn't know if he should feel better or worse, that whoever she was talking to apparently knew about *him*. Perhaps it would depend upon what she'd told this Barclay—that Lukas was an annoying suitor who would not take a hint . . . or perhaps someone with whom she enjoyed spending time.

Now that she'd spotted him, he could signal as he'd planned. Refrain from further interrupting her. Turn away.

Instead, he kept on leaning into the doorframe, watching her as she rolled her eyes—as if Barclay could see her—and perched on the edge of the desk. She really wasn't what one would call *pretty*. Her nose was a bit flat. Her hair was always slipping out of its chignon. And she hadn't enough by way of curves to be fashionable.

So why, then, did he so want to study her for hours? To memorize the way her eyes shifted and focused and saw what his couldn't? To draw close enough that maybe, just maybe, he could hear the music that whispered inside her? To wrap her in his arms until he sank through those brick walls she barricaded herself behind and emerged on the other side, where *she* was?

Her gaze lifted, settled on his. Such blue eyes she had. Tinged a bit with green, but still so vivid. Quite unlike the deep brown of his own family. And sharp—sharp and piercing.

"All right." She twisted a bit. "Give the girls my love. And Rosie, if you hear from her, and tell her to kiss the little ones for me." She set the telephone back onto the desk, still leaning over to speak into it. "All right. I will. Goodbye, Barclay."

Rosie. Barclay. Little ones, girls. *People* who obviously meant a great deal to her. He wanted to know about them but rather feared if he asked, she'd clam up as she often did. So he settled for a smile. "I am sorry. I did not mean to interrupt, only to let you know I was here."

She set the earpiece back in its hook and straightened. "You saved me a bit of frustration anyway. Barclay thinks it his sworn duty to torment me."

"And he is your . . . ?" It sounded casual, he thought. The sort of question one would ask of anyone who mentioned a random name.

Or perhaps not, given that teasing curl to her lips. "Jealous, Mr. De Wilde?"

Lukas pushed off the doorframe and took a step into the study. "Perhaps I would be, if you hadn't called him family."

She crossed her arms over her chest, kept her eyes locked on his. Tilted her head. "Shame. And here I thought I'd get to claim to have made Lukas De Wilde wild with jealousy. I don't know how many women can claim that."

"I am not the jealous sort." Or never used to be—though that could well be because he'd never cared about a woman enough to be jealous of anyone else in her life. The same couldn't be said for *this* woman, and that realization brought him another step into the room. "Though I admit it puts my teeth on edge whenever Cor Akkerman mentions you. He is back—so you know. And may well be seeking you out."

Her eyes flashed, yes. But not with longing. Not with desire. Not with affection. They flashed with suspicion and wariness and that sort of calculation that Margot would appreciate.

He prayed to God, silently but sincerely, that her eyes didn't flash like that over mention of *him*.

The calculation snapped and sizzled for a moment, two, then vanished behind her smile. "I appreciate the warning. Is that why you dropped in?"

"Partly." He eased another step in, half expecting her to straighten from the desk and edge away. Instead, she tipped her head a degree to follow him with her gaze. "I also had a favor to ask of you. Or rather, Jules has. I am merely relaying it."

"Jules." She blinked and braced her palms against the desk. "What favor could Jules possibly want from me?"

"That you join him and a lady friend of his and me for supper." He offered a smile, though it rested strangely on his lips. "It seems she is wary of him because of his association with me, and he hopes that we can convince her that he is benign. And boring. And that I have given up my old ways for you."

Another icy flash. Not quite to the level that it had been at mention of Cor, but enough to pierce him. "I am not certain how I can help with this, given that I certainly don't believe it myself—the part about you anyway. I haven't spent enough time with your friend to have any idea of how boring he may be."

He shrugged. And hooked his hands in his pockets to keep from reaching for her. It wouldn't exactly prove his reformation to kiss her out of the blue. "I do not know. I merely promised to ask you to join the rest of us tonight."

She said nothing as she held his gaze. She said nothing as she pushed off the desk. She said nothing as she took a step toward him, closing the space between them to a foot so scant he could barely catch his breath. Then she smiled. "All right. Come and pick me up. What time?"

What time? It was that easy? She would just . . . *come*? He forced himself to swallow. And to remember that he was no novice at taking a woman to a restaurant—his palms had no reason to go damp at the thought of it. "Seven, I imagine. If that suits?"

"Fine." She sashayed past him, not even pausing on her way out the door. "I'll see you then."

The room filled with air again, at least. He could drag it in, thank the Lord that she had agreed. And be grateful he had all the afternoon to lose himself in music and put thoughts of Willa Forsythe out of his mind for a few blessed hours.

SIXTEEN

Willa lowered her bow and opened her eyes. She stood by her window, closed against the cool air tapping at its panes, and the view of Aberystwyth's nicest streets greeted her. The last strains of the music seemed to echo long in her small chamber, sweet and high and . . . empty. That was the way her violin sounded now, in contrast to the Stradivarius. Like an imitation of the real sound, but not the sound itself.

No. It wouldn't do. She would go home soon, and this would be the only violin she would have to play. She would have to get used to its timbre again. Be content with it. And why not? It had been a faithful friend all these years.

Before she had known what she was missing.

Spinning from the window, she raised her bow again. Played, again, the first line of melody she had ever teased from the strings. It was nothing, really—a pub song she'd heard on the streets. Nothing special, something any child could hum. But it was *hers*. Because she had touched the bow to the strings and the music had been there, waiting for her. There inside this violin, it had seemed—she had simply asked it to come out, and it had.

It had been true with that pub song. She remembered thinking, in a burst of childish wonder she hadn't indulged in for

216

years, that the music must live inside the violin. And that if *that* music had, perhaps more did as well. The next day she'd gone out, when she was supposed to be finding pockets to pick, and found instead a few melodies. From gramophones in open windows. From other pubs with pianos. She'd walked about her familiar London with her ears open for the first time, and she'd heard it everywhere—music drifting from windows, from doors, from throats.

She'd gone back to their flat, pulled out that battered violin she'd shoved under the sofa, and asked it if *that* music would come out too.

It had. And so had the majestic, glorious stuff she'd gone in search of later, in the nicer parts of the city. When she'd climbed that forgotten half-wall, her ears sniffing out music like a bloodhound, and found the orchestra's practice room's windows. Her violin had brought it faithfully to life.

With a sigh, she sank onto her borrowed bed with its feather mattress. The music always came . . . But maybe it *was* just leaping from the instrument, maybe it wasn't in her at all. Maybe it had nothing to do with her and was just . . . luck. Or magic. A magic violin that would play for anyone at all.

She trailed her fingers over the precious wood, worn so smooth from the thousands of times she'd done just that. It wasn't the violin—if it had been, the Stradivarius would have been silent in her hands, or produced nothing but screeching nonsense as awful as that atonal mess Lukas had sheet music for.

But if it were her, in her, then why could she never pull it from her own head to her fingertips? Why could she only reproduce, never create? Why did the magic stop just short of what she really wanted it to do?

In a ritual she'd been doing for over a decade, she clasped the violin to her chest. The music had, those first days, felt a bit like . . . belonging. Like family. Like if she played the right notes, her parents would reappear. If she could just conjure up the right tune, it would summon them.

But none ever had. And she didn't want them to show up, not now. She didn't need to look into the eyes of the woman who had deemed her nothing but an imitation of love. Something to be cast aside when the real thing appeared again. She didn't need to meet the father who had never even wanted to admit she existed.

So why this yearning to bring out into the air the notes that clamored inside her soul? Why this unshakable idea that if she could, she would somehow have something she lacked?

"It isn't your fault," she whispered to the wood. "It isn't your fault I can't ever find the right notes. It isn't your fault you're not an expensive instrument. You don't *need* to be." It was *hers.* Her magic violin. She set it carefully into the scarred case and closed it up. She wouldn't think of it as less, as missing something—she wouldn't.

It was her. And it was enough. *She* was enough, her life was enough.

Laughter floated up from somewhere downstairs. She hadn't expected to like the sisters so much, but hearing their joy brought her back to her feet and pulled her toward the doors. They were sweet women. And she had a feeling that even if they knew who she really was, where she'd come from, they wouldn't look at her any differently.

Gwen had seen her violin, after all. And called it a friend.

She let the music of their voices pull her downstairs and into the little salon at the back of the house, where the afternoon sunlight shafted down. Where Daisy sat with her frizzy hair and Gwen rubbed her sore fingertips.

Miss Blaker was stationed by the window, embroidery in hand and a smile upon her face. Though she hadn't gone out today, she was still dressed in stiff, proper style with a high lace collar complete with a cameo brooch.

Worth a pound or two if she were to fence it, nothing more.

Daisy sat at the little secretary, a stack of papers in front of her. She held one in front of her, her gaze on her sister. Gwen had chosen the sofa and now motioned Willa to sit beside her.

"Come, sit. Help us choose which causes to support."

"Causes." Willa kept her voice even as she lowered herself to the cushions. She'd encountered plenty of people interested in *causes* in London. Ladies in large hats and taffeta gowns who paraded through a hospital in search of some *cause* to make themselves feel benevolent.

She hadn't, somehow, pictured Gwen and Daisy like those women, despite that she knew they volunteered at the local hospital. They had seemed genuinely concerned for the patients, that day she had accompanied them. They'd taken each one by the hand and prayed for them. It was more personal than a *cause*.

"We get so many requests." Daisy sighed and set the paper back onto the desk with a shake of her head. "Sometimes it is . . . exhausting. To try to discern which we should entertain and which we should dismiss."

Miss Blaker sent Daisy a tight, crooked smile. "I know many a person who would happily take on such exhaustion."

"Or simply waste the means, you mean." Daisy shook her head. "It was no work of our own that earned us this fortune, as well you know. It is our duty not to trifle it away but to see it does some good in the world. That is what the Lord asks of us."

Gwen nodded along. And sighed. "I wish we could do more."

"You are funding an entire orchestra." It couldn't be cheap— and was, in Willa's opinion, the best sort of *cause*. Bringing music to life. Enriching a whole town, a country once they began touring. And sending money back to Belgium besides.

"Yes, but . . . it isn't *us*, is it? It's the money."

Now it was Daisy who nodded along with her sister, albeit as she gently coughed. "It is all we can ever do, really, aside from visit a few people in the hospital and write letters for them. We can give of our abundance but never *do* anything."

Willa flexed her fingers against her knee. She had the opposite problem—plenty to *do*, innumerable ways to get her hands dirty doing it, but never enough pound notes to be sure the problem didn't return the next day. She could wash dirty children, brush the tangles from their hair, hug them, and whisper assurances that they mattered.

But what did her words really accomplish, when their bellies were empty and they shivered in the cold?

These sisters, however . . . What stopped them from doing both? "So then *do*. Do something active."

Miss Blaker snorted. "Don't encourage them, Miss Forsythe. They are of delicate health, and they cannot go gallivanting into gutters in search of orphans to rescue."

The snarl started somewhere in her toes and curled its way up through her middle. "So better to toss money at some organization that promises to go to those gutters for you? Is that what your precious Jesus did?"

She didn't know where the question came from. How she even knew to frame it. Something Rosemary or Peter had said—it must have been.

Miss Blaker narrowed her eyes. "Our Lord was a man. Not a young woman. A carpenter, not an heiress. We each have our purpose."

"Yes, but she's right." Gwen rubbed at her fingers. Were they paining her now, or had it just become a habit? "Christ went where He was needed. He didn't just send others, He *went*."

"Be reasonable, girls. It is perfectly acceptable to send others where you cannot go—TJ and the major, for instance, going into Belgium. Could you have gone to find the musicians? No—it wasn't reasonable. But you accomplished a great thing through them. You may have saved the lives of those musicians. You will enrich the neighborhood. And in the process, raise more money to send back to *their* neighborhoods."

"Yes, but . . ." Daisy rested her elbow on the desk. "It is so little in the face of an ongoing war."

"You don't think it will be over soon?" Willa regretted the question the moment she'd asked it. If they believed that, they wouldn't have gone to the expense of recruiting Belgian musicians and creating a relief fund through their efforts.

The sisters exchanged a glance. Burdened. Solemn. "I cannot think so," Daisy muttered. "The lads are digging in. The Germans have been repulsed at the Marne, it's true, but they have dug in as well."

Willa's stomach went tight and bruised. Trenches. Soldiers in them, with guns aimed and bullets flying. Georgie could well be in one of those holes in the ground. Shooting at other lads like him, just in different uniforms. Getting shot *at*.

She almost wished she knew how to pray. Or that she believed there was a God up there who would care if she did.

"Do you have someone in the war?" Gwen's words were so quiet, Willa scarcely heard them. A faint note caught on the breeze and nearly blown away.

Her face must have betrayed her. She cleared it. But couldn't bring herself to lie. "My little brother Georgie. He signed up nearly the minute war was declared."

"Three squares a day, Will," he'd said. *"Can't beat that, can you?"*

But you could. You so very well *could*. Better to be a little hungry and not have bullets whizzing over your head, by her estimation.

A soft, warm feeling started at her fingers and worked its way to her heart, stilling a few of the worries. It took her a long moment of blinking at the carpet to realize Gwen had taken her hand. And that she didn't mind.

"We shall pray for him," she whispered. "Every morning. Every night."

They would. Willa didn't doubt that. What she couldn't quite understand was why she was glad of it.

———◇———

So many years she had wondered what it would be like to sit with other musicians, to share in their conversation, to be *one* of them. An hour into the dinner, Willa sat at the elegantly set table in exactly that company and knew her fears from that first concert had been right: It felt like she was a thief, and she had stolen the seat of someone else. Like any moment someone would realize what she'd done and boot her back to the gutter.

She understood their talk now—mostly. A few times they mentioned a particular section of a particular piece, and she realized she'd not been pronouncing the Italian words properly as she studied them. And certainly she didn't always know the music by its name and composer. But still, the conversation she could now follow.

The place setting she could navigate well enough, thanks in part to having eaten at the Davies table these past weeks, and partly from the training the family had all given themselves with the aid of a book in order to blend in to the society functions they occasionally snuck into in order to lift a few pretty baubles.

The relationships she could understand. Jules, with his puppy-dog eyes aimed at Enora Peeters. Enora, who was wary but leaning toward being convinced. Lukas, who had spent the entire hour subtly complimenting his friend and deprecating himself.

That little triad was easy enough to categorize. Why *she* was among them, her place, she couldn't have said.

Enora laughed at one of Jules's jokes and sent Willa a look that said, *Men! What silly creatures.*

Willa smiled her reply. She knew the look. Had sent it herself to Rosie or Lucy or Retta. But she didn't know this round-cheeked

Enora with her enormous dark curls. They had no business exchanging looks.

Jules swirled deep red wine in his cup. "I, for one, will be ready to travel when the tour begins. This is a charming town, to be sure, but . . . so small, *n'est-ce pas?*"

"*Ja.*" Enora looked out the window, into the lamplit street. "Two more weeks, and then we will see more of Wales."

"*Oui.*" Jules's gaze traced Enora's profile.

Willa's lips twitched. It was sweet, watching him watch her. And funny how she would answer his French with Flemish and vice versa.

When Enora looked at the table again, Jules quickly glanced away, toward Lukas. "You will be ready to repair to a larger city, I imagine. Lukas quickly grows bored in small towns."

Did he? Willa turned to watch his reaction—and didn't bother correcting him on calling Aberystwyth a town, when it *did* meet the definition of "city." Lukas hadn't seemed particularly stir-crazy in her presence. Then again, she hadn't been particularly so in his either, though she was a London girl through and through.

That same self-debasing smile touched his lips.

She didn't like that smile on him. Which was strange, because she would have thought she'd prefer it over the self-possessed one. But there it was. Lukas De Wilde wasn't meant to put himself down. It didn't suit him.

"I prefer larger cities, to be sure." The unbefitting smile shifted to something better, something smoother, when he looked to Willa. "London I enjoy. I do, in fact, have to make a quick trip to London in the next few days."

He would be away? For *days*? She couldn't ask for a better opportunity for searching his room. Unless he took the cypher key with him.

Jules frowned at him. "London? *Porquois?*"

"I have heard of someone there who may have news of my

family." He reached for his wine, took a small sip. Sent Enora a polite gaze. "Is your family still in Belgium? Are they well?"

"Yes and yes. The soldiers did not come through our town. My family stayed and was none too pleased with me for leaving." The woman sighed. "They deemed it cowardly."

Jules cleared his throat. "Mine all went to France. But then, being from Louvain . . ."

Enora offered him a comforting smile and a few comforting words to go with it. Her eyes remained shuttered though. Her parents would judge his, by that indication. A mark against him.

Lukas *wouldn't* take the key with him, would he? Willa was all but certain it wasn't something he carried on his person. Not on the pocket watch, and he wore no other jewelry. It couldn't be in his greatcoat or shoes. But who knew what he might pack?

A waiter arrived with their pudding on a tray, and Willa leaned back to let him slide hers in front of her. Something apple and cinnamon and warm and gooey. Her mouth watered. Barclay would be so jealous—he adored apples.

Barclay. Her fingers closed around the fork. That was the answer. She could take the time to go through every speck and sheet of paper in Lukas's hotel room while he was gone. And she would get word to Barclay to check whatever bag he took with him. They could simultaneously cover every last thing he had with him in Wales.

She'd send him a wire first thing in the morning. A bite of the apple stuff melted on her tongue as she mentally composed it. *M coming home. Meet and greet. Check.* Anyone to intercept it wouldn't understand, but Barclay would. *M* for their mark. *Coming home* to indicate London. Find him, check his bag.

She had only to procure a bit more information and knew doing so would be a breeze. A simple smile aimed at her companion and a casual question. "When will you be leaving? For London?"

"I did not have time to check the trains yet, but I hope to go tomorrow." His eyes sparked, dark and deep as mystery. "I do not suppose you want to come along? We could meet your family as well."

A strange note laced his words. Something warm and yet frightened—frailty hidden under gumption. *Hope*, she realized. This man at her side, infamous for charming young ladies and leaving them behind, had actually pinned his hope on *her*. Invested a piece of his heart.

It made no sense. And made another strange note twang, this one inside her. She hadn't the name for it. But it made her almost, almost wish she could go with him. See what it felt like to bustle through a train station with her hand tucked into the crook of his arm. To sit beside him in the posh seats of first class and watch Wales and then England chug by. To tug him into Pauly's like Rosemary had done with Peter and introduce him to her family.

But he thought she came from a respectable one. If he saw where they lived, the Poplar neighborhood surrounding Pauly's pub . . .

And she had a job to do here.

She sighed, though, and made sure her returning gaze was warm and regretful. "I'm afraid most of my family is not in London just now anyway. And it would be rather rude of me to leave Gwen and Daisy during our visit, when I'll be going home for good so soon."

Disappointment flickered through his eyes, but it was swallowed up by logic. He was no doubt realizing that having her there would distract him from his true purpose in going anyway. He sent her that heart-stopping grin of his. "Perhaps absence will make the heart grow fonder then, as they say."

Heavens, she hoped not. But if it did, she would simply have to deal with it. Get herself under control. Remind herself that it was only allowed to hurt when *family* left, and he wasn't family. Far from it.

He was just a mark.

They finished their apple-things, chatted a few more minutes, and then Lukas claimed to have to get her home and made their farewells. Perhaps in truth he wanted to give his friend some time with his sweetheart alone.

Or, she granted when he tucked her gloved fingers into their place on his wool-clad arm once they were out in the street, perhaps *he* wanted time with *her*.

"I am not certain what time I may leave tomorrow." His voice was a breath against the quiet streets, a little white puff in the chill air marking each word. "I likely will not see you again before I go. Our lessons will have to wait until I return. Which will probably be the following day, or the next. I cannot think it will take me longer than that."

She nodded and wondered how much affection she should put in her eyes as she looked up at him. Then realized with more than a little frustration that it was a moot question. Because something must have been in her eyes without her even realizing it, given the way his softened in the glow of the lamp. A little sigh slipped out in a little cloud. "Would you send a note round when you leave, and when you get back?" So she could pass the word along to Barclay, that was all. Not because she would miss him.

"Of course." Satisfaction filled his voice. Hers must have reflected something more than she'd meant it to, as her eyes had done.

Blast it. She couldn't *like* him. She wasn't that stupid.

So why, when he drew her out of the lit path and into a little night-clad garden that probably belonged to one of the houses nearby, did she make no objection?

Because, perhaps, it could be viewed like . . . summer. Short, fleeting, to be enjoyed while it lasted. The autumnal winds of reality would prevail soon enough. Why not enjoy the warmth while it was here?

The night looked good on him. Better than it should, with the way the shadows carved each feature into something precise and extreme, chiseled a stronger ridge onto his nose, below his cheek, his jaw, and the moonlight kissed the planes. He was . . . beautiful. If she could wield a paintbrush as she did a violin bow, she would want to put him to canvas as some classical figure whose name she didn't even know.

The leather of his gloves touched her cheek and rested there. The dark of his eyes caught the moonlight and turned it into something more. "Will you let me kiss you again before I go?" The murmur wrapped around her like an embrace.

She hadn't, at the end of any of their lessons. For good reason. "No. That would be stupid. And Willa Forsythe isn't stupid." Except that she was, apparently. Because even while she said it, she leaned toward him, strained up on her toes.

One of his arms slid around her waist and helped her close the distance. "Ah. But *you* can kiss *me*. I see." And found it amusing, given the turn of his lips in the second before hers found them.

Music. It came in a burst, all brightness and joy and fast, high notes. But not the wispy kind, to be blown away in a stiff breeze. Undergirded by the deep strength of a bass. It grew as his lips caressed hers, increased in tempo, then slowed to a sudden pulsing when he pulled away just a fraction, enough to rest his forehead against hers.

The breath he dragged in was long and ragged at the edges. "Willa. I will earn your trust. Prove to you that you can risk a chance on me. I will. I need to make sure my family is safe, but—"

"Of course you do. I would never judge you for that."

"Just for . . . being Lukas De Wilde."

The last of the music ebbed away. She eased back, as much as the arm still around her would allow. There were easy responses. Things to dismiss the conversation. Words that would effectively place another brick between them.

But the truth slipped out instead. "My father was like you. Charming and handsome and sure of himself. And he left before I ever even met him—off to find the next woman to charm, no doubt. I'll not be like my mother. I'll *not*."

His larynx bobbed up, then sank below the cashmere scarf that screamed money as surely as that watch of his did. "You have every right to judge me so. I was that type of man—before. I realize this. And I regret it. I know I cannot ask you to trust me, trust that I have changed, when I have had so little time to prove it. But I will. There will be no next woman for me, ever. Just you."

Words. Words were so easy. No doubt her father had said similar ones to her mother. *Just you, no one else.*

But words meant nothing. She shook her head. "Perhaps were I another kind of woman, I could let you prove it. But I'm not. Even if you were faithful a year, a decade, I would always be waiting for you to leave. Expecting it. What kind of relationship could we possibly have with that thought always hovering?"

She was broken. Had been since she was six, staring at that note that said she couldn't trust anyone. That no matter how many times someone said *I love you*, it didn't matter.

Love was just a word. Three deceptive sounds linked together into a lie.

If he really had changed, he deserved better than that. And if he hadn't, then she was right to doubt him. Either way, this could be nothing but summer. Fleeting. Soon over. Swallowed by the cold winds of autumn.

His arm tightened around her, and he kissed her again. Fast and hard. Blaring trumpets and pounding percussion and a syncopated rhythm.

She let him. Savored the feelings that swept through her, crashing like cymbals. They would be a memory soon enough. Something to think about as she lay on her hard little cot in London, staring up at that battered poster on her wall.

When he pulled away again, it was by a whole step. His fingers left her cheek, and he took her hand with a deliberate, decisive motion. Placed it back on his arm and turned her toward the street again.

"I will prove it to you. I will never leave." A promise. Or perhaps a threat.

Or perhaps, maybe, an accusation. Because even if he didn't, she would still be broken.

SEVENTEEN

L ondon was about like Lukas remembered it—crowded and fast-paced and just how he liked a city. Without the charm of Paris, perhaps, but he had always enjoyed it. He could spend months or years in its bustle and be content, if this was where Willa wanted to live.

He strode out of St. Pancras Station with a glance over his shoulder in appreciation for the grand architecture. The enormous, graceful arches, the Gothic windows, the—

"Oh!"

"Pardonnez-moi!" The words spilled out by rote even as he reached to steady whomever he'd plowed into, dropping his bag in the process. A woman, apparently, and a young one. He noted carefully pinned blond curls, a somewhat faded hat, and big blue eyes that looked up at him and went wide.

Her mouth fell open. "You're . . . you're Lukas De Wilde!"

A month ago, he would have been pleased at being recognized. And would have immediately noted that she wasn't just blond and wearing a hat, she was pretty. Quite. But there was no catch in his pulse today. No hum of appreciation asking to gather in his throat. There was just the thought that she was pretty, and she wasn't Willa, and so he didn't much care.

Something went soft and relieved inside. No attraction, no compulsion. No rearing head of his past. It was too much to hope, no doubt, that he would never struggle with the man he'd been. But he wasn't now. Not yet. The Lord was filling him with something new instead.

He set the girl back on her feet and offered a vague smile. "*Oui*. I am flattered that you recognize me."

"Oh, well of *course* I do." She held out a hand, wrist limp. "Elinor Sayers. I have long been a fan, *monsieur*."

Because it was polite, he took her hand, raised it, kissed it. Because she wasn't Willa, he let it drop again as soon as he could. "How do you do, Miss Sayers. My sincerest apologies for running into you. I ought to have been paying better attention."

As he ought to be still. People swarmed, parting around them, a few sending scowls their way as they impeded other pedestrians.

Elinor Sayers didn't seem to notice. She beamed up at him, pressing her hand to her cheek. "Oh, don't be sorry. I'm certainly not. I can't believe it! I didn't know you were in London. Have you a concert here? If so, I shall go and buy a ticket to it straightaway!"

"Ah, no. Not this time. Though I am playing with an orchestra that will soon be touring Wales, if you ever make it there."

The girl pulled her lips into a pout and cast a glance past him, toward the station. She was probably on her way somewhere and in danger of missing her train. "I rarely leave London." A strange thing to say *here*. And come to think of it, she carried no bag. Perhaps she was meeting someone. "Such a shame—but I shall certainly keep an eye out for when you next come here for a concert."

A smile, a nod, and he bent down to pick up his fallen bag. It was light—had only the essentials, after all. "Have a lovely day. And again, my apologies for running into you."

"And again—no apology necessary." She gave him a pretty,

dimpled smile and walked away. The sway of her hips was, he had to think, exaggerated.

Lukas shook his head and redirected his attention toward Kings Cross. He had spent most of the train ride studying a map of London, trying to find where *L'Indépendance Belge* was located. From the looks of it, he could walk to it in fifteen to twenty minutes, without need to catch the tube.

In years past, he would have procured a room at the Midland Grand Hotel for the night after he had met with Monsieur Allard. But his money was shrinking too rapidly. He would find a cheaper place somewhere—perhaps the newspaperman could recommend a decent, economical room.

The day was already advanced, the sun hanging low and casting long shadows. Autumn's early dusk would catch up to him if he didn't hurry, so he gripped the handles of his bag and set off down the street.

"Lukas De Wilde?"

He nearly groaned when a man stepped in front of him—though something stopped him. Perhaps because the man—young, perhaps a year or two his junior but no more—didn't have the sound of a fan like the blond girl. He wore a derby at a jaunty angle and a wool coat in charcoal grey.

Something about the way he stood was familiar. Or, no, perhaps it was . . . something else.

The man held out a hand. "Barclay Pearce. Willa let me know what train you were on and said you might appreciate some help."

Barclay. Willa's . . . family, though she'd never said what kind. Cousin, he would guess. And he could scarcely believe she'd contacted him on Lukas's behalf. Would she do so if she didn't care for him at all?

Maybe. It was obvious she cared about reuniting his family. Just not for joining it in any capacity. Still. He would be warmed by the gesture of goodwill on her part. And be glad to have a

London native to help him find the press that was probably in some back-alley shop.

His shoulders relaxed, and he reached out to shake hands. "How do you do, Mr. Pearce. I did not expect Willa to go to such trouble."

Mr. Pearce laughed. "She has shown you her charming side, I see. And yet she hasn't scared you off completely?"

A smile tickled his lips. "I heard her play. Need I say more?"

Something sparkled in his companion's eyes—recognition perhaps. "She's good, isn't she? We always thought she was, but we're no judge of such things."

"She is . . . miraculous." He could think of no other word for it.

"Well." Pearce clapped a hand to Lukas's shoulder and held out his other in the direction he had been going. "You were going this way? Can I help you find what it is you're looking for?"

"Perhaps." He shifted his bag so he could reach into it for his map.

"Oh, you don't need a map, if that's what you're going for. I've got the whole city up here." Pearce tapped his hat and offered a grin that transformed his face from ordinary to notable.

The claim struck him as something Willa would say. A cousin, definitely. First cousin, he would bet. Lukas nodded and lowered his bag to his side again. "Thank you. According to the information I have, I am looking for Tavistock Place. Though I am not certain how accurate this information is. I do not suppose you have heard of any Belgian newspapers near here?"

Mr. Pearce's brows lifted. "You came to London to seek out a newspaper?"

Was that really so odd? Any number of refugees were, he would guess, trying to use such means to find their missing family members. "The man who runs it. My father's friend." He hoped. Prayed. Surely that was why the name Allard had sounded so familiar. "I am hoping he has news that can lead me to my mother and sister."

There was a hitch in Pearce's gait. "You don't know where they are?"

Lukas shook his head. And clenched his teeth against the emotion that surged. It took him a moment and a swallow to be able to answer aloud. "I know only that they are not at the house in Louvain—it was burned. And they are not at the house in Brussels. Germans have overtaken it."

His shoulder pulsed a reminder of how he had discovered that particular bit of information.

"I'm sorry." Pearce sounded it—truly sounded it, not as though he offered polite words to a stranger. "We'll help however we can, Willa and I. And my sisters." *The girls*, they must be. Though Willa hadn't mentioned names other than Rosie.

"Thank you."

Mr. Pearce motioned to the corner. "We'll want to cross there, to Euston."

They traversed the intervening distance in silence, dodging the many pedestrians going the opposite direction, the lampposts, the occasional tree planted in the pavement. It smelled of smoke from chimneys and the fumes from automobiles' exhaust, and horns and bells and shouts colored the air.

Its own kind of symphony, was a busy city.

They reached the corner and paused to await a break in traffic. Lukas was about to ask Mr. Pearce what part of the city he—and perhaps Willa—called home but managed no more than to open his mouth before he heard his name being called from the direction of St. Pancras.

His head swung to the left, and he sighed. The blond girl was hurrying down the sidewalk, hand waving. Another blonde was at her side—several years older, her hair a deeper shade of gold. A sister, perhaps, or a friend.

He was beginning to regret working so hard to achieve a level of fame. And certainly posing for all those posters. Though to be sure, he was rarely recognized outside his own circles, where people expected to see him.

Miss Sayers dug into her little handbag as she approached. "So sorry to bother you again, Mr. De Wilde. But I would have kicked myself had I let the opportunity pass by. Could I trouble you for an autograph? Please?"

Another sigh gathered, but he pushed it down and dug out a smile instead. "Of course. No trouble at all." And it wouldn't have been on a normal day, when he wasn't racing the sun toward Allard's.

But without patrons excited to see and hear him, he would have no career. He set down his bag again and reached for the paper and fountain pen she'd pulled out of her bag.

Not just a paper—an old program from his last solo concert in London. Where had she gotten that? Or rather, why had she been carrying it in her handbag? A glance up showed him she was blushing.

"I haven't carried this bag since last year—just got it out for the change in season and realized it was still in there. A happy coincidence today, though it must make me look a complete fool to you."

"Not at all." Hoping his smile put her at ease, he spread out the program against his left palm and asked her for the spelling of her name. Once he'd written it and added a short message, he signed his name and handed it back.

Her companion straightened when he did so, offering a smile. Her attention, however, seemed to have been on Barclay Pearce.

But the ladies said their farewells and hurried off in the other direction without detaining them any further, leaving Lukas to pick up his bag again and turn back to his companion. The day must be catching up with him. Already his bag felt heavier, and he'd scarcely begun walking.

Mr. Pearce looked amused. "Does that happen often?"

"Not really, other than at concerts." Or when he dared to approach his own house in Brussels when there were Germans inside it. Though having a girl come at him with a pen and program was a far cry from a soldier with a gun.

They'd probably torn the whole house apart, looking for Père's work. Destroyed what family mementos they hadn't burned. But none of that mattered, so long as he could find his family.

"Shall we cross?"

He followed Willa's cousin across the street and around another corner onto Judd Street. The hordes of people soon thinned out, giving them room enough to walk two abreast again.

Lukas cleared his throat. "Willa has said little about her home and family. Do you live near each other, Mr. Pearce?"

"A street or two apart. And you may call me Barclay. I'm not one for formality."

Not the sort of thing a gentleman usually said—nor a man of profession, actually. But he must be one or the other, given the cut of his coat and how well it fit him, the quality of the fabric. And the fact that he was a relative of Willa's, who dressed every bit as well, even if she claimed to be of limited means.

"Barclay. Thank you. You may call me Lukas." It was what Jules always called him anyway—though they'd been friends since they were in short trousers, so it hardly counted. Still, he would cling to the idea that someday this man could be *his* family too. Familiarity was not out of place.

"And Willa is . . . reserved, let's call it. Don't take it personally. I don't think she would have told me her hair color as a child if I hadn't been able to see it for myself."

Lukas chuckled. But it was more sad than funny. A consequence, he supposed, of the absent father she'd mentioned last night. "She is unlike anyone I have ever known, to be sure."

Barclay slowed, and a glance over at him showed Lukas that his brows were a knot of question. "I'd be the first to agree. Is that why you . . . are tutoring her? On the violin? Though to be honest, I was dubious that she really needs lessons."

"Oh, they will not change much about the way she plays. I hope only to polish what is already brilliant and teach her music theory. But it is an excuse to spend time with her."

Now Barclay came to a complete stop, and the question on his face went hard and stubborn. "She's about as friendly as a brick wall. Why are you looking for excuses to spend time with her?"

"She is not a wall. Just hides behind one." He met the man's gaze without flinching. Let him see whatever he wanted in Lukas's eyes. "She mentioned only the lessons?"

Barclay folded his arms over his chest. "She is about as communicative as a brick wall sometimes too. What else ought she to have mentioned?"

Lukas shrugged and kept walking. He may not know exactly where he was going, but he knew he hadn't any daylight to waste. "She eventually let me take her on a picnic. And we had supper with another couple last night."

"Hmmph." Barclay fell in beside him again. "I will ask again— why? If you think she's some wealthy heiress—"

"I think only that she intrigues me. That she looks at the world as so few people do, seeing more than what is on the surface. That she can touch a violin and make it sing with a skill beyond any I have heard. That if ever I can inspire her to love me, it will be with a determination that will never fade—she does not work in half measures."

Barclay stopped again. "Wait, wait, wait. Did you just say *love*? Are you aware that you've only known her for a few weeks?"

"Quite aware. But sometimes you know."

"No. You don't." Shaking his head, Barclay charged forward once more. "The world is going mad, that's what. First Rosie off and marries Branok Hollow without so much as a by-your-leave—

which is inexcusable, no matter how much I like him. No blasted way is Willa going to do the same stupid thing."

Lukas followed half a step behind. In part, he would admit, so Barclay wouldn't see the grin he couldn't quite tamp down. "No need to worry, *mon ami*. Willa thinks me mad for speaking of such things as well. Or rather, thinks me joking."

Amusement eclipsed the frustration in Barclay's green eyes. "That does sound more like Willa than being swept up in it all. Come to think of it, I would have liked to see her response if you actually said such things to her. She isn't much for romance, is our Willa."

"So I have learned. But I will win her through habit, if nothing else. I will simply stay right there by her side until she gets so accustomed to me, she cannot imagine me *not* there."

"If anything can win Willa, that might be it." But he sounded doubtful. Which didn't exactly light hope in Lukas's heart. "Though I maintain you're a fool if you really think you know so quickly you *want* to win her. Not that she's not worth winning, mind you—no one can hold a candle to Willa, unless it's Rosie or El or Lucy or Retta."

Lukas's eyes went wide. "Are they all your sisters? Her cousins?" He could not imagine so many girls, with their frills and trills and tears, in his home. But then, he had rather lucked out on the sister score with Margot. Even as a tot, she'd had no use for frills, preferred quiet over trills, and cried no more than boys her age.

Missing her was an arrow through his middle. He needed to see her hunched over her desk in that way of hers that always made their mother chide her for bad posture. He needed to feel that too-serious, too-heavy gaze upon him that was too old for her age. He needed to hear her complain about how stupidity made her itchy and writhe in that exaggerated way she did when someone said something foolish.

He needed to know she was well.

"I count Willa as a sister too. Be aware of that—you hurt her, you'll answer to me."

Lukas nodded. A year ago, it would have been a dismissive gesture, had a brother said such a thing. Today it was a solemn oath. "I will never do anything to put her at risk, either in heart or body."

"Well now, I didn't say no *risk*. If you risk nothing, you gain nothing." He paused and indicated the street sign fastened to the side of the building. TAVISTOCK PLACE. "Here we are."

The street Cor Akkerman had indicated. Now to find the right building. He led the way down the avenue, eyes hunting for a sign that would proclaim a printer's shop. There was nothing. But Wallonian-accented French caught his attention, pulling him toward a quartet of men standing halfway down the street.

One of those, praise be to the Almighty, held a copy of *L'Indépendance Belge*. Even if it were not housed here, perhaps they would know where it was printed. He approached with a polite nod and a hesitating, "*Pardonnez-moi, s'il vous plait.*"

The men all looked up, their welcoming smiles saying they recognized a fellow Wallonian. He indicated the paper. "I am looking for where this is printed and heard it was near here. Do you know where I can find their offices and Monsieur Allard?"

They all nodded, one of them motioning to a building just behind him, another saying, "*Oui, oui*, it is just here—and he has not left yet for the night, so you can still catch him if you hurry."

With excited thanks, he motioned Barclay to follow him and led the way to the brick building. The familiar scent of ink greeted him at the door, along with the steady *thwack, thwack, thwack* of the press running.

Had the men not told him where to go, these things would have done so.

He pushed inside, praying with every step across the floor that this would not be for naught. That even if Allard didn't know his father, he would be willing to help. He turned a bit so he could say to Barclay, "*Je vous remercie pour me mettre sur le bon chemin.*"

Barclay blinked. "Uh . . . I can tell that was French. Beyond that . . ."

"Sorry." Excellent. He could speak plainly to the printer, then, without fearing Barclay would understand. "I was merely thanking you for showing me the way."

"Ah. No problem at all." He motioned toward the back wall, where books and newspapers were stacked and shelved. "I'll just entertain myself over here while you speak with your father's friend."

Even better. With a nod of thanks, he followed a hallway out of the pressroom and toward what seemed to be offices, though the space was small and cramped. No doubt Allard had found it necessary to settle for whatever he could find, ideal or not.

At the end of the hall, a door stood open, the clicking of a typewriter's keys spilling out along with a lamp's light. He knocked on the doorframe.

The man at the desk looked up. He wore wire-rimmed spectacles, pomaded grey hair, and a mustache that looked as though he had twisted the ends in concentration all the day long. All of which dimmed in light of the way his eyes narrowed upon spotting Lukas, as if trying to place him.

An excellent sign. Lukas may take after his mother in most ways, but those who knew his father well could always see him in Lukas's features. "Monsieur Allard? I am Lukas De Wilde."

"De Wilde. Yes, that's it." His words were in French, and he motioned Lukas in and indicated he should close the door behind him. He didn't smile. "I heard your family home was destroyed in Louvain. It would have broken your father's heart to know that his private library had been burned along with the university's."

Praise God. A friend. Lukas nodded and didn't bother with a smile either. "You are right. And it would have broken it even more if he realized my mother and sister were forced from their haven. I do not know where they are."

Allard leaned back in his chair, fingers worrying one end of that mustache. "I am sorry to hear that. Are they in England perhaps, do you think? You can place an advertisement. Many have done so, occasionally with good results. Our paper has made it to all corners of the British Isles, into the hands of refugees everywhere."

"I cannot risk something overt. If you knew my father, you no doubt knew what kind of work he was involved in."

There, a bit of a smile, and a matching light in his eyes. "Ah yes, his puzzles. I never understood a bit of what he asked me to print, but I enjoyed knowing it was part of his research."

Puzzles. Was that all Père had called them? Perhaps a few knew of their import. Enough about it to be willing to help, at any rate. Lukas cleared his throat. "They were more than that—and the Germans have shown interest in finding his work." A twinge bit his shoulder. "Would you be willing to print another puzzle for me? To help me get word to my family? They have his work, you see. I need to be certain they, and it, are safe."

Allard muttered his opinion of the Germans and sat forward again. "Yes, of course. Anything you require. Do you need a full article printed or choice words in certain places? Your father rarely requested the same thing twice."

"I have prepared a series of things, if you would be so kind as to run one in each edition you publish." It had taken him most of the night to compose them, going back and forth from his writing to the key, transposing the letters, scratching it out and starting again.

He had managed. But cypher work had never been his forte. He was no Margot. And wouldn't have been able to manage even these short messages were it not for the key she had pressed into his hands before he left for his solo tour after the funeral.

"Here," she had said, handing it to him as he practiced on his last day at home. It had been bound with a blue ribbon as if it were a gift. "Papa and I made this for you. Before he died."

He had looked at the lines of music and smiled. Even as he frowned. "You wrote me music?" Neither she nor their father had an ear for it. None whatsoever. It was sweet that she had tried, but he could tell even by looking at it that all sweetness would end there.

Margot had smiled. "It's not music. It's mathematics."

A debate they'd had countless times. Music, she insisted, was all about the intervals and chords—mathematics. Music, he insisted, was about the aesthetic—feeling.

It hadn't been a desire to prove her wrong that had made him put the sheets on his stand and raise his bow. It was too soon after their father's death to want to cause his sister even a minor grief. He had played it because he loved her, and he wanted to honor the time she and their father had put into making him something.

But his expression had probably been exactly what Willa had worn last week when she'd pulled this paper from his crate.

And Margot had laughed. "It isn't meant to be played, Lukas! It's a code."

"A code." *A game*, he'd thought. But he'd play along. "Why do I need a code?"

Her face had gone too serious. Too old, as it too often did. "Because we never know, do we? When things will change. When we might need you, or you might need us. This way, we can always get word to each other."

He opened his bag now and reached into one of the twin compartments. His fingers met only the change of clothes he'd packed. Frowning, he spun the bag around and tried the other side. There . . . but odd. He never put his *clothes* in the side with the outside pouch—they made it too bulky. He must have been distracted last night after working for hours to remember how to use that key.

"It is a simple cypher," Margot had claimed as she tugged him into one of the chairs at her schoolroom table. She'd put the music in front of them, blank paper beside it. "Each note already has a letter anyway."

"But only seven of them."

"Twelve, if you count each black key as well. Seventeen, if you count sharps and flats separately, which I have done. That covers A through P. But they are all quarter notes. Longer notes indicate the subsequent letters. A half note A is really a Q. Et cetera. Do you understand?"

He had rolled his eyes. "I am not a dunce."

"Good. Now, that is the simple alphabet, but of course that is *too* simple, anyone could crack that code. So each line of the music indicates a different transposition. On line one, the first note is an E flat—that means that our alphabet begins on J. J will equal A, K will equal B, and so on. Line two begins with a half-note C, which is a U. U is A, V is B."

"Very interesting, Margot."

She'd rolled her eyes at him. "Not really. It's child's play. Even Mozart encoded messages into his music with cyphers like this."

Lukas had huffed. "Did you just say *even* Mozart? As if *he* were a dunce?"

"Well, he was no cryptographer, was he?" He could still see her grin. So condescending. So intelligent. So *Margot*.

He'd mussed her hair, solely because it made her squeal like a normal girl. Not because she thought it didn't look pretty—because, she said, it felt unorderly. Margot required order in everything.

She'd explained, then, how to actually *use* the code. One would have to convince an editor to put the word *Family* in the head-line somewhere. That was the signal to watch for a message. Then within the first sentence of the paragraph with the hidden meaning, include a number to indicate what line of the music they were using as their key. From there, it was a simple matter of beginning each word—or every other word, it didn't matter so long as he was consistent—with the encoded letter. If he were trying to spell out *Paris*, for example, using the first line as their key, he could say, "Yesterday I jumped up again and I shouted, 'Beautiful!'" The only letters that mattered were Y, J, A, I, B— which transposed to P, A, R, I, S.

Very flexible, she had insisted. Easy to use. Simple to decode if she had to send *him* one. But no one else would be able to decipher it unless they had the key. The music.

He pulled out the series of messages he'd devised and slid the papers across the desk to Allard. When he saw Margot again, he would have a few things to say about the supposed ease of this system. Sure, it sounded simple in theory, until one sat down to decide what one wanted to say and how to write a fake message around it. Then it became time-consuming, if not exactly complicated.

Not for her, though. She would be able to compose a message on the spot, no doubt.

Allard picked up the messages and read through them. "Very short. I should include them within a larger article as I have done in the past, yes? So long as the headline has *La Famille* in it."

"Exactly right, yes." Assuming this paper made it into her hands, Margot would need nothing more to find his paragraphs and decode them. Although he would certainly have a harder time of it if—*when*—she sent a message back to him. He cleared his throat. "I am not certain what my father usually paid for this sort of thing."

Allard smiled, and this time it was warm and true and exhausted. "It is my pleasure to help your family, *monsieur*, at no cost. For your father's sake. He was a good man. A good friend."

"Thank you." He peeked inside his bag again, just to assure himself that he hadn't been so exhausted as to forget to pack his music—the pieces he was memorizing for their first concert on the road as well as those sheets from Margot. The folder was there where it belonged, albeit in the wrong compartment, so he fastened it closed again and stood. "I am in your debt, *monsieur*."

"Nonsense. We must do what we can to help regain what was taken from us. I trust you will help another in need, when the time arises."

They shook hands, and Lukas let himself back out. In one respect lighter that this much, at least, was well accomplished. And in another respect, even heavier than before he entered, as he prayed that somehow, by some miracle, one of the papers with the coded message would make it into his sister's hand.

Barclay was still waiting in the pressroom, flipping through a book. At Lukas's approach he looked up. His gaze was less welcoming than determined. Less friendly than decided. "Have you a hotel paid for already?"

"Not yet, no. I was hoping someone could recommend a place." Though he'd forgotten to ask Allard.

Barclay snapped the book closed and put it back on the shelf. "You are welcome to stay with me. I've a room to spare."

Lukas opened his mouth, but no words came out. Not until he dragged in another breath. "Pardon me. It is a generous offer, but . . . why?"

Barclay lifted a brow. "Because if you're determined to get to know Willa, then I'm determined to get to know *you*. Come on." He turned for the exit, apparently not considering that *no, thank you* was on the tip of Lukas's tongue. "We'll have to take the tube."

Lukas followed. *No* hadn't really been on the tip of his tongue anyway. Getting to know Willa's cousin who thought himself a brother was sure to prove more interesting than a night worrying over his family in a cheap hotel room.

EIGHTEEN

Nothing. Nothing, nothing, and more nothing. Willa growled and kicked the bed—which was stupid and sent her hopping around on one foot until she finally sank down onto the mattress so she could rub her toes.

The curtains were drawn, but even so she'd brought her own small electric torch. No one should come in here though. It was well past housekeeping's hours, and Jules had gone out with Enora again—to a play, if she had overheard them correctly. So far as she could tell, no one else would really pay all that much attention to Lukas's suite. Still, it paid to be cautious, and light shining from the window of an unoccupied room didn't classify as cautious.

But there was nothing to be found in here. *Nothing*, blast it. His clothes, none of which had anything worth noting on them. The patent leather shoes that she assumed went with his evening attire—no odd markings on the soles. A French Bible on the bedside table, which had surprised her—though if *it* contained a key, she wasn't sure how she'd ever know it.

She scooted toward it, though, and ran her fingers over the

cover. It didn't seem particularly well used, but a marker stuck out of the pages. Were it in English, she would have flipped it open, just to see what he had marked. But she'd not be able to read this.

Her hand spread flat against the cool leather of the cover. They were so different. From worlds that were themselves worlds apart. This was just one small proof of it—even if he *spoke* English, spoke it to her, it wasn't who he was.

Even if he stooped to her level, left his world to spend time in hers, he'd never belong there. And he wouldn't want to. Not if he knew what her world really was.

She wouldn't regret it. She hadn't the time.

There were no more drawers or doors in here to look through. She'd already checked under the mattress, felt around for loose boards or panels—nothing.

Blast, but she hated to admit defeat. *Couldn't* admit it. Mr. V had never indicated the possibility that the key simply wasn't here with him. There had been no *if*. There had been simply *find it*.

She had to find it. If she didn't, then she would make an enemy of a man who had far too much knowledge of—and therefore power over—her family.

And then there was the man in the brown jacket.

Shuddering, she pushed up off the bed and smoothed out the counterpane. For a second—only one—it struck her. How odd and out of place she felt here in the bedchamber of a man she had kissed. Where he slept each night.

Doing a job, that was all. Or failing to do a job, in this case. She picked up the electric torch from where she'd set it on the bed and exited into the sitting room again. This hotel had no private bathrooms, so there was no other room to check. She took a quick turn through this outer room, but she saw nothing this time she hadn't before.

He must have it with him in London. That was the only answer. In which case, Barclay and the girls would have found it. They would run the job like they'd run other jobs before. Elinor to distract while Retta snuck up and slipped the contents from his bag into hers. Barclay to keep him occupied while Retta and Ellie looked through said contents. Then Ellie to distract again while Retta slipped her bag to Barclay and Barclay slipped it all back into Lukas's.

A simple Wimbledon, with the goods as a tennis ball, back and forth.

She would go back to the Davies house. Risk one more phone call to Peter's townhouse. The bill had to be adding up, but she would leave the Davies with pounds enough to cover it from what Mr. V had given her. A necessary expense, they'd call it.

A quick exhale extinguished the lamp, a quick check through the peephole told her no one lingered in the hall, a quick step out and she had her skeleton key in hand to relock it. Half a minute beyond that and she was padding down the stairs as she had done before. A job not so well done in terms of findings, but with no hitches to the procedure at least.

At the base of the stairs she paused to make sure no one in the lobby was coming this way, then slipped out the back door.

Cool air greeted her. And so did a rough hand, pushing her to the bricks of the hotel. A body followed, and lips pressed to hers. Not bruising. But certainly with no actual *feeling*. She had the odd certainty that he kissed her merely to keep her silent.

As if she were the type to scream when accosted in an alleyway—that was reserved for women who didn't slink through them with stolen goods in their pockets on a regular basis. The last thing she ever needed was a bobby coming to the rescue.

She could handle forceful men herself, in her own ways. Though this one she had only to shove away with a scowl. "Touch me again, Cor Akkerman, and you'll find my knee giving you injury in a place you really won't appreciate."

He chuckled and braced his arms against the wall on either side of her, as if he were a man with his sweetheart. But he angled his body, wisely, away. "Now, pretty Willa. Is that any way to speak to your business partner?"

"My *what*?"

He leaned his head close to hers, his mouth at her ear. "Had De Wilde been here, I would have thought you were in his room for predictable reasons. But he is gone. Yet you are here. And whatever it is you are stealing from him, I want a cut."

Breathing even. Pulse normal. No tells. No flinches. She lifted a brow. "I don't know what in the world you're talking about. I was simply here to return some music I'd borrowed—the clerk let me up to slide it under his door."

"Oh, *ja*, because music would not keep until tomorrow. Just like that man's wallet in London *jumped* into your hand? At the shoeshine's booth?"

Blast. She hadn't seen him there—which made the second person she hadn't noted following her about London. This wouldn't do at all. And no one—*no one*—ever saw her pickpocketing.

No one but another thief.

She leaned back against the bricks with a sigh. "I didn't get anything. He left nothing in his room worth taking, he must have had it all with him." Let him think it nothing but money she was searching for. It was the safest way to play it.

He clucked his tongue. "An easy story to tell, pretty Willa. But I am not such a fool as to believe you. Something brought you all the way here for this—it must be a big score. You let me in . . . or I tell De Wilde that I saw you in his room and let *him* try to determine what it is you were after."

Double blast. She didn't need Lukas's suspicions any more

249

than she did a bobby's attention. He would close up, at the best. Set those cops on her at the worst.

And she could just see the way he'd look at her. She could imagine the pain in his deepest brown eyes.

Triple blast. She couldn't think that way. Her breath hissed out. "You're right that it's a big score. But I didn't find it tonight. Check my pockets if you like. They're empty."

The sliver of moonlight trickling between the buildings caught on his teeth as he smiled. "Thank you for the invitation. I believe I will."

She gritted her teeth as his hand slid into one coat pocket, then the other. He reached next, of course, for her handbag and rummaged through it as well, snorting in what sounded like appreciation as he pulled out her picks.

"Nice ones."

"Thank you. Old friends."

"I could use new ones myself." He actually reached to slip them into his pocket. Actually thought she'd let him.

She jammed her heel into his toe and snatched them back. "Get your own. And try that again and you get the knee."

He muttered something in Flemish that she imagined to be a rather colorful expression of his opinion of her—and held out her bag.

She jerked it from his fingers. "I told you I didn't find it."

"But you will." He caught her chin and leaned close. "And when you do, you will split it with me—the price of my silence. And when you think that perhaps *I* have done something, you will also be silent. Or I go to De Wilde. Do you understand?"

"Why? What do you plan to do?" And why did it send a shiver through her to wonder? There were other thieves at work all the time, under each other's noses. As a rule, she had no problem with them, even if they didn't often obey the same codes she kept to. They knew, at least, to steer clear of the family that met at Pauly's.

No one ever picked *their* pockets. They all got out of their way when they saw them coming. They knew where to send little ones they found on the streets, sniffling and sniveling and starving.

But Cor Akkerman wasn't a London pickpocket, and he wasn't playing by the rules.

He grinned and backed away, all charm again. "You think I will ruin the surprise? No, no, pretty Willa. That is not the way it works. But you will know." He shoved his hands in his pockets and turned. "*Goeie avond*, pretty Willa."

He'd said it to her before. But the first time, leaving Pauly's that day she'd lifted the blighter's wallet, she had thought it *was* a good evening. Tonight, not so. She bit her tongue and said nothing while he sauntered away.

But she wasted no time in getting back to the Davies house and slipping in the back. Nor in tiptoeing down the hall to the study with the telephone. The sisters and Miss Blaker were still out, from the looks of it. No lights on anywhere down here, no noise from above.

She checked her watch—nine o'clock. Barclay should be home by now. And her hostesses no doubt would be soon, for they were not often out past ten. Unbuttoning her coat as she sat, she picked up the phone and waited for the operator's greeting.

"Hammersmith-1528, please."

"One moment."

It rang. And it rang. Willa shrugged off the coat and loosened her scarf while she willed her brother to pick up the blighted phone.

He did, on the thousandth ring—or perhaps the fifth—with a laugh. "Hello?"

"Tell me you had a better evening than I did."

Another laugh. "No doubt, given that I've been passing it with the person *you* have apparently been passing *yours* with, Willa. When were you going to tell me about the dates with our delightful Mr. De Wilde?"

"Barclay Reginald Pearce, you *didn't*!" That wasn't the way the Wimbledon worked! He wasn't supposed to introduce himself. Be *friendly*. Let the mark know who he was.

But the blithering fool just laughed again. "We're finishing up our supper now. Did you want to say hello?"

"You're . . . he's *there*? At Peter's house?"

"Well, why should I let the chap who's in love with you stay in a hotel when I've all these rooms? The girls were with friends tonight anyway. Other than Lucy, Lucy's here. She's entertaining ol' Luke with stories of discovering how our sister married a novelist."

The only *safe* stories. Though Lucy could make up others in a pinch and keep them all straight for the rest of her life—she'd probably begun tonight's tales with some fabulous tale of how she came to be Barclay's sister, when she quite obviously had Indian blood and he quite obviously did not. And Lucy was the only one not involved in the job—she wondered briefly where Elinor and Retta had gone for the night, but they had scads of places to fall back on. One never knew when a job would leave one in need of a corner to duck into.

Willa groaned. "Why are you so awful?"

"I'll have you know I've been an excellent host. And he's not a bad bloke, really, Will. You could do worse."

"Ha. Ha. Ha." And blast him, but it made her nose clog up and something hot press against the backs of her eyes. Which was stupid. "Will you *please* just tell me how work went today?"

A beat of silence, filled with nothing but static. Then the words that were no more telling, really. "Bust. How was *your* day?"

"I led with that, didn't I? Lousy. Though I ran into the puppy again—not the German shepherd, the other one. Finally puzzled him out for sure. His name's Robbie."

Barclay muttered something she couldn't quite make out. "What?"

"Just . . . I shouldn't be surprised, I guess. He give you trouble?"

"I'm fine. I . . ." She hadn't the words. Not that she could say over the telephone lines.

"Yeah. Listen, we'll take care of it. We will. We always do."

This felt different. There was more at stake than usual. There were governments involved. She wasn't sure how to "take care of it" assuming she succeeded at the primary goal, much less what to do with failure. "Right. Well. Good night, Barclay. Don't do anything stupid."

His snort came over the line loud and clear. "I wouldn't tell you if I meant to do so, as someone I know once said. But relax. I'm just getting to know him."

Stupid. "Mm-hmm."

"Night, Willa. See you soon."

Not if she didn't find this blighted key. At this rate, she'd be stuck here in Wales for a decade, searching for something that she suddenly doubted even existed. But there was apparently nothing Barclay could do to help, so she said goodbye and hung the receiver back in its cradle. Then let her head fall to the cold desktop with a whimper.

Antarctica was beginning to sound like a viable place to relocate. She didn't know where else she could go to escape from all the people she was in danger of making angry.

———◇———

Margot folded the papers back up and slid them into the box. She'd never given much credence to all the talk of feeling and emotion and such nonsense, but just now it felt as though her heart had sunk all the way to her stomach. And turned to stone.

Claudette had smuggled three different papers in this morning. *Three.* Two in English and one in French, but Belgian—printed in London, apparently. Her hands had shaken when she'd taken them, she'd been so excited. Her heart had rocketed into her throat when she saw *La Famille* in one of the headlines. She'd devoured the story about the king's family . . . but there had been no paragraph with a number. No coded words.

Coincidence. That was all. No message from Lukas.

She slid the box into its hiding spot under her bed and then sat there on the floor, trying to convince her heart to come back up where it belonged. Her stomach to unclench.

She counted the floorboards. Twenty-two planks, as always. The flowers in the wallpaper—seven hundred forty-eight. No, that wasn't factoring in the rectangle missing where the window was. What was wrong with her? How could she forget to factor in the window? Had she even subtracted the area of the door?

"Margot?" A knock accompanied her name and made her jump. She hadn't heard Maman's footsteps in the hall.

Something *was* the matter with her. "Yes, Maman?"

"The generalleutnant is back. He would like to play Go with you."

Her nails bit into the wood of the floor. She didn't want to play Go. She didn't want to look at his ugly, smug face. She didn't want to think about how he was here, his men were outside, and her brother was *gone*. Like her father was gone. Like everyone was gone. "I don't want to play."

"Margot." The door creaked open, and Maman's beautiful, frowning face poked in. "He is in a strange mood. Please. I cannot think that angering him would be wise. Come and play."

She wanted to say no. Plead illness. Plead *something*. But Maman didn't ask that much of her. And she was right that they ought not to invite Gottlieb's anger.

She nodded. "Just a minute. I have to . . ." Push this aside. Lock it away. But she could find no words for that.

Maman didn't demand any. She offered a small, apologetic smile. "Thank you, *ma petite*." The door clicked shut again.

She squeezed her eyes shut. Drew in a breath for *one, two*. Held it for *three, four*. Let it out for *five, six*. Repeated the process until the knot in her gut loosened a bit. Prayed. More with numbers than with words, but God would understand. He always did.

It took her three minutes and fourteen seconds to deem herself calm again, but then she tucked her legs under herself and stood. Walked with the same pace she always used toward the room at the top of the stairs and turned into it.

Maman was already in her usual seat, her knitting in her lap. Madame Dumont was in her rocking chair, a book open and held too close to her nose—she needed spectacles but refused to wear them, saying they were unwomanly.

Gottlieb stood at the table they kept set up with Go, surveying the board. They'd not finished their game yesterday, so the pieces still sat where they'd been left. He looked up when Margot entered, and his lips went up at the corners. But it wasn't a smile. Not a real one.

Only then did she realize that he usually *smiled* at her. Not baring his teeth as she'd first thought of him as doing, but smiling with sincerity. What was the matter with him today? Certainly *he* hadn't scoured a newspaper hoping for word of his brother only to get none.

"Ready, *fräulein*?"

She sat by way of answer. Pretended to study the board as he had been doing, though she had no need. She already had it all in her head. What she would do if she dared play honestly, what she would *actually* do, his likely responses to both sets of moves.

Gottlieb sat as well, but he didn't meet her eye as he usually did throughout the game. Didn't ask her if she had read anything interesting today, though she'd spent an hour this morning working through Hegel so she could quote it to him. Didn't ask her whether her friend had come by again.

Good. She didn't *want* him prying into her life. But Maman was right—he wasn't himself. And that could be a bad thing.

Well . . . he was, at the core, just a person, wasn't he? Perhaps he needed someone to ask him *why* he wasn't himself. His men probably wouldn't. Nor would Maman or the Madame. Margot picked up a stone, though it was his turn. "Are you all right, Generalleutnant?"

Her mother's sharp intake of breath hit Margot like a rebuke, though Gottlieb didn't seem to note it. He selected one of his stones and kept his attention on the board. "I am well."

"No, you're not." His respiration wasn't at its normal rate—it was slower, as if he were deliberately controlling it. His chin wasn't at its usual angle. And his heel kept tapping against the floor. "You're agitated. Have I done something to upset you?"

Adults never knew what to do when a child asked them a question like that. And sure enough, his gaze flew up to meet hers. "Of course not. What could you have done?"

She shrugged and pasted on a look she hoped came off as uncertain. "I rarely know what I've done when I upset an adult. Perhaps I insulted a book you like. Or was so very clever at our game yesterday that you cannot think how you will beat me, and it is a terrible affront to your pride."

A breath of laughter slipped from his lips. "You played well, *spatz*. But not *that* well."

His spine straightened a degree, bringing him closer to his usual perfect posture. Margot grinned. "Give me time. I will crush you."

"Perhaps. But not today." He put down his stone in an utterly incomprehensible position that gave him no benefit whatsoever.

So stupid it was itchy. And unlike him. "Are you quite certain that's what you meant to do?"

"What?" He blinked, took in the board again, and made a disgusted noise. "*Nein*. But it is done, I cannot take it back. Perhaps you *will* crush me today."

"Hmm." She fingered her stone. If she put it there, above his, it would give her a considerable advantage. If she placed it there,

below and to the right, it would be smart but not crushing—
though the more advantageous one was *obvious*. He would know
she'd seen it—anyone would see it.

Sighing, she put it to the right. "I'm feeling merciful. Though I
shouldn't, since you were obviously lying. About being all right."

"I am just . . . tired. It was a long day."

He looked exhausted, to be sure. A decade older than he usually did. He must be in his fifties, but he didn't usually wear the
years on his face like this. In ragged lines and deep shadows
under his eyes.

"Did you not sleep well?"

"I slept perfectly, as always." He leaned back against his chair
and rubbed his eyes. "It is nothing, *spatz*. Nothing you need to
worry about."

Something to do with his job, then, she would bet. She sneaked
a look at Maman. How much could she press him before she
earned another chiding breath? Her mother never drew the line
in the same place. Which made it unnecessarily difficult to know
where that line was.

Well, she would never know until she tested it today. "When
I was waiting in the bread line today—"

"When you were what?" Gottlieb's hand dropped from his face,
revealing tension in those too-ragged lines. "Why were you in
the bread line?"

He hadn't made her this itchy in weeks. "To get *bread*."

"No, I—" He paused, sighed, rested a hand on the edge of
the table beside the board. "I told you I would make sure you
had food enough. If you were running so low, why did no one
tell me?"

"We meant no disrespect, Generalleutnant," Maman said in
her sweetest, stubbornest voice. "But we cannot expect you to
provide for us."

He barely glanced at Maman. "I do not like it. Bread lines can get unruly—I have had to post soldiers there to keep the order. You ought not to be in such places."

True enough. But what choice did they have? "That wasn't the point of my story. May I continue?"

He looked as though he might refuse. His jaw was clenched, his nostrils flared. But he nodded.

"I heard in the bread line that your army has been dismantling our factories and shipping the parts back to Germany. Is that true?"

She'd scarcely believed it when the old men had whispered of it in line that morning. It was one thing when the army confiscated machines that could be used for weapons or other war-related operations. That was, at least, recognized as a valid move of an occupying force by the international community.

But these were just regular factories. And they weren't being pressed into use here or shut down to stop the production of items that could harm the German army. They were being torn apart, the pieces shipped away.

As if Germany were saying that when this was over, they had no intention of letting Belgium regain its footing. Of doing honest work again. Of *being*.

Gottlieb's swallow was visible. "It is."

No explanation. No apology.

Margot curled a stone into her palm. "And I suppose you do not question it. Because the German war machine makes no mistakes. Which means you *want* to destroy Belgium."

"Margot." He had no right to say her name on a sigh like that, as if he were a brother or a father or a friend. He had no right at all. "Do you really think I want to destroy your country? Me, Wolfgang Gottlieb? Do you look at me and think that my goal? Have I ever once acted in a way to indicate this?"

"You have never acted in a way that said you oppose such things. And not to act is to be complicit."

"War is a complicated business, *fräulein*. It involves more than you can understand."

Of course he would play the *you're a child* card. It was what adults always resorted to when they had no logic to defend their beliefs. "This is not that complicated," she said. "You saw what you wanted and you took it—and spat in the face of Belgium while doing so, out of revenge for having had a stronger economy than Germany until the invasion."

"*I* didn't."

"You are one of them! A generalleutnant!"

"*Margot!* That is quite enough." Maman, who at least had the right to chide her. Even if she wasn't right. It was far from enough.

But Gottlieb sighed. "We do not all agree with every decision. But we obey, because it is how we function. It must be enough for you, little sparrow, to know that I speak reason when I can. And that I will not let anyone hurt your family."

How was that supposed to be enough? She sucked in a breath. "It's your move."

"I know it is. I don't know what move to make."

Maman shifted in her seat, all but shouting her anxiety. "Perhaps you should rest this evening, Generalleutnant. You can play more tomorrow."

"No. I will gather my focus."

Silence grew as he did, seeming to expand with every second until it filled the room like a cloud. Long minutes later, he drew in a deep breath, let it out, and made a reasonable move.

Margot loosed a relieved breath of her own. "Better."

His brief smile still wasn't right though. "You will be hearing more news you will not like if you continue to go out. No doubt you have all heard already that anyone aiding a young man of military age in exiting Belgium will be arrested, correct?"

"Of course." Madame Dumont answered for them all, her tremulous voice iced over with disdain for the policy.

Gottlieb sighed. "It will get worse. A new command has been issued—anyone who has *information* on such a young man and fails to deliver it will be arrested as well. So if, perhaps, you have a son trying to escape Belgium and you do nothing to help but nothing to stop him . . ."

Maman's needles stilled. "And how will the army determine if a family knows such things?"

Gottlieb's lips thinned. "That is the question, of course. Because how could a family not have any information?"

So then anyone could be arrested on that suspicion. *Anyone.*

Them. If anyone knew who they were, anyway. Because Lukas was of military age, and though he hadn't fled to join the resistance or fight against Germany with weapons, he would be resisting them somehow. And so named an enemy.

Even though they had no idea where he was or what he was doing, they could be held accountable for his absence. Arrested.

Madame Dumont was again the first to reply. "How fortunate that you have no son, my dear."

Don't flinch, Margot willed her mother's way. *Don't blink out of turn. Don't drop your needles.*

Maman sighed. "Who would ever have thought that could be a blessing?"

Margot set her white stone in the spot she'd chosen two seconds after Gottlieb had made his move.

He pushed away from the table. "Perhaps you are right, Fräu Dumont. Perhaps I had better rest tonight. We will continue tomorrow, Margot?"

He was out of the room before she could agree. She turned wide eyes on her mother. "What was that?"

Maman shook her head, gaze still on the empty door. "I don't know. Perhaps . . . perhaps the Lord is working on his conscience. Perhaps he feels the burden of what his men are doing."

The madame snorted. "Or perhaps he ate too much sausage for lunch. That always sends *me* running from a room."

Margot had no idea how good laughter could feel when the proportion of fear had been so high. But now she did, and she owed the old lady for the lesson.

NINETEEN

Lukas clutched his bag in his hand and followed the line of people in front of him off the train, back into the brisk October air colored with dusk. Once on solid ground, he moved out of the way and then waited, eyes scanning the crowds. There would be a horse-drawn omnibus from the Belle Vue—one met every train. But that wasn't what his eyes sought.

He had no reason to think she'd be here—he'd sent a wire, yes, telling her what train he would be on. But he'd not asked her to meet him. She wouldn't have, had he done so.

Barclay stopped beside him. "She's going to be so cross. Can't wait to see it. Is she here, do you think?"

"I doubt it." But his gaze snagged on movement at the back of the crowd. He couldn't make out hair color, just a hat. And the woman's height. And a hint of the way she moved as she navigated through the crush of people. "Or perhaps so."

Barclay chuckled. "Perfect."

They'd hatched this plan somewhere around midnight the night before, in the middle of their second card game and with a pot of properly strong coffee made and drained—and keeping them awake. At the time, it had seemed perfectly reasonable—

262

good, even—for Barclay to come back to Wales with him for a quick visit with his cousin.

At the moment he wasn't sure *why* it had sounded like such a wonderful idea. Oh, it had made the train ride pass more quickly, to have someone with whom he could talk. But did he really want Willa's overprotective cousin looking over his shoulder as he attempted to win her?

Barclay had claimed he would stay only a night or two. But Lukas had his doubts on that one.

Ah, well. At least he liked the man.

She stepped into a clear spot, all business as she looked around for *him*. He ought to move forward, but instead he held his spot a while longer, just watching her. The way she never hesitated, even though she couldn't know exactly where he was. The way she looked over the crowd as if categorizing and filing away every bit of information about every last passenger or friend greeting them.

The way her eyes lit when she spotted him and the corners of her mouth bloomed into the beginnings of a smile.

The way that smile froze and the light flashed fury when she spotted Barclay at his side.

"Here we go." Barclay rubbed his hands together, grinning.

She'd smiled for him. Or started to. That was something to cherish. She'd actually come to meet his train, and she'd been happy to see him. Another decade or two and she might admit to some affection for him.

They met her midway, her simmering gaze locked on her cousin. "What are you doing here?" were the first words from her mouth. "I left London to get away from you."

Perhaps the words would have been more believable if she hadn't leaned in to give Barclay a quick, fierce embrace and smack a kiss onto his cheek.

The man's grin didn't flag. "I missed you too."

She shook her head and turned to Lukas.

The air between them felt heavy with their kiss of two nights before. Charged with his promise of staying. With her doubt that he would. Were they alone, without Barclay and the scads of people about, he would draw her close again. Taste her lips. Discover whether today she would bristle against or melt into him.

She held out her hand, wrist limp. He took it and raised it to let a kiss linger too long on her gloved knuckles.

Barclay cleared his throat with a loud *ahem* and put himself between them, slinging an arm around Willa's shoulders. "Lead the way, Will. Oh, the girls send their love."

Lukas could only see her face because she'd turned it to glare up at her cousin. "The Davieses sent me in their car. But where exactly do you think you're going to stay? I'm not going to impose upon them for you, and anyway, I don't think they have any extra—"

"Oh, I'll find a room somewhere. I imagine there's a hotel or two in this town, isn't there?"

She blinked.

Lukas cleared his throat—without any exaggerated noises. "If you cannot find a room, Barclay, you can always take the sofa in mine. I have a suite."

"There, see? Lukas to the rescue."

Willa rolled her eyes and leaned past her cousin to look at Lukas. "How did your trip go? Did you find your friend?"

"I did." His fingers tightened around the handle of his bag. "He did not have solid news of them, but he promised to help me discover whatever he could."

Her eyes sent a mixture of messages—gladness that he'd found him at all, regret that he had no more to offer. Hope that something would yet come of it.

He wished he knew her well enough to tell her more. Wished they'd known each other for years, that she were helping him in this from the start. That she were as comfortable with him as she was with this cousin of hers who could drape an arm around her. Who she could shrug off without any thought that it might hurt his feelings.

She stepped around Barclay, in front of Lukas, and took up position on his opposite side. Her hand found its usual spot against his arm, warming a cold place in the center of his chest. "Is there nothing else we can do now?"

We. Would she really help if he asked? Not that he knew what he'd ask of her. "We can pray. Just now, I think God alone can help us. I will trust that He will aid me in getting word to them, and them back to me."

Barclay hung back half a step, crossed behind, and fell in on Willa's other side. They were turning into a regular ballet. He leaned close to Willa, though he didn't bother pitching his voice down. "He sounds like Peter. You realize the irony of that, I trust, Little Miss I-Don't-Believe-in-God."

Her fingers pressed into Lukas's arm. "He didn't sound like this when I met him. And it doesn't matter if he does now, as I have no intention of running off and marrying him."

"Ouch." Barclay scowled, looking honestly miffed. On Lukas's behalf or over something else? "You could at least soften the blow, Will. This bloke actually *likes* you for some unfathomable reason."

"It'll pass." Her words were heartbreak wrapped in certainty.

Lukas's throat was too tight to allow for more than a murmur. "It will not."

"I'm hungry. Anybody else hungry?" Barclay increased his stride, cutting a swath through the crowd until he emerged onto the street.

Willa held Lukas back with that hand on his arm and looked up at him with those wide blue eyes. "I'm sorry—about Barclay. He can be an oaf."

A chuckle tickled its way out. "He just wants to protect you—I understand this. And I like him. We talked for hours last night about novels."

"Of course you did. Did he mention that Rosie just married—"

"Hollow, yes, who is really named Peter. He showed me his new collection of autographed Branok Hollow novels and told me that if you do not give me the boot by Christmas, I should spend it in Cornwall with your family."

She came to a halt and stared up at him, mouth agape. "He did *what*?"

He had begun to think nothing could ever surprise Willa Forsythe—but apparently her cousin could manage it. "Do not look so excited at the prospect, *mon amour*, you will turn my head."

"It just . . . It isn't like him. That's all."

"Should I take that as a compliment?"

Rather than answer, she sighed and looked ahead to where Barclay stood at the edge of the street, gazing across it with the kind of single-minded determination that he suddenly suspected was a family trait.

Lukas followed the direction of his new friend's gaze, but he saw nothing of particular interest across the street. A family of four hurrying into a carriage, two women standing in deep conversation, a man in a rusty-brown jacket on a bench, reading a newspaper in the dying light, and another fellow in grey with a cap pulled low against the wind, waiting for a break in traffic so he could cross.

Perhaps one of the women had caught Barclay's eye. Who could say?

Willa tugged him forward, her lips as thin as her hope. "Come on, then. We'll grab a bite on our way to your hotel."

Lukas sent one more gaze over the collection of people Barclay studied. And followed with a shrug toward the Davieses' car.

"Are you out of your mind?" Willa hissed the words under her breath—or would have hissed them had the words had any hissable S sounds. She glanced over her shoulder out of habit, though Lukas was safely up in his rooms, talking to Jules. She and Barclay were supposedly out in search of a room of his own for Barclay. Though they both knew he had no intention of spending the quid on one.

Barclay chuckled and led the way down the street as if he knew the place as well as she did. "I thought you would appreciate the chance to exchange information in person, without having to talk about dogs over the telephone."

"That's not what I mean." She caught the sleeve of the wool coat she'd helped make for him and drew him toward where she'd spoken to Mr. Brown. "You weren't supposed to introduce yourself to him at all. You *certainly* weren't supposed to invite him to stay with you at Peter and Rosie's last night. And you *especially* weren't supposed to invite him to holiday with us in Cornwall at Christmas!"

"Oh come on, Will, have a heart. The bloke doesn't know if his family's alive or dead or prisoners—he could use a little kindness."

The fact that she agreed didn't stop her from bristling. "I daresay there are thousands of Belgians who can claim the same. Should we invite them *all* to Cornwall? I think that might stretch even Peter's generosity to the breaking point."

"You know what your problem is with him?" Mouth in that annoying smirk of his, Barclay leaned close. "You actually like him. And it terrifies you."

"I do not. And it does not. Or wouldn't, rather, if I did. Which I don't."

Barclay rolled his eyes and strode out of the circle of light cast by the streetlamps, to the very bench where the German had been. "At some point, Willa-Will, you'll realize that you're letting them win by not letting anyone close. You're being nothing but what they made you—an abandoned child."

How dare he—he, who knew better than anyone what it felt like to be a scared child on a mean street? She stood in front of him, too mad to sit at his side. "I let *you* in, didn't I? And Pauly and Rosie. And the others, all of them. I *love* our family." It wasn't just a word, a lie, with them. They were all the same, floundering on the same sea.

"There's no risk in loving us, though, is there? We're safe."

A strange thing to say about a horde of thieves. But he had a point. Not that she'd admit it to him. "Look, maybe someday, someone will be worth that risk. But not Lukas De Wilde. Never him." He was a mark. And he was a gentleman. And he was a playboy. All the things she had no respect for, that she hadn't even had to swear to herself she would never get involved with, because it was too unthinkable to even need such a promise.

And really, what did she need with a man anyway? She had her family. Children aplenty who crawled up in her lap and snuggled against her. Perhaps they didn't call her *Mumma*, but that didn't mean she didn't love them like a mother should.

"Willa." It wasn't a chiding. It was a warning, delivered low and taut and half a second too late.

Something hard and cold and round pressed against the nape of her neck. The scent of pine drifted to her nose. Willa sucked in a breath but forced it back out. "Hello again."

Barclay had taken to his feet and narrowed his eyes, obviously trying to make out the figure in the mounting darkness. "Let me guess—Fido."

Mr. Brown pushed her closer to Barclay with the pressure on her neck. A gun, it must be. He was holding a *gun* to her *head*.

She missed London's thugs. They never acted this way. With her, anyway.

"I require an update, Miss Forsythe." He shoved her onto the bench and must have motioned Barclay to sit again too, since he sank down beside her. Just enough light reached them to glint off the metal of the pistol he held tucked against his side, where passersby weren't likely to notice it. "And an explanation of why your colleague has arrived with De Wilde after visiting a newspaper office in London. What are you about? I trust you do not mean to double-cross me?"

"If you trust so, you don't need *that*." Willa nodded toward the weapon. "Put it away, if you please. We're civilized enough to have a conversation without the need for threats."

Brown put the weapon into the pocket of his coat but didn't draw his hand out again. No doubt it was still pointed at them. "There. Now. An explanation, Mr. Pearce, as to why the leader of London's best gang of thieves is here in Aberystwyth."

Willa looked to Barclay, wondering if he felt the same nausea in the pit of his stomach that she did.

"You flatter me, sir." He leaned back against the bench and folded his arms across his chest. Half insolence. Half ease. "What is there to explain? Willa knew he was going there and let me know so I could shadow him. I decided I'd go the overt route and introduce myself, invite him home. Search his things at my leisure while Willa took care of business here."

Brown's face was nothing but shadows, wrought by hat and night. "So which of you has it?"

Willa swallowed, hoping Barclay would have some convenient lie to feed him. Perhaps he was hoping the same, because he said nothing.

Blast. Blighted spies—he must have cohorts in London. Did Mr. V know that? She cleared her throat. "I verified that it wasn't in his room."

Barclay shook his head. "The only items in his bag were the clothing he was wearing today and the sheet music for the concert coming up. He mentioned it later, that he was memorizing it." Her brother turned to her, brows drawn. "How can he memorize the music without his violin?"

"He is a professional, Barclay. He knows how he'll play each note without having to demonstrate it for himself."

"I don't see how."

"Enough." Brown edged closer. "The newspaper office. A Belgian resistance rag—why was he there?"

"Bloke who runs it knew his father. He thought maybe he'd had news of his family." Barclay shrugged. "Apparently he didn't."

The wind whistled through the silence. Brown stepped backward again. "You had better not be lying to me. Either of you. If you try to slip out of Wales with Mr. Pearce without giving me what I have asked for, Miss Forsythe, one of you will end up dead. Do you understand?"

She folded her arms too. "I liked you better before, when you spoke of the reward instead of the punishment."

"Deliver the goods, and you will have the reward. Do not, and perhaps I'll see if that Belgian thief scurrying about on De Wilde's errands would like a shot at this job instead—once *you* are out of the way."

A few choice words sprang to her tongue, but she bit them back. At least until the man had dissolved back into the darkness. Then she muttered a few.

Barclay tugged her up. "How about somewhere without ears?"

"The Davieses'. They were dining with friends tonight, so the house ought to be empty still."

Theirs was a family that knew the value of holding one's tongue about important things in public, so they said little on their brisk walk—they'd dismissed the chauffeur as soon as they reached the Belle Vue so that he could ferry the sisters to their engagement. Barclay filled her in on the goings-on of the family, the latest update from Rosie with all the little ones, how Pauly had tried a new recipe for his meat pies and almost started a riot.

On a normal day, the tales would have made her laugh. But with the feel of that gun to her neck still lingering, she had a hard time doing so. Once the house came into view, she hurried even more, using the key they'd lent her to open the door. The servants would have the evening off, since they were all supposed to be out.

She led Barclay into the cold parlor and slid the door shut. The lights she could turn on with a twist of the knob, but they'd have to lay a fire if they wanted heat.

Barclay just shoved his hands into his pockets. "That wasn't all that was in his bag."

Willa had no trouble backing up her thoughts to his answer to Brown's question. "What else?"

"A sheet of paper with a few paragraphs on it. Retta copied it." He pulled a folded sheet from his inside pocket and handed it over.

It was in French. Of course. "Very helpful, Barclay."

"She copied it again and is taking it to V. Or probably already has, today. Maybe it'll tell him something."

Willa sank onto the couch. It creaked and groaned and protested and filled her head with dreadful silence. She rubbed at her temples. "So basically, you accomplished more within five minutes than I have my whole time here."

"Now, don't be stupid, Will. If that was some sort of message he was sending through that newspaper, he wouldn't have *had* it when he was here, right? And we certainly wouldn't have known to look for it without your instruction." He sat beside her and bumped his shoulder into hers. "Besides, it wasn't the key. Maybe a message coded with it, but not the key. So how could it do them any good?"

She blustered out a breath and handed the sheet of paper back. Leaned over to rest her head on his shoulder. "I don't know what to do about Mr. Brown. Or Fido. Or whatever we want to call him."

"We'll let V handle him. He expects me to go back to London soon anyway—I'll get word to him." He reached up to pat the side of her head. "Just stay safe, Willa. I'd never forgive myself if something happened to you."

"Nothing's going to happen to me."

"You can't know that, can you? With Fido and Cor Akkerman and . . ." He shook his head.

She lifted hers. "He's planning something—Cor. Wouldn't say what, but I have a bad feeling."

"I'm sure. But you're right—you'll be fine, like always. Whatever he has up his sleeve, you'll handle it. *We* will." He tugged on a piece of hair that had slipped out of her chignon as usual. "I'll go back to London tomorrow. Catch up with the girls and with V. But I can come back to tell you anything we've learned. I wouldn't trust that information over the telephone lines."

It was awfully expensive to keep going back and forth—though if those paragraphs they'd copied were at all useful, Mr. V would probably be willing to pay for the tickets, like he had over the summer when he wanted Willa to go to Cornwall to check on Rosie.

There were benefits to a patron with deep pockets. Of course, there were also drawbacks. Who carried guns.

"I've some film I'll send with you—I don't know that there's anything helpful on it, but there could be. V can get it developed, I assume."

"I assume. You can fetch it in a moment."

Another beat of silence descended. Another sigh gathered in Willa's chest. "I'm glad you came, Barclay. Even if you *are* a pain."

He chuckled and pushed himself up. "You know . . . he's serious. Lukas. About you."

Willa shook her head and let her gaze rest on the sleeping fireplace. "He won't be, if he ever realizes who I am."

"People can surprise us, sometimes. Just look at Peter." Barclay ambled over to the window and looked out at the street. "He appreciates you—Lukas does. Your talent. Your soul. He called you miraculous."

"He's an idiot."

"No. He's not." He spun on his heel and squared his shoulders.

"I'd better get back to his hotel and claim that sofa. Get to know my future brother-in-law. Or cousin-in-law, as he thinks we'll be."

"*You're* an idiot."

"Am I? Way I see it, Will, you have a pretty nice score dangling before your nose, and you're snubbing it."

Her skin went prickly all over, pushing her to her feet. "You think I would *marry* him just because he has money?"

"Why not?" The gleam in his eyes bespoke a jest. Sort of. "It's the ultimate job, really. Ongoing. And you'd get everything you want out of the bargain—food, clothing, shelter, music. A man whose poster you've had on your wall for the past five years. A family."

"No."

He met her stubbornness with raised brows and folded arms. "Because you're afraid he'd hurt you?"

"Because . . . I'd hurt him." She wouldn't be able to help it. The doubts would eat her up from the inside out. And it wasn't like she had a warm and cuddly personality to begin with, so if it went colder and pricklier . . .

Barclay's breath slid out, slow and loud. "You've been thinking about it. I don't know if that makes me happy or terrified. Look." He lowered his arms. "When this job is done, just . . . stick around him for a while, maybe. Give it a chance. Don't rush into anything. I don't think I could survive it if another sister got married without telling me. But give it some thought. Make sure you don't want it before you throw it out with the rubbish. All right?"

There was nothing to think about. But he wouldn't let it go until she agreed. "All right."

"Good."

She spun away, ready for a break from his gaze. "I'll get that film for you." It was a quick trip up to her room and only took her a minute of fumbling to remember how to get the film out of the camera and put it in its protective canister. Not nearly long enough to make the words stop echoing in her head.

Barclay was waiting in the hall when she came back down, and he took the canister she held out, slipped it into his pocket.

Then he stepped close, pressed a kiss to her forehead, and turned for the door. "Pauly said to tell you the pub's too quiet without you, and he's waxing the stage for when you get home."

Weak as it felt, she smiled. "Tell him I miss him. And the girls."

"I will. Don't be too hard on yourself."

Impossible advice. She didn't know what to do but ignore it.

TWENTY

L ukas set down his fork when the entryway door was thrown open with enough force to bang against the wall. He'd been in the middle of telling the Davieses and Willa an anecdote about Margot when she was three—and already too smart for her own good—but the words dried up in his mouth. He couldn't see through the walls to know who was gusting inside the Davieses' house along with the wind, but he could hear panic in the fast, heavy steps.

A man burst into the dining room, the pale-faced butler a few steps behind but not attempting any excuse for the interruption. He must have recognized, as Lukas did, the orchestra's program director.

The roast that had tasted like perfection a minute ago churned in his stomach now. He darted a glance down the table. Willa's brows were knit—perhaps she hadn't met Mr. Rees. Gwen and Daisy Davies had both risen to their feet.

"Mr. Rees. What is it? Please, sit down." Daisy motioned to a chair.

Rees didn't sit. Instead, he set on the table a metal box with a clasp. "It is gone. I brought it home today after our return, as

275

usual. Counted it out, sealed it in my safe with what we have earned for the fund before. But it is *gone*."

The women drew in a collective breath. No one had to ask what *it* was. Rees had gone with the orchestra to Cardiff for the weekend, just returning that morning. He would have been the one with the concert's ticket money and donations in hand.

Gwen pressed her fingers to her lips. "How did you realize?"

Rees winced. "When I returned from a visit with my sister, I noticed my study door ajar. I went in and . . . the portrait over the safe was off the wall. The safe door open. They took everything, everything I had in there, though none of it matters as this does. I have failed you, Miss Davies. Failed them all."

"Now." Though her hand shook, Daisy placed it on Mr. Rees's arm. "It is not your fault. You did as much as any of us would have done—you are not the one responsible for the theft."

Lukas sealed his lips. Part of him wanted to scream that *he* would have put the money in a bank—the money from the concerts here, at least, even if he wouldn't have been able to deposit that which they had just earned.

But then, banks didn't guarantee anything either, did they? Especially in times of war. Lukas had plenty of money in a bank, and it might as well have been stolen too.

"Sit," Gwen urged, going so far as to pull out a chair for him. She motioned to one of the maids who stood against the wall. "A cup of tea for Mr. Rees, please. Quickly."

"Tea." Rees sank into his chair, swiping his hat off his head but then clutching it rather than handing it over. "Tea will not set this to rights. It was everything, Miss Davies. Everything the orchestra has brought in for the three concerts given, the donations that have come in for the relief fund. Over three thousand pounds, *gone*."

Lukas's gaze found Willa's and knit with it. Three thousand pounds would buy a lot of bread. And given that the British government *still* had not given that American ship permission to leave port with the aid for his country, they would need that bread. Soon.

"We will recover it." Her words may have sounded decisive, but Daisy's voice shook. Hands clasped, she turned to the butler. "Ring the police straightaway, Mr. Morgan, if you will. Or have you already, Mr. Rees?"

"I did, yes, of course. They were dispatching men to my home— my wife is there to welcome them and show them what we discovered. I let them know I was coming here. No doubt they'll be soon behind me."

"Then we will trust the law. They will find the thief, and they will find the money. Whoever did it could not possibly have spent it already. It is still there."

Willa dabbed her mouth with her napkin and set it aside. Lukas didn't know how to classify the expression she wore. A bit distressed, a bit confused, a bit worried . . . But then the more he looked, the more he thought all those things but an illusion. Underneath was a strange blankness. Or perhaps that calculation he had noticed that first day. She was filing it all away, a step removed.

She stood. "Lukas and I will get out of your way. Though do let us know, of course, if we can be of any help."

"Oh." Rees jerked up, his gaze flying to their end of the table for the first time. "My apologies! Miss Forsythe, Mr. De Wilde, I scarcely noticed you there."

"Quite understandable, sir." Willa offered a tight smile. "I am so sorry to hear this has happened."

"Don't go too far, Willa." Daisy smoothed her skirt, though it had no wrinkles. "The police will likely want to speak to all of us who have an association with the orchestra. Perhaps you noticed something at one of the concerts that we did not. Someone suspicious."

An excellent point. If anyone in the crowd had noted anything not as it should have been, it would be Willa. Lukas saw nothing beyond the glaring stage lights and the usual backstage clamor before and after.

She dipped her head. "I will try to remember anything that could be helpful." Then she caught Lukas's eye. "The parlor? It will give them some privacy to discuss this."

Gwen's eyes lit. "Perhaps, Willa, your . . . benefactor . . . could be of help. Are you in touch with him regularly?"

Benefactor? Lukas pushed to his feet. Of course—the scholarship for her schooling could have come from a private benefactor. He must be someone well connected.

"Not recently. But I can get in touch with him, of course, if the police cannot resolve this for you quickly."

"Thank you." Gwen looked near tears and averted her face to sniff and blink. She rubbed at one hand with the other.

Lukas rounded the table, barely keeping up with Willa as she dashed out the door. He trailed her into the parlor, where she halted beside the fire. And went still. So still she could have been a Grecian statue.

He eased up behind her and rested his hands on her arms, bared by the fashionable cut of her evening dress. In the week since Barclay had left, he'd convinced her to take tea with him twice. They'd had her lessons.

She didn't jerk away or even jump at his touch now. She was getting used to him. But was obviously upset. Why else would she close off like this? Knowing he pressed his luck, he dipped his head to press a kiss to her cheek. "They will find the culprit. He cannot have gone far."

Stiff, not just still. Like a Grecian statue. "He stole *cash*, Lukas. The easiest thing in the world to take and hide and use without anyone knowing where you got it. He won't get caught. Not for that. Their only hope is that something else in that safe is more notable—unique. And that he tries to fence it, and they can catch him then."

She said it in a way that indicated she *knew*. "Have you been through this before? Had someone steal from you?"

"No." Hard and cold and forbidding, that word. "But I've seen it. I know how it works."

It wasn't fear that kept her so stiff. He ran his hands down her arms, over the satin of her elbow-high gloves, until he could clasp her fingers in his. They were tense, but they curled around him and held tight. No, it wasn't fear. It was . . . something more sizzling. "You are angry."

"Well, of *course* I'm angry." She turned her head, just enough that he could see her blazing eyes. "This isn't money they were raising to pad their own pockets—it was all going to feed starving children!"

"I know." Children like Margot and Claudette and . . . no, not them, they were better off than so many, even with their homes destroyed. But the communes. The cities. They were swarming with families who lived from one payday to the next. And with all the factories shut down, the rail lines halted, normal industry at a standstill, they would have nothing left with which to purchase food. Even if there was food aplenty to purchase. Given the shortage, prices had probably soared.

It was his contribution, all of theirs in the orchestra—their way of resisting, supporting their home. And they had *all* been robbed of it.

He squeezed her fingers and rested his head against hers. "I will never understand why people do things like this. Hurt others for their own gain."

She pulled away, broke her fingers from his. "I can understand when it is the starving child stealing to eat, or a parent to feed them. But taking *from* them—no." Her face granite, she spun to face him. "Everyone in Wales knows every cent brought in by the orchestra is going to the relief fund. There's no excuse."

The front door's bell buzzed. The police, no doubt. Willa's eyes flickered, the fire in them banked, and she shrugged out of her anger like she would a cloak. In its place was the mix of masking emotions from before, all jumbled together.

But she'd let him see, just for a moment. She'd let him see her *real* reaction.

Before the butler could walk by to open the door, Lukas leaned down to kiss her. This woman really was all he could ever want. And maybe, maybe he actually stood a chance of convincing her of it.

———◇———

Willa let her bedroom door slam shut, knowing well that no one downstairs would even notice. The house was swarming with investigators and detectives and uniformed bobbies, with orchestra personnel and musicians and even stagehands. If another person came through the front door, the whole house might explode from the crush of bodies.

She'd had her fill. More than. It had taken everything she had and then some to answer all the questions of the police as if she were just another upstanding citizen and not someone they would be more than happy to slap cuffs onto, in another situation. Never mind she hadn't been the one to commit this particular theft.

She was still a thief.

She turned on the light. And jumped when she spotted the figure lounging on her canopied bed. He had his dirty boots propped up on the Davieses' pristine yellow counterpane, a satisfied smirk on his face—and her violin, which she'd left out on the mattress when she'd gone down for supper, in his grubby paws.

"Cor Akkerman! You have some nerve showing up here now." She marched to the bed and reached for the instrument.

He held it away from her, far enough that if she tried to reach for it, she'd end up sprawled over him. Not a position she fancied.

No matter. He'd put it down eventually. And she had bigger

things to deal with just now, so she settled for leveling a finger at his chest. "Where did you put it?"

He didn't wear innocence well. It sat on his face like a joke. "Put *what*, pretty Willa?"

"The money from the orchestra, for the relief fund. I know you have it. What did you do with it?"

She had known the moment Mr. Rees came bursting in and told them what had happened. Never for a moment had a question entered her mind, and seeing his eyes go wide certainly didn't convince her to doubt it now.

"My friend. You are certainly not accusing *me* of such a theft? Why, I am but a novice at our mutual craft. With not even a decent set of picks."

She hissed out a breath. "You're not amusing."

"All right, all right." He sprang up on the far side of the bed and produced a black bag from somewhere on the floor. Tossed it onto the mattress.

She stared at it. At the way the fabric molded to what were obviously stacks of something rectangular within. Pound notes, she would bet. But then . . . "What are you doing with it *here*?"

All pretense of playfulness fell away. Her violin still in one hand, he leaned against the wall. "My . . . entrance fee, let us call it. Into your gang."

Words buzzed around her head like out-of-tune strings, but it took her a long moment to sort through the fury enough to grasp hold of them. "I do not have a *gang*. I have a *family*."

He snorted. "You do not share a drop of blood with any of those people, and I will not believe you do."

"You don't need blood to be a family."

His gaze went patronizing. "Yes. You do. But whatever you call it." He motioned to the bag. "I want in. That should be enough to prove myself, *ja*? Three thousand two hundred pounds. My donation to the . . . *family*."

She didn't even look at it again. Couldn't, or it might make her ill. "We don't want that money."

He pushed off the wall, fingers tight around the neck of the violin. "I beg your pardon? Perhaps my English is worse than I thought. I thought, for a moment there, you said you did not *want* money."

"Not *that* money. And the fact that you think we would just proves that you are not—could never be—one of us."

He growled. Or huffed. Or some combination of the two that made a chill skitter over the back of her neck where the German's pistol had rested. He advanced to the foot of the bed. "You will pretend you are better than me, is that it? You are a thief, Willa Forsythe, as I am."

"I am a thief. But I have a code. I do not *ever* take from those worse off than I am. I don't take food from children's mouths—and that's what this money is for." She pulled off her gloves and tossed them onto the dressing table. "What kind of monster are you, to even consider such a thing? You're stealing from your own neighbors."

He regarded her with pure resentful incredulity. "And now you will try to tell me you have never stolen from another Englishman?"

"Not starving ones! And it's different now. We're at war—there's a greater enemy. You of all people—a *refugee*—should know that."

Cor snorted. Or perhaps laughed. Either way, it was an ugly sound. "You will refuse me—refuse thousands of pounds—for some stupid code? While you are here trying to steal from your boyfriend? And yet will lecture *me* on right and wrong?"

She pointed to the window, where he must have come in. "Get out of my room. Out of my life. I never want to see you again, and you'd be wise to respect that."

Jaw set, he shrugged—and reached for the bag.

She lunged and snatched it up half a wink before he grabbed it. "Oh no. This is going back where it came from."

"Give me the money, Willa." No charm remained in his tone now—it was all danger and darkness and warning. "I took it. It is mine."

"You called it your entrance fee? I call it the only thing that will stop me from having the police on your tail within ten seconds. Get out now, or I call them up here."

Fury crouched low and menacing on his shoulders. "You turn me in, I take you down with me. I will tell your darling De Wilde who—*what*—you really are."

"So then. We go down together, or we go our separate ways." She gestured to the window with a flourish. "Go."

His only warning was a low sound in his throat, somewhere between a cello and a bass. Then in the next second the world exploded. Or her heart.

He'd brought his arm back with force she couldn't have expected. And smashed her violin—her *violin!*—into the corner of the armoire. It cracked, splintered, wept. Fell to the floor. The sound of its cry rang in her ears.

He pointed at her, but she didn't see it. Not really. Her eyes were locked on the ruins of her soul.

"You will regret this, Willa Forsythe. Mark my words." He ducked through the window, left the room empty.

Empty. Her knees buckled and then smacked the floor. Something balled up in her throat, punched. Money bag abandoned, she crawled through the lamplight to that puddle of dreams on the floor. Something poked at her palms. She gathered the pieces, fingers convulsing. Broken wood held together by lax strings. Agony.

Something hot and wet scalded her cheeks.

She couldn't breathe. Didn't know if she would ever be able to again, much as she gasped. The jagged edges of wood pierced her hands, her heart.

There was no repairing it. Had it just been the neck that had snapped—but it wasn't just that. The back of the body had shattered, making a gaping hole that exposed the hollow meant to be there. And it wept and it keened and it screamed *Why?* into the room.

Or perhaps *she* did. It had been so long since she'd cried that she realized only gradually that she was. That the salty sting was from her tears, that the heaving was her own chest, that the gasps were from the sobs ripping her apart.

"Willa?" Her name joined a knock.

She couldn't answer. Wasn't entirely sure she heard it.

"Willa?" The door cracked open, then a gasp preceded rushed steps. "You're bleeding! What happened? Oh—your violin. Willa, your *violin.*"

Gwen. Willa squeezed her eyes shut. "He . . ." She could get out nothing more. What did words matter? They were just lies anyway.

Only music ever told the truth. And he'd destroyed it. Destroyed the one thing in the world that had made her more than just a street rat.

Gwen pried the broken wood from her hands and plucked a long, thick splinter from one of the bleeding places. "Sit up. On the bed. I'll go and fetch the bandages. Who did this, Willa?"

Cor Akkerman. She would hate that name forever. But couldn't speak it now. She shook her head, even as Gwen somehow convinced her legs to hold her until she reached the mattress. "No one who matters. But he . . ." She nodded, hollow, empty, to the black bag behind the door. "I'm sorry. I didn't take it—but he followed me here. It was my fault he did."

Only the little breath that slipped from Gwen's lips said she saw and grasped what the bag must hold. Otherwise she made no move toward it. Just muttered something about bandages and vanished into the hall. Returned before she seemed even to have cleared the doorway, with bandages and a small brown bottle in hand.

"Iodine tincture," she said as she set it on the bedside table. "After we get you cleaned up. What did you do, stab yourself with it?"

Willa stared at her hands. They were empty but for the streaks of red. No magic violin, ready to come to life in them. "I don't know. I . . ."

"Never mind. We'll get you right as rain in no time." She dabbed at the wounds with a wet cloth. Applied a smelly brown liquid to them from that little glass bottle. Wrapped them in crisp white bandages. "There now. All better."

"Thank you." But it would never be all better. *Never*. She wasn't even sure what the phrase was supposed to mean. "I didn't open the bag. You should. Make sure it's all there. Three thousand two hundred, he said. But I didn't count it. Didn't even look."

Gwen's warm hand touched her cheek. Did it hurt her fingers to do so? "Thank you, Willa. But it's just money. We could have replaced what was stolen. You can never replace your first violin, and if this happened because of it . . ."

It happened because she lived in a world with ugly people who did ugly things. She'd never get away from that. Should never have expected otherwise.

She shook her head.

Gwen sighed and stood, gathered her bandages and bottle full of smelly stuff. Then reached down and scooped up the bag. She didn't look inside either. "I'll tell them I found it outside. That someone must have felt badly and brought it back. You should . . . rest, I suppose."

It wouldn't help. She'd still wake up in the morning to a broken violin.

She ought to have known it would happen eventually—after all, the instrument was so very much like her.

TWENTY-ONE

The sun, she was sure, had never shone so brightly, despite the fact that it produced the same number of lumens as it had the day before. Margot bent over into the square of it spilling through her window and laughed into the rug.

He was alive. She'd *known* it! Alive and in Wales and ready to bring them there too, as soon as he knew how to find them.

She wanted to shout it, to run and find her mother and squeal it into her ear. But Maman was in the bread line. Madame Dumont was at the church, praying. Claudette had scurried away as soon as she had delivered this fresh batch of papers and collected the old ones to pass along to another neighbor.

There was no one to rejoice with her. No one but the sunshine and the Lord who sent it. "Thank you, God. Thank you, thank you, thank you."

The rug ate up her words, but she knew He heard her. And imagined Him chuckling along with her half-mad laughter.

Lukas was alive. And coming for them.

Or would be. She sat up straight again, eyes following one of the dust motes that danced through the light. How long had it taken the papers to reach her? She spun back to where she'd

286

spread the newsprint out on her floor and flipped *L'Indépendance Belge* back to the front page. Two weeks old. Not as slow as she had feared—Lukas should still be where he had been when it was printed. He would not be too distressed yet over a lack of response.

"Oh." A response. How was she going to get one to him? When she'd devised this key, it had seemed so simple. Fun, even. A private code between them, meant partially to give her a means of communicating family business without Maman knowing.

Not that Maman had sunk as deep into despair as Margot had feared she might. There had been no need to summon Lukas covertly home.

But had she needed to, she simply would have gone to one of Papa's newspaper friends.

Now, though. They were all shut down. That was one of the first things the Germans had seen to. A few were still being produced in secret, yes—the stack on her floor was evidence of that. But in other countries, outside the border. Not in Brussels, so far as she could tell.

Still. Someone could help her. Someone *must*.

She went through the list of all of Papa's friends while she folded the newspapers again. There was Georges Béranger. But he was in Louvain. Or had been. Monsieur Émile had been here though, hadn't he? And Jacque Allard. She was all but certain he was the one putting out *L'Indépendance Belge* in London. She recognized his editorial hand.

Allard had run the paper here in Brussels with his brother. Jerome. Where was *he*?

She couldn't just go out looking for him. After sliding the papers into their temporary hiding place, she left her chamber, needing more room than it offered to pace. Only certain kinds of thinking required movement, but the logistics of finding missing persons was one of them. It wasn't just mathematics. It was geography and social skills and other factors she couldn't readily think of names for.

Maman could help when she got home. Margot would tell her about the key she had created and given to Lukas—without mentioning *why* she had made it. She and Papa had long spoken of creating such a thing just for the family, and he had so loved the idea he had even told all his friends about it. But they never had done so. Not until this one, and then he had died so suddenly afterward, Maman had never even known. There'd been no time to tell her.

But she would tell her now. She would write down careful instructions on what to give to one of Papa's editor friends, if she could work out how to find them.

Except Maman could not go wandering the city, especially not the parts of it where their old friends lived. She could too easily be recognized. And then someone would shout a greeting, word of it would reach German ears, and their ruse would be over.

Madame Dumont, perhaps? But the old woman had scarcely recovered from the grueling trek from Louvain. She never walked farther than the block to church for Mass.

Claudette. It would have to be Claudette. The next time she came over, Margot would have the message ready. Claudette was already taking a risk by running papers around the city—she would not blink at a bit more. And probably knew better than the rest of them how to find Monsieur Allard.

Her feet had taken her through the upstairs parlor and then down the stairs. She stood now in front of the thick front door, staring at it.

She wanted to go. She wouldn't, but she wanted to. She hadn't stepped foot outside the door since she came through it two months ago, other than for Mass and that one trip to the bread line last week. After which Maman had forbidden her to go, apparently convinced by Gottlieb's claim that it wasn't safe. They had reasoned at first that it was safer for her to go—she wouldn't be recognized as quickly as beautiful, memorable Maman.

But after that, her mother wouldn't hear of it.

A sigh built, released, and Margot turned.

She meant to turn all the way around, back to the stairs. But her feet halted her at ninety-two degrees, when her eyes caught sight of something unprecedented.

Gottlieb's room. Open. Usually he not only shut the door but locked it behind him. Today, however, he must have turned the lock without properly latching the door first. It had swung open just an inch, the bolt out so it couldn't shut all the way.

Interesting.

She shouldn't. She *knew* she shouldn't. Or at least, she knew Maman would *say* she shouldn't. But something pulled on her. Usually if she felt such a tug she would think it the Lord telling her something. Though she wasn't altogether certain the Lord would instruct her to search Gottlieb's room either—He often sided with Maman on things like this.

"God? May I?"

Lukas always rolled his eyes at her when she asked Him a question like that, saying the Almighty had better things to do than answer a too-inquisitive girl, and that she wouldn't know an answer from Him if she got one.

But she did. When He didn't want her to proceed, her mind always filled with an impossible, ugly proof that she'd been laboring for years to make work. When His answer was in the affirmative though . . .

Beautiful, elegant numbers ticked along now in her mind. The Pythagorean Theorem. The proof of infinite prime numbers. That the square root of two is irrational.

She stepped toward the door without another moment's hesitation and into the generalleutnant's sanctum.

She had expected shadows, despite the fact that his room was directly below hers and hence also facing the sunny street just now. Golden light touched all the surfaces.

Most of them were bare. Any decorations that had belonged to the Dumont house had been removed to other rooms, and he'd not replaced them with anything of his own. Not unexpected, she supposed, of a military man. Dress regalia peeked out from a small closet. A shaving kit resided on the bureau top. A book sprawled open on the bedside table. Otherwise, it might have been unoccupied.

Why did he even bother locking it?

And why had all those lovely theorems told her to come inside? Frowning, she spun in a slow circle in the middle of the room.

The bed. It was positioned in the same place hers was. She crouched down and looked underneath it.

A box. Similar in size to the one she kept in the exact same place. Margot stretched until her fingers closed around the card-paper edges and she could pull it out.

It was plain and brown and utilitarian, which she could appreciate. She lifted the lid. And sucked in a breath that hurt.

Maman stared up at her. Maman and Papa and . . . Lukas.

No.

She knew the clipping. They'd had one too, once, in Louvain. It had been an article about Lukas's career, and she'd read it so many times Papa had told her to stop before she ruined the paper.

This one hadn't the attached article. Just the photograph in grainy blacks and greys. And the caption under it. *Renowned violinist Lukas De Wilde, with his parents in Louvain.*

Her eyes slid shut.

He knew. He knew who they were. Had he known all along? No, she couldn't think so.

That day last week when he had been acting so odd. That must

290

have been when he'd learned it. Why hadn't he turned them in immediately? For what was he waiting?

Fire danced over her nerves. Itching. Aching. She put the photograph back in its place, slid the box back under the bed exactly three feet and four inches, turned it to a degree eighteen off parallel with the wall.

Then she fled the room. Back up to her own long enough to grab her coat, her scarf, her hat.

Out the door. She didn't care if it wasn't safe. If Maman would cluck her tongue and scold her. If anyone recognized her. She had to find Jerome Allard now. Today. They had no time to waste. Gottlieb could decide any day to turn them in. They would arrest Maman. Probably Margot too. Because of Lukas and because of Papa and because of *her* and the work she'd done.

It took all her restraint to keep herself from breaking into a run out on the sidewalk. It would look strange if she did, and attention was bad.

"*Spatz?* What are you doing out here? Does your mother know you have left the house?"

She wished she knew a few curses so she could think them. Reciting the nines tables didn't exactly express the frustration and fear that filled her at Gottlieb's voice.

She turned to face him. And realized with a start that it was October 29. Which meant . . . She sighed. "Don't tell her, you'll ruin the surprise."

Gottlieb frowned. Rather, he had been frowning already and didn't stop. "What surprise?"

She glanced over her shoulder, as if afraid Maman would turn the corner. "It is her birthday on Wednesday. I thought . . . I have no gift for her. But I found a coin." She had, the day she'd gone for bread. It was still in her pocket, though it would buy next to nothing these days. A ribbon, perhaps. In black and red and yellow, for Belgium. They couldn't fly the flag anymore, but people were wearing the colors anywhere they could.

The frown not only eased, it turned into a smile. "She has said nothing."

"Well, of course not. It is hardly a year to celebrate."

Gottlieb motioned her to turn around again and jogged to catch up. "One should always celebrate the life of those one cares about though. You are a good girl, Margot, to remember the day for her."

"You won't tell her, then?"

"Of course not. And I will do better than that—I will see you safely to the shops and back."

Nine, eighteen, twenty-seven, thirty-six . . . No, not sufficient at all. Perhaps the powers of three would do a better job.

"What would she like, do you think? A book? Poetry, perhaps? Or—I know. Chocolate. It has probably been months since she has had chocolate, *ja*? I know where we can get some."

Margot told her mouth not to water at the thought. "I only have one franc."

He sent her a strange look. Chiding but warm. Like Maman gave her. "Pick out what you like for your mother, *spatz*. I will make sure it is paid for."

She scowled. "Don't look at me like that."

"Like what?"

"Like . . . like you're a father indulging his daughter."

She hadn't meant to say it. And doubly wished she hadn't when he dragged in a long breath and held it for a full five seconds before letting it out.

"Forgive me, Margot. I do not mean to make you uncomfortable. But you do remind me a bit of my daughter, when she was your age. Only a bit, mind you—I never could convince her to play Go with me."

Her feet came to a halt and wouldn't be convinced to budge again.

He turned when he realized she'd stopped, blond brows arched. "What?"

"You have a *daughter*?"

The brows remained raised. "Why is this surprising? Do you think a man of my age has never married, has no family?"

"But . . ." But if he had a family of his own, why did he chase after Maman? Follow her with his eyes all the time? Why had he never mentioned them?

She had a few suspicions, though they were all in the category of things that Lukas insisted she had no business knowing about.

Given the darkening of Gottlieb's countenance, he may well have the same opinion of that knowledge. "I see. You think me . . . She is dead—my wife. Eight years ago. My daughter is grown and has moved to America with her husband. I have not seen her for five years. My son did not live to his sixteenth birthday. What would I have said to you about them?"

Nothing. What could he? She looked away. First, for perhaps the first time with him. "I am sorry." Because it changed everything, somehow. Realizing he wasn't just a generalleutnant. Not even just a man. He was a *father*. Someone who looked at her and saw his own little girl, once upon a time, not just someone out to make her life miserable.

He sighed. "I am not a fool. I know your mother mourns your father still. And would never look at a German officer occupying her home as anything but that. But is it so wrong of me to want to see her happy on her birthday?"

"Of course not," she said. *Why do you have that photograph?* she wanted to say. *Why have you done nothing about it?*

Sentiment? He didn't seem the kind to be swayed by it. Or hadn't, when he'd just been Generalleutnant Wolfgang Gottlieb instead of someone's papa.

She started forward again. "Thank you. For walking with me."

She would have to find a way to escape him, of course. But she could be glad of the company for now.

"It is my pleasure." He clasped his hands behind his back, which was as straight and unmoving as a steel rod. But at least he didn't march without bending his knees. She couldn't have borne it if he did that. "But I will reiterate my advice of last week—it is not safe for you to be out here alone. And will soon be even less so." He glanced around, as if he needed to check and make sure no one was listening. Leaned down and pitched his voice low. "I have it on good authority that our governor-general will be soon sent to Turkey—replaced by General von Bissing."

She'd never heard the name before, but the way he said it . . . "Who is that?"

Distaste curled Gottlieb's lip. "I know you think *I* am arrogant. But von Bissing has rightly been called 'the only German general who can strut while sitting down.' He will be a cruel overseer, *spatz*."

Numbers beat against her skull like bullets. A warning. "When?"

"A few weeks, perhaps. A month at the outside." He straightened again, a muscle in his jaw ticking. "I intend to leave Brussels before he arrives. Von Bissing and I have never got along, but I have made it worse by trying to inject a bit of reason in the High Command's operations here. My friends in Berlin tell me I have jeopardized my career with such words, and von Bissing will be all too happy to destroy it entirely if I am directly under his command."

"So you will just leave?" Ten minutes ago, it would have made her want to dance. But no jubilation filled her. Not given those other words he'd said.

Was it her imagination or did his shoulders sag a degree? "I see little choice."

"And you . . . you have really been speaking reason to them?"

A breath of laughter escaped his lips and made a little puff of white in the air. "How many times must I tell you that I am not the monster you would make me, Margot?"

"Twenty-three. Apparently." She pulled her coat a little tighter. "Will it be better for you somewhere else?"

He shrugged and glanced down at her again, his eyes as serious and sober as they were when he looked at Maman, as if Margot were another adult. "Away from von Bissing will be a good thing. And worry not for me, my young friend. An enterprising man can always find a way to endear himself again to the High Command."

Her chest banded again. "How?"

He tried on a smile, but rather than looking flip and light, it looked pained. "I will simply await the right opportunity. Then . . . who knows? Take credit for the capture of a spy, or rooting out a double agent. That would prove my loyalty adequately."

The band went so tight she could scarcely breathe. *That*, then, was why he hadn't yet turned them in. He was waiting for the right moment, so it could secure him the most favor.

But it would pain him, at least. Clearly. He didn't *want* to hurt them, she was sure of that now. So she could still like him just a little, because he had gotten himself into this by speaking reason, and he was someone's papa, and he looked at her as though she was perfectly capable of understanding his dilemma. She could like him a little, and she could respect him. And she could know that he'd understand when they fled. He understood necessity.

They walked in silence for two blocks, Gottlieb matching his long stride to her shorter one. She caught a few sympathetic looks from people they passed, neighbors who no doubt thought her in some kind of trouble. She did her best to look recalcitrant. Or at least sullen.

At last, the shops came into view.

Gottlieb cleared his throat. "Margot—can I ask you a favor?"

"What?"

"This evening, I would like to start a new game of Go. Do you think you could bring yourself to play me as you want to, instead of holding back so that I think you stupider than you are?"

Three, nine, twenty-seven, eighty-one . . . It was no use. She wanted to scream. And she wanted to smile. She settled for saying, "On one condition."

"Yes?"

"Don't tell my mother."

He laughed and sounded like somebody's papa. "It is a deal. Now—where to first?"

She didn't know Brussels nearly as well as she did Louvain. But she'd come down this street with Papa a year ago and had counted the streets and cross streets they'd passed. He'd pointed out where all his friends lived and worked. Perhaps knowing, somehow, that she would need the knowledge someday.

The Allard press was five streets over—but the Allard home was only two away. And there was a bookstore on that side of this street. She nodded toward it. "A book. One that I can borrow from her."

He chuckled. "Good job, *spatz*. That sounded nearly like a normal child."

A bell jangled over the door when they entered, and Margot had to take a moment to close her eyes and breathe it in. Paper. Ink. Leather. *Home.*

"You are going to be here a while. I can see it already."

She grinned. She couldn't help it. "If you have other things to do, you can simply call back here in an hour. I'll have something for Maman by then. I promise."

He looked about to object, despite the prayers she was sending heavenward. But he glanced outside and nodded. "One hour. Do not start back without me—it is not safe."

"One hour. And I promise." She held her spot until he walked back out. And then dashed over to the proprietor behind the counter, who had been watching the exchange unabashedly. She leaned closer. "Have you a back door?"

The man asked no questions. He wouldn't need to—he had seen Gottlieb's uniform. He merely motioned her to follow him past the shelves, down a tight hallway, and through an office. The door was within it. "I will leave it open for you. And have a few books ready for you. For your mother?"

"That I could enjoy as well."

He nodded. "A novel. I have just the thing. Run along."

She would thank him later—she hadn't the time now. All her focus had to go toward checking each alley before she ran across it, to make sure Gottlieb wasn't on the other side. Remembering how many streets she needed to cover, when to cross, determine where crossing put her. And pray, with every step, that Jerome Allard still lived where he had a year ago.

Maman was always after her to get up and move about, especially before the invasion. *Go outside and play, Margot*, she had said in years past. *Take some exercise before your muscles turn to mush.*

Just now, she wished she had listened more. Within a block, she was short of breath and battling a stitch in her side. Losing the battle. But there were the eaves she was looking for, on the house Papa had pointed out.

No German soldiers were within sight, praise be to God. She hurried up the steps and rang. *Let it be the Allards. Please, Lord, let it be the Allards.*

A youngish woman answered. Unfamiliar, but not a servant. She wore a fine grey day dress and had well-styled hair. Her eyes went wide upon spotting a wheezing girl on her stoop. "How can I help you, young lady?"

Margot sucked in a breath. "Is this . . . Monsieur Allard's house . . . still?"

The woman's eyes returned to their normal size—and scanned

the street behind Margot. "Yes. Yes, come in. Quickly. I won't ask why you need him. It is always the same."

Margot stepped inside so the woman could close the door and then followed her through a tidy entryway and into a kitchen.

"This way," the woman said, opening a door to stairs and leading the way down them. "He is at the press."

Tinkering on it, apparently. It certainly wasn't running. The only sounds coming from the ancient thing were the clang of a tool against heavy iron.

Margot's heart sank. This thing didn't have the look of something that they ran regularly. "Monsieur Allard?"

The woman put a hand on her shoulder. "Jerome, come out. You have a guest."

"Coming. Coming." He said the words. But no action followed them to prove them true.

The woman patted her shoulder. "He will emerge eventually. If you will excuse me a moment, I must check on the baby."

"Of course. I can wait." Margot chose a spot that looked as though it couldn't be in the way when he finally emerged and knotted her fingers together. She could wait up to ten minutes. That would still give her plenty of time to talk to him and run back to the bookshop.

He emerged in two, wiping his hands on a cloth dark with oil. A smudge of it decorated his cheek, too, but it couldn't disguise the fact that he was young. Much younger than she'd expected, closer to Lukas's age than Papa's. Hadn't the other Monsieur Allard been much older? And they were brothers, she was sure of it.

This Monsieur Allard gave her a smile. "Wait a moment. I know that gaze—you are Professor De Wilde's daughter, aren't you? You looked at me exactly that way when you were only four years old."

Her brow furrowed. "I don't remember meeting you."

"Well . . . you were only four."

"Why should that matter?" Perhaps it had been in a crowd.

He laughed. "Yes, that is the mind that goes with those eyes. I suppose I should not be surprised you have found me. What is it I can do for you, *mademoiselle*?"

She sent a dubious glance at the press. "Is it running? Are you producing a paper?"

Allard sighed. "It runs. And it doesn't run. I produce what I can while it is being merciful, and I pretend that I have never run an old heap of junk like this in my life when in public."

"Is it being merciful now?" The grease stains said otherwise.

But the man smiled. "It will be tonight, when it is safe for it to be. Have you news for me to include?"

She pressed her lips together. "If I give you a message, will you include it exactly as I indicate? And will the papers make their way to Wales?"

"Wales?" Allard tossed the rag onto a table as depressing as the machine. "I cannot say, little one. I know they make it to my brother in London. Beyond that . . ."

"It will do." It would have to. "But the message?"

This time his smile was sad and old. "Trying to reach your brother? I just read that most of our musicians are in Wales, raising money to send home."

"Yes, I know where *he* is. I need *him* to know where *I* am."

"I will keep your message as you give it to me. You have my word." He held out a hand.

She stared at it for a moment. And then realized what he wanted. "Oh. I haven't written it down yet. If I could borrow a pen and paper?"

He set her up at the haggard table and made no pretense of giving her privacy as she printed the words in clear, careful letters so he could read them with ease. He leaned onto the edge of the table. "Is it a code?"

"A cypher." She wished she had a more concise way of giving

Lukas this information. It would take him half of forever to de-code it bit by bit. But how else could she direct him to Madame Dumont's house?

"I thought you needed some sort of master device for those."

"A key."

"Right." He leaned over. "Where is yours?"

She sighed and looked up just long enough to give him a *Do you mind?* sort of look. "It is in my head."

He shook his and eased back. "How old are you, anyway? Thir-teen? Fourteen?"

"Two hundred and thirty. I look young for my age."

When he laughed at her joke, she decided she liked him, de-spite his nosiness. And when he didn't ask her to explain the real meaning of the long paragraphs she'd written out and handed to him, she decided she liked him even more.

He scanned over it, nodding. "It reads like real news about the king and his wife."

That was rather the point. "Could you print the same thing each time you put out an edition? It can be nested in a larger article that changes around it. So long as *La Famille* is some-where in the headline."

Allard put the paper on the top of a stack of them. "Until you tell me to cease. You have my word."

"Thank you." She took a step toward the stairs, then stopped and turned. Fished the single franc from her pocket. "It's all I have right now. You'll say you don't need it because you pity me and feel affection for my father, but I want you to have it. My father always said that things are only worth what we're willing to pay for them. And this is worth everything to me."

He stood still for a moment. Then he reached out and took the franc.

She would count him a friend for the rest of her days. "God bless you, Monsieur Allard."

"And you, Mademoiselle De Wilde."

She hurried back up and let herself quietly out of the house. She still had plenty of time to slip back into the bookstore.

And she'd let Gottlieb pay for the novel. It would undoubtedly mean more to him than it did to her.

TWENTY-TWO

Willa listened for the *click*. Turned the knob. Slipped into the hotel room in what was becoming habit and slid the skeleton key back into her bag. She wasn't exactly sure what she expected to find on a third search that she hadn't on the first or second.

But she'd spotted Cor Akkerman that afternoon, trailing Lukas and Jules and the other musicians as they went for rehearsal. He wasn't going to vanish with his tail between his legs. He was going to cause her whatever trouble he could. So far as she could tell, he didn't yet know about Mr. Brown, to try to work that angle, but he was too observant. He could well realize soon that the German was trying to hire her, and use it against her, if V didn't arrest the agent soon.

Her hands still hurt from where the wood had pierced them. Her soul still hurt far more.

The pieces of the violin had been gone when she'd finally pulled herself out of bed the next morning at a ridiculously late hour. Gwen. She'd probably taken it to some luthier she knew and asked him if he could fix it.

He'd no doubt taken one look at the collection of splinters and declared it beyond redemption.

Her eyes burned as she shut the door to Lukas's hotel room behind her without a sound.

She'd begged off her lessons for the last three days, claiming to be unwell. It wasn't a lie. Never in her life had she felt so miserable. He'd come to see her, of course, but she had claimed she wasn't well enough to come down.

He would see the bandages and demand to know why they were there. He would look into her eyes and know the music was gone. Another something that would demand an explanation.

She hadn't one to give him. Not now.

Her time was running out. Cor would act again soon. He wouldn't realize that the blow he'd already dealt had felled her so completely. He'd think it nothing but an instrument. A *thing*. Something she could replace. He would think he had to strike again, harder.

She had to strike first. Get what she needed and get out of here before Cor could ruin it all with his quest for revenge.

Before Brown could ruin it all with his promise of violence.

Before Lukas could ruin it all with his blasted devotion.

Before Willa could ruin it all just by being who she was.

She sighed and looked around her at the scant belongings she'd already searched through. Wandered through the sitting room as she tried to engage her mind. She had to think. Not just look, but *think*. Think like Lukas—where would he keep something so dear? Something that allowed him to communicate with his family? Think like his father, who had given it to him. What would be a logical thing to hide a key in for his son?

His violin? No. No one but no one would dare to change a Stradivarius even slightly. And the bow had no room for any sort of key.

The case?

Maybe. It wasn't here now, of course. And hadn't been with him in London. And she'd looked all through it when she was getting the Strad from it and hadn't noticed any letters.

What *had* he had with him in London? Clothes. The sheet music for the symphony. Those paragraphs of French.

What if there had been something else, too, that Ellie and Retta had missed? It would make sense that he'd carried it with him. Unwilling to let it out of his sight. Unwilling to go off to send a message to his mother without it. Maybe it was still in his bag, even.

The bag was nowhere out here, of course. So she drifted into the bedroom. And halted. It smelled like him. Was like walking into his arms. She hadn't expected to miss that sensation after a measly few days apart from him. *Couldn't* miss it, miss him. It wasn't allowed. Though maybe she wouldn't have missed him quite so much if it hadn't gone hand in hand with that other loss.

Her nose ached, though she hadn't let herself cry again after that night.

"Chin up, Willa. Snap out of it." It was just a violin. A friend, yes.

But a *thing*. It wasn't Rosemary who Cor Akkerman had hurt, or Barclay or Lucy or Retta or any of them. Even Lukas hadn't been scathed by Cor Akkerman's fury.

It was just a thing. She'd find another one somewhere, and it would sing for her too. There'd been nothing magical about that wood.

And Barclay's words echoed in her head. *"You're letting them win."* He'd been speaking of her parents, but they were no less true here and now. If she couldn't stand up straight and keep going, then Cor Akkerman had won.

And he would *not* win.

Her head had been silent these past three days. Not so much as a strain of music, not a whiff. She'd been empty. Hollow.

Defeated.

"You won't beat me." She said it into the armoire, but it was for Cor. Her mother. Her father. She yanked open the doors and pulled out the small black bag Lukas had been carrying when he got off the train.

It was empty.

She tossed it back into its place with a halfhearted growl. What else? Clothes. The sheet music for the symphony. Those paragraphs of French.

V already had the paragraphs. She could check his clothes, she supposed. Or . . .

Her breath caught. The music. Of course! It wouldn't be in the symphony for the orchestra—but her family wouldn't have known the difference between that and any *other* music he had with him.

And hadn't she read in one of the old, tattered books on the subject that Barclay had found for her about composers hiding messages for their friends in their music? They hadn't hidden anything complicated—no secret instructions. Just their names. Or something special to them—one little word that the composers would turn into a motif.

But if she were a cryptographer with a musician for a son, wouldn't that be the logical place to put a cypher key?

Life pumped through her veins for the first time since Cor Akkerman had shattered her. It wasn't quite music, but it was life. Pumping and surging and making her head spin. Lukas's music crate was there, just inside the bedroom door. He must have moved it in here when Barclay stayed in the outer room, to be out of his way.

She moved to it, her fingers flipping through the sheets like they always did—quickly, searching for something she wanted to play.

No. She had to slow down. It wasn't as though the correct paper would shout, *Me! Look at me!* She must *think*.

How would she know which piece it was in? He had so many, and Barclay hadn't said anything about the titles of what he'd had with him in London. The Bach motif, if she recalled correctly, had been deliberately written to include notes that spelled out *B-A-C-H*, with the *H* being played by . . . wasn't it a B natural or something, with the *B* being a B flat?

But if his father had developed a key for his son, he could have based it on *any* melody and instructed him in how to use it. That was what keys sometimes were, according to the brief information Mr. V had given her—a book both parties had. A dictionary, perhaps. A map. Something both had been instructed in how to use a certain way, read a certain way.

It could be absolutely any of these pieces.

Maybe he'd marked whichever he'd chosen somehow. Willa pulled out a handful of sheet music and sat on the foot of the bed. Her eyes skimmed the margins for any notations, but there were none.

She'd played this one last week. It was lovely. A strand of it filtered into her silent head, distant and faint and tantalizing. She closed her eyes and reached for it, willing it closer like a man dying of thirst, seeing an oasis on the horizon. *Come, please. Please.*

She half-heard it for one second, two. Then it drifted away again.

Her shoulders sagged. She turned to the next piece. Scanned it again for any markings. And there were a few—pencil scratches.

She traced them. Not put there by his father, or by Lukas for any secret reasons. He'd simply scratched *legato* onto a section that she kept playing, according to *him*, too fast. Though the *composer* hadn't said it should be *legato*, had he? And what made Lukas De Wilde the authority?

Her lips felt a little lighter, not pulled so far down. Her fingertip settled on the first note and followed its successors. She liked it better as a rapid ascent up the scale, not a slow climb.

The music gathered in her throat. She wasn't one for humming usually, but she had no violin. And she needed to hear it.

Her eyes slid shut as the first note filled her mouth, her ears, without quite making it into that place in her head. She added the second to it, the third. Her shoulders relaxed, and that aching band across her chest eased a bit. She didn't have a very good singing voice, and there was no way she'd be able to hit the high notes at measure twenty, but she *heard* it. That sweet melody.

And a *click*. There was no *click* in the music. Her eyes flew open.

Lukas filled the doorway, frozen there with his brows arched and a smile at half bloom. "Willa. I must say, *mon amour*, I never expected to walk into my bedroom and find you waiting on my bed. You are not the type."

There should have been panic. Or a dozen excuses. Or *something* other than what there always was when she was with him—too much pleasure at seeing him, too much ease at knowing he was there.

She stood, but not quickly, with a roll of her eyes. "Get over yourself, Lukas De Wilde. I'm not here to throw myself at you."

The music settled. There, but muted. Present, but with its lips sealed, as a random thought spun through her head.

She would tell him.

It was stupid. But according to the music, it was right.

Lukas sauntered closer in that way he had. Pure confidence, never a frisson of doubt. "So I assumed, given that you would have expected me to be away another hour yet. If you wanted to borrow some music, *ma belle*, you need only have asked."

Her fingers tightened on the paper. Relaxed. She set the stack back in its crate. "I didn't come to borrow music."

"Did the clerk let you up? I really need to have a talk with that man." He stopped a foot away, his brows knit. He reached for her hands. "What happened here? You were injured? You were injured and no one told me?"

"Lukas." She tried to hide the bandaged appendages behind her back, but he was too quick. He already had them in his hands. Was already kissing them. Was already breaking her into more splinters. "I'm a thief."

He paused. But then he grinned. Loosed a sound that crossed a chuckle with a snort. "Perhaps that would be a better joke, *mon amour*, were the orchestra not still buzzing about that fickle thief from Sunday. Or will you tell me that was you?"

"No." A bit of the venom meant for Cor slipped out. "No, I would never steal from those worse off than me. *Never*."

His smile froze. And melted right off his face. "But you *would* steal from . . . ?"

"You." She'd meant to say it as a simple fact. It came out as a sorrowful one.

He still held her hands, but he lowered them. "You sound . . . serious. But you cannot be. You have known all along that all my assets are frozen in a bank in Brussels."

She had to look away. "I wasn't sent here to steal your money. I was sent to steal the key."

Her fingers went cold and lonely as his fell away. He took a step back. "Who are you?" His voice was ice. No, darkness. No . . . *silence*.

She sketched a bow, masculine style, just to try to bolster her resolve. "Willa Forsythe—one of London's best pickpockets."

"No." He hadn't moved a muscle. Not a single one, but for those in his mouth required to speak. "You are Willa Forsythe, violin virtuoso. Willa Forsythe, friend of the Davieses."

Her fingers curled into her palms. "I'd never even met them before coming here."

He shook his head. "Willa Forsythe. Woman I love."

It was a punch in the stomach. The eye. The heart. Her nostrils flared. "I'm not. Or you don't. Or . . . it'll pass."

He moved then. Exploded, more like. Spewing a stream of rapid

French, he spun, dragged his hand through his hair, gestured wildly with his other arm, and then turned back, jabbing a finger her way. His eyes blazed. Absolutely blazed.

What had the music been thinking? This was a stupid, stupid idea. He would never understand. How could he when she wasn't so sure *she* did? What, really, did V need with this key? It was just something to get a message to someone, right? Was it so brilliant that the government wanted to be able to use it with their own spies? Could they not compose their own? How in the world could it help them acquire a device?

She held her ground without flinching. If he wanted to rant and rave and hurl accusations at her that she couldn't understand, he had a right.

He stopped after another moment, chest heaving as if he'd just run ten miles. He didn't quite look at her. "You said you were sent. By whom?"

She lifted a shoulder, though he likely wouldn't see it. "The British government, more or less."

Now he didn't just look at her, he pierced her with his gaze. "By whom in *particular*?"

"I don't know. A man called V. I cannot say exactly who—"

He must not have needed to know exactly who Mr. V really was. He spun away again, an incredulous breath huffing out. As if that single letter said so much.

Perhaps it did.

He strode a step into the sitting room and held out an arm toward the door to the hall. "Get out of my room."

He looked like she must have three nights ago, when Cor stood there with her violin in his hand and that money on the bed. The righteous one.

Willa swallowed. "I can't. It isn't so simple anymore, Lukas. V isn't the only one who's come to me. There's a German agent here who has tried to hire me as well. Whatever this key is,

England and Germany both want it. Badly enough that the German threatened to kill me. Or Barclay."

"Barclay." His arm lowered. His eyes narrowed. "He is your *what* exactly? Husband? Lover, playing me for a fool?"

"Brother."

Lukas scoffed. "He is *not* your brother."

"Not by blood. But he is."

Lukas closed his eyes, jaw set. She watched the flicker of movement behind his eyes. "The girls. In London. Blondes. Elinor something and . . ."

"Retta. Two of our sisters. Again, not by blood. But sisters."

"They took my bag. Or took the things from it. They were in the wrong pouches."

Amateurs. Willa would have to speak with them about that. But that was hardly the point. "They had to. I couldn't find it here."

Another snort that may have sounded amused on a different day, in a different conversation. "All that talk about never taking the food from the mouth of a starving child."

"I *wouldn't*. It was Cor, not me, who stole that money! I got it *back*." She sliced a hand through the air.

He'd opened his eyes again and followed the motion. Something on his face shifted. Just a bit. "Cor Akkerman. Did he do this to you?"

He sounded as though . . . as though he cared about the answer. As though he would find him and do something about it if he had.

Willa tucked her bandages into the folds of her skirt. "Only indirectly. He broke my violin, and I grabbed at it without paying enough attention."

His expression didn't change in movement. Just in color. It darkened. "You said you had no violin with you."

It was her turn to try out that snort. "I confess I'm a thief, and you wonder that I'm a liar too? It was old and battered, Lukas. Not something a gentleman's daughter would own, that I could bring down into that parlor."

His larynx bobbed. "So you would stop Cor Akkerman from stealing the money for the relief fund because it was akin to taking food from a child's mouth. Yet you would help V—and perhaps the Germans—"

"I was never going to help *them*."

"—you would help them steal my sister from me. Or do children only get your consideration if they are poor?"

"Your sister." She shook her head, even took a step closer. "No, you misunderstand. They want your father's work, that's all. He said the key was the first step toward getting it. Some . . . some cypher machine. That's all."

He held her gaze. Held it so steadily she wanted to look away. "My *sister* was my father's work—the key is the only way to communicate with her and find where she is. There is no device. No machine. Just Margot."

Willa sank back down onto the foot of the bed. "No."

"I doubt they realize that she is what they are after. But yes. If they seek his work, she is all they will ever find. She is . . . She is with puzzles what you are with music."

Her shoulders sagged, her head following. She couldn't help them find his sister. That went against every conviction she had left. "I'll talk to Mr. V. I'll tell him he's on the wrong track, that there's no device, that—"

"You will not mention her to him. Do you understand? You will *not*. A man like that—he will not care if it is a girl or a mechanism that performs the task he wants, only that the task is performed. He would take her, he would sit her in some little room and call her a weapon. He would—"

"You're right." She wanted to deny it—who would treat a child that way? But V just might. "Of course. I . . . I'll just tell him you haven't the key. That you mentioned your father's work to me and that . . . it was all destroyed in Louvain."

Silence.

She lifted her head. He was still looking at her, a slight curl to his lip. Like she had looked at Cor three days ago.

She was better than him, wasn't she? She didn't steal from the poor. She didn't steal from refugees, or from the people left in their homes under an invading army. She would never hurt a child.

But in Lukas De Wilde's eyes, she was no better.

She stood. She'd known all along it would come to this someday. Today was no worse than tomorrow. At least today, she was already just a collection of splinters. He couldn't possibly hurt her any more.

He stopped her when she was sliding past him. Stopped her with a hand on her cheek. Not as gentle as it would have been an hour ago, but nowhere near as forceful as it should have been. And it trembled.

She looked up into his dark eyes. She chanted to herself, *He can't hurt me any more.*

His eyes wept without a single tear. "I loved you."

She was wrong.

TWENTY-THREE

L ukas stood inside the castle ruins, looking out at the bald hills that the Welsh tried to call mountains. The wind whipped him, the sun hadn't the grace to shine on him, and the ground beneath him didn't show him the kindness of swallowing him up.

No, he didn't want that. Much as one part of his heart demanded that he mourn, he couldn't. He hadn't the time. He had to focus on finding and saving Margot and Mère.

He wouldn't waste any more time, effort, or thought on Willa Forsythe.

Once he got back to the hotel, anyway. He'd grant himself this hour out here. That was all. She was worth no more mourning than this.

A thief. He jammed his cold hands into his pockets and turned into the wind. It made his ears ache. His eyes sting.

Echoes of his heart.

He would have preferred to learn she was the kind to steal the money. Money, after all, was just *money*. But of course it wasn't so simple. Nothing ever was. She had to be in the employ of that man. V.

Lukas turned it over, again and again, until it made him

queasy. What were the exact words V had used? Lukas's brain had been so fogged with the bullet wound, with the medication they'd given him. His shoulder throbbed now with the memory.

"I can help you. I can keep your family safe. Work with us, tell us how to find your father's work, and we'll protect you all."

Did he know? Did he know it was Margot he was looking for, not some encoding device that he could simply pick up and set down again on a desk? The words weren't enough to tell him. But he thought he recalled something in his eyes . . . something to make him distrust the man immediately, deep in his gut.

Why hadn't his gut given him the same warning about *her*?

It throbbed now like the bullet wound. Would probably fester as it had done too. Unless he could extract all the pieces now, from the start, so it could heal up properly.

That first day he'd seen her, staring at the building as Margot would do—casing it, probably.

He plucked it out and released it into the wind.

That evening the next day, when she had picked up his Strad and done the miraculous—probably all the while calculating what she could fence it for, or how she could take it with her when she ran off and keep it for herself.

He yanked it from his mind and hurled the memory into a gust.

The way he'd sensed her there that night outside the hotel when he had no reason to do so. The way she'd grabbed his tie and pulled him close and kissed him—gaining his trust, his confidence. Playing him. Nothing more.

He held that one in his mental hand. He never would have thought he'd be that kind of fool. Especially not with the first woman who had stirred him to want something more than a night.

"Lukas! You're a hard man to find!"

His hand had fisted inside his coat pocket. He released it, praying the memory would trickle out through the wool and into the wind. Then he turned to face down another traitor.

314

Barclay jogged up the incline with a grin, his hat low over his eyes and a bundle of something under his arm.

Her brother, she'd said. They acted like it. But should he believe her?

Did it matter? She was nothing to him anymore. If she were this man's wife or moll or whatever thieves called their conspirators, he didn't care.

He took a step back. A deliberate one. And kept his lips sealed.

Barclay was too keen to miss it. He slowed a few feet away, an amused question drawing a line between his brows. "Am I intruding that badly? Your friend—the one with that round-cheeked girl—said you'd come out here."

Jules. Not a traitor like these two. But so very absent these days. Busy with a life of his own.

Lukas unclenched his jaw. "You are wasting your time. My pockets are empty." He pulled out the lining to demonstrate.

One of London's best pickpockets. This man before him was probably another.

Barclay narrowed his eyes. "Why would you . . . ?" Then his face shifted. Into annoyance. "Blast it all. She *told* you. Why in blazes would she do that?"

Why had she? She could have bluffed her way out of his room, and he was fool enough that he would have believed she'd just come to borrow music. It was what he would have *wanted* to believe. He'd even handed her the excuse.

She hadn't taken it.

Barclay sighed. "Well. I suppose I'll not be sleeping on your sofa tonight. Even so, I brought you these." He pulled out the bundle from under his arm and held it out.

Lukas kept his hands in the pockets he'd tucked back in.

Barclay rolled his eyes and waved the package. "You'll want it. Trust me. Or don't, I guess, but still look. I've been haunting that little newspaper office we went to every day, waiting for—I

315

didn't know what I was waiting for. Until crates of *these* arrived. From Belgium."

Lukas curled his fingers into the lining. He wouldn't bite.

Barclay stepped closer, eyes bright. "They're from Allard's brother, Lukas. In Brussels. A newspaper. The moment they arrived, Allard shoved them at me and told me to get them to you as quickly as I could."

His hands itched. A trick? If so, he would find it out. The key wouldn't work.

But they could be lying in wait when he got it out and tried it. Watching. Ready to swoop in and snatch it.

They still wouldn't know how to use it though. How to write the headline and indicate the number and . . .

Blast. They very well could. He'd pre-written the paragraphs. They were in his bag in London. The blondes had no doubt seen them, copied them.

V had one piece of the puzzle.

The Margot in his head shouted numbers at him like expletives.

"All right." As if edging away from a snarling dog in the corner of an alley, Barclay slowly set the bundle on the ground and backed away, hands held up in front of him. "I won't take it personally. Just a prejudice against my profession—I understand that. You know, I never could bring myself to trust a baker. It's a bias I haven't been able to get over ever since one threw an old scone at me when I was rooting through his rubbish. Hurt like a rock."

Lukas clenched his teeth.

Barclay just gave him half a grin and finished straightening. "She's a thief. But she's the other things too. You know that, right? She couldn't fake her talent. Or her prickliness, which you seemed to like for some reason. She's still Willa."

Willa Forsythe—one of London's best pickpockets.

Lukas didn't say a word. And heard Jules in his head, saying, *"Would you just shout at me? Rant and rail as you usually do?"*

He'd always thought himself of loud temper. But maybe he'd just never known true depth of feeling until these last few months. He'd just never discovered that when something hurt enough, it didn't demand noise and fire—it demanded silence and ice.

Barclay didn't know him well enough to request the safer version. He just sighed and spun and disappeared down the hill.

Then, when the thief was safely out of sight, Lukas bent down and picked up the newspapers. His heart barely had life enough left in it to race. He looked all around him as he strode down the hill, but he saw no one beyond a few residents braving the wind and cold. No one lurking, watching.

He hurried through the eight-minute walk back to the Belle Vue, up to his room, and into the safety of dim light and empty chambers. Then—only then—did he unfold the newspaper.

The words were French. The first word of the first article claimed it was written in Brussels. And the article on page three had a headline that declared *LA FAMILLE ROYALE VISITE DES ÉTATS-UNIS*.

Lukas sighed. The royal family had, in fact, gone to the United States to try to drum up support from the Americans. But he hardly cared about the facts in the article, which matched the ones he had already read in other papers. He cared only for that *La Famille* in the headline. And that midway through the piece, a paragraph began with, "After a four-day tour . . ." *Four*.

He reached into the music crate, pulled out the one Margot had written for him, and looked to the fourth line.

It took him paper, pen, and an hour to work through the cypher—it would have taken Margot about ten seconds. But he worked at it as the light slipped down over the bay, then he stared at the message he'd revealed.

Margot's words. Margot's plea.

He knows who we are. Hurry. Two three one Rue de Florence.

Lukas jumped up to flip on the lights before darkness could obliterate the words. *Thank you, God, for getting this paper to me so quickly.* According to the date, it had been only three days since it was printed. It must have encountered no problems in being smuggled out. Taken directly to Allard in London.

And then Barclay had brought it directly to him. With a sigh, he slumped back onto the couch and dug his fingers into his hair. He couldn't quite bring himself to consider thanking the *man* for it. But he'd thank the Lord. Whatever else had gone wrong, those prayers were being answered. The Father was at work to restore his family to him.

He needed air. To walk as this settled. It would be cold outside, but he hadn't even shrugged out of his coat yet. He simply stowed the message he'd decoded in the bottom of his shoe—he could think of no other place safe from pickpockets—wound his scarf around his neck, and jogged down the stairs and out into the autumnal evening.

When he pushed outside, he found Cor Akkerman leaning against the glass enclosing the hotel's front door. His face was a mosaic of shadows even though he was bathed in light. "I have something to tell you, Lukas De Wilde."

This man broke her violin. Hurt her. He shouldn't care. He did. But it wouldn't change what he was about to do. "I already know it. But I could use your help. I need your cousins to get me back into Belgium."

Akkerman's eyes flickered from dark to pleased. "We can help you. For a price."

Lukas was keenly aware of the empty state of his pockets. "Name it."

"And you claim not to be stupid?"

Willa glared at her brother where he was sprawled on her bed at the Davies house, arms folded behind his head. She had half a mind to throw something to wipe that smirk off his face, but the only things handy were her gloves, and they wouldn't do enough damage. "Aren't you supposed to be supportive?"

Barclay pursed his lips and studied the ceiling. "No. No, I don't believe that's part of my job in these situations. I'm all but certain my job is to point and laugh."

She threw one glove at him. It fluttered to a pathetic rest on the very edge of the mattress.

It wasn't really fair how much better she'd felt the moment he showed up at the door. Not when she'd known very well that he'd have no mercy. And when he'd said all those photographs she'd taken were useless—and that V had failed to apprehend Brown thus far. "I was out of time, between Cor and the German. I had no other choice."

"Since when is telling the mark about the job even one of the choices?" But he didn't sound angry. Just annoyingly amused. "You know who you remind me of right now?"

"Shut up."

"Rosemary."

"I said shut up." She pulled her knees up to her chin. The armchair in the corner of her room didn't protest the position, though it had probably never experienced it before. Ladies, she was sure, never sat in such a way. "I'm not like Rosie. I didn't tell him because I've fallen in love with him or because I think he's a good man. I told him because the job couldn't be done otherwise."

Barclay could pack an awe-inspiring amount of doubt in one "Mm-hmm."

Willa sighed. "Do you think Mr. V knows? That it's his sister he's after?"

The amusement left Barclay's face as he pushed himself up to lean against her headboard. "If he does . . ."

He didn't need to say how he felt about it. It was Barclay who had made their family grow from the three of them—him and her and Rosemary—to a collection of twelve. He couldn't see a helpless child without wanting to be a brother to them. Without wanting to protect and provide. The twelve who had stayed, become family, were just a portion of the ones he'd taken in for a night or two, until they split again.

Street rats didn't often like to stay in one place for long.

Even after all these years, she wasn't sure what haunted him, to make him react in such a way. But she was grateful. Then, for making her a sister. Now, for saying without a word that he'd protect Lukas's sister.

From the Germans. From V. From anyone who tried to take her from her brother.

Something caught her ear. "Do you hear that?"

"What?" Barclay sat up straight, but he shook his head. "I don't hear anything."

"I do." She'd learned the house well enough to know where sounds were likely to come from—and which ones were unusual. The sisters may be quiet, but they enjoyed each other's company, and Miss Blaker's. They were all the time talking.

This, though, was a deeper tone. A neighbor, perhaps. Or the butler. Or . . .

She crouched down at the grate and put her ear to it. Sucked in a breath. *Lukas.*

"What is it?"

"Shh." She waved at Barclay to silence him and closed her eyes to better focus on the voices echoing through the walls.

Daisy was talking now. Or Gwen. It was hard to tell their voices apart at this distance, but one of them was saying, "Please, Mr. De Wilde, have a seat. Shall we call Willa down?"

"No."

She winced. Not at the tone of his voice—at the lack of it. As

320

if he weren't even angry, just stating a fact. That Willa didn't exist to him anymore.

That was the way it was supposed to be. The way it *had* to be. She wouldn't let it hurt.

Barclay settled on the floor too and leaned close to the grate.

"And no thank you, I hope not to be here long enough to need a seat. I have a favor to ask—but first a question. The men you sent into Belgium to recruit us. Who were they?"

"Oh." Daisy, she was fairly certain. "The man who administers our trust fund and one of his friends, I believe. Why?"

"What of the one called V?"

Willa squeezed her eyes closed tighter.

All was silence downstairs for a moment. Then Gwen said, "He knew our father. We know little about him, but he offered to help with the effort. Why do you ask?"

"You are not associated with him? Beyond accepting his offer to help?"

"Well. Not . . . especially."

He would put the pieces together. Soon, if he hadn't already. They were all there, laid out neatly in a row.

"Of course—and beyond asking you to host Miss Forsythe and pretend she was an old friend, I meant."

She couldn't hear the sisters sigh, but she knew they would have. "He assured us it was for a noble cause, Mr. De Wilde. Though, of course, we are never fond of deception. I pray you forgive us if this has somehow injured you."

"I am well. I assure you. But in need of assistance, and I would rather it have no connection to that man."

Willa opened her eyes when Barclay nudged her elbow. His brows were quirked. She shrugged.

"How can we help you?"

Lukas cleared his throat. "I need to return to Belgium, in secret, to locate my mother and sister and bring them back here with me. I have an . . . acquaintance who can help with this, but it will be expensive. And as I am sure you know, all my accounts are frozen."

Barclay's brows drew together by degrees until they all but flashed lightning. "An *acquaintance*?"

"Cor." Willa pushed to her feet and took off at a run. He couldn't trust Cor Akkerman with this—he *couldn't*. Was he an absolute idiot? She charged down the stairs and into the drawing room while Daisy was still speaking, assuring him with a smile that they would be happy to help.

The doors she'd pushed open smacked into the shelves behind them. "Are you an idiot? You cannot trust Cor Akkerman!"

Gwen had sprung up at the clamor of the door, a hand pressed to her chest. "Who is Cor Akkerman?"

"The man who stole the money from the relief fund."

"Oh." Daisy shook her head and held out a hand toward Lukas. "Willa is right, *monsieur*. You must not trust a man like that to help you."

"On the contrary." He looked at her so *evenly*. As if she were a stranger. "That proves exactly how far he will go for money. It is the only thing he cares about, the only thing he will seek. I give it to him, and he is trustworthy exactly as far as he agreed to be for a given sum." A tic in his jaw. "If any kind of thief can be trusted, I should think it is that kind."

Barclay must have followed her down, given that he leaned close and stage-whispered "Ouch" into her ear.

Willa batted him away. "And how far is that? Do you really trust him to get you into Brussels? Into the house where they're staying?"

Lukas's face didn't shift. But his hands fisted. "I do not need him for that. I know Brussels better than he does. Once I am there, I will be fine on my own."

She snorted and folded her arms over her chest. "The last time you tried to sneak into a house in Brussels under the army's nose, you were shot."

"Shot!" Gwen sank to a seat on the edge of a chair.

"Really?" Barclay, the oaf, sounded impressed. "That sounds like a story I'd like to hear. You obviously got away."

Lukas ignored them both. "I was unprepared last time. I will not be this time. I will find them, get them out, and—"

"Get *them* shot. Don't be an idiot, Lukas. You're a musician. You don't know the first thing about sneaking in and out of houses."

Barclay groaned behind her, obviously anticipating where she was going with this.

Lukas's eyes flashed. "What, then? Do I need a spy to help me?"

"Of course not. You just need a thief."

Daisy turned questioning eyes on her. "You said he shouldn't trust this Cor fellow."

"A *good* thief." She waved a hand between herself and Barclay. "You need *us*."

Barclay looked ready to smack her upside the head. "She means *her*."

She speared him with a glance. "It's his *sister*."

He growled. And sighed. "Fine. Us."

"No. Not fine. Not you—either or both." Lukas shook his head, slashed the air with a hand, that careful, even control slipping. "You think I would be idiot enough to trust you now? You would take her straight to him."

"No, I wouldn't." She stepped closer. Chin up, spine straight. Eyes begging him to see this one truth. "I wouldn't. We'd get in, get them out, and help you disappear. Safe, all of you."

Silence pulsed. In the room, in her chest. But not quite in her head. There was a hint of something stirring there, distant but melodic. Enough to say, *This is right.*

Lukas swallowed. "And how much will *this* cost me? Or the Misses Davies rather, until I can repay them."

Willa's lips turned up. "Not much. Just the key—after I deliver your family safely to you."

Confusion churned in his dark eyes. "It would be useless then."

Her smile grew. "I know that. And *you* know that. But . . ."

"They wouldn't." Barclay stepped to her side, even with her. "V and the German."

He studied her and Barclay, one and then the other. Looking for evidence that they lied. Knowing, probably, that he wouldn't be able to tell if they did. Weighing the risk—trusting them—against the reward—his family.

He sucked in a breath. "Why? Why would you help me—and ask nothing in return?"

"Because it's your sister," Barclay answered before Willa could wrap her tongue around a response. He bumped his shoulder into hers. "Family matters more than anything. And besides." A smile had entered his voice. "V will pay us for a job well done. Everyone's happy."

Sure. *Everyone*. Lukas would have his sister and mother. She would get paid. That was all either of them could want, right?

Daisy cleared her throat, drawing all gazes her way. "We will help you with this, Mr. De Wilde. We will have the funds delivered to your hotel first thing in the morning. Just . . ." She looked to Willa and Barclay. "Everyone be careful, please. TJ—our trustee—and his colleagues had no difficulties at all. There must be a way to achieve this that does not invite gunshots."

When all they were doing was secreting musicians out of the country, yes. But when they were trying to remove the De Wildes? Willa could make no promises.

Neither, apparently, could Lukas. He simply nodded and bowed toward the sisters. "I am, yet again, in your debt. And will repay it the moment I can." And then he was striding for the door, giving her and Barclay a wide berth. "We will catch the first train to London. Do not be late."

Willa pivoted when he passed her, followed him a step into the entryway. "Lukas."

But he didn't even pause. Just yanked the door open, walked through it, and slammed it behind him.

There were three people she cared about just a few steps away. But Willa hadn't felt quite so alone since she was six.

TWENTY-FOUR

Lukas paced to the window of the London house, wondering yet again if he were in fact trespassing—if this house, which they'd sworn belonged to their brother-in-law and were using with permission, in fact belonged to a random stranger who had left it vacant for a few months.

Wondering how long they could possibly sit there, poring over a map.

Wondering if it wouldn't have been more efficient for her to simply tear his heart from his chest and stomp on it.

"We need a bigger crew, Will, I'm telling you." Barclay tapped something against the top of the desk.

"*More* of us stumbling around a strange city? Barclay, it would be the gardens all over again."

"I'm thinking more the British Museum. We need someone who speaks German, who can be the mouth if we get stopped."

Willa sighed. "We're not pulling Rosie into this. She's got all the little ones with her."

"I speak German." Lukas said it to the window, not to them, watching the way his words frosted the glass. "And Flemish. So do my sister and mother."

"See?"

Barclay huffed out a breath. "He's too recognizable."

"Not to the general public." Lukas still refused to turn as he spoke. Their reflections were enough for him to see. "Only in my own circles, and perhaps to the army. If we avoid them and disguise ourselves appropriately, I daresay no one will look twice at me."

"See?" Willa said again. "We can handle it." Her words were light. Her tone carried another note in it though. An undertone. One that said, *Don't risk any more of us.*

He still couldn't quite wrap his mind around this group. A gang of thieves who seemed downright offended whenever he said they weren't really family. There were five of them in this house right now—the two behind him and three girls somewhere upstairs. Elinor, the blonde he'd bumped into. Retta, whom he had assumed she'd met at the train. Lucy, who had regaled him with stories at supper—he ought to have assumed from that one's darker complexion and almond eyes that she was no real relation to Barclay, but he'd rather assumed their father had behaved as so many had before, and then had the kindness to take in his illegitimate child.

There were apparently seven more of them in Cornwall. And the youngest, they said, was only six. *"Train up a child in the way he should go . . ."* Apparently they believed in training thieves young.

They *acted* like a family. They *looked* as though they belonged in this house, in the well-tailored clothes they all wore— Rosemary's handiwork, it seemed. The one leading the band in Cornwall and supposedly married to the owner of this house, the novelist.

Right.

Just like Willa had *seemed* to be growing fond of him, bit by bit. What an artist she was. And him the fool.

A buzzing sound filtered through their conversation, and footsteps raced down the stairs, along with a cheerful, "I'll get it!"

Lukas turned. Barclay had gone tense. Willa had popped out of her chair and was already halfway to him, her eyes flint. "Hurry. There's a cabinet here you can hide in."

"A what?"

But she'd already opened a door hidden in the paneling and was pushing him toward it, hissing, "Get in!"

Barclay was doing something with the atlas on the desk, turning rapid pages.

Lukas dug in his heels. "I will not be shoved into a hole."

Her eyes called him an idiot. "You think we have regular *visitors*?"

No. No, they wouldn't. He folded himself into the squat little closet and let her close the door.

He wondered if she ever meant to let him out. Or if he'd be able to open it from in here if it were the police, coming to arrest them all. He'd have a hard time explaining the position to the authorities if he had to ask for help with it.

"Mr. Pearce. And Miss Forsythe. I thought you were in Wales."

It was V. Lukas's throat went tight. Perhaps he couldn't quite explain logically the aversion he felt toward the man, but it reared up again at hearing his voice. Purely visceral. Overwhelming.

"She is. This is just a very clever disguise you see before you— I'm really Ellie."

A beat. Then, "You are amusing as always, Miss Forsythe. Perhaps I should ask *why* you are not in Wales. Here I came to assure Barclay that the German spy has fled the country, and I find you here when you are supposed to be about your task there."

Lukas could see her, though he couldn't *see* her. Rolling her eyes. Perching on the edge of the desk in that way that said nothing in the world bothered her. "I can't be about my task there, sir. I finally got some decent information from him, and the key's not in Aberystwyth."

Another beat. "Then where *is* it?"

Lukas held his breath. She had no reason to give him up—not now, when he was here, hidden in a closet she'd all but shoved him into.

"Paris."

His breath eased back out, silently. It was, he supposed, plausible. It was where he had been before he hurried back to Belgium after the invasion. He had, in fact, left many of his belongings there for the hotel to ship to him once he provided them an address.

A tap, like the dozens of others Barclay had made on the map. "We have the direction for the room he'd rented—paid up until the fifteenth of November, but we need to move fast to get in and out again before then."

He must have turned the page in the atlas to a map of Paris. Clever. And thorough. If he had to be working with thieves, these at least seemed to know what they were doing.

"Paris." V didn't sound disbelieving. Just thoughtful. "I thought for sure he would have it with him. How did you learn otherwise, Miss Forsythe?"

She didn't answer. Which would sound like an answer, especially if she summoned a blush to stain her cheeks. How did a woman *usually* get sensitive information from a man? Lukas's fingers bit into his palms. At least he hadn't been that kind of fool.

V sighed. "You are a thief, my dear. Not a spy. Not . . . I did not ask you to compromise yourself."

"Don't make assumptions, sir. They don't become you. Let's just say I know how to run a confidence scheme and leave it at that."

"Very well." A bit of rustling like paper being drawn over wood. "Where in Paris?"

Lukas squeezed his eyes shut, though it made it no more dark

329

in the little closet. Would this be where they tripped? They surely didn't know Paris that well.

But that *tap* came again. "The Rue de . . . Admiral Hamelin, however you say that in French. The Hotel Elysées Union."

Of course, he apparently didn't *have* to know Paris all that well, if he had a good memory. Lukas had told him about the month he had spent in the city. Mentioned turning onto the street and seeing the Eiffel Tower.

Though the man mangled the pronunciation of the hotel. He would have to keep his lips sealed whenever they stepped into Belgium or he'd give them all away in the first syllable. He might as well call out "Oi!" at the start of every sentence.

V made a humming noise. "Very well. Do you need anything for the trip? Documents? Passports?"

"V." Barclay laughed. "You haven't really met Retta yet, have you?"

"Ah. You've a forger already. I ought to have known." Footsteps, blessedly, toward the door. "Well, if you need anything you *cannot* procure within your own family, do let me know. Godspeed."

"Thanks." More footsteps followed the first. Barclay walking him out, Lukas guessed. They were too heavy to be Willa's.

And when the light came, blinding him, it was her face that came into focus after a few blinks. She held out a hand.

He ignored it and unfolded himself. Or tried to ignore it, until his foot caught on a strip in the threshold and nearly sent him tumbling into her. Grasping her fingers was instinct. And preferable to ending up draped all over her.

Her fingers curled around his to steady him. He could feel the uneven skin on her palm, the injury the bandage had covered yesterday. It was hot to the touch, swollen.

His feet had found their footing. But he felt all kinds of off-balance. He turned her hand over in his so he could look at the angry red cut. "You should put something on this. You do not want it to get infected."

Her fingers tried to curl over it, but his got in the way. And his heart made a strange little *thunk*.

"It doesn't matter." Not *It will be fine* or *I have* or *I will*. She tugged her hand away.

"Of course it does." He backed away a step. "You cannot play with injured hands or arms. Trust me."

"I won't be playing any time soon anyway." Avoiding his gaze, she turned back to the desk and clasped her elbows with those mangled hands.

She looked small. And fragile. And alone.

He didn't care. Couldn't. "What else do you need from me? For the planning?"

"Nothing."

"Then . . . I will see you in the morning. First light."

"First light."

Apparently that was all they had to say now. He turned and left the room. Went upstairs to the same room he'd borrowed before.

Or stolen. He still wasn't sure which. But if it got him to his sister and mother, he didn't care which it was.

———◇———

Antwerp was behind them. And so, thankfully, was Cor Akkerman. Willa pulled the scarf more securely over her head and tucked it into the ragged top of her old coat. They blended in rather well, she thought, with the poor farmers trudging along the road, always looking over their shoulders to make sure there were no soldiers galloping up behind them. Or zooming by in automobiles that rutted the road and scared the animals.

There was supposed to have been a wagon waiting for them just outside the city, but Cor's "cousin" was apparently about as reliable as Cor himself. No wagon had been there, but Lukas wouldn't wait. They'd started walking.

And would keep doing so—if they didn't find something faster—the thirty miles to Brussels.

She sidestepped a mud puddle and cast a glance to her left, where Barclay walked. And past him, to Lukas. "Do you think—"

"No talking." He didn't bark it. Just said it so calmly, so evenly. "You scream *English* the moment you open your mouths."

Well, yes. Because she was speaking English. She rolled her eyes and faced forward again. Did he really expect them to say nothing for the whole time it would take them to walk thirty miles?

The trip thus far had been painless—a train to the eastern coast of England, where Cor had led them to one of the fishing boats being used to smuggle goods across the Channel. Whereupon he'd barred their entrance until Lukas had handed over a thick stack of pound notes. The Davieses had, of course, come through.

And were praying for them. Both Daisy and Gwen had clasped her hands before she'd left—mindful of her bandages—and whispered a prayer then and there. That God would keep her safe. Show her where He would have her step. Guide her as she guided Lukas's family to safety.

Willa looked down at the road, pocked and spoiled by too many boots and wagons and automobiles in too short a time. Never in her life had she ever thought anyone guided her steps. Not God. Not parents. Not teachers or benefactors or the usual adult who ought to do so. It had always just been her. And then her and Barclay and Rosemary. Then the others who *they* cared for.

She brushed a fly off her bleak brown skirt and regretted it. Her hand stung.

Her chest ached.

She was tired. So tired, and it had nothing to do with the

three miles already behind them. It had everything to do with the silence inside. And out.

As if he heard her thoughts, Barclay started humming. A simple tune, one he'd asked her to play time and again in Pauly's pub. Some sort of lullaby, though she didn't know the words to it. And the tune must not scream *English!* since Lukas didn't hush him.

Willa drew in a long breath and savored the notes. He had the better voice, did Barclay. No natural talent with an instrument, but he could sing.

He went from one song to another as they walked, and when he stopped, clearing his throat, Lukas took over. Or no, he didn't hum. He sang, something soft and low and in what she assumed was Flemish, since it didn't sound like French.

Another lullaby, she would bet. It sounded like one. She could imagine a father bent over his little one's bed, singing this.

She curled her fingertips up. And regretted it. Her palms stung. Her heart ached. And the road stretched endlessly before her.

After another half mile, another three songs, Willa came to a halt. They'd just rounded a bend, and the green-brown autumnal fields stretched their way up to a house. It was all turrets and windows and spires and climbing ivy and perfection.

Aside from the wagon parked in front of it with the insignia of the German army. And soldiers scurrying around it, packing something or another inside.

"Do not stop." Lukas tugged on her arm, having apparently stepped past Barclay to do so. "Do not look their way. The Belgians do not, have you not noticed?"

Of course she had. In Antwerp, it had been almost comical, the way the natives would turn their backs whenever a soldier walked by, and shove their hands into their pockets. As if ignoring the soldiers' existence.

She would have apologized, if she dared. Explained that it was just the house, set back against the trees and looking so perfect, that had caught her eye. She would have said that Belgium was beautiful.

Instead, she kept walking.

The pressure of his hand on her elbow eased off, of course. He lowered his arm. But didn't leave her side. His fingers brushed up against hers as they walked the next step.

He should have jerked away—that was how he'd been all through the trip to London, *in* London, then to the coast. Other than in the study when he'd looked at her injury, which hardly counted.

But he didn't. He turned his hand and trailed the tip of his index finger down the length of hers.

Then he moved back to the other side of Barclay.

Willa fastened her eyes on the road ahead of them and told herself it had been an accident. Or something meant to confuse her. To punish her, even. He just wanted to make her feel like an idiot, to remind her of what he'd offered and she'd lost.

Well, she didn't need the reminder. She'd known all along she wouldn't be able to hold for long whatever it was they'd had.

They were closer now, and they could hear the Germans' shouts and laughter as they loaded boxes into the wagon. Boxes *not* marked with the German insignia. She kept her head down, the scarf pulled low so that she could still peek out.

A family stood at the corner of the house. A father in shirt-sleeves, with one arm around his wife, who wept into his shoulder, and another around a girl of maybe twelve. A young man, seventeen or so, stood half a step behind them, looking ready to charge past his father and light into the soldiers.

A bottle peeked out of one of the boxes. Green, like the ones used for wine. From another she could see a sack of flour.

Her blood simmered. They were taking their food—this family's food, and who knew what else?

"Head down, Will." Barclay barely breathed the words. "There's nothing we can do. Not for them. Focus."

"They are supposed to pay for what they take." Lukas, not but a breath louder than Barclay had been. "They do not. That is what Allard's brother reports."

Willa put her head back down. And clutched the scarf at her neck—more to have something to strangle than because the air was cold.

They drew even with the house just as the wagon lurched forward and started down the muddy drive. The men didn't need to tell her to move out of the way, they all leapt off the road together, into the muck and grass. Just ahead of them on the road was another wagon, old and plodding, which couldn't maneuver quite so quickly. The German driver shouted and barreled past, making the farm horse rear up and the driver yell something.

At the horse? Or at the laughing soldiers?

The horse, she assumed, or the soldiers probably would have leapt down to teach him a lesson for shouting at them.

Lukas took off toward the man's wagon, arriving just in time to keep a bale of hay from tipping off the side. He said something, smiled. The farmer smiled back, replied, motioned to the hay-filled bed of his wagon, and clucked to his horse until the wheels sat evenly on the road again. Then stopped.

Lukas waved her and Barclay forward, shouting something in Flemish. She smiled as if she understood. Which she did, given that Lukas had hopped up into the wagon bed and taken a seat on a bale of hay. And she'd caught the word *Brussels*, she thought.

Willa ran to catch up, accepted Barclay's hand up into the wagon. And sighed. She wasn't sure it was God directing their steps. But she was glad to be saved a few thousand of them.

They would be in Brussels by nightfall.

TWENTY-FIVE

Margot hadn't slept—not really—in a week. She napped during the day sometimes, when she deemed it less likely that Lukas would show up. But she couldn't sleep at night. One of these nights, he would come. It only made sense that he would sneak in under cover of darkness, when all the streets were empty with curfew, all the houses dark.

It could be weeks yet before he came. He may not receive the first message. Or the next, or the next. The paper might *never* reach him, if she were honest. But statistically, it should. Eventually. He had obviously found the older Allard brother in London. She had found the younger here. It was a solid connection, and that increased the statistical probability greatly.

And so, she couldn't sleep. Not until he came.

She had gone to bed as normal, of course, but then she had changed into tomorrow's clothes and taken her seat at the window. She had counted soldiers who walked by—nine. Cats she had heard meow—four, she thought, though perhaps only three. Madame Dumont had retired, and Maman would be padding down the hall at any moment.

"How *dare* you!"

Or perhaps not. Margot flew to her feet and out the door whose hinges she had oiled three days ago, in preparation for sneaking out. Her heart thudded, but she kept her feet silent. If Gottlieb were trying to hurt her mother—but she'd been sure he wouldn't.

She stopped in the hallway outside the parlor, out of sight. Gottlieb stood by the window, his hands clasped behind his back. Maman's shadow stretched across the floor from where she must be standing before the sofa.

His face flickered with some emotion Margot couldn't see clearly enough to name. "You act as though I am proposing something indecent."

Maman's breath hissed out in that way of hers. "Are you not? Why else would you invite us to join you in Antwerp?"

His cheeks went red. "It is marriage I am proposing, not . . . what you assume."

"Marriage." Maman sounded no less insulted. "You think I would *marry* you?"

Margot's fingers knotted in tomorrow's dress.

Gottlieb's knotted in his uniform jacket's hem. "No. Not for any reason of affection. But perhaps for logic. We both know you are not a Dumont, madame. I can protect you—you and Margot. We can detour to Louvain, so I can claim to have checked the rubble of your house there and verified that all your husband's work was destroyed. With your son shot and killed, what other protection do you have? For yourself? For your daughter?"

Would her mother's face flicker? Contort? Would fear be pulsing through her at the realization that he knew who they were?

Would it make her agree to the unthinkable?

She said nothing. Her shadow made not the slightest move.

Gottlieb sighed. "Consider it, at least. For Margot's safety, if not for your own. Even if you do not want to leave with me tomorrow, you need only send for me, and I'll come back for you."

Tomorrow? He was leaving tomorrow, and he'd said no farewell to her that evening? Margot edged back along the banister, sidestepping the squeaky board. Back toward her room. He'd kept it a secret from her. Yet asked her mother to marry him and go with him. What was he about?

And what would he do when she refused? Turn them in?

Hurry, Lukas. Hurry. Please, God, bring him soon.

She slid back into her room and whispered the door shut. A bare moment later, she heard Gottlieb's step on the stairs. Then Maman's traveling to her room across from Margot's. Her door closed with what was nearly a *bang*. Then all went silent.

After five minutes of such, Margot moved back to the window. Another patrol of soldiers was marching by. It would take only a shout from Gottlieb to have them inside, arresting them all. A shout he could have made any time, could yet make.

He had said he wanted to protect them. And perhaps, in a way, he did. But if spurned, what then? And what if it was all a ruse to get them peaceably to Antwerp, where he intended to make a show of capturing them before the governor-general?

The hours ticked by with her questions. By three o'clock, she'd given up trying to understand human nature and had taken to studying the stars instead. There was a pattern to them. God created things in such beautiful order. Perhaps from her perspective, her longitude and latitude and the earth's very position in the solar system, she couldn't quite tell what the actual pattern was. Something more than the pictures of the constellations though.

Counting them would be easier with a telescope. Were they at home in Louvain, with the house intact, she would have had one.

Of course, were she at home in Louvain, the house intact, she wouldn't be up at three o'clock counting stars.

Something below caught her eye. Shadows, but darker than the rest. And moving. Quickly. Finding the side of the house and merging into it. *Lukas!*

338

But not just Lukas. There were three of them.

Margot frowned. He must have recruited help in some form or another. Because it *had* to be Lukas. Had to be. Either Lukas or boys breaking curfew and using their little garden as an alleyway. Or thieves out to steal the half loaf of bread still in their cupboard. It couldn't be Gottlieb's men, for the shadows didn't move like the Germans.

She paused mid-reach for the bags she had packed a week ago and stashed under her bed. Then shook off her traitorous thoughts and reached the rest of the way. It was Lukas. Gottlieb wouldn't set his soldiers on them while he thought he stood a chance of convincing Maman to marry him.

She shouldered both bags—hers and Maman's—and pulled her door slowly open. Two normal steps, one long one, switch to the other side and hug the wall until she reached her mother's door without stepping on any squeaky boards.

Light glowed from underneath it. Evidence that Gottlieb's words were keeping her awake, because usually her mother was asleep long before now. Margot scratched at the door.

The squeak of the bed's ropes, and then the door opened. Maman was still in yesterday's dress, though her hair was braided for sleep. And she had apparently been knitting for hours, given the progress on the scarf on the bed behind her that she'd only started that night. "Margot." Her voice was quiet itself. "What are you doing up? And what do you have with you?"

Margot gripped her hand. "Lukas is here. Follow me."

Maman's eyes went wide. "I need to pack a few things."

She didn't question her. Not for a moment. Pure love welled up, and Margot grinned and patted one of the bags on her shoulder.

Maman gave her that familiar *What will I do with you?* look but said nothing more. Just went in, blew out the single candle she'd had lit—how did she knit with so little light?—and hurried back out into the hallway.

Margot led the way around the loudest of the floorboards, Maman doing a fine job of mirroring her movements. They paused long enough for Margot to draw out the notes she'd already prepared for the kind Madame Dumont, Claudette, and Mr. Allard. The Madame would see Claudette got the second two, and Claudette would deliver the one not for her to the newspaperman. Margot slid all three under the Madame's door. Then they crept soundlessly down the stairs.

She held her breath as they turned at the landing, away from the front door and Gottlieb's room. Toward the back hall that led to the kitchen. *Please, God. Please, God. Eight, sixty-four, five hundred twelve, four thousand ninety-six . . .*

A faint noise reached her ears once they were in the kitchen. Almost like a key in the lock, but not quite. It wasn't a simple slide and turn, but more of a . . . well, a pick. Naturally. How else would he get in? She ought to have come down each night and unlocked the door for him, but she hadn't thought of that.

More important—when did Lukas learn to pick a lock?

"Margot." Maman grasped her by the arm and pulled her back. Whispered directly into her ear. "I assumed he was waiting here—how do you know that is him outside? Did you see him?"

Before she could answer, the knob turned and the door swung open on its silent hinges.

It *wasn't* him. Not the one with the pick, anyway—that person was still crouched down. But his was the face directly behind.

His name wanted to tumble from her lips in a squeal, but she bit it back and hurled herself at him instead, nearly knocking over the one with the picks—a woman. That didn't matter. Margot threw her arms around her brother and held on so tightly he would probably complain that he couldn't breathe.

That didn't matter either. He was *here*.

He held her close, chuckled softly, squeezed her right back. "Margot."

"Shh. An officer lives here. He is sleeping in the downstairs bedroom."

"No, actually. He is not."

Maman gasped at the familiar voice, and the rest of them spun toward the corner just as a match was struck and touched to the wick of an oil lamp.

Gottlieb's motions were smooth and calm, his face betraying nothing. He was, for the first time she'd seen, not in uniform, and his hair was sleep rumpled.

Lukas tried to push Margot behind him, but she shrugged away. "Generalleutnant. We were just—"

"I know what you are doing, *spatz*." He had no weapon. He wasn't marching toward the door and calling for reinforcements. He was just *standing* there, with his hands resting on the worn top of the kitchen table. "So this is your brother. I have long been a fan, *monsieur*. Though to be sure, I only recently realized you were related to these ladies I have had the privilege of getting to know this autumn."

The other two with Lukas were edging farther into the room, clinging to the shadows. One whispered something to the other, but she couldn't quite catch what. It seemed to be in . . . English? She had heard it so little since Papa died and her lessons stopped. But of course that would make sense. Lukas had been in Wales.

Lukas eased farther into the room too, putting himself between Gottlieb and Maman. "Thank you, Generalleutnant."

"Though I confess, I am very surprised to find you in this kitchen. Word around the army, you see, is that you were shot and killed some two months ago."

Maman wove her arm through Lukas's. "It is what we heard too, Generalleutnant."

"Further." Gottlieb lifted one finger of one hand. "Further, this is not the De Wilde house. So I am *very* curious as to how

341

you found them." His gaze went straight to Margot though. "I am suddenly suspecting our trip to the bookshop was not so innocent as it seemed."

And what would he do to the proprietor if he was suspected of aiding the resistance? Margot shook her head. "The bookshop was just the bookshop. I am cleverer than that."

His smile looked like it had that day, though, when she'd agreed to play Go with him without holding back.

She'd beaten him in a mere two hours. And he had laughed the brightest laugh she'd ever heard from him.

"That I know. Well." He straightened and drew in a long breath. "I am glad I heard that noise outside and came to investigate. I would have hated to have awoken and found you gone without explanation. I would have worried."

Everyone remained still. It almost sounded like—but that couldn't be.

He lifted his brows. "Go on, then. I can hardly turn you in now, when I have known for weeks that I have the most sought-after fugitives in Belgium under my very roof and have done nothing about it. I would be court-martialed. You are safe from me, I assure you."

Margot huffed. "You could always claim that you suspected Lukas would show up and were waiting to arrest us until you could get him too. Or make a big show of it in front of your new superior to win back the favor you've fallen out of."

Lukas and Maman both spun on her. "Margot!"

She rolled her eyes. "He's not stupid. He would have thought of it already."

That bright smile settled on his lips again. "I believe that is the highest compliment I have ever been paid. But the standard belief is that your brother is dead. Who am I to resurrect him?"

Maman rushed forward and stretched up to press a kiss to his cheek. "We are in your debt, Wolfgang." His name came off her tongue awkwardly, as if she'd never said it before. She probably hadn't.

But his eyes gleamed. "I only wanted to keep you safe, Madame De Wilde. But I know there is no choice when the other option is your son. Perhaps someday, when this war is over, we will meet again under better conditions. But for now, you all had better hurry—and be cautious. You have only a few hours of darkness left and much city to get through."

One of the English shadows stepped forward a bit. Margot couldn't fully make out his features in the dim light, but what she could see she rather liked. "Is everything all right, Lukas?"

Lukas studied Gottlieb a moment more and then nodded. "It would seem he is a—a friend."

Margot took a second to work through the English and then nodded along. And forced her tongue to try a bit of it, to be polite. "We are ready. Come, Maman."

Her mother hurried back around the table and took one of the bags from Margot's shoulder.

"Wait!" Gottlieb, too, spoke in English. "The book I got for the two of you. Would you at least take that? To remember me? I can fetch it in only a minute."

The Englishman shifted, and his face said he didn't like the request one bit. "With all due respect, sir, I'd feel better if you stayed right where you are."

"It does not matter." Margot patted her bag. "I already have it packed."

He didn't move—perhaps because of the Englishman and whatever he might have in that hand he kept behind his back— but he held out a hand toward Margot. Sideways, to shake. Like an adult.

She slid her palm against his. "Thank you, Gottlieb." That name *didn't* trip strangely off her tongue, even though she'd never called him by anything other than his rank.

He smiled. "Good luck to you, Margot. Perhaps we will have another game of Go someday."

She smiled back, then turned away. The Englishwoman was at the door now, holding it open and herding them all through. She had an interesting face—it looked nothing like the man's, and yet it did. In the eyes. The way she looked into the night and took it all in. Even more interesting, though, was the way Lukas edged around her through the door, going out of his way to avoid touching her.

Which was not like Lukas at all. She was looking forward to figuring out who this woman was.

And asking her if she would teach Margot how to pick a lock. It seemed like a skill worth knowing.

———⬡———

It had been too easy. Willa knew it. And distrusted it. It made the palms of her hands itch and the hollow spots inside her chest echo with each thud of her heart. She wasn't sure if it was that man in the kitchen of the townhouse that caused the unease or something else, but trouble was brewing. She hadn't a doubt about that.

The De Wildes didn't seem to think so. As the sun came up, they visibly relaxed and even began chatting in Flemish as they walked the road back to Antwerp.

She hung back a step behind the family, beside Barclay. "If they are the most sought-after fugitives in Belgium, then . . ."

"I know. Someone will be looking. We have to get them off the roads."

Lukas turned to glare at them. "I was gracious enough to tell you what was said at the house—now please, no more English," he said in English.

Willa had a snarl ready, but she wasted no time on it when

ROSEANNA M. WHITE

the sound of distant thunder cut through the morning. "Off the road. Now."

This part of it thankfully had a few trees growing alongside and didn't just cut through open fields like so much of it did. They darted between the trees and all ducked behind a low stone wall a few seconds before the first of the horses cantered by. Followed by what looked like an endless stream of marching soldiers.

She could see them through a crack between the stones, and the others had found similar viewing spots. Lukas hissed out a breath.

She couldn't blame him. Had she seen a foreign army marching through *her* countryside like that, she would have felt it keenly too.

If she stretched out her hand just a few inches, she could brush his fingers with her own. Give a breath of comfort, maybe. A single note in a major key amid so much minor.

Or maybe it would just remind him of her betrayal and he would jerk his hand away—how was she to know?

"*Maman, regardes.*"

Willa turned her head toward the direction of the whisper, at the girl she still hadn't gotten a proper look at in full daylight. Margot De Wilde was pointing at the advancing ranks.

Willa sucked in a breath as she peered through the crack again. An automobile puttered along in the middle of the convoy, its top open. And sitting inside it was none other than the man from the kitchen—Gottlieb. "What is he doing here?"

Lukas's sister was the one to turn her way and whisper back, "He is transferring to Antwerp. And apparently taking his men with him."

She didn't like it. Not one bit. Why, of all the roads in the country, did this man who knew who they were have to be on *theirs*? Did he know where they were going? Did he mean, as

345

Margot had suggested, to make a show of capturing them, thereby securing himself favor?

As she watched, the man turned his head their way. He couldn't see them—he *couldn't*—but he was scanning the wall, the area behind them.

Barclay nudged her, nodded. "Down there. Hurry."

Willa craned her neck around to see what he had spotted. Cellar steps opened up just feet away from them. They looked old and unused in recent years, and were likely not connected to the farmhouse in the clearing.

It worked for her. They all crawled their way over, Barclay leading the way down. Margot followed without hesitation, her mother going next with a ginger step and a glance over her shoulder.

Lukas sent Willa a gaze as warm as an iceberg and jerked his head. In the face of such a gracious invitation, she had no choice but to jerk her own head toward the opening and whisper, "Stay with your family." She would feel better making sure no one had spotted them. That Gottlieb hadn't somehow sensed them and sent up a shout.

He growled but followed his mother down the steps. Willa edged down a few steps behind him but kept her head at ground level until she was certain the German general hadn't sent anyone to investigate.

"Willa, out of the way. I have a door."

She pulled herself into the dim space and backed down the steps, out of Barclay's way. The wood in his hands could only loosely be termed a door, as rotted as it was, but anything newer would have looked out of place. He managed to ease it up into position and wedge it there at an angle.

Not the most secure hiding spot they'd ever found when they had to duck away from authorities, but not the worst. She spun to take in the space, expecting darkness and spiders and rats and who knew what else.

346

Instead she saw, in the glow of an old lamp Lukas had lit, old wooden shelves with openings square and deep. Gravel on the floor. And scuffed work stations that had a strange bit of style to them.

"Wine cellar," Lukas said, setting the lantern on the counter.

His sister scanned the space, thoughts clamoring through her eyes. As if she were measuring it. Casing it.

Willa's lips twitched. Had she met this girl on the street, she would have tried to recruit her into the family.

Lukas sank to a seat at his sister's side. "How many bottles can it hold?"

Willa leaned against the stone wall, though it was damp and cold.

Margot tilted her head. "Two hundred and forty."

"Stones?"

"One thousand seven hundred twenty-eight."

Lukas pursed his lips. "Pounds of gravel?"

She lifted a piece of it, weighed it in her hand. "Half a ton."

He smiled and slid an arm around her, pulled her close to his side. "I missed you."

"Me too." She sighed as she said it and turned those inquisitive eyes on Willa and Barclay. "You never introduced us, Lukas. I am surprised Maman did not chide you."

"Mm." Their mother sat as well and closed her eyes. "Yes, Lukas. Introduce us."

He didn't so much as glance at them. "Barclay Pearce. Willa Forsythe."

Margot lifted her brows. "And?"

"And what?"

She rolled her eyes and motioned toward them. "How do you know them? Why did they come with you? And which of them should I ask to teach me to pick a lock?"

He looked almost ready to explode at that one. Willa laughed and slid down to take a seat as well. When had she last slept? She wasn't sure. "When we get to England, I'll teach you. If your mother allows it."

Margot looked to her mother with a hopeful lift of her brows, but Madame De Wilde made no reply. Her breathing had gone deep and even, her hands slack in her lap.

Barclay sat on the bottom stair. "Not a bad idea. Everyone catch a bit of sleep now, while it's safe. Let Gottlieb and his men get well ahead. We'll get back on the road later."

Willa stood again and nudged her brother's knee with her boot. "I'll take first watch. I've another hour or two in me."

"Are you sure?"

"Do I volunteer unless I am?"

He pushed off with a nod, mussed her hair fondly on his way past, and staked out a place on the floor. Lukas did the same without a word, and Margot leaned into her mother.

Willa drew in a long, musty breath and set her face toward the steep stairs and the bits of daylight that snuck through the crooked door. With her companions all quiet, she could still hear the steady steps on the road. How many of them were up there, marching to Antwerp?

Were they looking for them?

Instead of dwelling on it, she tried to conjure some music into her mind. It had been days since she'd played anything. More than days—a week. A week since she'd held a violin and heard it singing in her ear. The last piece she'd played had been one of Lukas's, but on her own violin. That Sunday evening before she went down for supper with him. Before Mr. Rees had burst in. Before Cor had wrecked it all.

No. She would think of the music, not him. She pulled it into her mind, rested her arms on her drawn-up knees to roughly imitate the correct position. And she played in time to the marching feet.

She finished her private, silent concert with a long exhalation and started when Margot sat opposite her on the bottom step.

"Violin or viola?"

Willa's lips pulled up. "Violin."

"Like Lukas."

"Mm." Her gaze found him of its own volition. His hair was tumbling all over his forehead. He was dressed in the rough clothes of a farmer. Dirt smudged his face and hands. And he was still the most beautiful man she'd ever seen. Blast him.

"Is that how you met him? Through the orchestra?"

She sighed. "He probably would not want you talking to me, Margot. I'm a thief. Fulfilling a contract for a job. Nothing more."

Margot gave her a look a fourteen-year-old ought not to be able to give. "I talk to whomever I want. And I have never seen my brother *not* look at a woman as deliberately as he was not looking at you this morning. He must be in love with you. And not happy about it. Is it because you are a thief?"

She didn't know whether to laugh or cry or do something else altogether. "A fine summation."

"I am good at sums." The girl rested her elbows on her knees, her chin in her hands, and studied Willa. "But you do not have to always be a thief. If you are as talented with a violin in your hands as you are with your invisible one, you can be a musician instead."

Willa picked at a dried-on glob of something or another on her ugly brown skirt. "I *like* being a thief."

"And he *liked* being a rake—but there always comes a time for change, *oui*?" She stood and dusted off the back of her skirt. "When you are ready, Jesus will forgive you. As He did Lukas."

Why did her life keep filling up with all these people who wanted to talk about Jesus? Willa shook her head. "Why would I want Him to do that?"

"Because"—Margot smiled as if it were all as simple as two plus two—"that is when He can start piecing us back together."

Willa's breath caught as the girl returned to her spot. Caught and knotted and made her eyes burn.

She turned back to the slivers of light and bit her lip until the tears marched away.

TWENTY-SIX

"Why are you telling me this?" Lukas dug his fingers into the dirt covering the stone steps. All was silent up above them and had been since he'd woken half an hour earlier and come over here to see if he could relieve Barclay of the watch.

He rather wished all had remained silent in the wine cellar as well. He ought to have objected the very moment Barclay had whispered, *"You don't understand, you know. Why she is the way she is."*

Lukas didn't need pity stirring in his chest for the woman asleep on the floor in the corner. What he needed was to build a wall around his heart, like the one she'd kept so well guarded around her own. He needed a way to force her from his heart altogether—a place she'd never wanted to be to begin with. As she'd said time and again.

Why hadn't he listened?

Barclay sighed. "You really mean to tell me it changes nothing in your opinion of her, knowing where she comes from?"

He breathed a laugh that felt as carefree as war. "She does not care what my opinion is. And even if she did, it does not matter from where she came, only where she has chosen to go.

351

And she has *chosen* to be a thief, as if it were the only option. As if there are not thousands in the same position who choose to lead honest lives." He stood, put a foot on the crumbling step. "But you know, that is not the worst of it. The worst is that she has tried so hard to avoid being like her mother that she has become her father instead—running from involvement that might risk her heart."

Barclay's eyes glinted, but any retort about Willa must have given way when Lukas took one step up and then another, because Barclay hissed, "Where are you going?"

"To look around. See if perhaps I can find a farmer with a cart who will drive us."

He didn't wait for a response, simply shoved the rotting door aside and blinked his way into the afternoon sun that assaulted his senses.

He couldn't stay down there a moment more, with *her* so close by, and so closed off. With the weight of responsibility for his family so heavy, and telling him every moment that he must hurry.

A wordless prayer surged through his heart. If they were to find their way back to the docks, find another boat, find a way across the Channel, it would be by God's grace. He was none too sure Cor Akkerman would still be waiting for them, regardless of the fact that Lukas still owed him fifteen pounds for the return trip.

"Hey! Where did you come from?"

Lukas started, biting back a choice word when a figure straightened from its seat on the low stone wall. The German uniform tied knots in Lukas's stomach. His gaze tracked to the automobile pulled off the road, its bonnet up.

He fastened on a smile, motioned toward the farmhouse in the distant clearing, past the bare trees, and prayed the man wouldn't hear the French in his German. "I saw you seemed to be having problems. Can I lend assistance?" Bluster was his only hope. Pretend confidence. With that in mind, he hopped over the wall and made for the automobile as if he had some clue as to how to fix the thing.

But the soldier narrowed his eyes. "I did not see you approaching when I looked that way a minute ago."

Blast. He'd rather hoped that the cigarette dangling from the man's fingers meant he'd not been paying attention to anything. *"Nein?"* He knit his brows together and leaned over the space left open by the bonnet. "Odd. Perhaps a tree blocked your view of me."

The man—if one could call him such, for he looked to be no more than twenty—took another drag from his cigarette, obviously contemplating the truth of that. At length, he shrugged. "I thank you for your offer. But my colleagues already know of the breakdown and have gone to fetch the needed supplies to fix it. They will be back in a matter of minutes."

No, no, no. That was no good at all. How was he to warn the others?

"Wait a minute. You look familiar. Almost like . . . but that cannot be, he has already been killed."

Would nothing go right this afternoon? Had they used up all their good fortune escaping from the house in Brussels? But no, God would not abandon them now. Lukas would just have to bluff his way out of this. He forced a chuckle. "I have been mistaken for many things in my life, sir, but never for a dead man."

"It is an uncanny resemblance. I'd studied his photograph for hours when we were watching for him. You—"

Thunk. Lukas spun back around just in time to see the soldier crumpling to the ground. Barclay stood behind him, a stone in hand. He tossed it down and bent over to check the soldier's pulse.

Lukas drew in a sharp breath. "Why did you do that?"

Barclay gave him a look he'd received no fewer than a dozen times from Willa. "He recognized you. What would you have *had* me do? But he's only unconscious, which means we haven't much time. When his colleagues return . . ."

They had better be long gone. Lukas vaulted back over the wall. "Margot! Mère! We have to leave now!"

But it was Willa, of course, who was the first to respond, and to urge his family to wakefulness and up the stairs. She didn't look at him—which was fine, because he certainly wasn't looking at her. Which meant he had no reason to note the angry look she shot her so-called brother.

He suddenly suspected she hadn't been asleep while Barclay told him about her childhood.

There was no time to worry about that. He set his sights on the distant farmhouse—and the wagon in front of it, with one horse hitched to it and another even now being led that direction by a figure too small at this distance to be discernable.

Friend or foe?

They had little choice but to gamble.

———◇———

It was better to rage than to weep, which was what she really wanted to do. Willa kicked at a little pile of hay that lay in the freshly scythed field across which they tramped—remarkably unsatisfying, given that it simply scattered in the wind—and debated the wisdom of slapping Barclay upside the head. She might, were it not so blasted *hard* a head.

"I'll not apologize," he said again, keeping his gaze fastened on the De Wildes, who were a few strides ahead of them. "Not for trying to see to your happiness. It's my privilege as your brother."

"As if *he* will make me happy?" She kept her voice low, kept her pace quick. And darted a glance over her shoulder. They'd trussed up the soldier and put him in the boot of his automobile, but he could wake up and make a racket at any moment. "As if he *could*."

"Willa." Barclay sighed. "What if life has more for you than this? Have you never considered it?"

More? More than the existence she had carved out for herself?

More than children who clamored around her, relied on her? More than music whenever she picked up a violin—assuming she got her hands on another? "I'm happy with our life, Barclay. It's what we are. What we're good at."

He squeezed his eyes shut for a second. "No, Will. It's something we did because we saw no other way. But wasn't the goal always to escape it? To give the little ones a chance for a different life? An honest one? We'll never be rich, that's a given, but working for V now, for the government . . . we could be better. *Normal.*"

"I don't *want* to be normal." And how could he do this to her? Start talking about changing everything, giving up on all they'd worked so hard for?

Barclay breathed a laugh. "Well, good. Because you, at least, don't have to be. Not with your talent. Don't you see? You can play your violin. Join an orchestra somewhere, put all this behind you. Give yourself a chance at happiness and entertain the possibility that maybe Lukas De Wilde is a part of that."

Why did it make her eyes sting? Oh yes. Because it was impossible. She couldn't undo all she was. She couldn't just become something else. "Next you'll start spouting the same nonsense as Rosie and Peter and Lukas. About God and prayer and Jesus."

Still he looked at her as if he couldn't fathom what went on inside her head. "Do you really never pray?"

"Do you mean you *do?*" She sidestepped a furrow in the field.

Yet he smiled a strange, crooked smile. "I have. Not often, mind you—didn't dare. An urchin going before the King, as it were. But when I prayed, He answered—He brought me to Pauly, to you and Rosie and the others. And it's made me think. Peter said something before he left about God calling us, drawing us while we're still sinners. And I wonder . . . I wonder if that's what He's been doing all along. Calling us to Him. To His work. If maybe that's what He's doing now, providing us a way out of the life we made for ourselves."

She shook her head, her back going stiff when a shout came from the farmer whose wagon they were approaching. Lukas had said he was amenable to taking them into Antwerp with him, but what if it was just a trap? Or if they came upon the friends of that soldier Barclay had bashed over the head and they got a good man in trouble? "Maybe I don't *want* out."

"Willa." Barclay moved close, rested a hand on her shoulder, and spoke in a bare murmur. "You can spend your life regretting what you've lost. Or you can thank the Lord for what He's given. We could have been alone. Each of us. We could have struggled and fought and starved and likely died or landed in prison. But instead . . . we have a family. A blamed good one, if you ask me. One I love every bit as much as I did the one I was born into."

More. More, because they'd chosen each other. Chosen to love and to stay and to sacrifice so they could.

He squeezed her shoulder. "Don't let stubbornness keep you from happiness. Seize it. Don't let it go."

As if the choice were only hers. Assuming she ever could have found happiness with Lukas, she'd already ruined everything there. He'd never trust her again. For good reason.

But it didn't matter. "Let's just get them back to England for now, Barclay. That's enough for today."

Barclay's sigh said he'd give up. For now. Which was just as well, because the farmer was speaking rapidly in Flemish, motioning them into the back of the wagon. And looking over his shoulder all the while, no doubt making sure no one saw them.

While Lukas handed over a few coins, the rest of them climbed up into the back of the wagon loaded with hay. They each tucked themselves among the bales so they'd be invisible from the road. Willa ended up sandwiched between Barclay and Margot, careful not to so much as crowd Lukas with her gaze once he joined them and the wagon lurched into motion.

Yet still it felt like he was pushing her away. Willing her out of his vicinity.

She didn't love him. So it shouldn't hurt.

Why, then, did it?

They were on the road no more than ten minutes, by her count, before the clatter of an engine broke in upon the monotony of horses' hooves, coming from the direction in which they were going. The Germans, coming to rescue their comrade, she imagined. She didn't dare peek out, nor did any of the others. Rather, they all burrowed deeper into the hay, covering themselves up as much as they could.

The others were praying—she could see lips moving, hear the breath of whispers. She could *feel* them all, straining upward. Willa squeezed her eyes shut, but she wouldn't have known how to pray had she wanted to.

This was where God would prove himself to be just like her father, right? He wouldn't show up. Or He would, on the wrong side. Maybe He meant to answer the prayers of those German soldiers instead of theirs.

The engine grew louder, rumbled past, faded off again. But it was no reason for relief. It was *after* they'd found their friend that there would be trouble.

The engine roared into hearing again, from behind. And a minute later, the wagon slowed to a halt. German shouts filled the air, though they didn't turn off their engine.

Willa pulled her knees up to her chest under her mound of hay, but it did nothing to ease the helplessness. In her mind's eye, though, soldiers were already coming at them, bayonets affixed to their rifles so they could stab into the hay in search of them.

The farmer answered the Germans in a voice loud enough to be heard over the engine. All she could make out was *"Nein, nein . . ."*

And then a miracle. The engine roared off again, back in the other direction, and the farmer clicked his horses back into a walk.

"He told them that he just entered the road half a mile back, from his farm," Margot whispered. "That he has not seen anyone else on the road yet except them, but that he'd noticed two men walking toward Brussels as he was hitching up the wagon."

Two men—Lukas plus one to hit the other across the head. The farmer was quick on his feet. And they may just owe him their lives. If Lukas had any spare coins from the Davieses, he ought to impart a few more to that man.

No other engines interrupted the jostling, jolting, uncomfortable hours of the ride, though they passed a few other wagons. Still, it would have been foolish to relax their guard for even a moment. Which meant that by the time the farmer pulled to a halt in the market district of Antwerp, Willa's nerves were jangling and her stomach was as clenched as after two days without food.

They slipped out of the hay under the cover of an awning and took a few minutes to pick the remnants of it off their clothing before they emerged to give the farmer their thanks and another coin—she hadn't even had to mention it. Then Lukas led them away from the market stalls and toward the docks.

Willa's chest tightened with every step. Perhaps it was just residual anxiety from the road, but she didn't think so. Something was wrong. Off. Skewed. She couldn't say what—she didn't know this city or who should be out and about at this time of day, but shouldn't there have been more of a crowd?

It was wartime in an occupied country. Surely that accounted for the largely empty streets and the sullen looks of those they passed.

The logic did nothing to ease the constriction. She met Barclay's gaze and noted that his jaw was clenched just as tightly as her own. His eyes darted to the left, blinked, then moved to the right.

She nodded and grabbed the elbow of Lukas's jacket to slow him down. Stretched up on her toes so she could whisper into his ear, careful to smile enough that it would look flirtatious to any passersby. "We need to split up. We're too noteworthy in a group this large."

Perhaps she had expected him to argue. Instead, he merely nodded and reached for his mother's arm.

Willa shook her head and leaned close again. "No. If anyone is looking for your family, they will be looking for you together. You and Barclay each choose a separate path. I'll stay with your mother and sister. Three women will draw little undue attention."

He didn't like it—she could tell by the way his hand fisted. But the logic must have been clear, because he just jerked his head and leaned over to whisper the plan to his mother in Flemish, then spun away.

Barclay peeled off too, leaving Willa with the De Wilde women.

She wove her arm through Margot's and had to make an effort to keep their pace measured, slow, and their heads down as they retraced the path toward the docks that Willa had taken before with the men. Occasionally she would catch sight of Barclay or Lukas, a street over on either side, walking parallel to them.

Then, finally, the tang of fish in the air shouted how close they were. Her eyes scanned the docks as they drew within sight—and snagged on the unbelievable.

Cor Akkerman was actually there, lounging against a wooden crate and in animated conversation with the fisherman he'd pointed out to them yesterday—the one taking them back across the Channel. He laughed, as did the captain of the rusty, rattletrap steamer they'd be boarding.

She looked to her left and saw Barclay emerging onto the pier from his street. To the right, Lukas was already approaching Cor and the captain.

Her stomach was as tight as a pauper's purse strings. So many soldiers were out and about—normal these days, she knew from when they'd landed. Normal, but dangerous.

Cor greeted Lukas with a nod and ushered him onto the boat. Barclay hung back for a minute before making his way there too, and also boarding.

Margot tugged on her hand, and Madame De Wilde increased her pace. Willa matched it, but her stomach didn't ease any. Not given the tiny little smile at the corner of Cor's mouth. He was up to something. She would stake next month's take on it.

But Barclay reappeared at the ship's rail and, as agreed upon to signal all was well, lifted a hand as if greeting someone far off.

The captain came toward the three of them as they neared, offering a warm, familiar greeting and going so far as to kiss Madame De Wilde's cheeks, as if she were a sister. Lukas's mother played along, laughing and tucking her arm into the man's, letting him lead her toward the boat. Turning to motion Margot to hurry.

Cor stepped into Willa's path. She released Margot's arm so she could keep pace with her mother and met his grin with an arched brow.

"It seems we work better together than you thought we would, *ja*?"

Her throat went tight. His words were friendly, almost teasing. But in English, as they shouldn't have been. And his eyes positively gleamed with hatred.

She stepped to the side, meaning to pass him. But never got the chance. As his lips bloomed into a full, nasty smile, the world exploded. Shouts, whistles, running feet. Every street-bred instinct she possessed screamed. Her muscles coiled, she sprang—but there was nowhere to spring.

Soldiers were everywhere. She saw clouds of uniforms, flashes of gleaming buttons. Heard the terrifying, earth-shattering sound of a gun.

It mixed in her ears with her own name, called out in a masculine tone. Barclay? Lukas? She lunged for it, but something collided with her back and sent her sprawling onto the damp, cold wood of the dock.

"Lukas!" It wasn't Willa's voice, though she'd been poised to shout for him. It was his mother's.

Willa tried to lift her head, to find him. She thought that maybe, perhaps, she saw familiar shapes on that rattletrap fishing boat. But she couldn't be sure. Her ears were too full of German shouts. Her lungs had no air. And a strange stinging warmth was clawing at her side.

And then *him*. Cor pushed through the soldiers, still grinning. He crouched down until he was just above her, his mouth hovering over her ear. "I told you, pretty Willa, that you ought not to cross me. Now look at you. Captured on suspicion of espionage." He clucked his tongue.

She bared her teeth, a retort curling her lips. But then pain exploded through her skull, and fog rolled over her vision like a dream before she could get out a word.

TWENTY-SEVEN

Margot curled into a ball, trying to slow her breathing. To count it into submission. But it was no use. It heaved and gasped, and mathematics could do nothing to calm it.

She was gone. Willa was gone, and now *they* were gone, chugging their way away from the wharf.

"Willa!" her brother bellowed, struggling against the hands holding him down. He was bleeding everywhere. It originated at his shoulder, but it had soaked his coat sleeve and had somehow gotten smeared all over his neck, his face, their mother—whose hands were among the ones trying to calm him.

But his eyes were still trained on the distant shore. "Go back. Turn back. We cannot leave her there."

Another round of gunfire sounded. Too far away to hit them, but it served as punctuation on the growl of the captain. "If we turn back," the old man said in heavily accented French, "we are all dead."

"Then put us off at the next stop." Lukas batted away his mother's hands and pushed to his feet. Or tried to do so, though he swayed.

Margot curled a little tighter into her ball. It shouldn't have

362

been Willa. She wasn't the one they wanted. They'd realize their mistake soon.

It wasn't that they'd then come after *them* that she feared, particularly. It was what they might do to the Englishwoman in the meantime. And upon discovering she had nothing to offer them.

Barclay all but shoved Lukas back down. His face was blank, but it couldn't be lack of feeling that made it so. Too *much*, perhaps. When he'd first stumbled against the rail as the boat charged from its dock, she'd thought he would leap into the river and go after his sister.

But Willa was already in the hands of the German soldiers. Ten of them, surging and hitting and pulling her limp form along, shoving it into an automobile.

Ten of them. Barclay must have done the mathematics on how unlikely it was that he could fend off ten soldiers and follow a car too. He'd spun back around without a single indication on his face of what he was planning.

Margot scooted back on her crate, until her back curved against the side of the boat. They would have a plan though. They must. That fellow they called Cor Akkerman—this had all been his fault. Urging the rest of them on ahead of Willa, drawing her away a step. Then giving some signal to the soldiers. They had appeared from nowhere.

Why? What lies must he have fed them, that they took the one who had nothing to do with anything and left their true targets unharmed? It ought to have been Margot they sought. And by extension, Maman and Lukas.

Not Willa.

Maman had rushed Margot onto the already-running boat, but Lukas had tried to dash after the woman he'd so stoutly refused to look at. And now a bullet had torn through him, and there was all that blood, and Willa was not here, and the captain looked etched from stone.

"Don't be an idiot," Barclay said to her brother in a voice like winter. "You've been shot. You go barreling back onto shore and you're a liability, not a help."

Lukas grunted as Maman wrestled his coat off his shoulder. "Well, you cannot go alone. You do not speak the language, you do not know the city—"

"You think I'm not aware of that?" It emerged in a shout that ripped the air, interrupted the engine noises, joined with the gulls screeching overhead.

It smelled like fish. And salt. And despair.

Margot hugged her knees tighter and prayed. That, by her calculation, was the best chance of a good outcome from this.

Barclay stabbed a finger into the wind. "That is my *sister*. You think I plan to leave her there a second longer than I have to? But we have to be wise."

Maman gasped. "Lukas. What is this?"

Margot craned her neck so she could see an angry scar on Lukas's bared shoulder, red even when their mother had swabbed away the blood that oozed two inches to the right.

Lukas grunted. "Where I was shot two months ago, trying to find you. It has healed. This one will too." Though he added a rather colorful opinion of the men who had dared to shoot him *twice*.

It was Willa who Margot's eyes saw then, though. She, too, had had red blossoming through her coat as the soldiers pushed her to the ground. *Keep her well, Lord God. Be with her. Eleven, twenty-two, thirty-three, forty-four . . .*

Maman heaved a sigh. "It went straight through, praise God."

"Better than the last one, then. I will be fine." He tried again to push forward, away from Maman's hands.

Barclay held him down this time with a boot to his uninjured shoulder. "Don't. Be. An idiot."

"This boat is not stopping until we reach England," the captain

364

added in English even more accented than his French. "You think I will compromise *my* family?" He motioned to a huddled mass of bodies beside him in the wheelhouse.

Lukas's face went darker than she had ever seen it. He *must* love Willa. Fiercely. "She could be dead by the time we return."

"She won't be." This Barclay pronounced with calm certainty, his hands fisted at his sides. "We're going to believe that. And we're going to go back to England, and I'm going to contact V—"

"No!" This time Lukas managed to lurch free of both boot and mother, struggling to his feet. "Not him."

"If anyone can get Willa out of their hands, it's him. You know it is."

But Lukas shook his head, eyes wild. "No. We will find another way. He cannot know you were in Belgium rather than Paris."

"There is no other way!"

Lukas's breath heaved. "Then you wait until I get them somewhere safe. Then you contact him. Tell him the trail led you there, but—"

"You think he won't discover the truth? That he won't talk to the people who took us there or wonder how we managed to push so far into Belgium alone?"

Margot scooted to the edge of the crate and let her legs dangle. "Who is V?"

Lukas swallowed but didn't look at her. "No. We find someone else to help, then. But I will not turn to him. He'll take her from me."

Margot stood. The *her* ought to be Willa. But it wasn't. She knew it wasn't. "Who is V?" she asked again.

Maman put a hand on his arm. Not to urge him back down this time, but to be an anchor to the look she sent him, pleading and somber. "Who is V?"

He looked at Maman, then darted a glance at Margot. "He would take her, Mère. Take her and make her a weapon, breaking codes all day."

Margot could say nothing. She had known—of course, she had known—why Papa's bragging about his "cypher machine" posed such a danger to her. She had known that she, as surely as Claude Archambault, could be forced to work for an enemy government. She had known that her skills would be sought in this war, even though she was only a child.

But she'd never once considered she could help those *opposed* to Germany.

The two men were glaring at each other again. Lukas said again, "No."

Margot's fingers knotted in her skirt. She shouldn't want to take part in the war, should she? It was a nasty, violent thing. It meant death and horror and things she'd only read about.

But ending it—ending it could mean life for her neighbors. For Claudette's family, for Madame Dumont, for Jerome Allard. If she could help put a stop to Germany's advance somehow with this gift God had given her . . . "Lukas." That was all she said.

But maybe he heard something more in it. His nostrils flared as he met her gaze, and he shook his head. "No."

Barclay folded his arms across his chest. "Sorry, Lukas. But it seems to have come down to this: your sister or mine."

———◇———

There was only darkness. Silence. And then worse than silence—words she couldn't understand barely reaching her from somewhere she couldn't see. Willa sat on a hard chair, her hands tied behind her, and wondered if this was death. Her whole body screamed in pain. Had they struck her? Or had she dreamed it?

How long had she been here? Hours? Days? Forever?

Her lips were dried, cracked. Her fingers could have been lopped off for all she knew—she couldn't feel them. Her side screamed. Why couldn't *it* go numb? Her head throbbed, each pulse an echo.

Alone. Alone. Alone.

Had she thought herself alone before? She'd never known the meaning of the word. Not like this. With the darkness. And the silence. And the worse-than-silence. *Alone.* No mother. No father. No Pauly. No Barclay or Rosie or Retta or Elinor or Lucy. No little ones.

No Lukas.

She would die here, in this silent darkness. It settled like yesterday in her bones—already known, unchangeable, certain. Whatever made her side scream had taken a lot of blood. It was a dried, stiff mess in her clothes. And made her head swim. It wasn't just darkness and silence. It was *swaying* darkness and silence.

She would die here. Of thirst or lack of blood. And no one would ever know.

Barclay would try to come for her. Try to find her. But how could he?

Her tongue was swollen. She tried to use it to wet her lips, but it felt strange and spongy.

Barclay would have to give up. He'd have to, for the sake of the rest of the family. They'd never lost one of their numbers before, but they'd discussed what to do if a job went bad on them, if one were already lost.

Cut and run. They'd all agreed the body didn't matter, not if they were dead—there was no point in the rest of them risking their necks to recover it.

She was already dead. He'd cut and run. He'd have to.

A crash sounded from somewhere in the unbroken night. Echoing. And echoing. And echoing. Thunder?

"Do you really never pray?" His words knocked around inside her aching head.

What was the point? It was like he'd said—she'd be nothing but a street rat petitioning the King. Nothing to recommend her. And no great need of the kind of justice she'd seen Him mete out.

But she was so very alone. Already dead. She'd come before Him in a few minutes or hours or days, anyway. . . .

God, are you there?

No answer came in the darkness. Nothing but a thudding growing ever louder. Her heart, probably, pushing all that life out her side.

Lukas. He wouldn't come either. He had his mother, his sister. And even if he hadn't . . . he wouldn't. Because she was nothing to him now. No, worse—she was her father to him. Someone who took and never gave. Someone who left before ever giving love a chance. Someone who stole the most important thing.

I'm sorry. God, if you're there, will you tell him I'm sorry? Tell him I didn't want to hurt him. Tell him . . . tell him that if I knew how to love, he's the one I'd want to.

A strange smell made her nose itch. Then she went blind. Only this blindness was painfully white rather than eternally black. She winced and turned her head away from the onslaught, but her chin was caught by something hard and fast and un-yielding.

It all swam. Light into dark into grey. Though her face was surely not moving with that solid something holding onto it, it rocked about. Maybe she was on the boat after all. Maybe this was all a nightmare. Maybe—

Words. Unfamiliar. Throaty vowels, sharp consonants. But the voice. The voice was familiar.

She blinked. Blinked again. But it was still just white and black and grey and . . . brown. A patch of brown.

The earth quaked underneath her, sending tremors through her whole body. Or perhaps it was the hands that gripped her, shook her. There were two of him. Or three. All moving in and out of each other. But she saw that brown. It meant something, but . . .

Brown.

She sucked in a breath. V had failed to arrest him. Said he

368

escaped the country. And here he was . . . with his fingers digging into her shoulders and a sneer emerging from the darkness.

He said something. Barked it, but she couldn't tell what words he used. Or if they were for her. A minute later, though, something cool and wet splashed against her lips.

Water. She sucked it up, gulped what was poured in until she choked and coughed and spat a mouthful out again. It settled, cold and cruel, on her shirt. And her side screamed in fresh agony. New wetness trickled there too, making her want to writhe away from it, if she could move. Were her legs tied too?

His face again. Familiar but fuzzy. Though there was only one of him just now. "I thought it impossible that it was you when I heard there was a female English spy captured."

I am not a spy. Her lips moved, but her tongue was still too swollen. Her throat too dry. Nothing came out.

"Yet here you are. And why is that, Miss Forsythe? Why are you in Belgium rather than in Wales, with your Belgian? Getting that key for me. Hmm?"

She was already dead. It wouldn't be thirst or bleeding that did it though. It would be him. Of course it would be him. Delivered into the hands of the Germans by Cor Akkerman—but at least his vengeance had only demanded her. The others had made it to the boat. It had been running. They would have gotten away. They *had* to have gotten away. And Cor would deem his vengeance complete. She was captured. Dead. And heaven looked a long way off. Hell, though—she could imagine it now. It would be dark and silent and scented with blood.

Knuckles connected with her cheek. The world spun again, this time keeping it up until it came to a crashing halt against something cold and damp and grey. It all went fuzzy again, but for the pain. Her side. Her cheek. And the opposite temple.

God, if you're there . . . I'm in pieces.

She was a violin, broken and shattered into splinters. Nothing left to fix. Margot had said God put their pieces back together, but how could He? Even the best luthier couldn't fix a ruined violin. Even God couldn't . . . couldn't . . .

A shout. Maybe it was English, but her ears were ringing too much to say. She saw Brown's shoes, twin smudges of black against the darkness.

She ought to be afraid. Shouldn't she be afraid to die? Someone like her, who knew well no paradise awaited?

But she heard the strangest thing. A note, high and pure. A violin's voice. Singing that note and then going up a third. Then a fourth, trickling back down. Five notes. That was all. The simplest of melodies. But it filled her head. Filled her heart. Drowned out the harsh noises coming from Brown's direction.

Her beginnings. Simple. Not sweet, exactly, but innocent. Five notes. Then the same five again.

The smudge of black moved. Drew back, flew forward. She tried to curl her stomach in, away from him, but there was nowhere to go. Just pain. More blood. Darkness.

But it wasn't silent. It stretched on and on, through the slamming of something metal. Through the pulsing of an ache in her head. Until her side dulled to a low throb. Darkness.

But the music serenaded her. Those five notes, then ten. Then the first note of the phrase dropped down a step, but the four to follow stayed where they'd been. Again.

It went back and forth for a while, then a beat of silence. Two. Only two, but she felt it—that sudden shift. The sudden change. *Alone.*

She closed her eyes against the darkness. It wasn't the *being* alone that had really bothered her, was it? It was the being *left.* That feeling of nothingness. Of not mattering. Of never being the one someone chose.

What made her father never care she lived?

What made her mother leave her?

What made Rosie start another family, without her?

What made her so certain she could never, *never* trust Lukas?

What made the darkness close in around her while Barclay and Lukas and his family all hurried onto the boat as Cor singled her out?

Not just alone—abandoned.

Is that all there was? In life, and now in death?

God, if you're there . . . I'm sorry. I don't know if you can fix me, but I want you to. I want to go back and listen. I want to know about Jesus. I want to have a chance to be part of your family, like Rosie said we all can be. Can you forgive me? Can you . . . can you love me?

The questions faded away. She'd never expected to hear His voice. Was sure she wouldn't know it if she did.

But she heard music. And for the first time in her life, she wondered if maybe . . . maybe this was what the Lord sounded like. If He'd been whispering to her all along, all these years. Little snippets of melodies she'd never quite caught.

But now the music filled her. Those simple early notes. The silence of abandonment. And then . . . then the life He'd given her, bursting onto the score with movement and light.

She kept her eyes closed against the darkness. And let the weakness tug her into the night.

She would die here. But it wasn't silent. And as the music filled her, she knew she wasn't alone.

That she never had been.

TWENTY-EIGHT

Willa must have been granted access to heaven, though she wasn't sure why. Could one cry to God really earn her a place there? Forgiveness?

It must have. And it was ablaze with electric lights as bright as day. She could feel the light behind her closed eyelids, through the hair that had tumbled down and was crusted to her face. With tears? Blood?

Though heaven hurt more than she'd thought it was supposed to. She blinked, trying to sort through the sounds that had interrupted her dream. They were so harsh compared with the music she'd been replaying over and over again. How many times? A dozen. A hundred. It hadn't mattered. It had lulled her, blocked out the pain.

Which reared again now as she dragged in a breath. No, not heaven. But not hell either, so there was still hope for that forgiveness. She was still in the cell, or whatever the room was. Her face was mashed into the concrete floor. Her left arm had gone numb. But the eyes she blinked couldn't find even a patch of darkness.

Words. In two voices. One nearly an octave deeper than the other, both speaking in German. Brown's and . . . it wasn't altogether unfamiliar. But wasn't altogether familiar either. She must have heard it at some point while she slept, if *sleep* was the proper word for it.

And they were near. In the room with her, though she couldn't see shoes or trousers or anything but . . . a door, cracked open.

A door. *Open*.

She could barely even open her parched lips, but she didn't have it in her to see escape and not try for it. She pulled up her knees as much as she could, dug them into the floor and scooted. An inch, maybe. *Maybe*. Another two hundred and she might get somewhere. *God, please*.

Now feet and legs filled her vision. Not Brown's—these wore high black boots polished to a shine, with grey trousers tucked into them that she saw only when he crouched down.

"My apologies, *fräulein*, for the poor care you have received. *Some* people do not understand hospitality." A hand slid under her head, warm and soft. The other seemed to grip the chair behind her. Then a grunt, and her head went light as the world rocked back to upright.

Willa tried to focus on the face. Blond brows. A ruddy complexion. Handsome features, though they showed their age. He must be in his fifties, but . . . she had seen him before. She blinked away the fog still possessing her mind.

And went utterly still. *Gottlieb*.

Brown seethed into view behind him. He snapped something in German, motioned to her.

Whatever it was, it didn't seem to faze Gottlieb. He reached to the side, took a step in that direction. A table sat there, at Willa's right. With a pitcher of water, a glass, and a stack of bandages. He dampened one of the pieces of cloth and came back to dab at Willa's temple.

She didn't mean to wince away. She just couldn't stop the reaction to the pain that unfurled at the touch.

"Again, my apologies. But we must clean you up, *ja*? Or you risk infection." His eyes were blue. And kind. That had to be a lie, didn't it? He ought to know who she was—unless the shadows in the kitchen had masked her. Even so, he ought to *assume*.

But he cleaned her face, tipped some water into her mouth—more slowly than whoever had done it last time. And only then sighed and crouched down beside her again. "Now. Are you able to speak?"

Speak? She wasn't sure her tongue remembered how. But she cleared her throat and forced air through it. "Y-yes. I . . . How long . . . have I . . . been here?"

"Two days. You have apparently said nothing, much to the dismay of my colleague." He shot a frown over his shoulder. "Though how he expects you to speak when he has neither cleaned your wounds nor given you water to drink, I do not pretend to know."

Brown, though obviously capable of speaking English, snarled a response in German and slashed a hand through the air.

Gottlieb turned back to her, met her gaze and held it. As if saying something his lips would not.

That he knew who she was. Knew she'd just been with Margot and her mother. But was that a good thing or a bad? Was *he* good or bad? He'd let them go in Brussels, yes. But if he'd been looking for a way to curry favor with the High Command, Cor Akkerman had just handed it to him.

And he wouldn't even have to turn on the family he'd obviously grown fond of to do it—he could just take it out on *her*. Willa was nothing to him. What hope did she have now, here, with this particular officer?

Two days. Two days she had been separated from Lukas and Barclay. If they were coming back for her, they would have done so already.

Her soul sagged. But only a shade or two. Because she'd already known it. And God had given her a song anyway.

Brown strode the three steps forward. *"Generalleutnant Gottlieb . . ."* The rest was incomprehensible.

Gottlieb didn't so much as look at him. He kept his gaze on Willa. His voice, when he spoke, stayed light. "This man here insists he knows you, that you are an English spy. But this, of course, conflicts with *my* information. Perhaps you can tell us which is correct, *fräulein*, now that you can speak. Are you a contact he made in England . . . or the daughter and protégé of the American reporter touring Belgium?"

She blinked. Reporter? *American* reporter?

Brown growled. *"Dummkopf!* You can tell by the few words she spoke that she is English, not American!"

Still Gottlieb didn't look away. "We both know many Americans send their children to England for their education. Accent means nothing. Just as we both know that the High Command is very eager for the Americans to write pleasant, positive articles about our occupation, *ja*? Now tell me, Herr Baumann. Is the reporter outside claiming his daughter is our prisoner likely to write a pleasant, positive article?"

"He is not a journalist! No doubt he is English too. Probably her employer. I have never seen him, but I have heard stories. A sly trickster of a man. I would not—"

"Enough, Herr Baumann."

Baumann—no, she couldn't think of him as anything but Brown after all this time—sneered. "You are a fool if you believe his story, Generalleutnant."

Now Gottlieb stood. Slowly, without bending his back, until he towered over Brown. *"I* am a fool? I invite you to remember that I am a general—and what are you? A *spy*. Who do you think the High Command will trust first, hmm? You? After I tell them you are a double agent?"

Brown flushed red. "I—"

It happened so quickly Willa hadn't even time to jump. In one motion Gottlieb pulled out his sidearm, aimed, and fired. The *crack* filled the room, filled her head, cut off Brown's objection. Her eyes felt as big as her face as she watched his eyes go blank. He slumped to the floor.

Other feet rushed toward the door, two soldiers bursting in together.

Gottlieb waved to Brown, casually, and said a few short words. Apparently not at all worried about what he'd just done. And the soldiers didn't seem alarmed either. They nodded, saluted, and then dragged Brown out of the door.

Gottlieb shut the door behind them. When he turned again, his motions were quicker. She heard the familiar gliding of a knife from a sheath, and then that of hemp being cut. When it snapped free, her arms sagged.

She had to bite her lip to keep from screaming at the pain as her shoulders rotated, as blood rushed into her fingertips like needles.

Gottlieb returned to the front and bent down to work at the ropes on her ankles. "That man has never once passed along useful information—he will not be missed. But you, *fräulein*, would do well to get out of Belgium as quickly as you can."

She didn't know what to rub first—her hands, her raw wrists, her aching shoulders. She didn't know what to trust. Or how to hope.

She'd been dead. Now she was . . . alive. "How?"

He lifted his brows. "With your *father*, of course. And if you would be so kind as to tell him that we went to great lengths to free you the very moment we realized the mistake that had been made, Germany would thank you. And we will be sure to find this local who turned you in and caution him against feeding us false information in the future. But that is no concern of yours. You need only go home with your father."

Her father. The words wouldn't settle, wouldn't set.

It couldn't be. She wouldn't know him if it were.

"There now." Gottlieb re-sheathed his knife and held out a hand. "You will be unsteady. Lean on me."

Unsteady was putting it mildly. Her knees buckled, her ankles turned, and her side blazed anew with the movement. But Gottlieb's arm proved strong and gentle as she leaned into it. He walked her slowly to the door. "I can take you to clean up first, if you'd like. Or directly to your father."

If she tried to clean herself up, she'd probably fall into a heap and not get up again. "My . . . father. Please."

The corridors blended together, one grey passage melding into another, until at last they emerged into a well-lit lobby.

It was day. And it was bright. And it was beautiful.

She scanned the faces in the direction Gottlieb led her, still not sure who she was looking for. Not until she spotted the bowler hat. The silver-gold hair. The fine—but not too fine—suit of clothes.

"Willa! There you are. Lands, girl, what did they do to you?" Mr. V rushed toward them, concern on his face and a strange accent tilting his words the wrong direction. American, she would guess, though she wasn't sure which region of it he was pretending to be from.

But when his arms came around her, she sagged into him. He wasn't her father. Not even close. In this moment, though, she'd happily call him her best friend.

"It was as I feared, sir," Gottlieb said. "She'd been apprehended by mistake. And questioned none too gently—though I have dealt with the man who treated her so harshly, I assure you. I pray you understand that he did not act in accordance with the German High Command. We would never condone treating a young lady in such a way."

"I'm just grateful you've returned her to me, General." Mr. V tucked her into his side and turned toward the door. "Now, if you'll excuse us—my daughter looks like she could use some pampering."

"Of course." Gottlieb bowed and walked them to the exterior door, even opened it for them.

Willa looked up at him, not sure what she expected.

He gave her half a smile, and his eyes were deep and . . . amused? Perhaps so. He'd done, after all, what Margot had said he meant to do—dealt with what his superiors would believe was a double agent. Found favor with the Americans. Made himself a hero. And saved the De Wildes—and her—in the process.

He pivoted away with a click of his boots.

They stepped out into the afternoon sunshine. Into freedom. Into life. Willa soaked it all in and listened to the melody of it as it danced through her veins. She waited until V had led her hobbling into an automobile before she dared to ask, "Where are they?"

V positioned his hands on the wheel and pulled out into the street bustling with German soldiers. "Safe in London. Except for Mr. Pearce—he's waiting at the boat. It was all I could do to make him stay there, but having him with me didn't fit the story I'd devised. And Mrs. Holstein and the little ones will be in London by the time I get you there, of course. I daresay she would have insisted on coming too, if we hadn't left before she'd had the chance to get to us."

Barclay hadn't cut and run—he'd run for help. *God bless you, Barclay. Thank you, God.* And of course Rosie would come—they were sisters. But that meant . . . "Then who's in London now?"

Mr. V angled her a knowing look. "The De Wildes, of course. I have seen that all their needs are met and have repaid the Misses Davies the funds for this trip. Young Margot is settling in at Room 40."

"At what?"

"Our new codebreaking headquarters—though mum's the word on that. You'll have to pretend you've never even heard the name."

"No." Willa turned on the seat, wishing she had the energy to lash out at him. But even that movement made pain shoot up and down her side. "No, she's just a child. You can't force her to work like that, she's—"

"A prodigy, Miss Forsythe. A miracle—and hardly a child. You, of all people, ought to understand that— think of where *you* were at fourteen. And you, of all people, ought to understand that we did not force her to do anything. We merely . . . offered her a violin. And asked if she would like to play."

Willa sank back against her seat. To Margot, yes, it would look like that. But to Lukas, it would look far different. It would look like he'd traded his sister's life for Willa's.

Her eyes slid shut. She wasn't alone. She had her family. She had this new, fragile understanding with the Lord that she would have to explore. She even, oddly, had Mr. V.

But Lukas De Wilde was as out of reach as he'd been as a poster upon her wall.

Lukas let the cold wind off Cardigan Bay whip him. Wrap him in its invisible arms. Chill him to the very bone. But he didn't rise from his bench. It was better just to sit here and listen. And to wonder at how much life could change in a few short months. A country invaded. A family lost. A love experienced. A friend . . . a friend grown so very distant.

"You should come," Jules said from beside him. "It will be great fun. Enora has convinced Nanette Georges to come along—she's a pretty one, *oui*?"

Lukas drew in a long breath and let it back out. "I cannot, Jules. But thank you. I must say my farewells and catch the train."

"But you can't mean it." Jules's smile caught at half-mast. "You can't leave. Not now, when the tour is just beginning. You love to tour. And what will we do without you?"

"There is always another violinist happy to play my part. And I will find a new position in London." It wouldn't have his friends. But it would be close to his family. And he couldn't bring himself to be more than a tube ride away from them just now for more than a day. "I have already spoken to the Davies sisters. I will send what I can to them, for the Belgian Relief Fund." His face went tight. "Our countrymen certainly need every bit of help they can get."

"But . . ." Jules sighed. "Is it your arm? Is this new injury bothering you?"

Lukas touched a hand to the sling he'd consented to wear this time, to hold his shoulder immobile for the first few days, while it healed. "Not overmuch. It will heal quickly. It is not that, Jules, that led me to this. It's—"

"Willa Forsythe."

He shook his head and focused his gaze on the slate-grey water across from them, the sweep of sand that disappeared into it. "I have not even seen her in a week." He wanted to. Oh, how he wanted to. To assure himself she was well, to thank her for risking her life for his family. To tell her that if she wanted his forgiveness for all she'd done, for being a thief, for lying to him, then she had it.

Even if she didn't want it, she had it.

He wanted to pull her close and tell her she had no *reason* to steal, not anymore. He could give her a different life, if she let him. She could give *herself* one.

But she didn't love him. She'd made that perfectly clear from the start. She hadn't loved him going into Belgium, so why would her stance have changed after suffering as she had for him and his? After, to her way of thinking, he had abandoned her like her parents had? She wouldn't see that he'd had no choice. She'd see only that he walked away in anger when they were still in Wales. That he'd left her to the German soldiers on the docks in Antwerp.

He would see her again, eventually. He would thank her. Offer that forgiveness. But not until he had the strength to withstand her dismissal and to walk away again without crumbling when all he wanted to do was gather her into his arms and beg her to be a part of his life forever.

Jules snorted. "I knew it wouldn't stick. That you'd realize soon enough she isn't your type and walk away. A man doesn't change so quickly, so thoroughly."

The pain yawned around him, threatening to strangle him. He couldn't speak. He couldn't look into his friend's eyes.

But Jules ducked his head to meet his gaze anyway, then scrunched his face in question. "And yet . . . you look heartbroken, Lukas. What happened?"

He dug his fingers into his leg, but it did nothing to distract from the real agony. "She doesn't love me."

"She . . ." Jules sighed. "But you love her? Then I don't understand. Since when does Lukas De Wilde not chase the thing he wants until he gets it?"

Since the one he wanted was too far out of reach to even hope to catch. He stood from his bench and stretched out a hand. "I owe you thanks, Jules. For saving my life. And I . . . I forgive you for it."

Jules breathed a laugh and clasped his hand. "That, at least, is the Lukas I know. I'm not sure what to make of a lovesick one— but you'll get your girl, if you really want her. You always do."

A ridiculous statement, since he'd never really wanted one in particular. Not like this. "I had better hurry. The train won't wait for me."

"You'll keep in touch?"

"Of course. And you'll let me know when Enora agrees to marry you?"

His friend's smile went boyish. "*If* she agrees. Certainly. You must stand up with me, you know."

"I would have it no other way."

They said their farewells, and Jules strode back across Marine Terrace and into the hotel. Lukas had no reason to follow. He'd already spent his last night in those rooms, packed his things, had them sent ahead of him to the train station.

There was nothing left for him now in Wales. But he stood there a minute more, taking it in. He'd come back someday. When it didn't hurt so much to relive the two months he'd spent here.

A quick check of his watch verified that he'd run out of time. The car would be waiting for him, so he moved toward it. Even managed to drum up a smile for the woman waiting inside.

Gwen Davies didn't look as if she felt any of his strain. "Are we ready, *monsieur?*"

She certainly seemed to be, in her traveling suit, a little handbag clutched in her lap, and pure light in her face. But then, she'd known from the start that Willa wasn't really an old school chum. She had no reason to fear seeing her again as much as she longed for it.

Lukas cleared the feeling from his throat. "Of course, Miss Davies."

"Thank you again for agreeing to let me accompany you. I do hate traveling alone."

He merely nodded. The other sister and Miss Blaker would follow Gwen in a few days, but someone had to be here now to help spread the word about the symphony's tour. Or at the very least, they had wanted to be. No doubt they could have hired it out had it not been something they'd anticipated doing themselves for months.

Miss Davies sighed. "You are certain she is well?"

"Recovering. That is what I am told." He had seen Barclay a few times—and V. Both gave him updates on Willa's well-being, obviously knowing he needed those morsels, even if he doubted that she'd approve of their talking to him about her. "The gunshot she took to the side did not hit anything vital. And the rest worked itself out in a few days." Sore muscles. Joints so stiff it took days for them to fully loosen. According to Barclay, she'd practically lived in a deep bathtub for the last week.

Even Barclay Pearce ought to know better than to mention such things to a man, born to society or not. Had he no sense at all?

"You have really not seen her?"

He didn't look at Miss Davies just now either. He wasn't exactly sure what he'd see on her face, but it would no doubt match her tone of voice—reproving, gentle, disbelieving.

"In deference to her wishes." She certainly had not asked after *him,* had she? And so he'd kept busy. Finding a house suitable for his mother and sister. Seeing Margot safely to her new position. Trying to push away the guilt for doing so that he couldn't quite shake, regardless of how excited his sister had been. How buoyant each evening when she came home. How right when she'd said, *"Would you not have jumped at the chance to join an orchestra at my age? Can you not see this is the same for me? All I have ever wanted, Lukas, is to be treated as an adult. To do something that matters with this gift God has given me."*

But she *wasn't* an adult. Or shouldn't be. Perhaps Mère had lengthened her hem and put up her hair so she looked older. But she was only fourteen. She was . . . She was . . . *not* a child, when it came to her mind. He knew that. It was unfair to expect her to want to spend her days embroidering or knitting or playing the piano when that was not who she was.

He had relented. And he was rewarded with her joy. With V's assurances. With Barclay's promises that he would stick as close as he could to her whenever Lukas himself wasn't nearby. Their mother went with her every day, both of them posing as secretaries. Apparently the whole codebreaking operation was so secretive that they all hid in a tiny cupboard of a room whenever an outsider came in anyway.

He had met the men she'd be working alongside. Good men,

if an odd collection. Few were military, despite working now in the Admiralty building.

But they all had the same instincts Margo had, to see the patterns. The puzzles. Though some had seemed baffled when she claimed they must follow it up with mathematics.

Perhaps she could teach them something.

"Are you quite certain that's what Willa wants?" Miss Davies said, pulling him back to the car and the streets passing by outside the window. "And that it isn't your anger with her keeping you apart? You realize, don't you, that the things you loved about Willa—those are not things about which she could have lied? If anything, knowing her past ought to make those things all the more remarkable. That God entrusted such a talent to a girl who, by rights, ought not to have had any means of exploring it. Who ought never to have even held a violin in her hands. Do you not ask why He did so? What plan He has for her?"

"I do not doubt the Lord has something in store. And I do not hold any grudge against her for lying to me." How could he, in the face of Belgium? She'd nearly given her life for them, to save his family. "But she is not the type to forgive so easily, *mon ami.*"

He'd long since known that if he could convince her to love him, she'd do so with her whole being.

Unfortunately, that no doubt meant she'd hate him just as fully for being the one to bring all this upon her.

TWENTY-NINE

Willa hadn't expected to actually *like* Gwen and Daisy Davies, it was true. But when she walked into the pretty little parlor of Peter Holstein's house in Hammersmith, which she'd called home for the last week, joy flooded her at seeing the woman who was, somehow, a friend standing there and rubbing absently at her too-sensitive fingers. Willa rushed forward and pulled Gwen into a tight embrace.

Perhaps it wasn't what one did in society. But Gwen hugged her back. "Oh, Willa! You look as though you've been through the very thick of it. Are you well?"

Her side still hurt. She couldn't sleep without nightmares rising—running through unfamiliar streets, someone chasing her. That terrible feeling of thirst. Being trapped in a dark, empty room. But when she awoke, it was with a sister by her side and brothers downstairs and the sure knowledge that no matter how lost she got, they'd come for her.

She wasn't alone.

She smiled as she pulled away. "Quite well. And so glad to see you. Please, sit. Can I get you anything? Tea?"

Gwen waved that away and pulled Willa down beside her on

the couch. "I am in need of nothing, I assure you. Only to see you again. I must apologize, Willa. I took your violin to a luthier, but—"

"He could not fix damage that severe. I know." That, too, filled her dreams.

But it was only a thing. She'd always known not to put too much value on things. Not when they could so easily be stolen or destroyed.

It was just a thing. And she'd have another—someday. She'd put back five pounds from what Mr. V had paid her. She'd put back another five after the next job, whatever it might be—Barclay had already announced to the family that they'd be working no more jobs outside of what V gave them. Legitimate ones, more or less, and Willa couldn't bring herself to regret it. Not anymore. She'd work for him, for her country, and she'd earn her keep. She'd save like the honest blokes did, until she could afford to buy herself whatever violin she decided on. She'd *earn* it—perhaps that would make it even more special.

"He couldn't, no. So I took it instead to a woodworker I know. He used the wood, at least, to make something new." Gwen reached down to a box sitting beside the couch and pulled out something flat and rectangular and covered with a scrap of muslin.

"Gwen. You needn't have." But curiosity overtook her, and she unwrapped the offering. Then couldn't quite breathe.

The wood had been arranged in a patchwork, creating a picture frame. She never would have thought that a frame could be so beautiful when made of ill-fitting pieces of scarred wood, but it was. She ran her fingers along it, wondering at how the craftsman had found enough good wood left to create anything new at all.

Then her gaze settled on the photograph cradled by her violin. The reason for her sudden lack of breath. "When was this taken?"

"At that concert in Cardiff, before the theft. We had a photographer there, did you not see him?" Gwen scooted close and looked at the photograph along with her. "You are a handsome couple. Look how he looks at you."

She touched a finger to the black-and-grey face of Lukas De Wilde. He looked down at the grey-and-white face of Willa with an expression she couldn't quite believe, even as she saw it.

He really had loved her. And she had ruined it. "Thank you, Gwen. It's . . . it's the best gift anyone could have given." Love, framed by music.

"Then you don't want my other gift?"

Willa looked up at the teasing note in her friend's voice. Saw the veritable blaze of a gleam in her eyes. "What other gift could you possibly give?"

"Well." This time Gwen stood and moved to the back of the couch. The sound of something large sliding across the wood preceded the appearance of a case whose distinctive shape could not be mistaken.

Willa stood, fingers itching even as she said, "You needn't give me a violin! I am saving. I will buy one myself."

Gwen lifted it, though, and held it out. "Please. It just sits there, never being played. It isn't right. I want you to keep it as long as you need—you can return it after you purchase one of your own, of course. But in the meantime, can't you bring it to life again? It wants it."

Her hands shook as she reached out. It was a fine case—no surprise for Gwen Davies. She set it on the cushions they had abandoned and flipped the latches. Then drew in that breath she'd lost. "Is that . . . ?" The wood was so beautiful, so gleaming. The wood grain impossibly tight.

Gwen chuckled. "Why do you think Mr. De Wilde brought his Stradivarius for me to see that first night, Willa? He knew I had one of my own to which I'd want to compare it."

"But . . ." She'd hoped to buy one for a hundred pounds or so—a solid, good instrument. But it would be nothing like this.

She could never, in a lifetime, afford anything like this. "It is too dear. I cannot. If something were to happen to it—"

"Then at least it will have spent time in the hands of a master again beforehand. Please, Willa." Gwen reached in when Willa didn't and lifted the precious instrument out. Placed it in Willa's hands. "Give it life. I never could do so as well as you."

Tears dampened her eyes, but she hadn't the hands to brush them away. Not now. One held the violin and the other the bow that Gwen also pressed against her fingers.

She closed her eyes. Raised the instrument. And played.

The vibrato moved from instrument to chin and straight down to her core. Its sound was as rich and full as Lukas's, of course. But today she didn't play one of the songs he'd pulled out for her. Nor one of the many she had heard over the years as she eavesdropped on orchestras.

She played her own. The one God had filled her spirit with in that prison cell. The one that spoke of beginnings and loss and a full, bright life despite it all.

When she lowered her bow and opened her eyes, Gwen wasn't the only one in the room. Rosie stood there too, a few of the little ones behind her. She had tears in her eyes—and a stack of papers clutched in her hands. "Beautiful. Did you write it?"

Willa's lips pulled up. "I think it wrote me."

"Well." Rosemary stepped closer, offering Gwen a smile but not asking for an introduction. Instead, she held out the papers. "Regardless. It looks like this arrived just in time."

Staff paper, Willa saw. With elegant lines stretching across the pages, all blank. Waiting for her to fill them. She set down the bow and reached for the stack. "Rosie! It's perfect." She had done nothing to deserve such friends, such family. Nothing. But she'd thank the Lord for them.

"So you can win that bet." Rosie winked and stepped back again.

Willa shook her head with a laugh. "That would be cheating."

"Oh, come now. What do you *think* Retta intended when she issued it? You were always your greatest obstacle, Will—we all knew it was yourself you'd have to find a way to get the music from."

They did? But *how* did they know?

Regardless. She would do it right, now. She would write down the song and play it at Pauly's that night, on the only stage she'd ever stood on—the only stage she needed. She'd win the bet and she'd issue another and she'd be with her family. And life would be good.

She made the introductions then and visited with Gwen for another hour before her friend had to leave. Then she climbed Rosie's steps back up to the room she was sharing with Ellie and little Olivia.

Elinor had moved all of Willa's things here while she was in Wales and they had decided without her input to let their flats go. The old cigar box stuffed with slips of paper with names of composers and their work that she'd wanted to look up sat on the bureau. Her clothes, stitched so aptly by Rosemary, filled the little closet.

Her poster of Lukas De Wilde had been tacked to the wall.

She stopped in front of it with a heaving breath. And positioned the photograph on the little table under it.

"I still can't believe you got to meet him." Ellie appeared at her side, looking up at it as well. "I mean, for longer than I did. It isn't right for a man to be so handsome, is it?"

Willa chuckled and slid an arm around her little sister's shoulders. "It isn't. It ought to be some kind of crime."

"And yet I bet that whole time you were there, you never thought to get an autograph. Did you?"

She turned raised brows on Ellie, with her too-pretty features and her rosebud smile. He hadn't looked twice at her, Barclay had said. Nor at Retta. Both of whom were far prettier than Willa. "No. Can't say as I did."

"Good thing you have me around, then." Ellie stretched up and moved the edge of something white under the tack holding the poster up.

A program. From that solo concert of his that she'd sneaked into—she'd rescued this from the street out front, where some careless patron with more money than sense had let it fall.

And scrawled on the front now was: *To Elinor, For the sake of the music. Lukas De Wilde.*

"Sorry it's to me. Would have looked a bit strange had I asked for your name instead."

"It doesn't matter. Thank you, Ellie." *For the sake of the music.* She turned back to the violin she'd set on the bed. To the promise of blank staff paper.

She had a bet to win.

"I am not taking you to a tavern."

Margot folded her arms over her chest and weighed the value of adding a pout. No, that would just cement in her stubborn oaf of a brother's mind that she was a child. Which would rather defeat her purpose. "It is not a tavern, Lukas. It is a pub. I have heard nothing but good things about Pauly's."

And more important, her brother hadn't. Or so Barclay had assured her when they'd concocted this plan this morning.

Lukas shifted from foot to foot and surveyed the room in which she spent her days. Sir Alfred Ewing had promised them more room soon, but at the moment it was little more than a cupboard of a chamber attached to his office. Still—it was a cupboard that buzzed with energy. A cupboard filled with all the most beautiful things—papers and puzzles and books.

Papa would have loved it. Even with the chaos of all those men in the close space, it was heaven.

Maman would be back any minute with their coats, and she

would help with the convincing, if necessary. But if Margot could not manage it beforehand, what kind of a little sister was she? "Please? Mr. Culbreth says the food is—what word did you use, Mr. Culbreth?"

"Hmm?" The man sitting nearest her desk looked up, his eyes still foggy with thought. Then he glanced between her and Lukas and seemed to sift through the words he'd no doubt overheard, even if he hadn't focused upon them. His smile said he knew her grand plan was underway.

He was a good sort, this new neighbor of hers.

"Brilliant. Had a meat pie there three days ago that's still filling my dreams." He wisely didn't mention that he'd had said meat pie when Barclay cajoled him into leaving his desk and going to Pauly's pub for a late supper.

Lukas's mouth was still far too tight a line. "But is it appropriate for young ladies?"

"Oh, there are hordes of ladies and little ones there this early." Most of them were Barclay and Willa's so-dubbed siblings, but Mr. Culbreth was too good to mention that too. "And I hear there will be music tonight. I've half a mind to knock off early and go over myself. I can show you the way, if you like." He leaned back in his chair.

"Please, Lukas?" It had to be tonight, Barclay had said. Willa would not only be there, she'd be playing. And according to what he'd told her, Lukas would be a "goner"—whatever that was—as soon as he heard her play again. And Willa, Barclay assured her, would be over the moon to see Lukas.

She wasn't entirely sure what Barclay did at Whitehall. He didn't seem to answer to Ewing, but she'd seen him once talking to the director of Naval Intelligence, Captain Hall—who seemed to count Mr. V a friend. Whatever the case, Barclay made an appearance on one out of three days. She was still trying to determine if she'd be able to count him a brother when *her* brother married his adopted sister. The mathematics didn't really seem in her favor there. But she would claim it anyway. His family didn't seem to care about such trifles as blood or legalities when it came to family. She could approve of that.

Lukas sighed. It sounded three times as heavy as it had before all this had happened. "I am really not feeling up to it, *ma petite*."

"And how long until you do? Must we all sit at home every night until then?" It was a low blow, she knew. But a sister had to resort to such things now and then. When it was for her brother's own good.

Another heavy sigh, but something in his eyes shifted. "All right. You win. Supper at this Pauly's pub."

But he didn't smile—she'd been able to count on one hand the smiles she'd earned from her brother since they got to London. They had to change that. It couldn't be healthy to have so few smiles.

Maman returned, her brows raised toward Margot, who gave her a confirming nod.

Lukas was questioning Mr. Culbreth, asking about the direction, apparently. Hopefully her brother didn't know London well enough yet to realize it was in a poor part of town. The tube would disguise the fact as they traveled, and hopefully the darkness of the November evening would aid them in the short walk from there.

Barclay had already drawn her a map of where to go. But she let Lukas get the direction as well—it would make him feel better, to think he was the one leading the way.

Margot slipped into the coat Maman handed her, not missing the prayer her mother muttered as she put on her own. A prayer for Lukas's happiness—and for healing of his broken heart regardless of what happened tonight. Margot added her own to it. *Nine, eighty-one, seven hundred twenty-nine, six thousand five hundred sixty-one . . .*

Then she followed her brother and mother down the bleak hallway filled with shuffling old men delivering their last papers of the day. Down the stairs and out into the cold London night. She missed Louvain, which would never be the same. She missed Madame Dumont's house in Brussels too. And the lady herself, and Claudette. She even missed, strangely, Gottlieb and his too-blue eyes and his too-slow moves in Go.

But she liked where she'd ended up. She didn't have to pretend to be stupider than she was anymore. She spent her days with people who forgot, more often than not, that she was a girl. Only a few of them were mathematicians as she was, but still they understood her. They saw her for the answers she produced. For the puzzles she could solve.

Like Papa.

She slid a hand into the crook of Lukas's arm and followed him toward the nearest tube stop. It was his turn, now, to find what made him happy.

He just had to take the risk and claim it.

———◇———

Pauly's place looked more dubious with every step toward it, and Lukas was about to say so, to insist these two females beside him give up their determination for a meal at this particular place. Except that Barclay jogged up beside them at that very moment, a grin on his face.

"Don't let the neighborhood fool you. This place is a gem."

Barclay—he should have known he'd be behind Culbreth having discovered the pub. Barclay, he'd learned, knew the best places for everything in London and gave advice about them freely. Still, it didn't seem the sort of place to take his mother and sister.

But Mr. Culbreth had been right about music tonight—he heard the lively strains of a violin, a guitar, a piano, and a trumpet. They weren't half bad either. Not exactly an orchestra, but a decent group for a pub in this section of town.

Warmth met them at the door, along with the smell of frying food and spices and roasted meat. His stomach growled on cue, and his gaze swung around the crowded room. If the number of people were any indication of the quality of meals to be had, he'd have to grant that Barclay and Culbreth hadn't led him astray.

He continued inside as he looked around, unwinding the scarf from his neck. It was when he turned to ask his mother where she wanted to try to find a seat that his gaze made its way to the tiny little stage jammed into the corner.

His feet turned to blocks of ice, frozen and immovable.

He saw the hair first, sliding as always from its pins. His hands tingled at the remembered feel of those stray pieces sliding over his fingers when he kissed her. The slender frame, standing with that same blasted bend to her back that he had spent weeks trying to correct—did she learn *nothing* from those lessons?

As if hearing his thoughts, she straightened her spine, turned just a bit as she played.

The violin—that snagged his gaze next. He could see from here that it wasn't the sort a thief could afford. She wouldn't have stolen it, would she have? He'd thought, somehow, that this whole ordeal would have changed something for her.

But maybe he'd been wrong. As he'd been to begin with, assuming he could win her.

"Gwen Davies lent it to her." Barclay kept Lukas still with a hand on his shoulder. "Until she could replace the one Cor Akkerman destroyed. I didn't know a violin could sound like that—but then, I suppose you did."

He swallowed and shrugged away from the hand. This had been their plan all along—his mother and Margot obviously conspirators. Later, perhaps he'd be angry about it. He should be. They were forcing him to certain heartbreak, and he was none

394

too sure he was ready to walk away whole. He needed more time to steel himself. To build that wall around his heart.

To be able to look at her and see someone other than the woman he loved too much, too fully, too disastrously.

But his feet took him a step closer. She must not be too upset about how everything had ended up, if she could play like that tonight. She must not miss him with the same soul-deep ache that overtook him every time he let his thoughts wander. She must not regret for a moment the way she'd handled it all.

The song came to an end, and amid the raucous applause, the other musicians climbed down.

Willa stood alone on the little stage, and her eyes were focused on a long table against the opposite wall. "This one's for you, Retta! Winning that bet!"

He spotted the blondes at the table then—the fairer Elinor, the more golden Retta, both smiling. Though Retta called back, "If you weren't the hardest composer to ever wheedle a song from, I'd say it doesn't count!"

Composer—she'd written something? Margot nudged him forward, and his feet thawed enough to allow it. Propelled more by intrigue than his sister's bony finger.

She'd written something. Lured it to her fingers and onto the page. It shouldn't feel like a victory for him—it wasn't his, after all—but it did. It made something go light that had been heavy inside.

A table cleared before them as if by magic. Or, perhaps, by the power of Barclay, who shoved him into one of the now-empty chairs and then leaned against the table with a smug little smile that might have been annoying if Lukas weren't too focused upon the stage to pay it any undue mind.

She closed her eyes, as she always did when playing from memory. Positioned the bow. And the din of the pub went muted, down to a dull hush ready to be pierced by the first note.

It had a slow start, almost wandering through those same notes played over and over. Then a pause, in which his soul recognized the question. The emptiness. The loneliness. He leaned forward. What would come next? A minor key, no doubt. Confused and forsaken and—

No. It wasn't minor at all. It was major and fast and full and . . . Willa. His breath seeped out. It was her song—or she was its. Full not of doubt, but of confidence. Of life. Of . . . gratitude.

"If you'd bother to talk to her," Barclay said into his ear, "she no doubt would have told you how the Lord spoke to her in that cell—through music. This music."

He had? It shouldn't surprise him. And it didn't, really. Except that it seemed odd she would have reached out. That she would have asked. That she would have admitted she needed anyone other than what she'd found for herself.

But she did. That was there too, in that line of melody. It wove around the notes, around his heart. And then it circled back to those same beginning notes. A restoration.

It was a simple song. So how could it say so much?

The crowd erupted again around him, with whistles and clapping and shouts of encouragement. He didn't know most of these people, but she was theirs. And the same pride that surged through him obviously surged through them as well.

She didn't need him. She had family here, a whole world happy to support her. To cheer her on and be her audience. And he had family too, who would support him if she rebuffed him, who would make certain he didn't sink too far into despair. Who would remind him that the Lord held his future in His capable palm.

But as he watched her bow, manlike, and smile toward the girls she claimed as sisters, he felt again that same recognition he'd felt in the Davieses' drawing room.

They could be two melodies, existing in the same world but never mixing. Counterpoint, each line unique. Or they could be a harmony, blending together and making something new. Something more than, as Margot would put it, the sum of their parts.

He pushed to his feet, dodging the hand that Barclay put out—no doubt meant to stop him from barreling from the pub. But he had no intention of leaving. Instead, he shouldered his way through the standing ovation until he stood in front of them all. In front of the stage.

She looked down at him, and her face froze. Her violin—Miss Davies's violin—lowered to her side. "Lukas."

That was a symphony all its own. His name on her lips, containing within it an apology, a recognition.

Hope.

He held up a hand to help her step down. And said, "Only my closest friends call me Lukas. If you do not want to give me false ideas, you had better call me *mon amour*."

Her lips smiled as she stepped down onto the crowded floor. But her eyes were still wary. "You have it wrong. You just told me to call you *idiot*."

"No doubt you think me one." He didn't release her fingers. Couldn't. Could only move his thumb across her knuckles. "That I proved you right. That I left."

She shook her head and gripped his fingers back. "No—I know you wanted to come back, Barclay told me. It was me who left. Who never gave us a chance. Who lied about so much—"

"But not about what matters." He nodded to the stage. "You could not lie about the music."

Her nostrils flared with the breath she sucked in. "I've turned over a new leaf—and not just because Barclay told us all we must. I mean it. So . . . can you forgive me? Someday, do you think?"

"Mm." He tilted his head, made a show of considering. "Perhaps. By our tenth wedding anniversary or so."

Her fingers went tighter still. "Lukas."

Someone shifted behind him and slid something warm and

round into his hand. His fingers closed around it, felt its outline. The smooth circle of metal. The jewel jutting out. He had to blink thrice to keep back the emotion. "I know I promised you London part of the year, Brussels the rest—but that will have to wait. London only, just now. Perhaps a day or two in Wales, now and then, to visit our friends."

She eased closer to him and handed off her violin to a brunette with curls who stood nearby. "And Cornwall. We'll have to visit Rosie and Peter in Cornwall."

"Naturally," the brunette said with a cheeky grin. Rosie, he assumed.

"Naturally," he echoed. And tugged Willa closer still. Then he reached for her now-free hand and slid his mother's diamond onto it.

Her eyes were the most beautiful things. Blue and green and brilliant. "Aren't you supposed to ask something when you do that?"

"And give you the chance to say no? I think not." But he lifted her left hand and settled it against his chest, where his heart raced for her. "I will be a good husband, Willa. I swear it. Give me a chance."

Yes, her eyes were the most beautiful things. Right up there with that smile that bloomed across her mouth. "I'll probably be a dunce of a wife. But if you'll have me, knowing all you do, then I'm yours."

"Kiss her already!" came from that long table, followed by hoots and laughter.

It was good advice. So he took it, inclining his head until he could capture her lips. Capture her heart. And blend her song with his own.

Willa's Song

If you'd like to listen to "Willa's Song," you can hear it in the video trailer at http://bit.ly/ASongUnheardTrailer.

Special thanks to Taylor Bennet, the talented young violinist who performed the music for me.

Kudos go out to Jessica Brand, the composer of "Willa's Song." I—and the voting public—love your beautiful melody, Jessica! To the other finalists in the contest, Thomas Reither and Melissa Merritt: I would have been thrilled and honored to have any of your compositions representing my heroine's journey!

I owe much appreciation, as well, to my old friend Harry Burchell, III, for taking pity on my overworked status and helping me turn Jessica's composition into sheet music for Taylor to play.

For the sake of the music.
RMW

A Note from the Author

Though there was no real Willa Forsythe, violin prodigy, or Lukas De Wilde, world-famous musician, these characters and their situations were, in fact, inspired by research I stumbled across when I first sat down to plan out the SHADOWS OVER ENGLAND series.

World War I is often considered a forgotten war—and this is true in Great Britain just as it is in America. For Britain, one of the great forgotten stories is of the hundreds of thousands of Belgian refugees who flooded England and Wales within the first few months of the war. No family, it's said, went untouched by these refugees, as nearly everyone opened their homes and neighborhoods to the influx. There were resentments, of course, by the end. But in the beginning, "brave little Belgium" was a rallying cry. After the soldiers returned home at the end of the war, however, refusing to talk of the horrors they'd seen, those left on the home front didn't feel they could talk about what they had experienced either. And so, these hundreds of thousands of refugees who went quietly home at the first opportunity were brushed under the rug, their stories largely untold.

There really was an orchestra composed of Belgium's most brilliant musicians, put together and funded by Gwendoline and Margaret Davies—two wealthy heiresses from Wales who are now viewed as among the greatest Welsh patrons of the arts. These sisters—neither of whom ever married—ended up opening a canteen in France in 1917 for the soldiers. After the war, they returned home to Wales and purchased and opened an estate called Greggynog, whose main purpose was to rehabilitate returning soldiers through art. They were soft-spoken, shy, very religious young women . . . who had a profound effect on their "dear principality" that is still noteworthy a hundred years later. I hope and pray I did these sweet sisters justice in my short portrayal of them and their good-hearted love of their neighbors. I tried to stick as close to the known facts about them both as possible. Gwen Davies really did have a Stradivarius violin, for instance, that she could no longer play—and though she didn't give it away to a poor prodigy in need, I like to think that it's a loan she would have been happy to make.

My portrayal of the German invasion of Belgium is based on the facts I gleaned from *The Rape of Belgium*, a great research book by Larry Zuckerman. I tried to weigh each side fairly, especially through Wolfgang Gottlieb, but historians today view the German army's actions in Belgium as a precursor to their behavior in the next world war. Far too many Belgian citizens passed the war without ever knowing what became of their relatives in the towns that were attacked—I wanted to capture just a hint of this with the De Wildes. My fictional family was quickly reunited, but others lived with the question of whether their loved ones were alive or dead for years.

I'd like to thank the staff at the Belle Vue Royal Hotel in Aberystwyth, Wales, who patiently and promptly answered my emails asking them strange questions about where the back entrance let out and where on the ground floor two violinists would have practiced a hundred years ago. Researching a book is made so much easier by helpful people—so thank you, Harri! And as always, big thanks to my early readers—Elizabeth, my England native, for making sure my dialogue sounds right, and Taylor for checking my violin terminology in the manuscript as well as playing "Willa's Song" for me!

I have to say that Willa was at times a troublesome heroine to write. So—stubborn! But I hope you enjoyed her story and the further glimpses of the family at Pauly's pub. I can't wait to dive even more into their world in Barclay's story, *An Hour Unspent*. We'll meet clockmakers, suffragettes, and pursue one of the strangest bets yet, when Barclay's family challenges him to steal an hour from Big Ben's clock.

In the meantime, thank you for traveling with me into the story of a violin prodigy with music trapped inside her. I pray that through her story your ears might be opened to new melodies in your life.

Roseanna M. White pens her novels beneath her Betsy Ross flag, with her Jane Austen action figure watching over her. When not writing fiction, she's homeschooling her two children, editing and designing, and pretending her house will clean itself. Roseanna is the author of over a dozen historical novels and novellas, ranging from biblical fiction to American-set romances to her series set in Britain. She makes her home in the breathtaking mountains of West Virginia. You can learn more about her and her stories at www.RoseannaMWhite.com.

Sign Up for Roseanna's Newsletter!

Keep up to date with Roseanna's news on book releases and events by signing up for her email list at roseannawhite.com.

More in the SHADOWS OVER ENGLAND Series

Growing up on the streets of London, Rosemary and her friends have had to steal to survive. But as a rule, they only take from the wealthy, and they've all learned how to blend into high society for jobs. When, on the eve of WWI, a client contracts Rosemary to determine whether a friend of the king is loyal to Britain or to Germany, she's in for the challenge of a lifetime.

A Name Unknown, SHADOWS OVER ENGLAND #1

BETHANYHOUSE

More from Roseanna M. White

Visit roseannawhite.com for a full list of her books.

When Brook Eden's friend Justin, a future duke, discovers she may be an English heiress, she travels to meet her alleged father. Once she arrives in Yorkshire, Brook undergoes a trial of the heart—and faces the same danger that led to her mother's mysterious death.

The Lost Heiress
LADIES OF THE MANOR

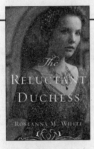

After a shocking attack, Rowena Kinnaird is desperate to escape her family and her ex-fiancé. She finds an unexpected protector in the Duke of Nottingham, but will she ever be able to trust him—let alone fall in love—when his secrets threaten to endanger her once more?

The Reluctant Duchess
LADIES OF THE MANOR

Lady Ella Myerston is determined to put an end to the danger that haunts her brother. While visiting her friend Brook, the owner of the Fire Eyes jewels, Ella gets entangled in an attempt to blackmail the newly reformed Lord Cayton. Will she become the next casualty of the "curse"?

A Lady Unrivaled
LADIES OF THE MANOR

◆ BETHANY HOUSE

You May Also Like

Gentlewoman Rachel Ashford has moved into Ivy Cottage with the two Misses Groves, where she discovers mysteries hidden among her books. Together with her one-time love Sir Timothy, she searches for answers—and is forced to face her true feelings. Meanwhile, her friends Mercy and Jane face their own trials in life and love.

The Ladies of Ivy Cottage by Julie Klassen
TALES FROM IVY HILL #2
julieklassen.com

Fleeing a stalker, Kaine Prescott purchases an old house with a dark history: a century earlier, an unidentified woman was found dead on the grounds. As Kaine tries to settle in, she learns the story of her ancestor Ivy Thorpe, who, with the help of a man from her past, tried to uncover the truth about the death.

The House on Foster Hill by Jaime Jo Wright
jaimewrightbooks.com

After a tragic mine accident in 1954, Judd Markley thought he had abandoned his Appalachian roots forever by moving to Myrtle Beach. Then he meets the privileged Larkin Heyward, who dreams of moving to Kentucky to help the poor of Appalachia. Drawn together amid a hurricane and swept away by their feelings, are their divergent dreams too great an obstacle to overcome?

The Sound of Rain by Sarah Loudin Thomas
sarahloudinthomas.com

⬥BETHANYHOUSE